T0354336

A Journey To Freedom

A Novel

STEVEN W. MOORE

iUniverse, Inc.
New York   Bloomington

A Journey to Freedom
A Novel

iUniverse books may be ordered through booksellers or by contacting:

iUniverse
1663 Liberty Drive
Bloomington, IN 47403
www.iuniverse.com
1-800-Authors (1-800-288-4677)

ISBN: 978-1-4502-3488-7 (sc)
ISBN: 978-1-4502-3486-3 (ebook)
ISBN: 978-1-4502-3487-0 (dj)

Library of Congress Control Number: 2010907919

Printed in the United States of America

iUniverse rev. date: 6/22/2010

Contents

Chapter 1   Trapped

"Is someone watching us!? I can't see it, but I can feel it!" A voice echoed from the deep, dark, recesses of the woods. A slight pause ensued, then another outburst. "There's someone out there!" The voice speaking was that of an African-American female walking along a path cut out of the thick woods, while with her, walking alongside her; was her African-American male counterpart. It was an extremely dark, frigid, wintry night in the rural, dense, back woods of Kentucky. It had just finished dumping a cold rain an hour earlier; this made the leaves that were stuck to the ground slick as ice. The thick clouds that were above began to break, making it possible for the moonlight to stream through the branches of the trees. There was enough light for the both of them to see their own breath as they exhaled. There was a thin fog that had formed due to the earlier rain. The only thing this did was aid in keeping their clothes damp and moist. They had been walking at a brisk, steady pace for hours, when the girl suddenly heard the sounds. After she thought she noticed something out there, they instantly stopped dead in their tracks. The girl was frightened. "It sounds like there is movement all around us!" The girl said. They noticed, slightly to their right, a log jutting out onto the path. The log had once been part of the remains of a giant oak tree. The female slave imagined herself as an heroic figure, using the log as a barricade to stop the passage of some fat merchant weighed down by all the riches of the world. "Come on, be more practical," the female slave thought to herself. It could be used as a hiding spot should their assailants close in. She frowned at the thought. She'd prefer being a hero assaulting the rich, rather than a scared child hiding behind a log like a rabbit. But that's what she was, a terrified young girl, stuck in these vast woods. The log was more than ample size to use as a barricade. It was roughly split between the wooded forest and the open path. The opening of the path the two were walking on was about ten feet in width. The path was dirt based, littered with tiny rocks and stones. Clearly the path was well worn and trampled upon by many feet in the past. It didn't have defined boundaries, so it didn't look like it had been carved out by hand. "Where do you think you saw someone?" Her black counterpart asked. "I don't know, it's too dark to tell," the girl responded. The girl began rotating her head in every direction. "Hold on, let me try to figure out the direction of the sound," she said. There were little sounds coming from every direction, making it hard to distinguish one sound from another. "It sounds like it's coming from all around us," she said. "Be quiet, I heard something. It sounds like it's coming from over there," her male counterpart said. "Where?" The girl asked. The male was facing in the direction of where they had been walking, standing to the right of the girl, he turned completely around and pointed toward the girl's side of the woods. "It's coming from over there!" He pointed. "It's definitely something," he said. The girl was now turned completely around as well, facing in the direction of where her male counterpart had pointed. "What could it be?" She asked. "I believe I know where it's coming from now; but I can't make out what it is," the girl said. "Why's it could just be a raccoon or a squirrel," the male said. The girl became emphatic. "Or it could be a bear, or worse, a bounty hunter!" She said. "No, that's not a bounty hunter," the male replied. The girl hits her male counterpart on the shoulder. "How can you tell?" She asked. "If it was, we's a heard him along time ago," the male replied. The girl began to panic. "What do you mean!?" She asked. The male was adamant. "If they is bounty hunters, we would have heard them earlier in the day following us," he said. "You don't know that, they are professionals, they know what they're doing. They could have been stalking us all day and we wouldn't know it. Besides, it's been raining most of the day, that blocks some of the sound out, you know," she said. The male turned his head downward toward the ground, seemingly dejected by the girl's response. "You is right," he said.

She was the more educated between the two. His lesser education, which showed in his grammar during his speaking, was once far less advanced than what it currently was now. He had spent some time up north, time he had spent as a freed fugitive slave, and during that time he had a small window of opportunity to get educated. While staying in safe houses in the northern states, he had some brief good fortunes to get some education; at least he had some time to learn some proper grammar.

"I had lived through years of scrounging for food," the male slave recalled. "Years of never being able to clean myself, years of watching over my shoulder, fearing abuse at any moment. My female counterpart was in the same precarious situation as me. She was actually in worse shape than I was when it came to looking over her shoulder for the alluring enemy on the plantation. We were both tough and mentally strong as a result; it came with the territory when you had lived your whole life on a plantation as we had."

"I could have sworn I just saw a shadowy figure move from behind that tree over there," the girl said, pointing with her left arm across her body to an area twenty feet ahead, to a tree surrounded by bushes. The yardage between them and the supposed shadowy figure was open territory. The open path was the only thing separating them from those bushes. There wasn't a tree to be found to block them from what she saw. "How can you tell. It's just too dark," the male slave replied. The girl began to panic. "Where do we go from here, what do we do?" She asked. "Shhh, be quiet, whisper. If there is someone out there, we's better be quiet, you's a making too much noise," the male slave said to the frightened girl. Suddenly, there was the sound of limbs cracking and bushes rustling, right in the general vicinity of where the girl had pointed just seconds earlier. With the both of them now facing in the direction of the bushes, the sound came directly in front of them. This time there was no doubt they thought, there was something behind those bushes. The location of the sound was up a slight incline from where they were. They both turned back around and noticed the log in front of them. They quickly ran to where it was. They immediately stepped over it so that the log would become a fortification between them and the location of the noise. They both had one knee touching the ground, as their other knee was leaning against the log. They were positioned in such a way that their heads were even with the top of the log, having to crouch just slightly to remain completely hidden. "What do we do now?" The girl asked. "Stay calm and very still," the male slave replied. "We's a don't want to draw any attention to ourselves," he continued.

The silence was deafening during those next few minutes; "I'm so cold, I'm soaking wet, and all I have is this raggedy old sweater, I'm thirsty too," the girl said, her voice was shaky from the shivering. She had just taken her clear coated poncho off and had it tightly bound in her hand. Her partner, having the same type of poncho, still had his on. "I know, I know, I can't stop shaking either," the male slave replied. They were exhausted. The long trek, over a great many ridges and up many steep, mountainous terrains, about twenty miles in length, an all day journey to their current position, had drained them. "You know, you are tired, you could of just been seeing things," the male slave remarked. "Let's just surrender. I want to go back. I'm scared." the girl said with a tense, trembling voice. "How do you even know they is people up there? Like I said before, it could just be an animal. And anyways, are you's a crazy!? It's too early to talk about surrendering; we just simply don't know what made those noises. Let's just step back for a moment, catch our composure, and figure out what we just heard," the male slave said. The girl was almost at the breaking point of crying hysterically. The male slave was intense when he spoke. "If they are peoples over there, and we surrender now, they's a definitely will kill us. We's not goin back to that damn plantation anyways, and that's final. Think of your freedom," he said. "What freedom? Its pitch black, I can't see a thing, I'm lost in woods I've never been in before, and there are men chasing us that I can't see, only hear. These men are itching to either capture us, or kill us, not knowing which is the worse part. Now that's too close for comfort in my book. I'd rather take my chances and surrender, think about it, on the plantation, at least there, we knew what to expect, at least we had that. Here, there's no food, only the same old food we have been lugging around on our backs for days, we're lost, and I can barely see my hand in front of my face." Her male counterpart was shaking his sweater under his poncho, trying to dry it, when he spoke up. "We is not lost. You is just saying that because it's so dark," he said. "Do you know where we are?" She said, hoping for a definite answer from him. "It's so dark, but I think I have a rough idea. "Do you, or do you not know where we are?" The girl insisted. "Is you trying to get under my skin here?" The male slave, harboring some frustration, replied. The girl chuckled as she wiped away the fluid from her wet, cold, nose. "Is it working? Should I try a little harder to irritate you, or should I just zip my mouth?" She asked. She was trying to be humorous to forget her fear; but it wasn't working. "Listen, there's no need in you is getting so agitated. I have been tracking our heading all day long. I know where we are. You is jumping to conclusions anyways. Listen, I don't want to upset you any more than you already are, but if they is indeed human beings and not animals, we's in trouble," the male slave said. That remark he just made, made things worse for her terrified spirit. She became desperate. "Please God, do something!" She said. "I knew what I just said would worsen things for you. I'm sorry, I'm just thinking out loud. Just try and think like this; it's too early to tell what made that sound, and you is with me, I'm not going to let anything happen to you. Now just be quiet and let me think," the male slave said.

If there are human beings out there, were they bounty men or marshals they wondered? Worse yet, they could be hit men hired by some slave owner. Bounty men or marshals usually just captured their fugitive slaves, while hit men had just one goal in mind, to kill. It really didn't matter to the two slaves that night in those dark woods, as far as they were concerned, at least to the female slave, they were threatening; trigger happy stalkers, out to get them. To her, they were trapped; her thoughts began to rest on the worst case scenario. They were going to die. They had to find a way to escape. After a few seconds had passed, the sound that had occurred behind those bushes began to sink into the conscience of the male slave; he too, began to think. He was now full of fear, not a gripping fear like his partner, but he did feel a sudden fear come upon him. He was not thinking of the worst case scenario like his partner, but of a lesser, more lenient outcome. Unlike the girl, his outcome was much less jeopardous than the one she was thinking. To him, the scenario that was playing out in his mind had a much simpler solution. He wasn't thinking of the worst cast scenario of those stalkers killing them, no, he was thinking to himself, "They're only out to capture us. They're not going to kill us," he said to himself with assurance. He didn't realize that he was thinking out loud. "Are you kidding me!?" The girl said. "I know what slave haters do. I've been beaten and verbally abused my whole life. I know what they're capable of," the girl replied in a strong whisper. "Don't you think I know too? I've been there, I've experienced the same things you have; I know what life on a plantation is like. I've been beaten, I've been verbally treated bad; but listen, I've been through this, you haven't. I've walked these woods before," the male slave said. "Then why are we lost?" She inquired of him. "As I said", he continued. "I've walked these woods before. I know what's out here. I've dealt with the evil hit men, and the racists Marshals and bounty men. You have to remember girl, I've conquered this journey one time already, I've tasted the sweet savories of freedom. So listen to me, I'm talking from experience here. When I tell you it's going to be alright, it's going to be alright."

He was referring to his first journey up north, escaping from his Natchez plantation in Mississippi. He had only done it one time before, but that one time was enough to know what it was like, the dangers involved, the snares attached to it, the bounty men, marshals, and hit men that were involved. He had been through it all. It's one thing though to have been in this situation before, the situation he currently found himself in, it's another thing to keep control over your emotions, your fears, regardless of how many times you've been pursued or stalked. "Listen, I've been through this before, you haven't, I know what men like these in front of us are capable of. They can murder us, simple is that, and they wouldn't give it a second thought," he said. Suddenly he realized, he too was getting caught up in the same reaction that his female companion was going through. This time, he thought to himself, not out loud, but in his head, "I've got to keep it together here. I can't lose it, not in front of this frightened girl." In the girl's paranoia she suddenly realized, thinking out loud, "I could actually die! And worse yet, I could die in these cold, wet, scary woods, far away from home. Yeah man, I know it sounds ridiculous, but yes, I consider that horrible, retched place of my Plantation, home. Getting beaten was petrifying I know, but it was still home." He was trying to think of a way to calm her nerves, "I know exactly what you mean, but you is far away from that place," he said. She interrupted to continue, "But compared to this, I don't know, getting beaten suddenly sounds less menacing." "Are you crazy!? Don't you be goin and bein ridiculous now, there's nothing worse than plantation life. I know we're in a tough spot here, not knowing what's on the other side of those bushes, but you can't turn back." The girl became overwhelmed with emotion. "But I don't want to die!" She said. "This can't get any worse," she continued, "I don't want my journey to end, not when we've come so far," she said. "Compared to the plantation life, I'll take my chances out here any day of the week. I know it can be scary, lonely, and sometimes you just don't know what awaits you on the other side of the corner." "Like right now!? She interrupted with a strong whisper. He continued, "It's just a matter of weighing your options. Do you want to spend the rest of your life being property, working hard for nothing? Or do you want to take your chances out here; at least out here you have a chance at being free. Yes, you have to work hard out here, work hard at running, but at least out here, you're free. No boss men yelling at you, no picking cotton at five in the morning." The girl spoke up, straining in a loud whisper. "Were fugitives, man! We might as well have a bull's eye attached to our chest. You know what I mean. Yeah, I get the part about being free, running toward a goal, not repetitively running toward the same cotton field at five in the morning day after day. But man, right now, in these woods, I don't know, it just seems like we may have made the wrong decision." He interrupted, "You've got to remember, we didn't have a decision, we didn't have a choice regarding our lives. We were born slaves. We never got the chance to speak up, to let our voices be heard. I don't remember anyone asking me if I wanted to work for free. Do you?" "No," the girl said. "Okay then, the way I see it, we only had one option, to run as far away from that God forsaken place as possible." "And what now, run, only to get stuck right here, in these scary woods. The way I see it, the plantation, this journey, we really didn't have any options did we?" She asked, hoping to get some type of reassurance. "What do you mean?" The male slave asked. "I mean, on one hand, we were trapped on the plantation, and on the other hand, we're now trapped trying to leave the plantation." "I still don't understand what you mean." "It's a no win situation man! Either way you look at it, we're slaving under the hot sun or the harsh winters, working for free, or we're out here facing death," the girl said. The male slave looked over at her, in a continued kneeled position beside her. "Well, that's the way it is, I'm not going to sugar coat it for you," he said. By now he had his hand on her left shoulder trying to console her. "So, here we are huh, trapped, it's like that?" She said with a mean, bitter tone. He quickly removed his hand from her shoulder. "Yeah, it's like that!"

There was tension beginning to mount between them. After a slight pause, he continued. "Listen, I don't want to fight, okay. We have to stay united if we're going to get out of here in one piece." "I know." She said calmly. "I'm just feeling like my back is against the wall here," she continued, "it's rough when your hope is just snatched away from you in an instant. I mean, one minute we were walking along this path, minding our own business, and then suddenly we're forced to huddle behind this log, you know. I don't know, I just feel overpowered by fear that's all," she said in a frustrating tone. "It's okay; we're going to make it." He was trying to reassure her, but to know avail. "I just want to scream!" She said, hopeless, tired, and frustrated. "Keep your voice down," he whispered. "I just want to say" she was now speaking once again in a whisper, "that no matter what happens here tonight, you have been a great companion along this journey. "Hey, don't give up on me now. We're not even sure what it is that's out there yet." "I know. I guess I'm just thinking of the worst case scenario that's all. You know, if we don't make it and all," she said. Her pessimism was getting the best of her. The male slave spoke up with tension in his voice. "Okay, I just have to start thinking. Let me think. I just have to think."

For the slaves, the moment was intense. Were they just seconds away from being caught? Even worse, were their lives getting ready to end? Were they moments away from being executed? Were all their efforts up to this point in vain? For those moments crouched behind that log, the tough lives they had lived began to flash before them like snap shots on a movie reel. The darkness; and the acute silence surrounding them, only fueled the situation. The tension was insurmountable. Any slight noise, from any direction, caused the log in which they were crouching behind seem like a tiny, narrow box. Their feelings of being helpless and trapped grew with each passing minute. They were gripped with fear. Although the male slave was being the level headed one between the two, the young teenage slave girl's pessimism had finally started getting to him. He was trying to stay calm, but her fear was increasingly rubbing off on him with each passing second. His head shook toward her direction when he spoke up. "I'm trying to stay calm here, but your panicky behavior is making things worse on me," he said. "I'm sorry, I don't mean to be a hindrance, I'll try my best to stay calm. It's just that I'm scared that's all. The fact that you're much older than I am, and you have done this before, helps though. And you being a man doesn't hurt either."

Suddenly, the smell of burning wood filled the air in the dense, dark woods. The female slave panicked. "Are they going to burn us alive!?" She said. "No, they can't be, I don't see any fire up there. They're not going to burn the entire woods just for us. "They hate us man," the girl blurted out, "they would do anything to kill us." "Remember, we still don't know what, if anything, is on the other side of those bushes." The reassuring attempt by the male slave was not succeeding. Both of them, at this point, were thinking the worst, he wasn't even buying into what he was saying. Nonetheless, the smoke that by now was surrounding them, had successfully taken their attention off of their dreary thoughts. "Where is that smell coming from?" The male slave asked.

For what seemed like an eternity, they just sat there, stooped behind that log, trying to figure out that smell. What did it mean? Where was it coming from? They looked all around, trying to pinpoint the origin. "Maybe it's coming from a house nearby," she said. "Good thinking. Let's begin looking around for lights," the male slave said. "Please let it be a safe house. That's our only chance right now," she thought to herself out loud. As they peered through the heaviness of the dark night, suddenly, they noticed a small flicker of light way off in the distance. Could it be!? A burst of hope came upon them. The light quickly made the once unending woods, seem smaller, less intimidating. That tiny little box of a log they had been cringed behind suddenly widened. The feelings of being trapped that dominated them, suddenly dissipated. Thoughts of being captured or murdered had no longer consumed them. He put his right arm around the frightened teenage girl and gently squeezed her. "We have a chance!" He strongly whispered. After focusing their attention on those bushes twenty yards ahead of them for what seemed like hours. It had in fact been an hour since they first heard that shuffling behind the thick shrubbery ahead. By now, it was three a.m. If they didn't do something soon, the night sky, which was both a hindrance and a shield to them, would suddenly dissipate, giving way to the dawning of a new morning. In daylight, those men, if it was in fact men behind those bushes, would have no problem seeing them. The slaves had their bearings about them now. They quickly had direction. Like a lighthouse on an island surrounded by the mighty ocean, this light was a beacon of hope for the two slaves.

With the hour gone by, and paranoia and terror really beginning to set in at this point, each crack, each sudden movement of a limb, with the exception of the area twenty yards ahead of them, seemed to them like an ambush just waiting to happen. The sounds they were hearing were just the drops of rain from the trees falling on the leaves, and the wind whistling through the woods; but to the slaves, the continual rustling caused them to envision men surrounding them at every turn, with rifles and nooses. They quickly began to feel claustrophobic again. The log that shielded them from their attackers became increasingly smaller, just like before, before they saw the light. Each sound was amplified in their ears. To make matters worse, they kept hearing the crack and swish behind those bushes in the direction of that infamous location. The sounds in that location were constant, about every five to ten minutes. There definitely was something behind there, man or animal. At this point, the slaves just didn't know. But oh, this light, this radar in the night, each time they noticed it, it made these intimidating sounds immediately more tolerable. Though it was some distance away, it felt to them like it was right over their shoulder. Someone else was in the woods with them. It was no longer just them and whatever was on the other side of those bushes; in this vast, dark, wooded space. They were caught between being scared and having hope. Yes, they felt closed in and trapped; but at the same time they were experiencing a kind of breaking free feeling, breaking free from the twenty yard enclosure they had been experiencing for an hour. It's as if they had hammered their way out of a concrete crate. The light was directly behind them, but it was about a hundred and fifty yards away. It was located below them, extremely below them, all downhill. And the terrain from the source of that light to the log in which the slaves were hiding was terrible. From where the log was located, it was about a hundred yards of steep slanting slope, toward the light. The next fifty yards, well, it got remarkably steep. Plus, there were the slippery leaves, rocks, and fallen limbs to deal with. Not to mention the fact that it was extremely dark. The clouds that remained above, hindered the moonlight from giving off its full light.

The area of Kentucky in which this middle of the night standoff took place between the two slaves and whatever was behind those bushes, was in an extremely rural area. Most southern states during this period were extremely rural. In the most rural of areas, areas such as the woods the slaves were in, one house per every ten miles would be considered populous. To elaborate more on the rural conditions of Kentucky; not only were the houses spread remotely apart, but the mountains and hills that surrounded them made those homes secluded and isolated. The state had a very rocky terrain. If you lived in one of these homes during the nineteenth century, it was as if you lived in your own little world, covered by an insurmountable barrier of rock that nature had created. Kentucky was covered with one giant rock after another. It was full of many underground caverns and mines. The rocky landscape made for some steep, mountainous terrain. And the terrain in those woods that night was excessively steep. If you lived in one of those homes during this period in rural Kentucky, sure, there were stores nearby, but it meant getting on horseback and making a day of it just to get there and back. There was no doubt; Kentuckians lived a very isolated life, which meant they enjoyed their privacy. Although the land was rocky and curtailed with mountains, they had enough open land to build farms to help sustain their private lives. This could mean, in some instances, that these rural citizens didn't want to be bothered by outsiders. With a gun always handy, some Kentuckians, especially those living in very isolated areas, were the kind of people who shot first and asked questions later.

Kentucky was also a state that was covered with a vast expanse of extremely dense wooded areas. This meant that the slaves were lucky that there was a light at all that night. And the winters in Kentucky, well, they were harsh. The temperature in that part of the state in which the slaves were located would get as low as twenty degrees in the wintertime, especially at three a.m. Those that lived in Kentucky experienced everything from snow, to sleet, to freezing rain, and, like on that night, cold, stinging rain. Kentucky is a beautiful state, especially in the summer time, with its rolling blue grass hills, and its deep underground caverns. But in the winter time, it's harsh, and the slaves were feeling it first hand. All they had on that night were a pair of long johns, two pairs of thermal socks, which of course were soaking wet thanks to the pouring rain that transpired previously that night; two pairs of old, thick cowhide gloves that were designed for farmers; two pairs of leather sandals which completely wrapped around their feet all the way up and over their ankle bones, and a pair of faded overalls with a wool sweater tucked underneath it; and last but not least, a poncho. Not to mention the bags of bread, and smoked ham, they were carrying for their meals that they allowed themselves to eat twice a day, with each bag weighing about eight pounds a piece. In twenty degree weather, or a temperature hovering close to that mark, it clearly was not enough to keep them warm. The slaves were dealing with a lot that night, the noises, the emotions, and most definitely, the weather.

They didn't have much in the way of supplies that night to handle what was going on around them. They did however have heart, determination, and willpower. Ever since they left the plantation they could taste freedom; and it was that taste that would fuel and propel them onward. They had the fortitude to endure anything that came their way. And this journey, the same journey that brought them to the back woods of Kentucky, would be a journey filled with many ups and downs. There would be a lot of things that would come their way. They would have to fight and claw their way through rough terrain, deal with racist, evil men with the goal of ending their dream of freedom, by one means or another; and white men and women they would meet along the way who could either be pro-slavery or anti-slavery. They would live in constant fear of these white people; never being sure if these whites were setting up a trap or a safe haven. Those were the obstacles these two slaves faced in their hazardous road to freedom. The snares and traps made them vulnerable. They had no weapons, except maybe for a knife; but what would a knife do to a man who was pointing a rifle at them? The chance of being caught or killed was at a high percentage. But yet the experiences they had on the plantation, the beatings, the verbal abuse, the being treated like disposable property, the daily degradation at the hands of the slave owner's hired hands, or overseers as they were known by around the plantation, made the risk worth it.

These two slaves had ideals, ideals of becoming their own individual person, with rights of their own, and the freedom to choose their path to happiness. Something that's taken for granted now a days. Before this journey began for these two brave slaves, they had no path to happiness.

Their path was chosen for them. They were not their own individual persons. Their white slave owners, or their overseers, took away their individuality, stripping them of any means to acquire any sense of self-worth. The slave owners and overseers running the plantation debased them of their humanity. They were merely meat, a means to an end, and the end being a profit for the plantation and its owner. They were not viewed as human beings with creativity and dreams of their own. They would wake up at five a.m., do the same job, sometimes until the wee hours of the evening, and receive no reward for their efforts. The harder they worked the less productive they seemed to be. One step forward and two steps back type of process. It was to no avail, they would never see themselves as successful. The only reward they would receive was to get up the next morning and do it all over again. For some slaves, like the two here, it would come to an eventual breaking point. They thought to themselves, "Something has to give", they couldn't, and wouldn't, keep living in this hopeless, valueless environment. To plan an escape though took great courage. Besides, the only world they knew of was on a nine square mile plantation. Or worse yet, their world was even smaller, a world subjected to a small living space and a small plot of land in which to work on day after day. Some slaves never ventured beyond this tiny bit of a much larger plantation. That was their world, a box, or better yet, a boundary that they could never cross, never venture out from. So this 'leap in the dark' venture into this outside world that they barely knew, much less heard of, would be daunting. Living in their small, confined boundary of a world, never even getting a chance to venture around the big plantation house, much less the entire plantation, made the world outside seem like an immense black hole. Yet, somehow these two slaves mustered up enough courage to take the plunge. It seemed like a desperate move, a kind of writing your own death sentence type of move. After all, if they were caught while trying to escape, they would return only to find that the life they were used to would be turned upside down.

Slave owners would make sure that returning fugitive slaves would be welcomed to a much harsher life than the life they had once previously lived on the plantation. Harder work would be given, they would be assigned worse living conditions than before, and the abuse would become much harsher. They would be used as an example for the other slaves on the plantation to show that this is what you get if you escape. But compared to the previous despairing plantation lifestyle the slaves had been going through before their escape, it was a chance they were willing to take. Even though plantation life was hard, and it took a lot of guts to escape, one slave that night, in her precarious situation she was facing in the Kentucky woods, had thoughts of returning back to her plantation. There is just something about facing death that makes a person think that their terrible life they fled from, suddenly becomes less gruesome than before, if indeed death is what she was facing, after all it could be just some varmint behind those bushes. She wanted to go back though. It was a tremendous strain on her; she had to weigh out the options. Does she stay and face certain capture or death? Or go back to the plantation in hopes that apologizing to her master will lessen the blow of her punishment? This of course, is hypothetically speaking. She doesn't know if death or capture is even a possible outcome, yet.

Her male counterpart however had no dreams of going back to his plantation. He had experienced a taste of freedom. He was a fugitive slave who was successful in his first escape attempt. He had made his first desertion from plantation life an "over the hump" type of experience. He had not only escaped from his plantation; but he had triumphantly made it through the back roads of the deep south, through many safe houses along the way, and finally to his destination, a northern free state. While up north, he had a brief taste of what life was like outside the confines of the slave world in the Deep South. Why did he come back down south? We may never know the answer to that question. Maybe his first hand accounts of freedom were so overwhelmingly great that he couldn't help himself but to go back and share this newfound existence with any slave that would listen. Maybe the feelings he had experienced while up north were so overwhelming, so fulfilling, that he was bursting at the seams to share these feelings with someone who had never experienced this wonderful sensation before. One thing is for sure however, he could say from first hand knowledge, that there was indeed life outside of the plantation boundaries that slaves were retained in. That one bite of freedom, however long or short it was, was more than enough for him. The time he had spent up north made everything he had been through previously pale in comparison. Whatever he saw, whatever he did, whoever he talked to during that time, had made such an impact on him, that it made him want to leave those free surroundings and risk his life once again by returning back to the Deep South. The taste, that taste of people, both white and black, treating him as an equal. The taste of being able to walk around in pubic unrestrained, not having to look over his shoulder at every step, at least part of the time anyway, he still had to worry about slave- catchers; but that swallow of freedom must have been enough of a dose to last him a lifetime. With that taste still fresh in his mouth on that shivering, wintry night in Kentucky, the thoughts of going back to his plantation never even entered his mind.

Kentucky had a component in the nineteenth century that characterized it. Something most Kentuckians probably didn't want to have on their résumés. The State was pro-slavery. The reason most Kentuckians probably didn't want this stigma attached to them is because in the nineteenth century, Kentucky was thought of as an Upper South, or Border State, rather than a Deep South state. African-Americans made up a substantial percentage of the population back then. Although early Kentucky history was built on the labor of slavery, it was in fact, from 1790 to 1860, just a small minute enterprise, compared to the state's Deep South sisters. The slave population in Kentucky was never more than one quarter of the total population, with lower percentages after 1830, as planters sold slaves to the Deep South. Slave populations were greater in the "bluegrass" region of the state, which was rich in farmland. The woods, in which the two slaves were in that night, was to the far western part of the state, they were far away from the "bluegrass" region which was in the eastern half of the State. In 1850, 23 percent of white males in Kentucky held enslaved African Americans, compared to their white male counterparts in the Deep South. In the Deep South, over 70 percent of white males owned slaves. Farms in Kentucky tended to be smaller than the plantations of the Deep South, so ownership of large numbers of slaves was uncommon. Many slaves found spouses on neighboring farms, and were able to raise families in Kentucky. Unlike the Deep South plantations, where many slave owners did not allow slaves to raise their own families. Because of Kentucky's proximity to Free states, separated by just the Ohio River, it was an enticing, targeted escape route for slaves who wanted to escape their Deep South taskmaster's plantation. The abolition movement had existed in Kentucky since the 1790's, when Presbyterian minister

David Rice unsuccessfully lobbied to include slavery prohibition in each of the state's first two constitutions, created in 1792 and 1799. David Barrow and Carter Tarrant, both Baptist ministers, formed the Kentucky Abolition Society in 1808. By 1822, it began publishing one of America's first anti-slavery periodicals. The small-farm nature of Kentucky meant that slave labor was not as critical to profits as it was for the labor-intensive crops of the Deep South, such as sugar, cotton, and rice farming. Laws in 1815 and 1833 limited the importation of slaves into Kentucky, which created some of the strictest rules of any of the slave states. *The Nonimportation Act of 1833* banned any importation of slaves for personal or commercial purpose. The ban was widely violated, especially in the counties near the Tennessee borders. Once again the two fugitive slaves are located on the opposite side of this area of the State, away from the more hustle and bustle slave operations to the east. In Owensboro, just miles from the site of this tense, emotional happenings in the secluded woods, newspapers were being published on anti-slavery. Networks of abolitionists' schools had sprung up all over the state, especially in the western half of the State. If there was any southern pro-slave state to be stuck in, facing possible capture or murder as our slaves could be possibly faced with, with a chance of finding someone who was on their side, it would be Kentucky. There was no doubt; Kentucky was leaning toward abolitionism in the early to mid nineteenth century, the same period in which our slaves' dangerous plight was occurring. The state was full of African Americans, and many white anti-slavery activists, especially around the same region as the rural woods in which the slaves found themselves cornered in. How does this apply to the two subjects who are entrapped inside the deep, western recesses of this Bluegrass State? It applies to them on several fronts. First of all, being in Kentucky, they have a better chance of finding refuge, especially on the other side of that distant light. Secondly, upon reaching that light, they have a better chance of encountering someone who may be the same color as them, or at least someone who is sympathetic to their cause. In any event, they were fortunate to be stuck, or in the girl's point of view, lost, in the western part of this state.

The girl was looking intensely at the light, squinting her eyes to try and see if she could notice any more details about what was around that light. The clouds opened above, just enough so that she was able to see what other details she could pick up surrounding the light. "Hey, I see smoke coming from what looks like a roof, here, check it out," she said as she grabed her male counterpart by the arm and points to the source of the light. The male slave could hardly contain his excitement. "Yes, it looks like a house!" He said. The source of that light was indeed coming from a house. But was it a safe house? They didn't know what awaited them on the other side of this visible, yet distant glow. Their thoughts ran wild. "What if we walk right into a trap?" They thought. "What if those men in front of us came from that house? What if the people inside that house are slave owners? What if they're Marshals or hit men living in there? What if they're just white people who hate blacks?" They continued thinking. The more they thought, the more scared they became. For the girl, those thoughts compounded her fears. The thoughts of who might just be on the inside of that house caused her to panic even more than when she would think of who just might be on the other side of those bushes. "If we walk into a trap down there," she said with heavy breathing, "there's no way out! We'll be definitely done for then! Our enemies could double in size if we go down there. At least out here in the open, we have places to run. And we have this path that we've been walking on all day." "So what!" Her male counterpart said. He became frustrated at her. "What's a path going to do for us?" He said. "It could lead us out of here, that's what it could do for us," the girl said with optimism. "We have to make a run for that house, we have no choice." the male slave said. The panic in his voice suddenly made the girl's once secure feelings in her male companion dimmer somewhat. She began to panic. "Why are you freaking out?" She asked. "You don't think we have a chance do you?" She asked.

She was trying to coax him into giving her some more reassuring words like he had done before. Some more consoling words like the time he told her everything would be alright when she felt hopeless. "That really worked before. I need him to console me like that again," she thought to herself. "Tell me, do you really think we're going to make it?" She asked. "I need to know that you believe we're going to pull through this." She was trying her best to pull the words out of him. Her plan worked. "Yes, we is going to make it. I told you, I know what I'm doing. I need you to get it together here and calm down; I'm going to take care of you, okay. Now, we have to concentrate on getting to that house."

She became nervous. "I don't know, like I said, it could be a trap?" She said. "Can you think of a better idea?" He asked. "Yeah, I told you, let's run through this path." "If there is someone out there," the male slave said, "Don't you think they will just chase after us if we simply run down the path? Plus, they could shoot us. Running to that house is just simply our only choice. Listen, if we don't get to movin, we's gonna be hanging from one of these trees we's a under. Do you understand what I is a tellin you?" Now that remark really set the girl into panic mode. "What, they could hang us?" "Yes!" he replied forcefully. "Oh my God, I don't want to die." The thought of being hung caused her to start crying as she said that. "Just the thought of being hung, that's the worst way to suffer. You're not helping me to calm down any by saying that." "I'm sorry", he said, "I'm just trying to be realistic here. Anyways, you haven't been calm since we got behind this log." "I just need to know that you're here for me," she said, "that you have my back, and more importantly, that you know what you're doing." "I know what I is a doin, alright." She felt somehow reassured. She felt safe with him there by her side. He gave her a sense that everything was going to be alright. "Now listen, on my count, let's start running." "I'm scared," she blurted out. "There's no time for being scared. We gots to move!" She observed the landscape. "What about the wet ground? It's steep down there," she said. They were in a tough spot, dangerous men after them in front, and a slippery slope in back. They were caught between a rock and a hard place they thought to themselves. Guns, nooses, slave-hating men with one goal in mind, to capture or kill, or running down this hill and possibly breaking our necks, they were thinking. Between those men and the slope, they thought, the slope was far less perilous. By this time they were convinced that there were indeed men behind those bushes. To be honest, they had thought that from the outset. Not only the girl thought that way, but her male companion believed that as well. He was just telling her it could be something else to ease her mind; but deep down he knew it was something more than just a harmless animal. They were making plans ahead of time, plotting their escape, not taking any chances. They didn't want to be caught unprepared if indeed it was someone, or some group, ready and armed to come out of those bushes.

If it was not a safe house, it would automatically become an ambush, making their escape attempt futile. "What if those men chasing us know the people that inhabit that place?" They were questioning to themselves. Their thoughts continued to run wild thinking about the "what ifs" of that distant house. The girl slapped her hands on her thighs. "This just can't get any worse," she said. "Um, actually it can." He responded. She raised both her arms for a second. "My mind and heart can't take any more!" There was a slight pause as she stared at him with her eyebrows raised and her mouth open. Finally the pause ceased as she said, "Well, out with it! What could possibly be any worse than what we're already facing?" Once again there was a slight pause as she watched him rubbing his hands together while he stared at the ground. "Well, you see, these men, these men out here, they could torture us." "Torture! Torture! What the hell do you mean torture?" He raised his shoulders while slumping his head. "Well, I mean torture."

Some bounty hunters, marshals, and hit men would sometimes use homes as torturing grounds for fugitive slaves. They didn't want to just capture, or even kill the slaves, no; they wanted to torture them for their rebellious ways. "Would you is a rather be hung or tortured?" He asked. "Hung!" She said punching her fist against the log. She began shaking violently. The male slave extended his right hand out to her shoulder. "Calm down girl, they will hear you," he said. "I can't take any more of this! That's it, I'm going to get up, go over there, and tell those men that I'm surrendering," the girl said, now determined to give up. "Whoa, wait a minute now, you's can't do that." He was trying to calm her down by putting his right hand on her shoulder. After a few minutes of her smashing the log with the side of her right fist, she calmed down a bit and continued. "I really don't want to know this, but, well, what do they do when they torture you?" He raised his eyebrows. "You really want to know?" He said. "Yes, tell me." She said hesitantly. "Lot's of things. Sometimes they burn your skin, electrocute ya, and pull your teeth and fingernails out, just lots of things." She became emphatic as she buried her face in her hands. "Okay, that's enough!" She said. His goal of consoling her was backfiring. She began shaking her hands up and down. "This can't be happening! This is like a nightmare, please pinch me? I want to wake up from this," she said. "You have to stop thinking the worst," he said. "But this isn't a game; this is our lives at stake here!

Electrocution, burning, pulling of teeth and fingernails, getting shot, being hung, it can't get any worse; it just can't get any worse. I just can't take this anymore," she said in a whispering panic. She was loosing it. The male slave had to think of something to say to calm her fears. "We can't think about these kinds of things, our only choice is that house," the male slave said. "But we're in Kentucky! We're still in the south! Do you know what that means? Our chance of this being a safe house is diminished greatly. Look! We're stuck, okay!" The girl vehemently said. "I know you're scared, I'm scared to." She buried her face in both her hands again as she spoke. "Scared is not the word, my bowels are about to give way here. I'm about to have a serious meltdown here, you know." "We have to take this chance," he continued. "If it's a safe house our plan worked, if not, our lives are all over." "You forgot about one thing," she said. "What?" She grabbed his poncho around his neck with both hands. "The torturing!" She said. If they did make it to the house, and it was indeed a safe house, what about their stalkers? Could the people inside that house stop them? She felt doomed. With her head now buried in her hands, she slumped over and laid the top of her head on the log. She was at the breaking point. She desperately wanted this to be over. The only way she thought, was for them to surrender. She became emphatic. "We're surrendering and that's final." She said. "Do you want to be tortured? Is that what you want? Do you know that by surrendering we could still be tortured? I'm telling you the house is our only option!"

"I didn't hear half of what he said," the girl recalled. "His voice was fading in and out of my mind as he was talking about surrendering. I was too busy thinking about one thing, torture. I could only think about what he had earlier said about the acts of torturing. I tried my hardest to feel the pain. To feel what it would actually be like to have my tooth pulled or to be burned. I tried my hardest to experience those things in my mind. I was trying to make it as real as possible. I could visualize sitting in a chair inside that house below, with men bearing hot branding irons, applying it to my skin, or having my fingernails pulled out. I just couldn't get the vision out of my mind, no matter how hard I tried. I wanted to kill myself at that point, and I'm not the suicidal type. Torture was just too much to bear for my young teenage mind. My companion wasn't helping matters much by bringing up the subject and telling me the specifics. I know he was only helping, but damn, he didn't have to get so specific on the subject. Looking back now, I'm so glad I didn't kill myself."

Her breathing got short, she began gasping for air. "Are you alright?" He alarmingly asked. "I, I can't breath." Her breathing suddenly got shallow. "Oh my God, here, just lay back." "It's too wet." She said faintly. "Okay, come here." He quickly picked his knees up and sat on the cold, wet ground with his legs crossed in an overlapping fashion. "Put your head on my legs, come on," he said. She lifted her head off the log, removed her hands from her face, and began to lie on her left side; with her head resting on his legs. It still didn't help though, although her breathing strengthened, she still had a visual image in her mind of being tortured. She just laid there on his lap, thinking of being tortured for what seemed like an eternity.

Many slave owners practiced this ghastly ritual to slaves who were disobedient on their plantation; most of the time it was on a regular basis. It was carried out mainly by the overseers. They found ways of making sure that all the slaves on the plantation knew when a slave was being tortured. For example, the overseer would make sure another slave watched as his or her friend was being tortured, whether it was out in the field, or in one of the slave shacks. They would even torture slaves in front of little children, this was especially savage. A permanent emotional scar was left on those little ones who observed this brutal practice. The slave owners and their overseers had one goal in mind when torturing; to make sure every slave on that plantation knew about it, from adults to children. They wanted to send a clear message to the slaves, don't mess with authority. According to an account by one overseer to a visitor, "some Negroes are determined never to let a white man whip them and will resist you, when you attempt it; of course you must kill them in that case". Slave owners and overseers were vicious. They not only worked their slaves to the bone; but they brutalized and terrorized them as well.

Slaves, especially female slaves, were subjected to sexual exploitation by their slave owners and overseers. These men of authority had no legal obligation to respect the sanctity of a slave woman's body. These slave women had no formal protection against their owner's sexual advances. Without legal protection, these women were subject to the master's whim and were constantly at risk. Eyewitness testimony, like that of Frederick Douglass, who grew up as a slave in Maryland, reported the systematic widespread rape of slave women. Slave owners did this, in a very perverted way mind you, to increase or boost slave numbers. As a result, there were many mixed-race child slaves living on a plantation. For example, Thomas Jefferson used many mixed-race slaves on his plantation. Many of them belonged to his father-in-law John Wayles and the enslaved woman Betty Hemings. More often than not, mixed-raced children in the Deep South were sometimes the recipients of transfers off of a plantation as property and social capital. There are many accounts of enslaved women being sexually violated by individuals who held power over them. A plantation was not just simply large fields and a big beautiful home; it was an orgy of violence, torture, murder, and rape. The plantation landscape was a chaotic operation masked by its outward beauty. On the outside looking in, it was a pretty and attractive place; but on the inside, the slaughter and violation of innocent human beings was transpiring.

When slaves were brought over from Africa in the early seventeenth century; stuffed tightly in ships, like large amounts of luggage stuffed in a tiny trunk of a car; they had lost their identity. From that point onward, they were no longer considered a person, they were considered property. Nearly one million slaves were brought over from Africa to the United States during the seventeenth century. Slavery got its start in America in Virginia in 1607. By the mid-seventeenth century, slavery had taken off in the south, due in large part to the success of Tobacco as a cash crop. Its labor-intensive character caused planters to import more slaves for labor by the end of the seventeenth century. Slaves were subjected to bad water and inadequate nutrition while working in the fields, causing large casualties. In 1705, slavery was defined as people, with the word people used lightly here, who were imported from other nations that were not Christian. Adding to this point, many religious affiliates endorsed slavery. The Southern Baptist, whose origin was derived in the Deep South, endorsed it literally from its inception. This religious denomination formed the Southern Baptist Convention on the premise that the Bible sanctioned slavery and that it was acceptable for Christians to own slaves. Later on, in the twentieth century, the Southern Baptist Convention renounced this interpretation. In 1810, a migration of slavery took place. Over one million slaves were uprooted from their plantations and shipped from one state to the other in the Deep South. Most of them were moved from Maryland, Virginia, and the Carolinas. Georgia, Alabama, and Mississippi benefited the most from this slave transfer. By 1820, a child in the Upper South had a 30 percent chance of being sold to a plantation in the Deep South. In 1860, a census was conducted. Nearly four million slaves were held in a total population of just over twelve million in the 15 states in which slavery was legal. An average plantation held up to 50 slaves, while a much larger plantation held over 100. By the nineteenth century, the wealth of the United States was greatly enhanced by the labor of African-Americans. Slavery was the major issue of the American Civil War, which lead up to the abolishment of slavery. They were bought, sold, used, and discarded away when no longer of value. Southern slaves were not the only ones who were bought and sold. Strong, healthy blacks in the North, who were productive and reproductive, were highly valuable commodities to southern plantation owners. Free blacks, who had lived their entire lives in freedom, were often kidnapped and sold into slavery. "Certificates of freedom", signed, notarized statements attesting to the free status of individual blacks, could easily be destroyed, with no reason needed. To help regulate the relationship between slave and owner, including legal support for keeping the slave as property, slave codes were established. While each state had their own codes, most of its codes however, and the basic ideas behind them, were shared throughout the slave states. In the codes for the District of Columbia, a slave is defined as "a human being, who is by law deprived of his or her liberty for life, and is the property of another." In South Carolina, death was declared in its Black Code for anyone who dared "to aid any slave in running away or departing from his master's or employer's service." In the Deep South, in the case of a slave child, if the father was free and the mother was a slave; then the child must be a slave. While working on plantations and farms, women and men had equal roles in labor-intensive work. In some cases, women were more productive than men. Which every way you looked at it, which every angle you took, one thing was constant when looking at slavery; they had no right to speak up in the every day affairs of their lives.

Turning back to the torturing of slaves; why did slave owners feel the need to torture? Why do people go on killing sprees? Their compass, directing them to moral and descent behavior, was skewed. Slave owners and their overseers wanted to send a clear message to their slaves; but did they have to go that far? From the slave owner's vantage point, they did have to go that far, namely for economic reasons. For example, in 1793, there was the invention of the cotton gin by Eli Whitney, a device designed to separate cotton fibers from seedpods and the sometimes sticky seeds. This invention revolutionized the cotton industry by increasing fiftyfold the quantity of cotton that could be processed in a day; the result, an explosive growth of the cotton industry. This, in turn, greatly increased the demand for slave labor in the South. Mounting pressure was now on the slave owner to produce more cotton than their partnering plantations. The slave owner also faced surmounting competition from foreign cotton producers such as Egypt and India. This pressure to produce, and therefore to make more money, led to greed, greed then lead to pushing their slaves harder. There was also surmounting pressure on rice and sugar producing plantations in the south as well. Not to excuse their barbaric behavior, slave owners felt that by applying pressure to their slaves, visa vies, by making an example out of some; that production would increase. This was carried out in the following manner. The plantation owner would torture the slaves, showing that the slave owner was not going to put up with their slack behavior. The slave owners would show the slaves the seriousness of getting their work done by making an example out of a fellow slave, making the other slaves watch him or her getting tortured in hopes that it would scare the slaves into working harder. He would turn his plantation into a fear based environment. No longer would he be satisfied with the hard labor the slaves were already executing; but he wanted to manipulate them into thinking that, if they didn't work harder than they had been previously, terror would await them. Slave owners also used torture to prevent slaves from escaping. The overseer, the one who actually watched over the slaves and their productivity, played a key role in the owner's new found strategy. Maybe the slave owners panicked and cracked under the pressure of trying to be prosperous and have the most productive plantation in the State, or the entire Southeast for that matter. Who knows? But one can't deny the fact that their acts of torture were just plain wicked; whatever the reason behind it.

Slavery was a cruel way to exist back in the seventeen, eighteen, and nineteenth centuries in the deep rural south of America. The white man dominated this part of the world. They were in a class all their own. Except for tea parties and bridge playing, which was often organized by their wives, white men controlled every part of society. They owned everything, from occupying businesses to heading up social gatherings. The world of the rural south was the property of the white man. For the slave owner, his plantation was handled much the same way. Like a judge ruling over his courtroom, white slave owners were methodical and organized, sometimes cruel and evil. Day after day, they held the rod of command over their families, their overseers, and especially their slaves. To the slave, the slave owner was like a dictator of a country, dictating his plantation. And like a citizen under the control of a dictator, slaves were constantly looking over there shoulders, fearful of punishment at any time, for any reason.

Not all slave owners were barbaric and sadistic. George Washington, for example, treated his slaves, on his Virginian plantation, with the utmost care. In the Revolutionary War, he had fought alongside many black soldiers. One such case involved a 12 year old African-American named Joque Graves. In Washington's crossing of the Delaware, Graves was left behind at camp. He was a groomsman for Washington. He wanted desperately to make the crossing with the army. Washington, aware of the danger, ordered him to stay on the Pennsylvania shore. Discouraged and dejected, Graves did as he was ordered to do. Washington, however, had a task for the young Graves. He was ordered to shine a light, so upon the return of the company, they would be able to retrieve their horses. After the surprise attack on the Trenton barracks, Washington returned to the Pennsylvania shore to find Joque frozen to death, guarding the horses, the lantern still ablaze and frozen in his hand. Washington loved the boy's devotion and commissioned a statue, "The Faithful Groomsman" to stand at Washington's plantation at Mount Vernon in Graves' honor. What makes this story so ironic is that this statue, commissioned and made popular by the slave owning Washington, would eventually become a symbol of freedom for runaway slaves. Fugitive slaves during the early to mid nineteenth century would use this statue, not the actual statue itself, but replicas, to guide them to safe houses, during what was known as the Underground Railroad period of slavery in America. No doubt, Washington's favorable treatment of his own slaves was due in no large part to the experiences he had in the war with slaves from the south and freed black men who lived in the north. Washington, in 1797, would give each of his adult slaves a quarter of a bushel of corn per week and twenty salt herring a month. This was a lavish amount of goods given, compared to the average slave owner. Washington was just one of many decent slave owners that existed during the years of slavery in America. One would almost call it an oxymoron to put decent and slave owning in the same sentence. After all, slave owners did treat their slaves as property, being men of good will or not. Whether they thought of them as human beings or worthless meat, they still used them like they would use their own farming machinery; buying them and using them for their own gain, without having to pay them mind you. So calling slave owners decent should be used loosely, after all, if they were really decent slave owners, why didn't they ever let their slaves go free? I guess one could say it another way. Instead of saying slave owners were decent; one could just simply say that they treated their human property well. Much like one would treat a car, washing it constantly, waxing it, detailing it inside and out, taking a tooth brush to the wheel spokes; really vigilant in caring for it.

Being the property of slave owners meant that slaves were at the mercy of their masters. They had no rights, no freedom to come and go as they pleased. Slave owners could ship them away at any moments notice, for any reason, to another plantation. Slaves were simply at the whim of their owners, not knowing for sure what would happen to them with the dawning of each new day. Imagine not being able to count on having a stable routine on a daily basis, knowing that you have a sense of security when you lay your head down at night. What a helpless feeling that must have been for them. Slave owners controlled every aspect of the slave's life, even to the point of what their slaves could eat. Feeding them only what the owner thought they should eat. They also controlled the quantity they ate.

The replica Joque Graves statues, which George Washington originated, played a pivotal role in the Underground Railroad movement.

The Underground Railroad was an informal network of secret routes and safe houses used by nineteenth century slaves with one goal in mind, to escape their Deep South plantations and make their way toward the Free State territories and Canada; with the help of course from abolitionists who were sympathetic to the escaping slave's cause. Other various routes lead to Mexico and overseas. The Underground Railroad was at its height from the period between 1810 and 1850, with over 30,000 slaves escaping enslavement, mainly to Canada, via the network. The Underground Railroad thrived during this period. Despite this however, fewer than one thousand slaves from all slave-holding states were able to escape each year. A quantity that was much smaller than the natural annual increase of the enslaved population. Although the physical impact of this movement was small, the psychological impact it had on slave owners was immense. Although under the original Fugitive Slave Law of 1793, which stated that runaway slaves were the responsibility of officials of the slave holding states whence the slaves came from, plantation owners were at a heightened sense of awareness during this period. With the pressure of productivity at an all time high resting on the slave owner's shoulders, the last thing they needed were rumors spreading like wild fire throughout their plantation of slaves learning that there was a system designed for escape, routes already carved out that would lead them to the north. Slaves lived in tight, bunched in quarters on a plantation; if one slave got wind of anything, much less a plan of an escape, rumors could easily spread quickly to the other slaves. Slave owners applied pressure to the overseers during this time to make sure rumors of a possible escape didn't get started on the plantation, much less spread. This is when overseers used violence as means to quell the escape rumors. From the slaves prospective however, this treatment by their overseers and master only fueled their urge to think, eat, and sleep escape, not to mention the desire to spread the news about it. Three questions that plagued slaves since the inception of slavery was not *"Do you want to escape?"* No, escape had been on their minds since they first realized they were slaves; but it was rather *"Can you escape?"*, *"How can you escape?"*, and finally *"When do you escape?"* The *Can, How,* and *When* of escaping seemed unanswerable for the slaves for centuries; that was, until the Underground Railroad movement. This movement suddenly gave slaves answers to those impenetrable questions. Before the Underground Railroad movement, the world outside the plantation seemed like an unreachable place to the slave. Once the Underground Railroad movement was in full force, slaves suddenly thought of the world on the outside as attainable and reachable; with its many, already carved out escape routes.

How were these escaping routes formed? How did these routes get established, with so many created throughout the country? They were formed and established by slaves who decided, after they had successfully reached the north, they would return back to the Deep South to rescue more slaves. There were routes established as far east as Florida and as far west as Texas. They went up as far north as Maine, Wisconsin, and Michigan, leading into Canada. Without these slaves risking their lives for their fellow slaves; returning from the north to the very place they escaped from, the Deep South, there would be no escape routes. Many slaves who returned from the north only knew their part of the operation of the Underground Railroad route system and not the whole scheme. Many more died than did survive trying to make the long journey back down south to rescue their fellow companions; but to those that survived; they made the Underground Railroad movement thrive. Without them, we wouldn't be talking about it today. Sure, anti-slavery abolitionists helped the cause; but it was the returning slaves that were the backbone to the operation. Without them, there would be no rumors started on the plantation of a possible escape. Slaves would just go about their business as they had been doing for centuries. But those slaves who risked it all, made the Underground Railroad movement a reality for those slaves who would have other wise never heard about it. Those returning slaves opened the window for those southern slaves' little world. For example, Harriet Tubman made 13 trips to the South, helping to free approximately 70 slaves.

The escape network was solely "underground", in the sense that it was such a secretive operation. The network was known as a "railroad" by way of its routes, which sometimes went along railroad tracks. The Underground Railroad consisted of meeting points, secret routes, transportation, and safe houses, and assistance provided by abolitionist sympathizers. Individuals were often organized in small, independent groups; this helped to maintain its secrecy. This provided slaves with having to supply few details of their immediate area. Escaped slaves would move along a specific route from one way station to the next, steadily making their way north. "Conductors" on the railroad, who assisted slaves northward, came from various backgrounds and included white abolitionists, free-born blacks, former escaped slaves, and Native Americans. Churches also played a role, especially the Wesleyans, Reformed Presbyterians, Quakers, as well as certain sects of mainstream denominations such as the American Baptists, which mainly had its ties up north, and the Methodists. The resting spots where the runaway slaves could eat and sleep were given code names such as "stations" and "depots" which were held by "station masters". They were also those known as "stockholders", who aided the slaves by providing them with money and supplies. Slaves would generally make their move along the routes at night, travelling ten to twenty miles per night. They would stop at the "stations" and "depots" during the day to rest. While resting at one station, a message would be sent to the next station to let the station master know the runaways were on their way. Sometimes boats and trains would be used as transportation. Although real railways and wagons were sometimes used by fugitive slaves, the primary means of transportation was by foot. Communication between the 'Stationmasters' and the 'Conductors' were even more disguised, in some cases, sermons were encoded to inform parishioners of the week's reception schedule.

A certain color handkerchief would be worn on a certain day signaling, or suggesting from one railroad worker to another that "The wind blows from the south today", alerting a safe house to a visit in the coming evening from fugitive slaves. The traditional 'who goes there' password is said to have been 'A friend of a Friend', which makes sense when remembering that a 'Friend' was another name for a Quaker. The Quakers spearheaded the Underground Railroad campaign in its earliest days.

During the Underground Railroad movement, southern newspapers would often fill its pages with notices, soliciting information about escaped slaves and offering sizable rewards for their capture and return. It was a difficult road to hoe for runaway slaves during the Underground Railroad movement. To make matters worse, many northern states granted police protection for slave-catchers who were trying to bring runaway slaves back to the south. The Fugitive Slave Law was instituted for suspected fugitive slaves. If caught in a free state, and not by a southern slave-catcher, the law stated that a slave would have to appear before a magistrate or commissioner and had no right to a jury trial and could not testify in their own behalf, since technically they were guilty of no crime. The marshal or private slave-catcher only needed to swear an oath to acquire a writ or replevin, for the return of property. Indiana for example, a free state, passed a constitutional amendment that barred blacks from settling in that state. So even though the purpose of the Underground Railroad movement was to get from southern slave states, north, to Free states, it did not mean that the fugitive slaves were in the clear. For many routes leading to the north, the goal was simple, get to Canada. For people along the routes that helped runaway slaves, they were referred to as "agents" or "shepherds". Abolitionists would be known from time to time during the movement to fix the paths that slaves traveled on along the route, the paths would later be referred to as "tracks". Those that helped fugitive slaves along the way referred to them as passengers or cargo. The Railroad itself, that slaves would sometimes ride, was referred to as the "freedom train" or "Gospel train".

How did the runaway slaves guide themselves, besides the help they received from anti-slavery men and women along the way? How did they know if they were headed in the right direction, north? One way was by using the Big Dipper asterism, whose bowl points to the North Star. It was known by runaway slaves as the "drinkin' gourd". It was the plantation owner's design to keep his slaves illiterate so they would never learn east from west, or south, much less which way was north. The more the plantation owner kept the slaves in the dark, the less likely they would be to learn about the North Star. The Joque Graves replica statue was another means of direction used by slaves. This statue was used throughout the Deep South by compassionate anti-slavery white men and women, and their families. During the Underground Railroad movement it was referred to as the black "lawn jockey". Today it would be considered a sign of poor lawn decoration at best and an overt racist post at worst. This lawn jockey was an important signal on the road to freedom on the Underground Railroad. Its name and the manner of dress have been corrupted over the years; but its significance to the fugitive slaves during their escape cannot be debased. The statue was about two feet tall. The only black part that was exposed was its face and right hand. Its left hand was tucked in its white pants, the pants extended to its gray shoes. It had a white, long sleeved button up shirt, with a white tie attached around its neck, covered by a red vest that was buttoned halfway up its chest. It had a red hat on its head with a triangular white spot in the front, just above the bill of the cap. Its right arm was sticking out, just slightly bent at the elbow. Its right hand was folded, with the top of the hand to the side, so as to make a fist. There was a hole running completely through the fist. This was so, during the Underground Railroad, a lantern or an American flag could be placed on the forward reaching hand. With spies and bounty hunters everywhere, even safe houses were not always safe. It became necessary to convey, in a low-key fashion, what condition any Underground Railroad stop was in at any given time. The answer was the tiny little lawn jockey. It was placed in the yards of safe houses to alert runaway slaves that the house was indeed a safe house. If a safe house was under scrutiny or compromised, the lantern or flag would be removed, signaling to the slave that the house was unsafe, and to move to another house down the road. The signal on the statue changed the further south you went. Even slave states used the statue. Green and red ribbons were tied to the statue in this part of the country. Red ribbons alerting danger, green ribbons announcing safety.

The safe houses that contained these statues were a key component of the Underground Railroad. Without them, slaves could not have made the journey. They were used as hideouts and aided in the slaves escape journey. These safe houses provided food, shelter, rest, and clothing for the slave. In some cases, as was the case with the male slave stuck in the Kentucky woods, they provided some education. The safe houses provided the slave a place to unwind and rest from the stressful journey. It gave them a safe haven, a break from the chase. It was also a cheerleading post. People living in those homes would encourage and root on the slave. The people living there would foster hope and reassurance, giving the slave confidence to march onward. The safe house was a refuge, an escape of sorts, although be it for just a brief while. Without the safe house, there would be no means for the slave to survive. It would be this same type of safe house that would be the only chance of hope for the two slaves in those cold, dark woods.

"If there were indeed bigoted slave-catchers on the other side of those bushes we were staring at," the slave girl recalled. "That house at the bottom of that hill would be our only chance of escape. Yes, our chances of dying were much greater than our chances at survival. That's why I freaked out so much that night. But we had only two options, get shot at, or the more obvious solution, run like hell. Sure, the house was some distance away, and we weren't sure who was on the other side of that house, but it was, flat out, our only option. I felt so trapped leaning against that log that night."

"Can we make it?" The girl asked with a slight optimism in her voice. "I don't know. We have an advantage though. The darkness will make it harder for them to shoot us," the male slave said. The girl chuckled. "Yeah, and it will make it harder for us to run too," she said. "My leg is asleep," she said as she was holding on to the top of the log with both hands, trying to extend her right leg. "Well you is a better try and wake it up. Don't stick your leg out that way; they can see it poking out. Stick it out behind you." The girl did as she was told. "Is it working?" Her male counterpart asked. "Yeah, it's starting to come around," the girl responded. "You know, we have been behind this log for a long time, maybe it was just an animal," she said. "I don't know," he said with concern in his voice. "It could be that, but we is just can't be sure," he continued. The optimism he had shown her earlier, the same optimism that kept her from coming completely unglued, had begun to fade somewhat. She quickly picked up on it. The same panic she had experienced when she first thought she saw the shadowy figure suddenly began to bubble up inside of her once again. The panic caused her to burst out into a series of rambling questions. "What if they have big spotlights? What if there's a gang of them? What if they are faster than us?" She asked. "It's too dark, it's just too dark, they won't be able to see us," he said, trying to calm her down. "Yeah, but what about the spotlights?" She asked. Her panic was at the breaking point, he had to do something quick to calm her down; if there were slave-catchers out there waiting to pounce, her panic would blow their cover. He began rubbing her shoulders. "Relax, relax," he said. "Remember, we have a way out of here, we have that house behind us," he said. His words were not relieving her anxiety in the slightest. She was about to cry. "Yeah, but that house could be a trap, remember? I just want this to be over!"

She said. "Listen, it's going to be alright," he said as he was still rubbing her shoulders, "I'm here to protect you, I have this knife, I'm not going to let anything happen to you, okay." Those words he had just spoken, and with him rubbing her shoulders, made it feel like a warm blanket covering her frightful body. Once again, he had come through for her, calming her down. He definitely was the glue that held them together. If he wasn't there, there is no telling what she would have done. She probably would be dead by now, bounty hunter or animal, it didn't matter, her panic would have gotten the best of her. Even though he felt like panicking, just like her, or worse, his age and his experience came to the forefront. Nothing takes the place of experience, especially when faced with possible death, and he had stared death in the face many a times before, during his first northern journey. "I don't know, what I would do if you were not here with me," she said. "When I first heard that you had been through this before, I knew I was making this escape with just the right person." He grinned. "Thanks," he said. "We have to do this now; we must make a move before they do," he said with fervor. There was one problem for them however, their fear of whoever was in those woods, or how many of them there were, was so intense, they were paralyzed by it. The fear gripped them, so much so it hindered their thought process. They had trouble thinking, trouble planning how to get from point A to point B. She became frustrated. "I can't think!" She said. "We have to do this!" He said strongly, trying to convince himself. Fear is a funny thing, the intense emotion of it can sometimes cause experience to take a back seat; and that's exactly what had happened to him. Even though he had been through this before, he could never expect to get use to this gripping emotion of panic and apprehension that had a grip on him, no matter how many times he had felt it. You can experience it, but you never get use to the feeling. All they had to do was run toward that light, as if their lives depended on it, which of course, it did. They were nervous though, their hearts were about to leap from their chests. The same fear that paralyzed them would also be the same fear that would propel them from out behind that log. "What if we trip over a log, or a rock, and break a bone? We will be sitting ducks. It's so dark, what if we run into a tree, or worse, fall and hit our heads on a rock? I don't want to die," the girl said. The panic that had been by her side during the entire time behind that log was still just as strong as ever as she rambled on. "What if we fall and roll down that steep embankment? We will role forever!" She whispered. "Would you please quit with the negative thoughts, stop thinking about such things, we have that light to guide us, and this small lantern in my hand." Oh yes, that promising yet distant light. It was a beacon of optimism, their only way out. "I think we can make it," he said with confident hope. "When I say run, don't think, just run." "Okay," she said with some nervousness and hesitance in her voice.

As they planned and prepared for their sprint, there was some more movement in the bushes ahead. This time, it was louder than it had ever been previously. They could hear the shuffling of feet. From the sound of it, it was more than just one person. To the slaves, it sounded like an army. They both slowly raised their heads up over the top of the log. Their eyes were as wide as saucers, their jaws dropped, and their hands were gripping the log so tight that their knuckles were white. As they peered through the open path to the bushes ahead; they could see what looked like two crouching figures moving from behind the bush closest to the path. From the looks of it, the shadowy figures were about to step onto the path. For the first time, the both of them new, this time with certainty, that it was not an animal behind those bushes. Their worst nightmare had come true. They were being stalked. And worse yet, they were being stalked in the darkness, and in these horrible weather conditions. "I have an idea," the male slave said as he quickly crouched back behind the log. "Well hurry, what is it?" She said crouching down along with him. "This lantern, it's our only hope of safely getting out of here."

Suddenly, a deep voice echoed from the woods, "I'm going to enjoy killing you!" It was a menacing, deep voice, slowly and teasingly coming from behind the bush. "Hey, I recognize that voice!" The girl said instantly. "Shhh, keep it down!" The male slave whispered. "Yeah, come on you spooks, come out! We've been listening to you niggers whispering this whole time!" Another man shouted from the bush. "I told you to keep it down!" The male slave said to the girl in a strong, low whisper. "You niggers always think you can get away!" The man with the deep voice said. "Don't come any closer!" The girl shouted with a frightened, shaky sounding voice. "What'cha doin? That's not gonna work," her male counterpart whispered. "I think them there spooks is a scared of us Junior." The taunting voice was loud enough as the man with the deep voice was talking to his partner that the two slaves could clearly hear him. "Yeah, they's a nothing but some worthless cow dung, looks like we're going to do a little jungle hunting." Both of them were laughing out loud at this point. By now, they were standing on the path. The two slaves could now see the two men's figures. They both were well over six feet tall. It was too dark to tell if they were thin or fat. The slave's eyes quickly fastened to the shotguns both men possessed, flashing in their hands. And the two men wanted to send a clear message that that was indeed what they were carrying. "Ker boom!" One of the men's shotguns blasted a shot into the cloudy nighttime sky. "What do you say we kill ourselves some coons and make ourselves rich Junior." There was no doubt; these men were hit men, ordered by some slave owner to do one thing, kill. "They have a gun! They have a gun!" The girl shouted in a whisper. By now, her panic had reached an all time high. "That's it, we are going to die, did you hear that old country bumpkin, he said he was going to kill us and get rich. These men are hit men! I bet you they can hit a target from a mile away! We don't stand a chance!" The girl said. "Calm down, it's still dark, we's a still have that goin for us," the male slave said, trying to reassure her. This stand off in the cold damp woods had been going on for quite some time now, and it was getting closer to daylight with each passing minute. "Come on out you coons, or we are coming down there after you!" One of the men said in an agitated yell. "Yeah, come on out you breeding wenches!" The other man said. Suddenly another shot rang out. This time it was aimed at the log. The male slave heard the bullet hit the tree just off to his left. "We is gotta go now!" This time the male slave didn't whisper, for the first time since the girl had seen the shadowy figure, he yelled!

Those men may not have necessarily been ordered to kill those two slaves by a slave owner, or anyone associated with a slave owner, a plantation, or the slave business. It was not just the slave owners that ordered hits on fugitive slaves. No, there were other parties involved as well. Many fugitive slaves were murdered by orders given from a different source. There were some contract killings of runaway slaves that were ordered by many of society's elite, from high-ranking politicians, to local business owners. The south, as a whole, benefited from slavery. So it was in the best interest of white successful men throughout the south to keep slavery going; which meant getting involved in the business of slavery despite the fact that they didn't actually own a plantation, or work on one. To the white man in the South, they believed that their economy was thoroughly dependent on slavery, and therefore defended it strongly. In other words, they believed that in order to put food on the table, support their families, and support their businesses, they must support slavery. In the south, if you were not white, you were the enemy. So it did not matter if you had a stake in, or reaped the benefits of the slave owning business, to a white man, slave owner or not, you still thought a black person was the property of someone else, namely a white man. If you were black, slave or not, in the South, to the white man, you deserved death if you tried to escape or interfere in any way in the operation of the plantation. To the white man living in the south, if you didn't have the same skin tone, you were the opposition. In retrospect, if you had the same black skin tone, you were the helpless victim.

Chapter 2   Springing Forth Life

*I*t was an unusually warm, breezy, sunny morning on the Defour Plantation. May 8th, 1829, this was a day that the plantation was bustling with springtime activities. The dogwood trees that lined the long dirt and rock driveway that lead up to the main house were coming to life with beautiful thick, fresh green leaves and colorful white and pink flowers. The apple orchards were budding with green foilage, and the apples were just beginning to show themselves. The horses were being prepped and ready for their afternoon ride at the plantation stable. The sounds and smells of freshly cut grass echoed and permeated throughout the grounds surrounding the big house. The smell of fresh lumber being cut at the lumber yard located in the far corner of the plantation; filled the air. Birds were chirping all around as the morning dew began to dry resulting from the beautiful sunrise. The giant cotton fields were springing to life. Life was coming alive once again on the plantation grounds with the arrival of spring. Life was also springing forth elsewhere on the plantation grounds.

"Do we have a way of getting it out of here, and out of here quickly!?" A voice echoed from a downstairs bedroom. "Yes a ma'am!" A black woman yelled from the adjacent hallway. The afternoon sunlight streamed through the hallway windows of the house and into the bedroom. "Now listen, I don't want any panic going on here. We've planned for this moment for nine months. We must execute this as planned. I don't want anything to go wrong. It can't go wrong. It just can't." "Relax ma'am we is got it all under control. It should be just any minute now," a slave announced in the crowded bedroom. The tension was growing with each passing second. There were five ladies packed in that bedroom, four of them slaves; while one woman, Harriet, was in the adjacent hallway, also a slave. There were two slave women, Kabuka and Coni, located at the entranceway to the house as well; not to mention the four male slaves located just outside the house on the rocky driveway. All primed and ready for the exchange. They had practiced the drill over and over again, like a football team getting ready for a big game. Each of them knew their role in this grand scheme. They knew where to go and what to do at the exact moment. "Make sure everyone is ready, Harriet, no mistakes!" The woman yelled in a panic from the bedroom. "Yes a ma'am!" Harriet yelled back from the hallway. Harriet walked briskly from the hallway to the entranceway of the house. "Is you girls ready?" "Yeah, we is ready," Coni and Kabuka said. "This doesn't feel right," Coni said while standing guard at the door. "What do you mean this doesn't feel right. We is been goin over this for months, and now you is just all of a sudden questioning this thing!" Harriet yelled. "I don't know, it just don't feel right. I feel uneasy about this whole thing, I have from the beginning, I just didn't say anything," Coni said. Harriet put her hands on her hip. "And now, when it's time to act, you decide to grow a conscience," Harriet said. Harriet was dressed in a cotton one piece maid dress. An all white dress from top to bottom with a black vest buttoned around her chest. "Listen," Harriet continued, "were goin to go through with this thing whether you agree with it or not." She turned from Coni and fixated her eyes on Kabuka. "Do you have a problem with what we're doin?" She asked Kabuka with a sharp tone and an obvious attitude. "I don't know, maybe," Kabuka responded. "The both of you is in big trouble if you back out now. Both of you will be hangin from a tree if you don't go through with this. You understand what I is a sayin? Hangin! From a tree! Now I gots to get back to my post and get ready, I expect the both of you to do the same." As Harriet was walking away, the two slaves began talking amongst themselves. "I don't like this one bit!" Coni said." "I know, this just aint right," Kabuka said. "Is there anything we can do?" Coni asked, with concern in her voice. "You heard Harriet. If we don't cooperate, we is be hung!" Kabuka shouted. "I know, I heard, but I feel so bad about what's goin on, don't you?" "Yeah I do, but I don't want to get hung. Do you?" Kabuka asked. "Psst, psst, hey you," Kabuka was trying to get the attention of one of the male slaves outside. "Yeah you, come here," she said in a whisper. The male slave walked quickly up the steps to the front door. "Is it time!" He said feverishly. "No, I didn't call you up here for that." Kabuka begins shaking her fist at Coni. "This girl here thinks that backing out of this thing is more important than getting hung from a tree," Kabuka told the slave. "Is you crazy!" The male slave yelled at Coni. "Shhh, keep quiet, I don't want Harriet to hear us," Kabuka quickly responded. "I didn't say that," Coni said. "You is putting words in my mouth. I just simply said that I didn't necessarily agree with this whole thing. I don't want to get hung; but I don't want to be a part of this either," Coni said, desperately trying to defend herself. "Well, you have no choice in the matter," Kabuka said sternly. "We is never had a choice since the day we is born," she continued, "we is been doin what we is been told all our lives, we don't have any choice here, don't you get that? It doesn't matter if I agree with this or not, I do what I'm told, my personal feelings come second." "She's right," the male slave said, "we is slaves, nothing more. We do as we is told. Now shut up with all that disagreeing business, like you is white or something, and do as you is told." Coni began shaking her head while looking down. "Your right," she said. "I'm a slave, I have no rights here, I'll do it whether I agree with it or not." "I'm glad you is come around. You were headed in the direction of getting us all hung for this nonsense," Kabuka said. Coni began shaking her arms. "So you do agree that this aint right?" She asked Kabuka. "Drop it!" Kabuka said sharply. She continued, "Now man, go back to your post." "You is better keep quiet Coni!" The male slave shouted back at her as he was walking away.

"I can't believe this is about to happen. All the planning we have put into this, we must execute this right. Slaves are you ready?" The woman asked. "Yes a ma'am," all four of the slaves in the bedroom said in unison. "How's it looking down there?" The woman asked. "She's almost there," the doctor said, kneeling at the foot of the bed. Doctor Wilson was one of only two doctors in the entire town of Natchez. "Harriet, is the mother ready!?" The woman yelled out to Harriet who was standing out in the hallway. "Let me check, ma'am." Harriet runs to the entrance door, "look out!" She yelled as she breezes past the two female slaves, Kabuka and Coni, to the place where the male slaves were located. "Is she ready?" Kabuka asked one of the male slaves. "Yeah, she's right over there." The male slave points directly behind him to the woman standing about ten yards away. By now the sun had drifted toward the edge of the sky. It was late afternoon now, and the slaves who were a part of the plan had been standing at their post since the darkness of the early morning. Harriet, after seeing that the mother was in place, rushes back into the house to her post in the hallway. "Yes, ma'am, she's in place!" Harriet yelled out. "Great! This is all coming together just as I imagined it would. Doctor, how's it going?" The woman asked. The doctor is silent. The silence seemed like hours even though it had been only a few seconds. "Doctor! Talk to me!" The woman yelled. "We're having a slight problem here, ma'am." "Slight problem! Slight problem! What do you mean, slight problem!?" "It's nothing to be concerned about at this point, ma'am, we were just going at a steady pace, and all of a sudden things have slowed down," the doctor said. Suddenly the woman's plans had taken an abrupt nose dive. "Harriet, come in here! Now!" The woman yelled. Harriet quickly rushed into the bedroom. "I need for you to tell me that everything is going to be alright," the woman said. "What happened, ma'am?" "Something has gone wrong, terribly wrong!" The doctor, hearing the woman, realized he had said something that sent her into a panic. Once he realized this he instantly got up from his kneeled position at the foot of the bed and went over to where the woman was standing. "Listen, ma'am, I didn't mean to upset you, things like what's occurring now happen all the time. The reason I said it was a problem was because, up until this point, things were moving right along; and then suddenly, it just stopped." The woman grabbed a hold of the doctor's shoulders with both hands. "What do you mean stopped!?" The woman asked. "In cases like this, ma'am, timing is everything, and when this timing is interrupted, I get a little concerned." "Can you be more specific!?" The woman yelled hysterically. "I could have used my words better, it's not a problem, it's just a slight concern that's all. Nothing to worry about." The doctor was trying his best to reassure the woman that everything would be alright; but in the back of his mind, he was very concerned. The woman began shaking the doctor. "As I said before, can you be more specific!?" The woman asked. The doctor took a moment to compose himself in order to say just the right words. He had to be careful here, one wrong word, and it would cause the woman to lose it completely, and thus, causing the patient to undergo even more stress than was already occurring. After a few seconds of thought, he believed he had the right words to calm her nerves. He took a deep breath, looked her square in the eyes, and with a sideways grin he began to speak. "Moments like this are normal in the process. It never goes completely as planned. You want it all to just flow, without any interruption; but in a hundred percent of my cases there is always a small bump along the road. I've never had a case without a bump, it's just natural. It's only natural. And what I mean by bump is a momentary pause, that's all." After a slight pause, his words had seemed to begin working on her. She was no longer clutching his shoulders, her eyes returned to their normal size, and she was taking deep relaxing breaths. "Are you alright, ma'am?" Harriet asked. "I believe so, Harriet, thanks. I'm alright now I think." She quickly went back to her routine, the same routine she had been doing all day, pacing back and forth in the bedroom. After an hour had passed, there was still no progress. "Doctor, is everything okay?" The woman asked. "Yes, ma'am, everything is fine." The doctor knew in his heart though, that everything was not fine, he was just telling her that to keep her calm; but he was growing more worried as the afternoon wore on. It had been a long day on the Defour Plantation for those involved in executing the plan; but the day was far from over.

The Defour Plantation rested on an area in the Deep South known as Natchez, Mississippi. Natchez is located in Adams County, on the banks of the mighty Mississippi River, on the far western border of the State. The terrain around Natchez is very hilly. The city sits on a high bluff above the river. In order to reach the riverbank, one must travel down a steep road to the river landing. Natchez is the oldest city in Mississippi, founded in 1716 by French colonists. Mr. Defour, who is the Plantation owner; has French blood flowing through his veins. His father migrated from France to Natchez before he was born. His family came from a long line of rich Aristocrats in France; they were an extremely wealthy family. The original site where Natchez is located was the ceremonial village of the Nochi Indian tribe. The Nochi tribe occupied this land until French settlers took it over. In the late eighteenth century, an overland route was formed known as the Natchez Trace.

This route ran from Natchez to Nashville, Tennessee through what are now Mississippi, Alabama, and Tennessee. Produce and goods were transported by flatboatmen and keelboatmen. The boatmen were called "Kaintucks" because they were usually from Kentucky. In 1798, when Mississippi was first formed, Natchez was its first capital. Throughout the course of the early nineteenth century, Natchez was the center of economic activity in the State. Its main product was cotton, which was shipped up north via the Mississippi River. The city flourished economically during this time, due in large part to their close proximity to the river. Being located on the banks of the Mississippi River made transporting goods, which of course was mainly cotton, a very productive mode of operation. The city was also known for its lumber factories, which produced and shipped tons of wood each year. Also during this period, Natchez was considered to be one of the wealthiest cities in the nation. Natchez had the most millionaires per capita of any city in the United States. The city's prominence on the river brought many different steamboats from up north to the city during the early nineteenth century. No doubt, without the mighty Mississippi river, Natchez would not be the prosperous, hustle and bustle city that it was during the nineteenth century. In the nineteenth century over 55% of the entire population of Mississippi was comprised of slaves. The success of cotton productivity, which was mainly supported by the need of international countries for the commodity, caused a large-scale increase in the number of slaves in the State. And on the Defour Plantation, where over three hundred slaves resided, this made for a large operation on the Plantation. The Defour Plantation was over nine square miles in size. It was over half the size of the entire town of Natchez, which was sixteen square miles. The Plantation consisted of cotton fields and apple orchards. The plantation was mainly comprised of cotton fields and received over eighty percent of its profits from cotton alone.

Several hours had past, and it was well up into the evening now. The lights were on, the drapes were closed, and there was still no progress with the patient. The doctor had made his decision; it was time for some action. "I'm going to have to use my instrument now," he said in a concerned voice to the ladies gathered in the room. "Why, what's wrong?" Asked the woman, who was pacing back and forth in the room, the only woman in the room who was not a slave. She was expecting a straightforward answer from the doctor. The doctor gathered his instrument and headlight. "Breathing has slowed," he said. It was clear to the woman that the doctor had no time for chatting, so she remained silent; yet fear and panic were coursing through her veins. "It can't end like this," she thought. She was now sitting in the rocking chair at the head of the bed. She had her hands together rubbing them back and forth, while biting her bottom lip. After an intense, silence deafening thirty minutes, the procedure was over. Was the patient alright though? "Is everything going to be okay now, doctor?" The woman asked. "The patient is sleeping now, must be quiet," the doctor said in a stern voice.

Suddenly it was time. The plan had to be quickly executed, and right away. There was no time for delay. No time to make mistakes. The woman rose from her chair. "Harriet, it's time!" The woman yelled into the hallway. "Quick slaves, we must hurry, now!" The woman yelled. She was thinking of the steps they had planned for months. Her mind was so busy with the thoughts of what to do, what her steps were suppose to be after this one, and the next one, and so on. She could barely keep her focus. Her body was having difficulty keeping up with her mind. She was nervously scurrying about the room, making sure everyone knew what to do at that exact moment. "I can't freeze up now, I've put to much time and effort into this mess," she thought to herself. "Quick slave, grab it!" "I is, ma'am, I is!" The slave said while grabbing the delicate package. The woman in the room, the same one in charge of this whole plan, demanded that it be called a package during the execution. The other three slaves were lined up at the entrance way to the bedroom; one on one side, and two on the other, all of them had a towel in their hands. "Hurry! Get it out of here!" The woman shouted. "Please, ma'am, you're only making things harder," the slave said as she was holding it in her hands. Two of the slaves ran over to the foot of the bed and began using the towels. "Get it out of here!" The woman shouted even louder. "Please, ma'am," one of the slaves said as she was toweling off the package. The slave who was holding it said to the other slaves with the towels, "Okay, I think that's enough." "Move, move!" The woman barked out the orders. At this point, she sounded like an army commander directing her troops into battle. After several minutes of toweling; the slave got up off her knees at the foot of the bed, "quickly get out of the way!" The slave told the other two slaves as she brushed them back with her left arm while holding the package with her right arm. "Harriet, are you ready? Here it comes!" The woman in charge screamed. "Yes, ma'am, I is ready!" Harriet hollered back at the woman. The slave, by now holding the little thing with both arms, quickly ran to the doorway of the bedroom leading into the hallway. "Hold on," the slave said with a concerned voice as the abruptly stopped. The woman walked up to her, now just a few feet from her. "What are you doing, slave? Get!" The woman yelled. "Ma'am, it's bleeding." "So what; give it to Harriet, don't even look at it!" By this time the woman had put her hand on the slave forcefully, and began to push her. The slave only had a few seconds to ponder over the situation as the tiny package was bleeding in her arms. "But, ma'am, this isn't right, we is need the doctor." The doctor was on the other side of the room, with the bed blocking him from the entrance to the bedroom. His back was turned to the situation as he was putting up his equipment in his tiny black bag. "We're not getting the doctor, now damn it, move!" The woman hollered out. All she could think about was her plan, executing it to perfection. The thoughts that raced through her mind of pulling this plan off, were making the slave's voice seem faint, even though she was right up close to her. The slave desperately wanted to turn around and run to the doctor; but then she quickly had thoughts of what the consequences would be if she did. She would receive a severe beating. She took her eyes off of what she was holding; this caused her to abruptly begin thinking only of herself. That fear, now flooding her mind, caused her to forget completely about the little package she was holding. "I definitely don't want to get beat. I've heard too many horror stories of what it's like, to go through that myself," she thought to herself. "If you don't move, you little wench," "yes, ma'am," the slave interrupted. The slave couldn't move though, her body was frozen, as she suddenly began fixating her eyes on the package once again. "I can't just hand this thing over with it looking like this," she thought, as tears began welling up in her eyes. The woman pushed her hard in the back. "If you don't move!" The woman yelled. Suddenly a dose of bravery came upon the slave, "Doctor!" The slave yelled out as she stepped away from the woman, far enough so that the woman's arm could no longer reach her. "Doctor!" The slave shouted even louder. The doctor, with his back still turned to all the commotion going on behind him; by now having put up all his equipment, was just staring down at the dresser he was leaning on. "Doctor help!?" The slave woman yelled out again in distress. The doctor didn't budge an inch.

"I wanted to help," the doctor recalled. "All I could think about was, my God, my God, that poor little thing. It was my calling, to help people. That's what I was born to do. But on this day, I was just frozen in time. I felt helpless."

"Harriet! Get in here, now!" The woman yelled out into the hallway. By now, she was beyond enraged. "Coming, ma'am," Harriet said as she rushed from the hallway into the entrance of the bedroom. "Give it to her," the woman told the slave. By now she was trying her best to say calm. "Don't you see it!?" The slave yelled at the woman. She lifted what she was holding to the woman's face, but the woman just turned away. When Harriet had entered the room, she saw the little thing, and her heart sunk into her chest. After the slave had held the package up to the woman's face, Harriet said with a shaky voice, "ma'am, my goodness." "Get it out of here, I said!" The woman said that with such fervor, that her body was now leaning toward Harriet.

Meanwhile, outside, Coni and Kabuka were listening at the yelling. "What's going on in there?" Coni asked Kabuka. "Something is definitely going wrong in that house," Kabuka replied. "Should we go in there?" Coni said. "Is you crazy!" Kabuka said, pushing on Coni. "That woman is yelling at the top of her lungs, I is not about to go in that place." "But what if," "what if what?" Kabuka interrupted. "I know what you is thinking," Kabuka said. She continued, "Listen, the more we think of this thing as an operation of delivering a package, and nothing more, the better off we is be. Don't make this personal, we is just delivering a package, that's all." "It's more than a package Kabuka, and you is know it." "I do what I is told, Coni, and you is better do the same. When you is a slave, your conscience doesn't matter. Hell, we is don't matter!"

Meanwhile, in the bedroom, Harriet was trying to get over the shock of what she was looking at. "That poor thing," she thought. "Harriet, take it!" After saying this, the woman slapped the slave that was holding the package in the face. "Ouch!" The slave woman shouted in pain. "How could you slap me, why I is a holding this thing!" "You are crossing the line, slave! If you don't do as I say, you will be in the pit for months!" The woman screamed. The pit was located on the eastern side of the giant plantation, near the lumber factory. Misbehaving slaves would sometimes be subjected to it. It was a ten foot deep hole, circular, about ten feet in circumference, surrounded by concrete, with a steel ladder extending from top to bottom. It had a gate on the top, with six bars going across, and a lock on it to keep the slaves from escaping. The woman put her fingers in the slave's face. "Do you want that!?" She said. Once again, the slave went from thinking of what she was holding, to her own future. The other slaves were just standing in the background, in a semi-circle. Their job was finished. They had done their part. To be honest, they were just glad their part was over with, and the woman wasn't focusing her mad behavior on them. But they were emotional over the situation. After all, they had seen the little thing first hand, and even though they were used to the woman's mean demeanor, because of the circumstances, they just couldn't believe she was acting the way she was.

The circumstances surrounding this event were indeed unique. Because of the sensitivity of the situation, the woman in charge should have been more compassionate; but all she cared about was getting that little thing out of the house as quickly as possible. She should have been thinking of her family at that point; but her hatred for her slaves was too much, and was overtaking her during this long, spring day in May. She couldn't stand to look at the little thing, the blood on it didn't matter; getting her plan completed was far more important than doing the right thing. She didn't care who she was hurting, and that night, she was hurting some very important people dear to her life.

The patient was just lying on the bed sobbing. The pain was excruciating; but the emotional pain was drowning out the physical pain. The woman in charge was like a wolf focusing on its prey; she didn't care about who was going through what, and how important they were to her life. She wanted that thing out of there. And what about the doctor, why was he not doing anything? Was he getting paid extra money to stay out of the way? He wanted to help, it was his natural instinct being a doctor; but for some reason he just stood there, silent, still. He thought by having his back turned to the situation, it would make things easier. But he had seen the little thing as well, he knew how grave the situation was; but yet, he did nothing. The tension was great in that room that night, everyone was going through some type of emotion; from the slave holding the package, to Harriet, the doctor, and the three other slaves, who were sympathetic to the little thing, and desperately wanted to help it. And what about the patient, who was physically and emotionally in pain? And then there was the woman in charge, her emotion was very opposite to that of everyone one else. She was not sympathetic, exactly the opposite. She was void of any feelings toward the package. Her emotion was one of anger and resentment. Sure, she had been concerned earlier in the day; but to her, that seemed like months ago. She was thinking to herself as she stared down the slave holding the package, "I am going to kill these worthless little ingrates, they are about to ruin this plan I've been preparing, and preparing for such a long time."

In the meantime, Harriet was standing in front of both the slave, and the woman. She was rocking back and forth while biting her nails. What she had seen in the slave's arms when she first entered the room had caused her once certainty about the plan, to waiver. She was now torn between helping the little thing and saving her own skin, just like the other slaves in the room. The woman noticed it. "Harriet, get a grip here. You know what to do." "Yes, ma'am." Harriet was intimidated by the woman. The woman's constant threats toward her had caused it. The woman began pointing at the package. "Now get it, and take it outside, just like we planned," the woman said. "Yes, ma'am," Harriet said.

Coni and Kabuka were standing at the entranceway to the house, growing more nervous with each passing moment. "I'm goin in, Kabuka." "No don't!" Kabuka shouted, while holding on to Coni's shirt. "I hear adults yelling, but I don't hear any crying. Does that not concern you?" Coni asked. "Maybe it's not time yet." "It's been a long time, Kabuka, don't you think? It's not going to hurt for me to go in there and take a peek." "Don't you remember what Harriet said earlier, we could get hung if we interfere." "I'm goin in." "Coni wait!" Kabuka tried to grab her, but it was too late. Coni had slipped into the house. She slowly and gently walked down the long hallway toward the bedroom. She was approaching the bedroom entrance, and could see Harriet. From Coni's vantage point she could only see Harriet's backside. She noticed Harriet's nervous demeanor. "I knew something wasn't right," she said to herself in a low whisper. She was close enough now to where she could hear them talking. "Harriet, I need for you to take it from this slave; now is not the time to choke, we have been going over this for a long time, and you know your role." The woman was talking in a calm tone, she had been yelling and screaming most of the night, but she realized that was not getting her anywhere, so she tried a different approach. "Harriet, take it please," the woman said calmly. Even though Harriet had agreed to the woman's command, she couldn't help but look at the package, and then look up at the patient lying there like a helpless victim. Then it suddenly dawned on her, "Hey, I'm the slave here, I'm the one that's the helpless victim." This quickly created in her the courage to proceed with what the woman was demanding of her. She no longer looked at the patient as a victim, and she certainly no longer had compassion for the thing in the slave's arms. She was going to save her own skin. Just like the other three slaves in the background, and the doctor. She was going to look out for number one, herself. "I'm going to do it, ma'am." She quickly grabbed the package, ripping it out of the slave's arms. "No, Harriet!" The slave yelled out. The other slave women standing near the foot of the bed said nothing. "Damn it, no" the doctor said in a whisper, it was the only thing he could say, as he remained in his standing pose, facing the dresser. "Yes, go!" The woman shouted. Coni, listening in the hallway, yelled out, "shit!" She turned swiftly and started running for the main doorway entrance. Harriet, with package in arms, started for the hallway. "Is there someone out there!?" The woman screams out in the direction of the hallway. Coni runs as fast as she can, like a sprinter running toward the finish line, except for Coni, the finish line was the front door. "I must get there before Harriet, or that woman, sees me, or else." Coni could envision, in her mind, hanging from a tree. Her heart was about to leap out of her chest. "What happened?" Kabuka said after Coni had made it to the doorway, completely out of breath. Kabuka waits for Coni to catch her breath. "The package is in trouble! I saw it!" Coni said. They had been prepped for so long on the plan, saying package came naturally to them. That was the intention of the ring leader of this whole thing, the woman in charge. She wanted to dehumanize the situation. Make the subject seem like a worthless object. "What do you mean, you saw it?" Kabuka replies. "It's damaged!" "What do you mean, damaged?" "I saw it, it's, it's bloody!" Coni said, still breathing heavily. "Oh that's only natural in cases like this," Kabuka said with a smile. "No, you don't understand, it was cut something awful." "The doctor!" Kabuka replied as she snapped her fingers. "The doctor?" Coni asked. "Yeah, the doctor must have hurt it. Was it serious?" "I don't know, I couldn't tell. I only was able to get a glimpse of it." Kabuka placed one arm on each of Coni's shoulders. "Did anyone see you?" She asked. "I don't think so, but I'm not sure." The woman walked out into the hallway to see if anyone was out there, but the only thing she saw was Harriet's backside running away from her. "Oh yeah, hey, Harriet!" The woman yelled. Harriet stopped abruptly. "Make sure the little Nigger is still breathing!" The woman said with no feeling, as if she was just saying it just to have something to say. That remark by the woman was too much for Harriet to take. She herself, had been used to being talked to that way; but under the circumstances, with what this little thing had been through, to say it that way, was unbearable for Harriet. She thought seriously of turning on the woman. Yes, she had thought about it before when she first entered the room that night and saw the little thing. But this time, this time, she was really thinking about abandoning the plan. "What if I just go back in there and say I'm not going to go through with this plan," she thought to herself out loud. "I will certainly die then." She just stood there in the hallway for a second with the package in hand. With the remarks still fresh in her mind, she turned around and looked at the woman right in the eyes. The woman was looking at her with raised eyebrows leaning against the entrance to the bedroom. "Did I stutter?" The woman said with a smart tone. Harriet opened her mouth, ready to give the woman a piece of her mind, but nothing came out. Something in Harriet suddenly caused her to turn back around and start running again. Was it fear of the woman that drove her to turn around? Or had it been the years of being a slave, years of being tore down to nothing by the verbal abuse? Could it have been all the stories she had heard her whole life growing up on the Plantation, of punishment and torture at the hands of the overseers? It certainly was one of those questions that caused her to give up on ruining the mean hearted woman's plan. Harriet arrived at the front door, breathing heavily. "Here, take it." "What in the hell!?" Kabuka said shockingly. Kabuka took a few steps back from Harriet in total shock. "Look at it!" She said.

"The doctor has buchered it." Coni began shaking her arms at Kabuka. "I told you, Kabuka," She remarked. "We is gotta take this thing back!" Kabuka demanded. "Now you is listen here," Harriet said sternly, "we is not taking anything back. How many times do I have to tell you; we is slaves and that means we do as we is told! I know you were in there Coni, I heard you, and I saw you." "But," "no buts," Harriet interrupted Coni. "Now you is trying to get us all killed here, this is white folks problems, not ours; get that through your thick head. "But the package, it's not," Coni was about to say the reason why all the slaves involved were upset, until Harriet interrupted her. "This package is white folk's problems, I know what you were going to say Coni; but the fact remains, that white woman in there wanted it done this way, and that's exactly what we're going to do." "That's bad," Kabuka remarked with an expression of concern on her face as she looked at the little package. "I know it's bad, but I'm looking out for myself here," Harriet said. "But Harriet it's," once again Coni was interrupted by Harriet. "I know it's that, and that's why I thought about revolting on this whole plan and telling that white woman where she can stick it; but then I thought about dying, or being stuck in that awful pit. We is slaves, we don't have any control or say so in anything; but at least we can keep from being punished." As the woman walked back into the hallway, she could hear the commotion outside. "They better not still have that thing out there when I get there." Harriet peeped around the corner of the front door into the hallway. "Hurry, she's coming!" Harriet strongly whispered as she quickly held the package out in her now stretched out arms. "I'm not," Coni said. Kabuka reluctantly held out her arms. "Here, give the package to me." "Where is that damn thing!?" The woman yelled out toward the front door as she quickly approached the front entrance.

Kabuka, with everything she had, careful not to drop it, ran down the steps and across the rocky drive to where the group of male slaves were gathered. She quickly handed the package to one of the slaves. "Quick, give it to her!" Kabuka said, breathing heavily. By now, the woman was at the door. "What's going on out here?" Harriet looked at the woman, then looked down at the ground. "We is just talking, ma'am," she said. "Where's the Nigger?" The woman demanded with her hands on her hips. The woman could see in the distant darkness, the package being delivered. The male slave rushed the package over to the woman slave, who was standing about twenty yards from the drive, in the dewy green grass of the yard. She had been standing there, as had the other slaves involved in this plan, for fourteen hours straight; but for her, her day was far from over. "Finally, it's over, Harriet," the woman said. "Yes, ma'am." "That little animal is finally out of my hair," the woman said with a deep sigh. "Yes, ma'am," Harriet said. "You're a good piece of property," the woman said, staring at Harriet. Harriet just stared at the ground as she replied. "Yes, ma'am." "You're actually worth your keep." "Yes, ma'am," Harriet replied. Coni just stood there seething inside. The woman walked back into the house in the direction of the bedroom. "Why did you let her talk to you like that?" Coni asked. Harriet gave a mean look to Coni. "She's been saying things like that to me for years. I'm used to it," Harriet answered. "She's just an old cracker," Coni said. "Keep your voice down!" Harriet said abruptly. "Someone could overhear you! You know you is been trying to get us in trouble all day long. Your job is finished, go back to your shack." Coni placed her hands on top of her head. "I'm going to have nightmares about this night for a long time to come, that's for sure." "Yeah, me too," Harriet said.

Meanwhile, the woman was walking back into the room, the place that had experienced such emotions that day. She was heading in the direction of the doctor. The doctor, now turned, facing the entrance into the bedroom, was slumped slightly forward with his black bag in hand, leaning against that same dresser he had been staring at for the entire evening. The woman walked up to the doctor with a slight grin on her face. "Doctor Wilson," the woman said. "Yes, ma'am," the doctor said. "Now, Doctor Wilson, you know our agreement don't you?" "Yes, ma'am." "Now the slaves, I don't have to worry about, their worthless and their not going anywhere anyway; but you, you on the other hand, you, I worry about." The doctor was now standing straight up, face to face with the woman. "Why is that?" He was taking the woman's tone in her voice as a personal insult. "You see doctor; you have connections, very prominent connections. You stay in contact with some of the most influential people in this town, don't you?" "I guess I do," the doctor replied. "That means that there is a high percentage of a chance that you could talk to some of these highly influential people about what just happened in this room today, right?" "Ma'am, you don't have to," "I just want to make sure I make this very clear to you doctor," the woman interrupted. "We have paid you very well for what you did here today, and then some. I expect, no I require it of you, to keep things secretive around these parts, you understand what I'm saying here?" The doctor was really feeling insulted at this point, and threatened. "What are you saying, ma'am?" "What I'm saying doc, is this, keep quiet about this night and you won't have to worry about a thing." "What is that suppose to mean?" The doctor said with concern in his voice. "Doctor, just forget what happened here today and you won't get hurt. Is that simple enough for you?" The doctor was intimidated by this woman, just another one who was intimidated in a long line of people who were a part of this plan. He was not about to say anything to anger the woman. He knew exactly what she meant, and he was scared. "If I hear from anybody in this town," she continued, "about what took place in this room, we *will* come after you." The doctor had received the message loud and clear. The scare tactic had worked, he was petrified. "Ma'am, I get the message loud and clear. I know now that my very life is on the line with regards to what went on here, so I understand very clearly what you're saying." "Very well then, now that we're both on the same page, we can go about our everyday lives." She began patting the doctor on the shoulder. "Would you have rather I not been so blunt with you, Doc?" The doctor remained silent. "You know, life can turn on you when you're not loyal to your word," she said sarcastically. The doctor had heard enough, "good evening, madam" he told her. He then quickly left the room. He approached the front door where Harriet was standing; he looked at her square in the eyes. He gave a deep sigh. Harriet didn't need any words from the doctor to know what he was thinking. She could see the fear in his eyes. She knew he had been threatened. She had been around that woman long enough to know her ways, and her ways were written all over the doctor's face. After looking at Harriet for a few seconds, he tipped his cap at her and walked out the front door.

The slave woman, with package in arms, walked briskly through the yard and into the six foot tall weeded field. On the other side of the field was where her shack was located. "It's going to be alright, Sweetheart, hang in there. Don't you is goin and dyin on me now. Not now," she said, choking back the tears. "We is goin to make it, yes we is." The weeds were striking both her and baby as she marched through them.

Suddenly to her right, right as she came out of the weeded field, she heard a loud, deep voice yell out. "Who goes there!?" It was an overseer; he had been assigned that night to guard the weeded field where the slave was walking. The slave froze stiff in her tracks. He could hear the sound of a weak, faint cry coming from the sickly baby. "What are you doing in this field at this time of night, Nigger!?" He was about ten yards away and approaching her fast. The slave suddenly began to panic, her heart was about to leap from her chest. In a shaky voice she softly spoke out, "I is takin care of some business, sir." "What kind of business?" The man said, now just feet from her, wielding a shot gun in his hands. "Owner business, sir," the slave woman said. As the man approached her, she quickly turned in the opposite direction of him. He could see she was cradling something in her arms. "What do you have there?" He said in an ill-tempered voice. She still had her back turned to him. By now she was humped over the baby, and was turning her head slightly toward him when she spoke. "It's, it's, it's a baby, sir." "Turn around and address me, slave, when I'm talking to you!" He was yelling at the top of his lungs at this point. "What kind of owner business!" He yelled. "I is can't tell you, sir, it's owner business." The fact that she said that it was owner business caused him to back off somewhat. He was still curious however. "Turn around, wench, and let me see what you have in your arms?" The man was no longer yelling, but he was talking with a mean tone. "Come on, turn around," the overseer demanded. The slave, scared and shaking, turned around slowly. She was clutching the baby now tightly. When she turned around she looked the man in his eyes with her head still drooping. All she could see was the man's eyes. They were pure evil looking she thought. "Is that a damn nigger baby, slave?" "Yes, yes, sir," the woman said hesitantly. She thought not only was she going to get a beating now, but this baby was going to surely die at the hands of this mean, wicked man. "I should kill you, and this little Nigger for being out here so far away from your pitiful shack." "Yes, sir," the woman said, now holding the baby even tighter. "You say you're doing owner business are you? Well I don't see any of our kind around you. What kind of owner business are you doing?" "I would tell you, sir, but it's of a private matter." She was trapped. She had been threatened for months if she told anyone of the plan, and now she was facing certain death at the hands of this overseer, not to mention the danger this sick baby was now in. "Sir, my baby is very sick, if I don't get it back to my shack it is certainly to die" "I don't care about that, you whore. That thing could die right here in front of me and I wouldn't bat an eye. I am considering, however, of letting you go by because you said that you were going about the owner's business." She had already gone too far by telling him it was owner business; but what choice did she have? That decision to tell him that would cost her a many sleepless nights. "Alright, go on, Nigger, but I will remember your face." She gave a deep sigh of relief after he said that. She didn't need to be told twice, she quickly stood back upright, and began walking vigorously toward her shack. "I will check your story out in the morning!" He yelled from a distance. That caused her to stop momentarily. "I will never make this out alive," she said out loud to herself, "nor my baby." She took a quick glance at the baby and immediately forgot about the man. She had to make it to her shack before it was too late.

Sam was standing, bent over, peering at the sickly baby which was now inside the mother's shack. "Is it goin to be alright?" He asked. Sam was one of ten slaves, including the mother, who lived in that tiny wooden shack. The shack had cracks in the walls which was often times stuffed with rags to keep the cold out. In a typical shack at the Defour Plantation there were about ten slaves to each shack, a mixture of men and women and a few children. Mr. Defour did not allow families to live in the same shack. This was done, in part, because he didn't want families meshing just in case he decided to ship one of the family members to another plantation. Keeping families separated made the shipping away of slaves less dramatic and hassle free. He would allow tiny children up to about age two to live with their mother in the same shack; but after that, he would split up mother and child. Once again, in case one of them had to be shipped off. He only allowed men and women to live in the same shack for breeding purposes. Their beds were made of hay, which meant of course, that they had to sleep on the dirt floor. It was an extremely degrading means of existence.

The baby had been placed on a bed made of hay immediately after the slave woman had entered the shack. All the slaves had gathered together, forming one big circle around the baby, with the mother knelt down by the hay fashioned bed. They had no warm water, so the mother used stale water in a small bucket about a foot deep, to apply on the baby. Because it was springtime, the water was not cold. She had a small worn out cotton rag in her hand that she used to dip in the water and apply it to the baby. The baby had several extensive gashes on its body. It had a cut going horizontally across the top of its head from ear to ear. It also had a gash going across its stomach and a small cut on its right leg just above the knee. The concern however for the mother, was the two cuts on the baby's head and stomach. The cuts were about an inch wide, and a quarter of an inch deep. There was a serious problem however; the slaves had no means of getting stitches. "Find some more rags!" The mother shouted. By now she was engrossed in her baby's cuts, blocking out every sound, and every person around her. All they had to go on for light was a little candle inside of a six inch lantern. "Quick, more rags!" The mother shouted. She was not acting hysterically; something inside her was making her calm. Maybe it was the encounter she had with the overseer just minutes ago, facing death right in the eyes and overcoming it. Or maybe it was the early morning, all day, into the evening, standing around waiting for her baby, that made her calm. She had been through a lot that day, maybe she was too worn out to be hysterical, whatever the reason, she was calm. "She is goin to die!" Sam said, weeping with his hands on his knees still bent over the baby. Sam was a big, muscular man; six foot five and two hundred fifty pounds, with a heart of gold. He was a teddy bear inside. He cared for all the slaves he lived and worked with. And this night, he cared for that little baby who was on the brink of dying. With more rags now at her side, the mother alternated between the wet rags and the dry ones, applying them to the cuts. She just needed one dry rag for the cut on the baby's leg; she just laid the rag on the cut and left it. Her main concern and attention was directed on the other two cuts. "My baby is a losin too much blood!" The mother said in a mad tone, looking at Sam. The baby, who had been faintly crying the entire time the woman was cutting across the field, had now stopped. "We're losing it, my baby is a not goin to make it!" The mother yelled out. "We need alcohol, gauzes, stitches, and a pair of tweezers," Sarena said. "How do you know this Sarena?" The mother asked. Sarena had once observed an overseer's child getting stitched up after a fall from her bike. "I is seen it done before, just a couple of weeks ago, I seen a little girl get stitched up on her leg. I believe I can do it!" It was the break the mother needed. Hope suddenly burst through the mother from the inside. She began shaking her arms and pumping her fists. "My baby is goin to make it!" She said. "Yeah, but where is we goin to get the supplies we need?" A slave shouted in the background. "I know where the medical building is!" Sam shouted.

The slaves caught a break they so desperately needed. Sam had routinely been working at the medical supply building for the last six months, loading and organizing the supplies into the building. "I is been workin there for the last few months. I know exactly where it is!" Sam said emphatically. "It's too dangerous, Sam," Sarena exclaimed. "It's dark, there is overseers everywhere, it's just too dangerous," she continued. "What about my baby!" The mother yelled at Sarena. "I'm sorry, I know your baby is about to die; but if we send Sam out, he is a most assuredly goin to die. Then we is have two dead people to mourn." "I understand what you is a sayin, Sarena," Sam said, "but I is got to do this. I can't stand to watch this baby suffer like this. It's just an innocent baby, it hasn't had a chance to even live yet, and it's goin through this!?" "What life does it have to look forward to, Sam? This life, the life we is been livin for so long. We is never had a future, what makes you think this baby has one? What future? We is doin it a favor if it doesn't make it," Sarena said. The mother, with her arm in the air, and her hand balled up in a fist, yelled out. "How can you say that, Sarena!? You don't know what the future holds. My baby could have a chance at a great future. Maybe this nightmare of a life will be over and done with by the time it's grown up." "The woman has a point, Sarena," Sam pointed out. "We don't have much time," one of the slaves yelled out from the back of the circle. "He's right; I've got to do this now!" Sam said with impatience about him. "It's too dangerous, Sam." Sarena said as she points to the door. "You is writing your own death sentence if you walk out that door." "I can make it, have faith, Sarena. I know where I is a goin." "You is too big," Sarena continued, "you'll make too much noise!"

The medical building was located to the right of the shack, about a hundred yards away. He would have to go across the dirt road that separated the shacks from the cotton fields and apple orchards. He would then have to go through one of the cotton fields, in a diagonal direction, and across an open grassy area to finally get to the building. "What if the building is locked?" Sarena asked Sam. "It's never locked; I've never seen it locked." Sam replied. "But what if it is?" Sarena continued. "Then, I'll take my chances," Sam adamantly said. "You better do it now, Sam, we're running out of time!" The mother yelled at him emphatically. Sarena points to the corner of the shack with her head. "Sam, come over here a minute," she said. They both walk to the corner. Sarena grabs Sam's overalls by the upper part of his chest. "I don't want to lose you!" She said. "You is not goin to lose me, Sarena, I can do this, I'm confident about this. I have to do this for that baby. Do you understand?" Sarena, still holding him by the overalls, lays her head on his shoulder. "Why you though, Sam. Why can't it be someone else?" Sam lifts her head from his shoulder. "Because I'm the only one who knows where it is. I'm goin to be alright," he said in a comforting voice. "You were always the caring one out of this bunch," Sarena said with a smile. "Now, let me go and do this okay?" Sam said to Sarena. Sarena held his cheeks with both hands. "You better be careful!" She said. "We don't have much time, Sam!" The mother yelled out from the other side of the shack. "I have to go, Sweetheart," Sam said to Sarena as he turns and rushes out the door. "Sam!" Sarena yelled out with her arm stretched out toward the doorway, it was too late; Sam had already disappeared into the night. "I just wanted to say, I love you," Sarena said to herself in a soft tone.

While walking across the dirt road slowly, Sam peers to both his right and left, looking for anyone white, or anyone with a rifle for that matter; "so far so good," he said to himself. It was a clear, warm night. The moon was a full one, providing plenty of light on the Plantation. Sam entered the cotton field; the dangerous part of his journey was still yet ahead. The open area beyond the field was the danger zone. If he was going to be seen, it would be in that area. He walked through the field, taking it one step at a time. "I don't want to get caught," he said to himself, "but I must hurry, that baby's life depends on me." He picked up the pace just slightly, stopping every few seconds to observe his surroundings and listen for any footsteps. All he could hear though were sounds of dogs barking way off in the distance. That meant that overseers were indeed around. He finally got to the edge of the field. He could see the building; but he also noticed the long, open field between him and his target. It wasn't far to the building, about fifteen yards; to him however, looking at that intimidating open vast space, it looked a whole lot further than it actually was. He stood still, in a crouched position for about five minutes, listening intensely for any sound. The dog's barks were still far away, on the other side of the field. He felt comfortable with his surroundings; with the dogs at a distance, and no sounds around him, he felt it was time to make his move. He quickly darted across the open area. He was quickly making it to the building, but to him it seemed like the building was moving away from him. It was as if the building was taking one step back with each forward progress he was making. For what seemed like forever to him, he finally reached the building. Now the big question, was it locked? He had to be quiet; the building was made of tin, so any sudden jolt and the noise would echo throughout the Plantation. He carefully and gently, with fine precision, pulled on the door. It wasn't locked! "I knew it!" He said to himself in a whisper. He quickly closed the door behind him and entered the large building. There were windows going along the sides of the building along the top, so the advantage of the full moon was paying off. He could clearly see. Because he had worked in this building for six months he knew where everything was located, so it didn't take him long to gather the much needed supplies. He had brought with him a leather sack to carry back the supplies in. Once he gathered what he thought would be enough he made his way back to the entranceway to the building.

There was a window on the entrance door. He used this window to look through as he slowly pushed the door open to hear for any sounds. Once again he waited for about five minutes. The dogs were still at a distance and he heard no sounds. He was ready to make his move once again. He stepped out; the door he was holding was wet from the nighttime dew. As he turned to close the door it slipped from his hand. The door made a sound that reverberated throughout the area as it slammed against the building. Suddenly, he heard a dog bark twenty yards directly in front of him. Because of the moonlight and the open area, he quickly noticed the dog; but more importantly he noticed the rifle. His eyes went from the dog to the rifle, and finally to the most important thing, the large white man standing there. "Hey, you, Nigger, don't move!" The overseer yelled out. Sam didn't waste any time; he swiftly darted diagonally toward the cotton field, sprinting with leather sack in hand. "I must get this stuff to that baby," he said out loud. A gunshot explodes into the air. "Hey, Johnny, we got us a runner!" The man yelled to his fellow overseer who was further down the way, closer to the shack Sam was running to. Sam was flying, busting through the cotton field, trampling over the cotton stalks. He was thinking of that baby, and Sarena. He had strong feelings for both, and those feelings were fueling his drive to make it back safely. "Should I stop when I get to the end of the field," he thought. He wondered if he should stop once he got to the edge and hideout for a few minutes, and see if the men would give up on hunting him down. "I'm big enough to take them and their dogs, but I can't compete with their guns," he said out loud as he was running. The overseers were running toward the shacks. They decided to split up at the middle of the shacks; one would go down toward the front and the other toward the opposite end. Sam got to the edge of field. He stopped and bent over, he was so out of breath that he couldn't stand up straight. "Did they see me go into the field?" He thought. If they had seen him there would certainly be dogs in the field by now, and that's what he was thinking. Sam couldn't move, there was no way he could. He couldn't see the overseers and he didn't hear their dogs, so he had no idea if it was safe to cross the dirt road, so he waited.

"Sam is taking too long, something has gone wrong," Sarena said with deep concern. She began pacing back and forth while holding her head. "He should be back by now," she continued, "if he dies." She was looking directly at the mother as she said that. "What, Sarena? What will you do? Do you see my baby? Have you really taken a good look at it? That doctor butchered it! It's barely breathing. What are you going to do to me? I'm trying to save my baby here and Sam is risking his life," "that's right, he's out there risking his life," Sarena interrupted, "why couldn't it be someone else, huh!" "He's doin the right thing Sarena," the mother said, trying to calm Sarena down despite the fact that she herself was panicking for her own child. Meanwhile, outside, Sam was patiently waiting to make his move. He couldn't wait too long though; he knew that baby wasn't going to make it much longer. Sam listened intensely. "I don't hear anyone," he said to himself in a whisper. "I'm goin to make my move." He positioned himself in a sprinter mode, with one leg in front of the other, one arm in front of his body and the other behind him. He leaped from the field and began running toward the shack directly in front of him.

"Johnny, there he is!" The overseer yelled out. Sam got to the shack and opened the door. A shot rang out; Sam hit the floor face first. He had been shot in the back. The bag that had the supplies in it went flying across the dirt floor, scattering the contents everywhere. "Oh my God!" Sarena shouted out. After seeing the bullet hole in Sam's back, she began screaming deliriously. "My Sam! My baby! My baby!" She yelled out during her delirious screaming. Some of the slaves quickly pulled his body in and shut the door. Sarena ran to where Sam was lying and fell on top of him. "Why? Why?" She said sobbing uncontrollably. Suddenly the door busted open, it was Johnny. "Give that Nigger to me!" He demanded. Sarena became frantic. "No! Please no!" She screamed. By this time the other overseer had arrived onto the scene. The slave children living in the shack, three of them in total, between the ages of seven and nine, were awakened by the screaming and carrying on of Sarena, and also from the shotgun blast to Sam. They covered their faces with their blankets, hoping to somehow escape the madness that was occurring right in front of them. "I is scared," one of the children whispered to another. "Just keep the blanket over you," one of the other children whispered. "I never got to tell you that I loved you," Sarena said, sobbing over Sam's lifeless body. No sooner had she got those words out of her mouth than suddenly, and without hesitation, the overseers grabbed Sam's dead body and dragged him out, with Sam still face first on the ground. "We're going to hang this dead Nigger," Johnny said in a sarcastic voice. "No!" Sarena continued to scream. "Shut up wench!" The other overseer said. "Or we're going to hang you right along next to him!" Suddenly Sam's body was gone. The slaves could hear the overseers laughing and yelling from inside the shack. "Woo hoo! Yeah! Alright! Nigger time!"

Sarena pointed to the mother. "You!" She yelled. Sarena rushed toward the mother. "Hold on!" Martin said, he was one of the slaves in the group. He grabbed Sarena with both arms, holding her tightly. "Now just hold on, attacking her, Sarena, is not goin to bring Sam back," Martin said. The other slaves had gathered together in front of the mother and child, blocking the two from Sarena. Sarena was swaying back and forth, trying to break the bear hug Martin had on her. "Let go of me, Martin!" "Now we have a dying baby here. Sam would not have wanted it to be this way. He died to save this little thing,

Sarena. He wouldn't have done all of this to see you get in the way of that. Now, I know you is hurtin, but you have to think of Sam's wishes here, and the baby's. Sam wanted this baby to live and he risked his life to make sure that happened," Martin said, trying to be the voice of reason in this chaotic scene. "Let go of me!" Sarena screamed. "Are you calm?" Martin asked, still holding Sarena tight. Sarena jerked her way out of the grasp of Martin. She pulled on her overalls, stood there for a minute, and turned away from the mother and child and began walking to the corner of the shack opposite them. "Now, quickly, let's gather these supplies up and give them to the mother," Martin said while he and the other slaves picked up the scattered pieces and handed them to the mother. "Sarena," the mother calmly yelled over to the corner where Sarena was trying to compose herself. "I can't do this without you. You know how to do this, I need your help, please," the mother begged. Suddenly the baby let out a sickly cry. Sarena could hear it. The sound suddenly made her anger dissipate. Her thoughts went from Sam to that little baby. All she could think about now was helping that innocent child. After a few more seconds of thinking, she responded to the mother's plea. "Okay, I'll help," she said in a soft voice. Sarena, with a calm pace, walked over to where the mother and the child were. She received the supplies from the mother and began to work on the baby. After almost an hour, Sarena had completed her work. The bleeding had stopped. The baby's eyes were now open, and it was respondent to the mother. The mother began breastfeeding the starving baby. After being knelt by the baby for quite some time, Sarena got back up, turned, and slowly walked back to the opposite corner of the tiny shack. After the mother made sure the baby was alright, and could be left unattended to by her, she looked up and noticed Sarena standing in the corner, slightly slumped over. After taking a deep breath, she stood up from where she had been sitting for hours now, and walked over to Sarena. "Thank you, Sarena. You saved my baby's life. Listen, Sam didn't die in vain. He saved my baby too. He's a hero, you both is. And I will make sure my baby knows that about you two when it's all grown up, and what you two did for my little child here tonight. You two worked together as a team to save my baby here tonight, Sarena. Don't you see how beautiful of a picture this is? My God, your love for each other, the same love that brought the two of you together, was the same love that saved my little baby. Sam would be proud of you." Sarena was touched by the words of the mother. She turned around and faced the mother. She looked into her eyes and smiled. With the fresh stains of Sam's blood still on her cheeks, arms, and overalls, she said calmly, "we did do this together didn't we?" The mother hugged Sarena. "Yeah, Sarena, you guys did." After a few seconds, Sarena returned the favor.

As Sarena and the mother were hugging, there came a sudden tap on the closed shack door. Martin slowly went up to the door. "Who is it?" He asked tentatively, fearful that it might be an overseer coming back for some more fun at their expense. There was no response from the other end. Martin stepped back a bit and turned to Sarena. Sarena let go of the mother and stepped to her right. Now facing Martin she said "what's wrong, Martin?" Martin looked back at her with obvious fear in his face. "What if it be another one of those hired hands, coming back for some more of us?" "If it was a hired hand he wouldn't be a knockin, Martin," Sarena replied. "Good point," Martin said with a relief look on his face. "Who is it?" He yelled again, this time he was quite some distance from the door. "It's Coni, Kabuka, and Shilo," a woman said in a loud whisper from the other side of the door. "Shilo, who's Shilo?" Martin said out loud. Shilo was one of the male slaves in the group outside the house that night. He was the one who handed the baby off to the mother. Martin walked to the door slowly, "who else is with you?" "It's just the three of us," the woman whispered. It was Kabuka's voice Martin was hearing. With a slight hesitation, Martin opened the door. "Quickly, get in," he said forcefully. "What's wrong?" Kabuka asked. She could see the fright on Martin's face. The three of them, once they entered, quickly glanced over at Sarena. They immediately noticed the blood that was covering her. "Is, is that from the baby?" Coni, nervous now, thinking the worst, asked. The three of them glanced over at the baby in a hurry. They observed the baby from head to toe and noticed the work that had been done to it. They also noticed that the blood that had once been gushing from it, had stopped. "Thank God," Coni said as she gave a big sigh of relief. Shilo pointed up and down at Sarena's body. "What is wrong with you, I mean, uh, look at you, Sarena," "Is it from the baby?" Kabuka asked. Sarena took her eyes off of them and suddenly looked at the ground. "No guys, it's not," she said. The mother was also looking at the ground, except she was shaking her head. "It was Sam," the mother said. "What about Sam?" Coni asked with a concerned tone. She and Sam had been close friends for years. "What about him Sarena?" Coni continued, this time taking a few steps toward them. "He's dead damn it!" Sarena yelled out at her. "Oh my God!" Coni said while bending over and placing her hands on her knees. Kabuka spread her arms apart and asked. "What happened? I mean, I mean, where is he?" "He's probably hanging from a tree by now," Martin said with a seemingly uncaring voice. Sarena marched right up to Martin. "Shut up, Martin, just shut the hell up!" She shouted, by now her voice was horse from all the screaming she had done that night. "You is an insensitive ass!" Sarena shouted, now face to face with Martin. "I'm sorry Sarena, but it's true. I didn't mean to sound insensitive, I is only stating the facts." "What do you mean?" Coni asked. "He was killed by overseers tonight returning from a mission of getting medical supplies for the baby. He went to the medical building and came as close as where you're standing from making it; but they shot him right were you are." Martin explained. "What a great man," Kabuka said. "Yeah, he saved my baby, guys," the mother said. Sarena just looked at the floor. "Yeah, a real hero," she said. "Sam and Sarena both saved my baby," the mother continued. "Sam risked his life getting the supplies, and Sarena performed the surgery." Coni stared at Sarena and said. "Wow, you're love worked in harmony; even at the point of death." A tear fell from Sarena's eye. "I understand that our love we had for each other worked to save this baby; but I still wish I could just look into his eyes one more time." Coni and the mother went up to Sarena and embraced her, one on each side of her.

"My name is Martin," Martin said as he extended his arm out to Shilo to introduce himself. "Shilo," Shilo said as he extended back his arm and shook hands with Martin. "I'm goin over to look at the baby," Kabuka said. "I'll go with you," Shilo responded. "Hey, Sweetheart," Kabuka said gently to the little baby. "It was a tough ride for you wasn't it?" She continued. She grabbed the baby's tiny, little pinky and said. "I remember when I was holding you in that house; I didn't think you was goin to make it." "Yeah, we is thought you wasn't goin to make it little one," Shilo said while leaning over the baby. Coni came up behind them. "You know, if it wasn't for Sam and Sarena you wouldn't be here shining your beautiful eyes at us," Coni said in a whisper to the baby.

The mother began waiving her arms from the corner of the shack. "Guys, can you all come together over here for a minute," she said to Sarena, Coni, Kabuka, Shilo, and Martin. She had her arms stretched out around the group that had now formed a circle. "I just want to say thank you," the mother said. "I know none of this will bring Sam back; but I know he's in heaven smiling down right now at us, and my baby, the baby he gave his everything to save." "Or he's watching upside down from a tree," Martin said out loud. He meant to be just thinking it silently, in his head, but it just slipped out. "You son of a bitch!" Sarena shouted. She lunged at Martin, grabbing him by the throat. "I'm goin to kill you, you bastard!" She yelled. Shilo struggled for a bit, but finally was able to get in between the two to break it up. Coni stared at Martin with her eyebrows in a downward position. "How could you be so vain and uncompassionate?" She asked Martin. "Martin, I think it would be a good idea for you to just retire for the night," the mother said, trying to solve the discourse between him and Sarena. "Thank you for your help though, Martin," the mother continued. Martin did as requested and went over to the corner where the children were lying, and laid down on his hay bed. "This is a nightmare, Martin," one of the children said. "Don't you is goin and worryin about nothin kids, it's all over now, you is safe, go to sleep now." The combination of having Martin close by, along with his comforting words, eased the tension the children had been feeling this entire night. They quickly went back to sleep.

"As I said earlier," the mother began again as she addressed the four now. "I know none of this is goin to bring Sam back; but each one of you can be proud of the role you played here tonight. Each of you played an important role in saving my baby, especially you Sarena, and Sam as well. I don't know what I would have done if it had not been for you two." Sarena stood there, slightly slumped over, with her hands on her hips as she spoke. "You know this has been a tough night on me guys, emotionally; but at least something good came out of it." Coni placed her hand on Sarena's shoulder. "How did you manage to stay so calm to perform that procedure on the baby, right after you had just witnessed with your own eyes the death of Sam? I would have been a nervous wreck." "I don't know, I didn't have much time to think about it I guess," Sarena said. "Well, she's a hero in my book," the mother said. "Her, and Sam, what they did, as I told Sarena earlier, my baby will know about it, I'll see to that. And all you guys, I'll make sure my child knows about what all of you did; the sacrifices each one of you made for my baby." She hugged each one individually, as the night turned into morning.

Chapter 3   Appearances

"I can remember when I was three," Koweena recalled. "I mean, I know you can't remember your entire childhood; but yeah, I remember when I was three."

"What is yo name?" A little slave girl asked as she approached Koweena. "Koweena," Koweena replied. "That is a pretty name. You know who I is don't you?" "No," Koweena answered back. The two just stood there eying each other intensely as little children often do; both of them checking each other's physical characteristics out. "You look different. Why is that?" The little girl noticed. "I don't know," Koweena responded. She became quickly embarrassed. "Well anyways, I am yo sister," the girl said, rubbing her leg while wearing her old, torn, cotton overalls. "What is yo name?" Koweena asked. "My name is Josi." "How old are you?" Koweena continued. "I'm is three just like you is." "How is you know how old I am?" Koweena asked. "My mom told me," Josi replied. "What is yo mom's name?" Koweena asked. At this point Koweena had stepped back a few inches from Josi. She was a little suspicious at just how much Josi knew about her. "My mom name is Amitha," the little girl replied. Koweena thought to herself, "Hey, that's my mom's name." Koweena had a surprised look on her face. "My mom has the same name as you mom," she said. Once again Koweena stepped further away from Josi. Koweena was a little uncertain and shy of this little slave girl who acted so forthright, as little children often are when they encounter another child of the same age. Josi reached out, trying to touch the now distant Koweena. "Yeah, we's have the same mom,"

Josi said. "You mean my mom is your mom?" Koweena asked with a puzzled look on her face. "Yeah, we's got the same mom," Josi confirmed again. "We is sisters!" Josi said with a big smile on her face. "How come I is never seen you before?" Koweena asked. Mr. Defour had it set up to where some mothers would have multiple children living in different shacks spread throughout the shack location. The shacks were clustered together on the Plantation which made it somewhat manageable for the mother to at least attempt to breastfeed their children. But children for the most part would grow up their entire lives on the Defour Plantation and never know their brother or sister. They could even be working along side their siblings in the field and never even know that they were related. "The reason you is never seen me is because I live in another shack than you. Yeah, I live in the shack that's way down yonder." Josi points to an area way down the little dirt trail that's littered with slave shacks all along the right side. Her shack is too far to see with the naked eye. "I can't see it," Koweena said, trying to strain her eyes to pinpoint the exact location of Josi's home. "It's right down there, see it." "No." "Well it's down there. You's need new eyes. Maybe I's get to show you later sometime," Josi said with an optimistic voice. "Do you want to play in the dirt now," Josi asked. It was the only thing slave children could do for fun; they didn't have toys or dolls. Suddenly Koweena's curiosity got the best of her. She began to let down her guard, forgetting about her once skepticism of Josi. She began walking toward her. She approached Josi, getting real close to her, by now; they were just six inches apart from each other, staring each other down, as three year olds often do. "Okay, I'll play with you," Koweena said with a smile. Out of nowhere a man's deep voice yelled out, "Get away from each other! Now! You little niggers." The big man pushed the two apart violently. "Go back to your shacks where you belong!" The man forcefully commanded them. Koweena looked up at the man, who to her, seemed like a ten foot giant. She noticed the rifle he was carrying in one hand, and the whip he was carrying in the other. "You better get along now before I punish your parents!" Koweena had visions of her mom getting beaten, that was the last thing she wanted. The girls took off running, with dust flying off the back of their shoes as they kicked the dry dirt while sprinting away; they both were breathing hard from the fear they had just experienced, quickly passing one shack after another. They finally reached Koweena's shack; and now safely a good distance from the man, they stopped running. They stood there for a few minutes trying to catch their breath. Finally Koweena spoke up, "that was scary." "Yeah, those men are evil; at least that's what momma told me. Momma says those men use those guns and whips all the time." "Do they use them on little people like us," Koweena asked fearfully. "I don't know. I don't think I wants to know. Is this yo shack?" Josi points to a shack that was next to Koweena's. "No, it's this one," Koweena points to the shack beside it. "Get in your shacks!" This time, it was another man that yelled out, wielding the same weapon as the other one. Josi took off down the road. Koweena was standing there, by now the man had approached her, and was standing directly in front of her. "Why aren't you working, Nigger!?" The man yelled at her. "I, I, I," Koweena was too scared to talk. She was only three; she didn't deserve to be talked to like that. She was too young to understand what she had done to deserve this man yelling at her so meanly. "I said, you little spook, why aren't you working!?" The man was yelling even louder at her now. "Leave her alone!" A male slave shouted from a distance. The man turned from Koweena and began taking giant, violent steps toward the male slave. He grabbed him with one hand and threw him to the ground. He started whipping the slave, striking his back, arms, and face. Koweena could only stand there in horror, watching the violence. To be so young, and watching this brutality must have been scarring for the young child. She was too scared to move, she was frozen in her tracks. After several minutes of the beating, another overseer came upon the scene. "Whip him harder!" Shouted the other overseer. While the beating was going on, the overseer glanced over his left shoulder and saw little Koweena standing there, witnessing the whole thing. As the one overseer was still beating the man, the other one approached Koweena. "You want that same thing done to you!?" He asked her while yelling at her. "No, sir." "Then get back in your shack and don't come out you little bitch!" Koweena didn't have to be told twice; she scurried into her shack and slammed the door behind her. She was alone now in her shack. She fell to her tiny knees. To ease the shock of what she had just gone through and witnessed, she just started writing in the dirt. But tiny tears fell from her eyes onto the dirt she was playing in.

"Yeah, I clearly remember when I first met my sister on that sunny, hot, dry summer day on the Natchez plantation," Koweena recalled. "My innocence had been shattered that day. I witnessed something I was too young to understand. Why was that slave so deserving of that punishment? I didn't know why. And why was I getting yelled at so harshly? I was so scared. Yes, my conscience had been warped that day. But it was only the beginning, it would get much worse. Why did that day stand out in my mind so clearly? Well, I guess you could say, at that age, I was very observant. I thought to myself, 'I look nothing like my sister.' Then I thought, 'I look nothing like any of the slaves that were around me either.' It hit me that day, I was different. My skin was much lighter than my sister and the other slaves. My hair was different; I didn't look like hers, I didn't look like any of the slaves. I was the only light skinned slave on that whole plantation. I just couldn't figure it out. Why am I so different? I did in fact have a unique look about me that separated me from the other slaves on the Plantation. My skin had a pale butterscotch color to it, compared to the dark, black skin of my fellow slaves. I also noticed something else different about myself. My hair was not like the other slaves either. It was long, soft, and curly, with a mixture of brown with some light brown streaks in it, flowing down just below my shoulder blades. It was not rough, coarse, and nappy, like the other slaves. The question of why I looked so different; would become my companion, haunting my thoughts almost on a daily basis as I grew and matured on the Plantation. It caused me heartache and confusion. My future would be filled with thoughts of why I looked the way I did. My complexion however, the same complexion that caused me this heartache and confusion, would also become the same complexion that would make me so pretty. From the time I could walk, I stood out, apart from the other slaves, as the cutest and prettiest slave on the Plantation. At least, that's what I was told anyway. It still didn't alleviate the stress and embarrasement that came along with looking different. I wanted to be just like the other slaves, and that meant looking like them as well. I loved the attention it brought me though from the other slaves. They would always tell me how pretty I was, I loved that. I guess you could say, it was like a two way street. It troubled me yes, but it also helped to get me through those tough days on the Plantation. The problem with being pretty on a plantation is, it causes you to have a bull's eye on your chest. And that certainly was the case with me."

"Momma." "Yes dear." "Why do I look so different?" Koweena asked weeks after her encounter with her sister. The words Josi used that day, "you look different," stood out in Koweena's mind. It was like a tape rewinding itself over and over again in her little brain. For a three year old, those words were crushing. Koweena felt confused and humiliated. She had suddenly felt ashamed to go out of her little shack. She didn't want to be seen by anyone. The feelings of being self-conscience had planted its roots in Koweena's heart. "You don't look different, Dear," her mother said. Amitha was very protective of Koweena. Of course she had no say so in making sure Koweena stayed in the same shack as her, that was just luck; but it did make Amitha even that much more guarding of Koweena. Amitha had two other children besides Koweena; but there was no doubt, Koweena was her favorite. Koweena was holding her hair with one hand. "Momma, my skin is different, my hair is not like the others," she said. "Koweena, Dear, God made you the prettiest slave here. He made you this way so that you would be special, the best among the children, the best among all the slaves, shoot, even the best among the white folks. It's not a bad thing, Dear, God made you to shine like a star. You is the most beautiful little thing around. Be proud of that, not ashamed." "God made me special, momma?" Koweena asked. Her mom's talk had made Koweena suddenly feel better about her appearance. She had been depressed. After what she had witnessed just weeks earlier, with the beating, and those men yelling at her, and the comment by Josi, she was at a low point in her young life. Being three years old is just too early for a child to be experiencing such low emotions. Amitha knelt down, facing Koweena with her arms outstretched, placing them on Koweena's shoulders. "Yes, Dear, God made you special. He took extra time in creating you." "Wow, God took extra time in creating me," Koweena thought, "that is really something." Koweena now felt better as she looked in the tiny mirror on the wall. "You is not different, Koweena, you is unique, one of a kind," Amitha told her. Amitha knew this subject would come up at some point. She had been planning just the right words to say when it did, and she came through with flying colors.

Koweena had forgotten that day about the comments of Josi, and she was no longer depressed. She was no longer depressed until the day she encountered an overseer during one of her many trips to the fields. Koweena was four now, and she was working as a babysitter in one of the overseer's house. When she wasn't babysitting, she was running errands for the overseers, taking and bringing back buckets of water and food to the slaves working out in the fields during the hot, sunny days. On such a day, and on such an occasion, Koweena was taking a bucket of water to the slaves, when an overseer stopped her in front of the main water station where the water was being gathered. The overseer was a giant of a man. He was muscular and was about six foot five and two hundred and fifty pounds. "You know what you are don't you, you little Nigger?" The man said, while holding his whip with one hand and slapping it against the other hand, as if he was going to use it at any second. "You are a little half breed," the overseer told her in a very mean, sharp toned fashion. Koweena was taken back by what the man said, she had never heard of that word before. She did know however that it was name calling, and it was meant to hurt her, she knew that much. The overseer didn't know, he was just guessing, but he did notice something different about her complexion. His main objective was to hurt the little girl. If he was not going to do it with his whip, he certainly was going to make an attempt with his mouth. It worked; Koweena was crushed by the word. The man moved his arm up and down in front of Koweena. "I mean, just look at you, you have it written all over you!" "No, sir," Koweena replied. The man got in Koweena's face. "What did you say to me, you little wench? Were you trying to say something to me?" "I just want to be left alone so I can do my job, sir." "Oh, you want to be left alone do you? Hey Charles! Come here!" The man yells to another overseer five yards away. "What is it, Ray!?" "Just come over here a minute!" Charles walks over to him. "Do you think this little spook here is a half breed?" He asked Charles while pointing his whip at Koweena. Charles chuckled. "Sure as hell looks like one Boss." "Well, you know what Charles, this little half breed talked back to me." "No, I didn't, sir, I was, I was," "you was what!" Ray yelled out to her. "I was just trying to go about my business, sir." Koweena was at the point of crying she was so hurt and scared. Tears began welling up in her eyes. These men were picking on a little four year old, an innocent child. Children at her age just don't understand why things happen to them the way they do. "Should I do something about that, Charles?" Ray asked. "Please don't, sir, I won't say another thing, I promise," Koweena said, choking, trying to hold back from crying. What had Koweena said to get herself in this mess in the first place? Absolutely nothing. "Hey Boss, we have more important things to worry about than this little Nigger, let's go," Charles told Ray. "Yeah man, you're right, forget this," Ray said while looking at Koweena in a disgusted manner. As Ray was walking away he suddenly stopped. Koweena thought it was all over with and started walking toward the fields, still choking back the tears. Ray went back up to Koweena and leaned into the side of her face. He whispered in her ear. "You better be careful from now on. With the way you look, you stick out like a sore thumb; you make for an easy target. You're going to be easy to find if I ever need you for something, you hear?" The threat made Koweena instantly drop her bucket. She did nothing to deserve that. At such an innocent age, she was already placed in the situation of having to look over her shoulder each and every day from now on.

"Momma, I'm scared," Koweena told her mom that night. Amitha grabbed Koweena and sat down on the only small wooden chair in the shack, placing Koweena on her lap. "What is it, Sweetheart?" It was just the two of them in there that night. "A boss man today approached me and said I is an easy target." "What!?" Amitha said. "What happened, Koweena, tell me everything?" "Well, these men walked up to me, I didn't do anything, they just walked up to me for no reason. They called me a half breed. I didn't do anything, momma." That word was a nightmare for Amitha. She had been fearful this day would come ever since Koweena was born. "Momma, what's a half breed?" For a few seconds, Amitha was speechless. Although she had thought about this moment for a long time, she was unprepared to give a response. After giving it some careful thought, Amitha responded. "It doesn't mean anything, Koweena; it's just a bad word. Don't let words hurt you, they is just words." That was the only thing Amitha could think to say at that moment as she stroked Koweena's long flowing hair. "Were they tryin to hurt me, momma?" "Yes, Dear, that's what they was a tryin to do." "It worked," Koweena said with a depressing tone while staring at the floor in her mom's lap. "Listen, Koweena, I'm goin to try and explain somethin to you okay?" Koweena leaned against her mom's chest. "Okay, momma." "You see, white folks is above us kind, us kind of people who don't look like them, do you understand? And sometimes they abuse their authority. They pick on us for no reason." "Like that man I saw get beat last year." That episode was obviously still fresh in Koweena's mind. Little children Koweena's age tend to forget things easily, especially things that happened a year ago. But to prove that that incident was scarring to her psyche, she could easily remember the incident even though she was only three when it happened. "You still remember that, Dear?" "How can I forget, momma?" "You see Koweena, that's how they can hurt men like that slave." Amitha made sure she explained to Koweena that physical abuse was only subjected to men, not women. Amitha felt bad, after years of telling her daughter that she was special and unique, and a star; she was now trying to explain to her that she was different for another reason, a more negative reason. "You see, Koweena, the white folks is more powerful than us, stronger than us." "Why do they want to hurt us, momma? Are we bad people?" "No, Dear, don't even think that, they just have authority over us that's all. They tell us what to do. They is the boss and there is nothing we can do about it." Koweena understood what her mother was trying to tell her. "The white folks are in control," Koweena thought to herself. "Can they do anything to us, momma?" This question disturbed Amitha greatly. The answer was yes, that was obvious; but how was she going to tell that to her four year old daughter without worrying her even more than she already was. So she did the only thing she knew to do to protect her daughter, she lied. "No, Dear, they can't do anything to us." It pained Amitha to say that to Koweena. She had just lied to her child, a lie Koweena would sooner or later realize was a lie at some point in her life. But Amitha was hoping for the day when slavery would come to an end, or at least the day when her daughter would be set free. If that would be the case, Amitha thought, Koweena would never have to know it was a lie. Those white overseers wouldn't have a chance to do anything they wanted to with her, if she were free. Thinking this Amitha went on, "you see Koweena, they can't hurt you physically, so don't worry about that. You don't have to be afraid of that. Sure, they can talk to you mean, but that's all." A tear fell down Koweena's cheek. "I don't like it when they talk to me mean. It hurts me bad, momma." "I know it, Sweetheart, but it's gonna to be alright. You is gonna live a great and

happy life, Sweetheart." Somehow, someway, Amitha was trying to paint
a pretty picture of their barbaric life. Koweena had already endured and
seen what no young child should ever have to endure and see at such a
young age. Amitha was just trying to smooth it all over for her daughter.
Koweena, so young and so innocent, at least deserved that much from
her mother at this point in her brief life. "You know, Koweena, those
men is not gonna bother you again," Amitha continued her lying, "you
know what you have to do to make sure of it?" "What, momma?" "Just
keep your head down and mind your own business, don't even look at
the white folks." "But what about when I baby sit, I have to look at them
then." "Well, let's see," this was a very important moment for Amitha,
she was trying to teach her daughter how to survive in the white man's
world; and she wanted to make herself clear to her young child about
this. "Just don't talk, Honey, just say 'yes ma'am' and 'yes sir' to them,
that's all you need to say, and don't ever look them in the eye, never look
them in the eye." Amitha knew Koweena was scared; after all, that's
what started this whole conversation in the first place. She was trying
to ease her child's fears, even if that did mean lying to her.

Koweena felt better that night. For one, she was in her mom's lap,
safe and secure. For another reason, her mom had promised her that
she was going to be alright, that nothing bad was going to happen to
her. Koweena was impressionable at that age, and with her mom's body
language and comforting tone in her voice, Koweena put the bad events
behind her. But Amitha pressed on, her motherly instincts told her to
really make sure that Koweena understood what she was telling her.
"Do you understand what I is trying to tell you, Koweena?" Amitha
really wanted to drive the point home about making sure her daughter
understood how to survive out there. Amitha gently shook Koweena
to drive the point home. "You must mind your own business. Do as
you is told." Koweena was now getting the message loud and clear
from her mother, that she was all of a sudden inferior, a weaker person
to the white people. It broke Amitha's heart to have to explain this to
Koweena. She had been pumping Koweena up her entire four years.
Telling her how great she was and how much better she was than the
other slaves; and now she was telling her that she was a weaker person.
Tears began welling up in Amitha's eyes. She thought to herself, "all of
that hard work of lifting my daughter's spirits for four years, and now,

with just a short conversation in this tiny little shack, I have destroyed that."

"I believed my mom that night, about how white folks couldn't hurt me. Why should I not? She was my mom, she wouldn't lie to me." Koweena recalled. "At that point, I just didn't realize what lie ahead for me. If I had, I would have never come out of that shack. I would have never walked back out into that sick, twisted world referred to as plantation life. That's what I would have thought back then if I had known then, what I know now, but looking back, I know that would have been impossible, just a fantasy. Regardless of how scared I was, I still had to get up the next morning and go through the motions all over again. Looking back, it was a very tough road. I had a disadvantage when I was born" Koweena remembers. "I was born with some strikes against me right off the bat. I was born into slavery, and I was born black. No choices, no decision to make as to whether or not I wanted a life filled with being able to make my own choices. No rights, no chance at becoming my own person. It seemed like a hopeless endeavor. I had no hope, no aspirations, and no dreams of my own. People talk about living for the now or even for tomorrow; but when you were in my situation, there was no living for anything. I had no future. I had nothing to look forward to. Oh yeah, sure, at age four I didn't think of my life as hopeless. But the more I experienced on that Plantation as a young child, the more that hopeless feeling began to creep into my conscience. I was not a human being, I was property. Like some cattle or horse on the Plantation. I began to think back then as a little child, 'what kind of hope do I have? What kinds of dreams do I have to achieve?' All I had to look forward to was what I had witnessed when I would bring water and food to the slaves out in the fields, sweaty, backbreaking, blood blistering hard labor under the scorching hot Mississippi summer sun. I can remember handing cups of water to the slaves, and noticing that when they held their hands out to grab the cup, all I could see was blood, and huge gaping sores all over their hands. It frightened me. And it hit me back then, that was what I had to look forward to in the future. My optimism was robbed from me when I was a young child. Every young child experiences optimism and excitement and hope about life; but not me, not a child born into slavery. All of that is robbed from a slave child before they even take their first breath. Imagine growing up in my shoes for a moment. You're yelled at from the time you could walk, you're called names when you don't even understand what they mean. You're laughed at and mocked for the way you look, something I had no control over, and you're working barely after you start walking, and not getting paid for it to top that off. You're the property of some man you have never met before. And don't even get me started on play time. There was no playing for me. Sure I could write in the dirt, but what child would truly call that playing. I had no toys, no friends, and no chance to run around and let the wind breeze through my hair. I was trapped, and at age four I knew it. Looking back, no human being, little own child, should be subjected to that kind of living. What child deserves such a dreadful and depressing beginning? But yet, that is in fact what awaited a child, if that child were born black in the south. If only white folks could see it from our prospective, then maybe, just maybe, they wouldn't be so harsh. That's what I thought growing up anyway. But now, at this point in my life, I realized that those white people on that Plantation were just plain evil. It wouldn't have mattered if they did just walk a mile in our shoes, they still would have abused us. People always told me growing up, that not only was I beautiful, but I was also charming and witty, despite what I had been through. People would tell me that I always seemed to make them smile. No matter how hard life was on me, and it was hard, I was always outgoing and jovial."

Koweena and Josi were walking with their buckets in hand toward the fields. "You is so crazy, Koweena!" Josi said. "Seriously, let's go up to the slaves and instead of handing them a cup of water, we just dump some of it on each one of them. It would certainly cool them off, right?" Koweena said. "That is a smart idea, but it's crazy," Josi said. Koweena was committed to carrying out the plan. When she got up to the slaves, she dumped a little on one of the slaves. "Is you crazy, girl!?" The slave yelled out, drenched by the water. "It cooled you off didn't it," Koweena laughingly said. "Come here, you!" The slave yelled. Koweena laid the bucket down and started running, just laughing all the way over the field. Josi soon followed. Josi began laughing. "That was funny!" She said. You is funny, Koweena." "Hey, let's go up to the water station and begin splashing water on the slaves," Koweena said with excitement. Josi became adamant. "We could get in trouble for doin that, Koweena!" She said. Koweena was running away from Josi with her arm stretched out to Josi, motioning for her to come on. "Come on, it will be fun!" Koweena said. "She is goin to get us in trouble," Josi thought to herself out loud. When Koweena got to the water station, she quietly tippy toed up to where the water was running. She swiftly began to splash water on the girls gathered around it. They didn't know what hit them. Before long, Koweena had all the girls there laughing and giggling. She had made the girls forget about their dreary lives for at least a few minutes. Josi arrived on the scene. "You is so crazy!" She said, laughing out loud. "Stop that," she continued. Koweena was laughing and splashing water on the other girls. "Come on Josi, join in, it's fun!"

"Yep, that was me, the jovial one," Koweena said, while looking back at that moment in time. "Although I was going through the same nightmares as the other kids, I tried to have a little fun along the way. I was five then, and for several months I had been going through my daily routine without any run-ins with the overseers. I thought things were actually improving for me. But oh, how I was wrong. It would get much worse for me in the near future, very much worse. I didn't know it then, and looking back now, part of me is glad I didn't, but at age five the worst was yet to come. I'll never forget the day, that cool autumn, sunny day, when my innocence would truly be shattered. With it being cool, it only made my experience worse."

"Hey, Charles!" "Yeah, Ray." "Come over here a minute!?" Ray asked him from a distance. Charles approached him. "Hey listen, do you remember that little half breed that walks around here?" Ray said. "Can't say as I do Boss, why?" "You know, that little Nigger that looks different. The one that's lighter than all the other spooks." "Um, oh yeah, now that you mention it, I do seem to remember her. You had that little run in with her last year didn't you?" Ray nodded with a sideways grin. "I sure did." "Why, what are you thinking?" Charles asked. Ray was rubbing his mustache with his fingers while holding his rifle with the other hand. "I'm just thinking," Ray said. "What is it, tell me? You have that look about you." "What look!?" Ray said with a mean tone. "You know, that look you get when you're about to do something to one of the slaves." Ray chuckled. "What makes you think I'm going to do something?" Charles raised his eyebrow. "Like I said, that look." "I was just thinking Charles; maybe we should give that little bitch a calling."

"A calling, Boss?" "Yeah, maybe we should pay her a visit man, you know, let her know we're still around." "Why, Boss?" Charles asked. Ray leaned back, with his arms folded by his chest as he sat the rifle down next to his leg. "What do you mean why? We don't need a reason around here to talk to Niggers. Or to, let's say, for example, beat them." "What are you saying Boss?" Charles asked. Ray chuckles. "I'm just thinking out loud. You know, we don't need a reason to beat them do we?" "Wait a minute Boss; you're not thinking of beating a little child are you?" Ray snaps back at Charles. "She's not a child, she's property!" Charles stretches out his arms toward the ground and opens his hands as if to try and put on the brakes of Ray's thoughts. "I don't know Boss, we've never beaten a child before." Ray now had his hands on his hips. "There's just something about her Charles, just the way she looks, she gets under my skin. I've been itching to do something to her for a long time now. Where's our whips?" Charles shakes his head. "Come on, man, no." "Shut up Charles, it will be fun." "But a child, Boss!?" "Charles, a child is white, not black, remember that." Charles was tore between his conscience, telling him that this little girl was just property and not a human being, and visualizing hitting a small child who didn't deserve it. "Now, go get our whips!" Ray commanded Charles. "I have a plan, now hurry, go!" Ray continued while pointing in the direction of where the overseer's supplies were laying, supplies such as whips, hats, vests, gloves etc., some twenty yards away. Charles returned with two long leather whips with thick soft cowhide for handles. "Okay, here's the plan Charles. She usually goes to that water station several times a day." They both point to that water station down the dirt road. "That water station. The one you had that run in with her, right?" Charles interrupts. The two were standing on that road that separates the fields from the slave shacks. "Yeah, that one," Ray continues. "We will just stand to the side of the station and wait for her to come by." "What then?" Charles asked. Ray just smiled. "Don't you worry about that, I'll take care of the rest," he said.

Koweena, after she had just completed taking a load of water to the fields, was returning to the water station. She was humming to herself, no particular song, she didn't know any songs; she was just humming as she was skipping across the dirt road, with empty bucket in hand, toward the station. She had just started to get into a routine, not having run into any overseer since that encounter at this same water station a year ago; she was finally starting to feel good about her situation. Yes, she was working for no pay; but she was too young to realize that, she just thought this was part of her everyday life, and she had accepted it. As she was skipping along the road she was planning in her head another funny trick she was going to pull on the slaves working in the fields. Suddenly, as she approached the station, Ray bumped into her intentionally as he was walking by her. "Watch out, you little half breed!" Ray yelled. Koweena instinctively looked up and noticed that it was the man she had had that run in with before at this very place. She quickly remembered her mom's now infamous words that were imbedded in her mind. "Don't ever look them in the eyes." Those words were ringing loudly now in Koweena's head. "I just looked that man in the eyes," she thought to herself. "I shouldn't have done that." "You know, you think you're something special don't you? Looking the way you look and all, don't you, bitch? Hey, I'm talking to you!" Ray yelled. Koweena was just staring at the ground. Her heart suddenly began to beat at a high steady rate. "No, sir, I don't," Koweena said in a low soft voice. Ray grabbed Koweena's long, curly hair and began pulling on it. "I can't hear you, Nigger; speak up so someone can hear you!" "Sir, you is hurting me." By now the girls surrounding the water station had dispersed once they saw the overseer Ray grabbing Koweena's hair. Ray knelt down, so as to be face to face with little Koweena. Still with a handful of her hair in hand, he looked at Koweena right in the eyes, or at least he tried to. Koweena would not look him in the eyes. She still remembered the promise her mom made to her that if she didn't look at the white folks in the eyes she would not get hurt. Ray jerked Koweena's head by her hair so that she was forced to look at him in the eyes. "Look at me!" He yelled. He spoke to her in a calm eerie tone. "You think me pulling your hair hurts now, you haven't seen anything yet, you little whore." By now he was just inches from her face as he whispered that to her. "Take me to your shack," Ray said to little Koweena. He let go of her hair, and pushed her to the ground, she fell hard on her knees. Tears had filled her eyes when Ray began pulling her hair, now they were flowing freely from her eyes and she began to sob. "Quit your noise, don't make a sound!" Ray demanded of her. It was tough for Koweena to sob quietly, but she tried nonetheless. "Come on, Charles, let's go!" Charles followed behind, carrying both whips. Koweena had yet to see those whips, so she had no clue what was going on, or what she could have possibly done to make Ray upset at her. She was only five, but she had been verbally abused already; and those feelings she had experienced before, came rushing back as she continued to sob.

Ray kept pushing her ahead of him until they arrived at her shack. She didn't even get a chance to open the door when Ray threw her through the door. The force of the throw caused her to skid across the dirt floor about five feet along her knees, ripping the skin from her knees. Hitting the door face first also created a one inch gash along the top of her left eyebrow. The blow to her head caused her to loose consciousness, as well as a lot of blood. She just laid there, still and silent. Charles tugged on Ray's shirt. "Okay Boss, we've done enough, let's go now." "No, we haven't even started yet." "But she's unconscious Boss. There's nothing more we can do." "Give me the whip!" Ray jerks the whip from Charles' hands. He begins laughing uncontrollably. "We will wait until the bitch wakes up, and then the real punishment will begin." "But Boss, she didn't do nothing!" Charles had never beaten a slave who wasn't disobedient before; especially a child. His partner Ray, had never beaten a child before either; but he had beaten a slave for no reason before. After several minutes, the overseers noticed movement on the dirt floor where the already battered little Koweena lay. After she came to, she had temporarily forgotten why she was in the position she was in, that was until Ray grabbed her overalls from the back and jerked her to her feet. He didn't even wait to make sure she was alright. His desire to beat her was too strong to wait. "Get over there!" Ray yelled as he threw Koweena again, this time to the center of the shack. The shack was empty; all the slaves were out in fields working. Koweena, still stunned from being unconscious, was too confused to begin crying again. She was on her knees when Ray yelled out, "take off your shirt!" Suddenly Koweena realized what was about to happen. The thoughts of that slave getting beat when she was three came flooding back to her. "No, sir, please don't! I'll be good; I'll be a good slave!" Though she had done nothing to deserve this, she was still apologizing for her nonexistent bad behavior. "I promise, sir, I won't do it again!" At this point she was crying hysterically. Ray was directly over top of her, leaning toward her as he yelled. "Shut up bitch, and take off your shirt!" "Why?" Koweena pleaded. "I don't want to. Please don't make me." Ray yelled even louder. "Come on you little rat, take it off!" "Take it off you little piece of trash!" Charles hollered, once just an observant to all this, was now yelling at her. He now had begun to get caught up in Ray's madness. The men grabbed her forcefully again, one on each side of her arms and jolted her to her feet. At this point Koweena was barefooted, the fall from being thrown into the door had shaken her sandals off. "Rip her shirt off, Charles!" "Come on you little animal, here we go!" Charles grabbed her shirt, he didn't bother to pull it up over her head, the desire was so strong to beat her as soon as possible, that he just violently ripped it off her. What must be going through the mind of this innocent little five year old? One minute she was skipping and humming along as a child her age would normally do, and the next minute she had been slammed through a door, made unconscious, verbally abused, jerked around violently, had her shirt ripped from her, and worst of all, she was now getting mentally prepared for a beating. Mentally, she was just too young to endure this kind of punishment. The first lash penetrated deep into the skin on her back. The pain was greater than she imagined. She suddenly began to grit her teeth. With her four foot tiny frame stretched out over the dirt floor, they continued lashing out on her back; the pain was so great that the tears welling up in her eyes would not come out. She screamed out, "mommy, mommy!" The overseers were holding nothing back, they were putting all their might into each strike; with each thrust from the overseers, little Koweena's body was taking an intense jolt, shaking her body from head to toe with every blow. At this point Koweena was in too much pain to open her mouth. She just laid there with her eyes full of tears, still gritting her teeth. The coolness that was in the air only added extra pain to the stinging she was already feeling with each whip to her back. The scene of that little body lying on the dirt floor with hands and feet stretched out, taking the whippings from those big men, raring back and giving it everything they had, would be too much for anyone to take, let alone the slave boy that had just walked in on the horrific scene. "Oh my God!" The little boy shouted out in disbelief. The overseers quickly stopped, "get out of here!" Charles yelled. The boy quickly left the scene. "Come on Boss, let's get out of here." "One, two, three, four, five," Ray was counting the lashes on Koweena's back; "six, seven, eight, nine, ten, eleven, twelve, hold on Charles I'm not done yet! This little bitch deserves some more!" He lashed out on Koweena's already ripped, bloody back two more times with everything he could muster. "Alright, now we're ready."

As the men left the shack with their bloody whips in hand, Koweena just laid there on the cold dirt floor. She didn't even feel the coldness on her stomach, chest, and face, as she lay there; the excruciating stinging sensation on her back was all she could feel. She was still gritting her teeth. The mental anguish of taking the blows, one after another, had been so great that she was completely in shock. She was so tired that the stinging sensation she had been feeling took a back seat to her fatigue and shock. She was overwhelmed with emotion. Her thoughts began to race; from the verbal abuse, to being thrown around like a rag doll, the beating, and of course, the pain, it was all just too much for her five year old brain to try and wrap around. So she just shut down. Her mind ceased to function for a moment. The pain and the tiredness was all she could feel. Her breathing had slowed somewhat as well. Little children are resilient. After a few moments of shutting down, her mind began to start up again; despite her bloody back, she livened up a little and began to think again. All she could think about as she lay there was the time she sat in her mom's lap in this same shack, and her mom plainly telling her that she would never have to worry about being hurt physically by those white folks. Thinking about her mom's promise coupled with the tremendous pain on her back, finally made the tears that had been in Koweena's eyes since the beating, begin to flow. Koweena thought to herself as she lay there now crying; "I must be a terrible person to have been beaten like this? What have I done that was so bad?"

Suddenly, three male slaves busted through the door, followed by the boy who had entered moments earlier. "Damn!" Martin shouted. "What the hell!?" Another slave yelled out. They couldn't believe their eyes as they looked upon Koweena's beaten body. "A child, Martin!?" The slave said with intense emotion. "Quickly, get her mother!" Martin told the little boy. The little boy hurried back out of the shack. Martin ran over to where Koweena was laying and knelt down beside her. Completely exhausted, Koweena's face was buried, face first in the dirt floor. Martin spoke with pain written all over his face while rubbing Koweena's hair. "Oh my, Sweetheart, I'm so sorry! Tell me what I can do, Koweena, to try and make things better for you?" "Don't touch me," Koweena said faintly. Martin quickly removed his hand. "I'm sorry, Koweena." "I want my mommy," Koweena said, with barely enough strength to talk. Martin grabbed his head with both hands. "She's coming, Dear, she's coming. Oh my God! Oh my God! I can't believe what I'm looking at!" Martin had never before seen such a sight. He was just kneeling there, staring at Koweena, with the fresh bloody stripes all down her shirtless back. He felt helpless. Martin couldn't help but count the number of stripes on Koweena's back. "Fourteen!" He said in a whisper so as to not let Koweena hear him. "My God, a child," he continued to whisper. Martin tried to reassure her. "I know you're hurting, Dear, but it's goin to be alright," but deep down, he knew her pain was unbearable and there was nothing he could do to alleviate it. "Koweena, can I move you to the bed?" "No, don't touch me." Koweena had just been viscously violated by some strange men; she wasn't about to let anyone else to touch her. "Listen Koweena, we need to get you up off this floor, okay?" "No Martin, don't touch me." "Koweena, we have to get you up. I will be gentle with you, I promise." "I don't want anyone else to touch me, not now, not ever." Martin was thinking to himself, "Is she ever going to recover from this?" "Sweetheart, it's Martin, it's me, I'm not going to let anything happen to you." "I don't care who you are, you is not goin to touch me; and that 'I'm not goin to let anything happen to you' bit, I've heard that one before." She was referring to her mother of course. She spoke up in a low whisper, with barely enough strength to speak. "Martin, just let me lay here, please."

Her mom suddenly rushed in, with the boy tailing behind her. "My baby!" Amitha screamed in horror. Martin quickly jumped up and ran over to Amitha. "Listen Amitha, I think it be best if you don't get too upset here. I know it's hard, and I know you feel like yellin; but that's not goin to do Koweena any good here. You must stay calm, alright." Amitha began shaking Martin, with her hands wrapped around his shoulders. "Martin, look at my baby, look at her!" "I know, it's bad Amitha, but like I said, you must stay calm." "Okay, okay, I understand what you is sayin, but look at her!" After a moment of thinking, Amitha gathered herself. "Okay, I think I can. You is right Martin, getting upset and letting Koweena see me like this is only goin to make things worse." Amitha ran over to Koweena. "Oh, my baby, my baby," Amitha wanted to wail out but she controlled herself. Tears still flowed down her cheeks, she couldn't control that. "What have they done to you?" Koweena began to cry out loud for the first time since the beating. "Momma, you told me this would never happen. You promised me." She had been quietly sobbing before, but now she was in a full blown crying state. "I'm sorry, Dear, I'm so sorry." That was all Amitha knew to say. When she made that promise to Koweena, she truly believed it. It never entered her mind that an overseer would beat a little child. And now the nightmare for Amitha had come true. The child who she never thought would be beaten, was now her very own daughter. "I never thought this would happen, Koweena, never in a million years." Amitha began to cry. "My God, look at you!?" She said. Her emotions were starting to overtake her, she tried to remain calm, but the visualization of her daughter's back was too much for her. Martin could see that she was beginning to lose it, and quickly put his hand on her back. "Remember, Amitha, stay calm." "Look at her, Martin! Just look at her!" The yelling of her mother made Koweena even more upset than before, she began to cry all the louder. "Listen, Amitha, you have to understand what your daughter has been through emotionally here today. She can't afford to get upset anymore than she already has, okay? Now be calm and composed." "Okay, okay, Martin," Amitha made herself stop crying; she took a deep breath and turned back around to Koweena. "I'm so sorry this happened to you, my child. Shhh, it's goin to be okay. Get some rags, Martin." "Wet or dry?" Martin asked. "It doesn't matter, just go get some, hurry." Amitha began to stroke Koweena's hair. Koweena allowed it. She was mad at her mom for the promise she made about the fact that no white person would ever physically hurt her; but even though she was mad at her, she had made up her mind that her mom was the only one who was going to touch her. "How did you get that mark above your eye, Sweetheart?" Amitha said calmly. "Those men threw me through the door and I cut it on the door." Her mom stared at her back. "They threw you around on top of all of this?" "They did everything to me, momma." With her mom gently rubbing her hair, Koweena had stopped crying for a moment. "Would it be too painful for you, Koweena, to tell me everything that happened?" "I was just minding my own business, momma. The same boss man that I had that run in with last year bumped into me at the water station. "The same water station as before?" Her mother asked. "Yeah." Her mother quickly began to think that something was fishy about this story. Why would the same man bump into her at the same water station as a year ago? "That man planned this," Amitha thought to herself. "He called me that word again, half breed, and started talking mean to me. There was another man, his name was Charles," her mom now had a name to go by. "The next thing I know, momma, I was flying through the door. Everything suddenly got dark, momma." Her mom at this point couldn't bear to hear anymore; but she clinched her fist and bit her lip and continued listening. "The next thing I know, one of the men ripped my shirt off and made me lay on this dirt floor, stretched out. I knew what was coming after that, momma. The pain, momma, the pain was terrible. I thought they was never goin to stop. They just kept hittin and hittin, I thought they was goin to kill me, momma." Koweena began to cry again. "Shhh, it's okay, Baby, you don't have to tell me anymore."

Four male slaves came barging into the shack. "Tell us how this all happened?" Alias, one of the slaves demanded. "I'll be right back, Koweena, I just have to go talk to these men. I'll be right back, okay?" "Okay," Koweena said, sobbing. She was still lying face down on the ground with her back still exposed. The men could see the damage that was done to her. As Amitha approached the men, Alias spoke up, "what can we do?" "I have a name," the mother said. Alias spoke up with a mad tone in his voice. "What is it?" "Charles." "Do any of you guys know an overseer named Charles?" Alias inquired of the others. "I do," one of the other slaves spoke up. "What does he look like?" Alias demanded. "I don't know. He's tall, heavy set, light brown hair that comes down to about his shoulders." "Does he have any hair on his face?" Alias asked. "No, I don't think so, I don't know." "Do you, or don't you, know what he looks like man!?" Alias asked impatiently. "If I saw him, I would know it was him, but I would have to see him first before I knew for sure." Alias was thinking hard when he spoke up. "Okay, here is what we is goin to do. Martin, where is you?" Martin raises his hand in the background. "Right here, Alias." "Martin, come here!" Martin hurries up to where Alias is standing. "Okay Martin, I want you, and these other men, to go and gather up ten other men from the field. Be quiet and very careful, we is don't want any overseers catching on to what we is about to do here." "Okay," Martin said, intensely listening to Alias' every word. "You can't be seen Martin, you got it?" "Yes." "I want you to bring these ten men back to this shack. We'll all meet up here." "And do what Alias?" Martin inquires. "I'm not sure yet, just worry about goin and gettin them first without getting caught, then we is think of the rest when they get here." Martin gathered the other slaves that were in the shack and they headed out. Meanwhile, Amitha was bent over Koweena trying to clean up the mess on her back left by the two overseers.

It was a risky plan. The sun had gone down, but it was still daylight, and they could easily be seen. There was no doubt, Alias was thinking of this plan on pure adrenalin after seeing Koweena. He really hadn't had much time to think this thing through. The plan had been hastily thought through, and it was about to become evident in the field. Martin and the other slaves were talking to one of the slaves in the field. There were about eight of them gathered around the slave, including the slaves that were in the shack with Alias. "Listen man, some overseers beat a little girl today," Martin told the slave. The slave dropped his bucket. "What!?" "Yeah," Martin continued, "she was beaten pretty badly. They threw her around and everything." The slave put his hand to his head. "Man, I is never heard of a child gettin beat before." Martin had his hand on the slave's shoulder. "That's why we have to do somethin here, okay," Martin said. "You is talkin about hurtin an overseer aren't you?" He asked Martin. "Yeah, somethin like that. Are you in?" "Um, huh," the slave stepped back a couple of feet. "I don't know. I mean that is terrible what happened to that little girl, but hurtin an overseer? I don't know, we is could get in some big trouble for that." "Come on, man," Martin pleaded. "They is gone too far this time, we have to do somethin. It could be another child next time, and another one, hell, it could get to the point where they is hurtin little babies." The slave began rubbing his head, thinking about whether or not to join in on this rushed plan. "You have a point," the slave said. "Do you know who it was that did this?" The slave asked Martin. "We have a name, Charles. This guy over here says he knows what he looks like."

Meanwhile, an overseer some twenty yards away, in the same row in the cotton field as the slaves, notices the gathering and talking. "Hey, Robert," the overseer motions over to his partner who had his back turned looking in the opposite direction. "Yeah," Robert said. The man points to the slaves. "Check this out." The slaves were so engrossed in their conversation that they failed to notice the two overseers further down the row. "Look at those Niggers just talking over there, Robert?" "Yeah, something definitely aint right about that." "Should we yell at them?" The overseer asked Robert. "No, let's just watch them for a while and see what's up." After a few minutes of observing the slaves, the overseers noticed that they were jumping up and down, punching each other in excitement. The whole emotion of Koweena getting beat had clouded the judgment of the slaves in the field, as well as Alias back at the shack. "Yeah, there's definitely something going on here," Robert said. "Yeah, something is up," the other overseer said. "Hey, Robert, go get a couple of the other overseers and tell them to come here. I'll be a few yards ahead by the time you get back. I want to get closer to them." As Robert was leaving, the overseer moved in closer, crouching down behind the cotton stalks as he walked slowly toward the gathered slaves. After a few minutes had passed, Robert came back with three other overseers. "Hey, what's up?" One of the overseers asked, crouching behind the cotton. "We got us some spooks here looking to cause some trouble," the overseer who had been watching the slaves this entire time said. While Robert was gone getting the other overseers, the overseer who had been watching the slaves had managed to get within ear shot of the slaves, and could hear everything they were saying. "Their planning on attacking one of us," the overseer said. "It's a Code Red!" Robert shouted. A Code Red was a system derived by the overseers to wrought off a slave attack planned upon them. "Yeah, and Charles is one of the targets," the overseer said. Robert spoke out in excitement. "Should I go back and tell the other guys we have a Code Red in effect?" "No Robert, there are five of us here, and right now I'm counting eight slaves; with our rifles and our training, we can take them." Before the overseers actually became overseers they were trained extensively in how to take down disobedient slaves by force. They were trained in how to whip the slaves, how to shoot the slaves, how to hang them, and how to use their rifles as weapons when they couldn't use them to shoot. They were also trained in different fighting techniques. So they knew how to handle defiant slaves.

"So, are you in?" Martin asked the slave. "Yeah man, count me in." Martin raised his arms into the air. "Alright, we is goin to kick some overseer ass," he said. They were completely oblivious about the possibility of being watched while they were talking. Once again their emotions were getting the best of them. It was dark by now as they arrived back at the shack. Koweena was now lying on the bed. It was much too painful for her to lie on her back, so she laid there with her face buried in the hay. It was also too painful for her to put on a shirt either, so she remained shirtless. She had a few wet and dry rags on her back. The shack was filled with the sounds of her moaning and groaning in pain as she sobbed. Martin spoke with a disappointing tone. "We were only able to get a couple of guys, Alias." Suddenly, the door exploded open. Martin, Alias, and the other slaves were staring at five overseers brandishing rifles. Robert chuckled as he spoke. "Planning on hurting one of us huh, Niggers!?" The men swiftly ran toward the slaves. The slaves only had time to get their fists in a cocked back position when the sound of rifles smacking against their skulls resonated throughout the shack. The bodies of the slaves, one by one, smacked against the dirt floor. Just like that, Martin, Alias, and the other slaves who had planned the attack, were lying on the ground unconscious. The only ones not attacked were Koweena and Amitha. "What are we going to do with them, Robert?" "We are going to hang'em that's what we're going to do; they're much too dangerous to be left alive." "No!" Amitha blurted out without thinking. She and Martin were close, they had been through so much together, and she didn't want to lose him. Robert pointed toward Amitha. "Wench, if you don't shut up you are going to be joining them, is that clear!?" He said. "Momma, don't," Koweena faintly hollered out. After all that had happened to her that day, she couldn't bear the thought of losing her mother as well. Koweena tried to get up, the rags feel from her back exposing her bloody lashes. "My God!" One of the overseers yelled out upon seeing Koweena's back. "Look at that!" He continued. "Are you kidding me? Who did that to you?" The overseer asked. "It was," "shut up!" Robert interrupted Amitha. She was trying to tell the man who did this to her daughter. She had the name; maybe if she said Charles, the man might be able to carry out some kind of justice on him. She had temporarily forgotten her circumstances however. She had forgotten that she was just a slave. Those men didn't care one bit about justice for her daughter; she was just surprised that the overseer had such a concerned voice about him. It was the first time she had seen one of them care to even ask about the condition of a slave, much less her daughter. For a split second she had thought of herself as an equal to the concerned overseer. But the quick response she got from Robert brought her back to reality. "Look at her though, Robert. Her face and back. I thought we're not supposed to beat a child." "She's not a child!" Robert quickly responded. "She's just a piece of meat!" Robert said laughing. The other overseers joined in on the laughing. It couldn't get much worse for Koweena. After all she had been through; they were all just standing there, now laughing at her condition. "Yeah, she's just dark meat," one of the overseers remarked as they continued laughing and taunting her. "Come on, you little Nigger, role over on your back and see how that feels!" One of the overseers shouted. Her mother could only stand there and painfully take it as she choked back the tears. Koweena just lied back down on her stomach and let the tears flow down her cheeks. It was a day where she had been abused both physically and emotionally, almost to the point of it being fatal. "How much more violence in one day can I take," Koweena thought to herself. She put both her arms to the side of her head to block out the taunting going on at the entrance to the shack. She was thinking that she would have to endure more punishment that day than what she had already been through; but the men had gotten their bellies full of the taunting. Their focus now was on the unconscious slaves lying in front of them. "Come on, boys, let's get these Niggers up," Robert said, ordering the other overseers to start dragging the bodies out. "Where are you takin them!?" Amitha shouted. Robert began walking over to where Amitha was standing. "I told you to shut up, bitch!" An overseer stretched his arm out toward the direction of Robert. "Come on, Robert, it's not worth it. Let's take care of these bodies and get out of here. We still have to hang them," he said. Robert, now just a foot from Amitha, was pointing at her. "Yeah, you're right, you're lucky, Nigger. I've got more important things to do," he told her in a disgusting tone. The overseers left, and along with them the bodies of the unconscious slaves.

Koweena's innocence had been completely shattered that day. The language she heard, the verbal abuse she had taken, and yes, the terrible, almost deadly beating she received. It was way too much for a five year old to have to bear. But there it was, all of it, weighing down on her shoulders like a giant weight, crushing her already damaged emotional state. Would she ever recover from what happened to her on this autumn day? One thing is for sure, if someone with some authority on that Plantation doesn't step in on Koweena's behalf, she very well might not survive.

Chapter 4   The Meeting

"Several months had passed since my terrible beating, and I had been working non stop since that dreadful day," Koweena recalled. "I was not even allowed one full day of recovery from my injuries. I had learned, through the grapevine, that slaves on the Plantation were sometimes beaten that afternoon, and expected to get back to work that very same day. Even though I didn't have to go back to work that very same day, I still had to go back to work the very next morning. Hey, I did have that one night to cry myself to sleep, right, fortunate me. That one night was not enough, not even close to repairing the damage that had been done to me the previous day. The very next day I was back at it, carrying buckets to the slaves, and babysitting. During my many trips to the fields, I would sweat. I thought the pain was going to kill me as my wet clothes stuck to my sores and rubbed against them. I spent many a weeks gritting my teeth. The act of grinding my teeth almost became my best friend. Having no time to recover only made my emotional and physical scars worse. Staying busy made my emotional pain well up inside me like an untreated mold spreading throughout an abandoned house. My scars seemed to never heal as a result. I slept on my stomach for months. I had no time to deal with the deep emotions I was experiencing. I became more and more depressed. That little shack didn't help matters much. It was already depressing in there as it was. It didn't help that the beating occurred in the very same shack in which I lived either. Each night, as I lay there on my hay bed, I was reminded, over and over again, of the beating, I couldn't escape it. My mom tried to help by applying wet cloths to my sores, but it was to no avail. Each night I would hum, not a song, but just a melody that I heard my mom hum. And sometimes my mom would do the same to me as I lay there in my bed. It wasn't enough, not nearly enough. Something else happened during this time. I had grown very distant from everybody I knew, including my mom. I didn't speak. The only thing I said was 'yes sir' and 'yes ma'am' to the white folks, other than that, I was silent. I cut off all contact with my sister. I stopped with the jovial acts out in the fields and at the water station. I quit skipping around the Plantation. I just cut myself off from the outside world. I shut down emotionally. It was just too much to handle at my tender age."

One Friday toward the end of those few months, Koweena found herself in the main house of the Plantation, the Defour home itself. Leading up to that point, previously, earlier that day in the Jenkins' household(Mr. Jenkins was the head overseer of the Plantation), Koweena was babysitting their baby Samuel,the one year old child of Mr. and Mrs. Jenkins. "Okay, were going up to see Mrs. Defour now," Mrs. Jenkins told Koweena. Koweena just stared at the ground. "Yes, ma'am," she said. While spending time babysitting at the Jenkins', they never once called Koweena by her name; they either called her nigger or nothing at all. Babysitting Samuel was her first and only babysitting job up to this point. She had been babysitting Samuel for about six months now. She spent most of her days just looking at the ground in a blank stare, void of any life in her eyes. As Mrs. Jenkins, holding her son tightly in her arms, and Koweena , were walking up the long gravel drive that lead up to the big house, Koweena could slowly begin seeing the house off into the distance. As they got closer, Koweena became amazed. For one brief moment since the beating, Koweena's eyes came to life. It was the biggest, most beautiful sight she had ever beheld. For the first time since the beating, she became excited about something. She couldn't believe the sheer size of the house. Before this, her world consisted of cotton fields and tiny little shacks. Sure, the Jenkins' house was nice; but the combination of the Defour house foyer, living room, and dining room was bigger than the Jenkins' house itself. Before now, the Jenkins' house was the prettiest thing Koweena had ever seen; but now, just upon approaching the Defour house, they were not even at the front steps yet, Koweena's jaws dropped at the sheer sight of the house. As they approached the steps, Koweena was getting nervous. She was scared of white folks, especially now after what had happened to her; and now she was about to meet the most powerful white people in her world. Mrs. Jenkins rang the doorbell; Koweena's hands were now sweating profusely. She was continually wiping them on her overalls to dry them when the door suddenly opened. "Welcome, Mrs. Jenkins," a slave woman in maid attire said. One look at the slave and Koweena was taken back. She had never seen a black person so made over before, so dressed up. In fact it was the first time Koweena had seen a black person who was not in overalls. As Koweena walked in, alongside Mrs. Jenkins, through the front door, she glanced up at the maid; the maid looked down at her and winked. Koweena thought that was strange, for one thing it was the first time she had ever been winked at; and for another, the black woman looked actually happy. It was a new expression Koweena had never seen before. "A black woman happy? How strange," she thought to herself. The black woman seemed relaxed and comfortable to Koweena, not stressed and gloomy like the slaves back in her little world. The maid was also standing straight up, not slumped over like the slaves she was used to seeing on a daily basis. When Koweena focused her attention away from the maid, toward the inside of the house, it took her breath away. Everything her little eyes gazed upon was so shiny, colorful, and sparkling. With the scars still fresh on her back and the visible mark above her eye still prevalent, Koweena's spirit was about to be lifted by what her eyes would behold all around her. She glanced up at the woman slave once again, puzzled as she was by her, Koweena then turned and focused her attention back on the furniture, the paintings, and the giant clock with its huge pendulum swinging back and forth, and what seemed like a never ending staircase leading up to the second floor. Koweena noticed a woman coming down the staircase. She was dressed in the most beautiful attire Koweena had ever seen. "Welcome, Dorothy," Mrs. Defour said to Mrs. Jenkins, greeting her with a hug as she approached her after coming down the long staircase. Koweena, after experiencing one amazement after another the last several minutes, was now experiencing another as she gazed upon Mrs. Defour. She scoped Mrs. Defour out from her neckline down to her feet, looking keenly at her.

"I had never before seen such a beautiful piece of something that I couldn't quite recognize," Koweena recalled. "It was a silver, shiny thing around her neck. I had never before seen something that looked like that. I wasn't familiar with jewelry, but Mrs. Defour was wearing a thick, silver necklace with a blue diamond about one inch in circumference hanging from the necklace. I couldn't take my eyes off the diamond. The dress that Mrs. Defour was wearing was even more stunning than the necklace. After staring at the diamond for a few seconds, I went right to the dress with my eyes.It was a long, flowing, velvet dress trimmed in lace. It was red, with a low cut top and puffed sleeves. It had a corset with lots of flowing crinoline petticoats. I couldn't believe my eyes. I'll never forget that visual image I had of her. Mrs. Jenkins wore some nice stuff, but nothing compared to this. I was suddenly experiencing a strange feeling. I began to feel like an important person being inside that house. I was beginning to understand why that maid had that strange look on her face.I suddenly forgot about my violent, dreadful little world. Inside that house, my little world seemed like a million miles away. For the first time in a long time, I stood straight up, no longer slumped over. Also for the first time in a while, I began looking up instead of down. Everything was looking up for me, that was until I gazed upon Mrs.Defour."

Mrs. Defour glanced down at Koweena with a disgusted look on her face, a "why do you have to be here?" look. Koweena's much needed lifted spirits had taken a quick nose dive. She was reminded of something that she carried with her in her mind daily, routinely; and that was to never look up at the white person, under any circumstance. Koweena quickly went back to staring at the floor. "Will I ever get away from the white person hurting me?" She thought. The feeling of being in such an important place however still made Koweena excited, despite the glare she had just witnessed from Mrs. Defour. She was at an in between state now, in between the feeling she had carried on her shoulders since the beating, and the feelings she began to experience the moment she saw the grand house. The look from Mrs. Defour was like a gavel slamming down on her lifted spirits though, it deflated her somewhat. She was sad yes, but despite that, she was also excited, which lead to her to being somewhat happy. After the disgusted look Mrs. Defour gave Koweena, Mrs. Defour focused her attention back on Mrs. Jenkins. "Come on in the living room, Dorothy, for some tea," Mrs. Defour said while pointing to the living room area. Mrs. Jenkins moved her head in the direction of the living while staring down at Koweena. "Come on," she said to Koweena. "Yes, ma'am." Koweena said as she followed behind Mrs. Jenkins. She couldn't help but lift her head to look around at the beautiful scenery around her. Her curiosity had gotten the better of her. It made her forget about looking down to avoid looking at the white folks. Instead, she was like a kid in a candy store, absorbing every color, the beautiful floor and carpets, the little antique decorations, and the giant mirrors and pictures that surrounded the place. It was a cloudy and overcast late afternoon day, and the lights were already on in the living room. "Here," Mrs. Jenkins said to Koweena as she handed Samuel over to her as they sat on the long sofa. "So, Dorothy, how's Donald?" Mrs. Defour asked. "He's fine. You know he really takes being the head overseer on the Plantation seriously. He works all the time, he's very proud of his position." Koweena was experiencing, yet again, another new sensation she had never experienced before. She was listening for the first time to a white folk's conversation. As she scanned the room looking at Mrs. Defour and Mrs. Jenkins, careful not to look at them in the eyes, she couldn't help but notice how they were sitting and drinking their tea. Their mannerisms were much different than that of her fellow slaves. First of all, she was not used to seeing two people talk on furniture, and secondly, they were talking while sipping tea, both of which were something she had never seen before. "So, Dorothy, does he like being the one in charge of the Plantation, only having my husband above him?" Mrs. Defour asked. "Oh yes, he takes great pride in being in charge. He respects your husband greatly, and he appreciates the opportunity your husband has given him." Koweena hears the doorbell ring. The sound of the long musical melody it made, made her smile. It was her first smile in months. She hears the sound of boots thundering on the wooden floor, getting closer with each step. "Mrs. Defour, Dorothy Honey, how are you beautiful ladies doing this afternoon?" It was Mr. Jenkins. Koweena was definitely afraid of this man. In her months of babysitting she had only met him once; but the way he looked, looking tall and heavyset, and what he wore, a white, long sleeve shirt with a black tie wrapped in overalls, made Koweena only think back to the beating and of those two overseers. "How's

Samuel?" Mr. Jenkins asked. "He's fine, Dear. He just woke up from his afternoon nap and I thought we would come over and visit the Defours for a while. What are you doing?" Mrs. Jenkins asked. "Oh, I just need to speak to the boss about some business," Mr. Jenkins responded. As Mr. Jenkins said this, he was walking over to where Koweena was sitting. When he approached her, every muscle in her body tightened as if she was embracing for a hit from the tall white man. "Let me see my boy," Mr. Jenkins said while leaning down over Koweena and grabbing his son from her arms. Koweena, after holding her breath the entire time Mr. Jenkins was approaching her, exhaled after he took a hold of his son. This was the reaction she had every time an overseer got anywhere near her since the beating. She was constantly on pins and needles, even while in her own shack at night. "Donald, Dorothy tells me you are really enjoying being in charge out there," Mrs. Defour said while sipping her tea. "Yes, ma'am, it's a lot of responsibility, but I enjoy the challenge." "Do you have much contact with the niggers?" Mrs. Defour asked. Koweena, now use to that word, she had been called it so many times before from the white folks that the word seemed like any other word to her. "No, ma'am, I leave that up to the men I'm over, the overseers I'm in charge of. I rarely have any contact with them." Just hearing the word overseer gets Koweena's stomach to start churning. After enjoying her time in the house, she suddenly began to feel uneasy and scared. Just being around all of these white people with authority was nerve wrecking for her. Mr. Jenkins handed Samuel back to Koweena; once again she took a deep breath. "Ladies, if you'll excuse me." Mr. Jenkins said as he walked out of the living room. "Good bye, Donald," Mrs. Defour said. After Koweena had held Samuel for a few minutes, Mr. Jenkins turned around, walked back over toward Koweena after saying good bye to Mrs. Defour, and once again Koweena's entire body clinched up. She took a deep breath and held it as Mr. Jenkins leaned over her and touched Samuel as she was holding him. Koweena exhaled once more and relaxed her body as Mr. Jenkins kissed his wife one more time and walked away. Mrs. Defour flung her arm in the direction of Koweena. "So how's this little Nigger babysitter doing for you, Dorothy?" Mrs Jenkins gave Koweena a disgusted look as she responded. "She's doing okay, for a nigger I guess." Koweena's little five year old brain was getting used to being talked to and stared at like trash. With all she had been through up to this point, she couldn't feel any lower. With all she had experienced, her mom's talks she gave her growing up about how great she was, was now only a distant memory.

How did Koweena land the role of babysitting the son of the second most powerful man on the entire Plantation? It was because of her looks. Her bubbly personality which existed at least up until the beating; didn't hurt her either. But it was mainly because she was so pretty. The Jenkins' figured that if they were going to get a slave to watch over their child they at least wanted a slave that their child could look up to in the face and see someone looking back at him that was so beautiful.

"What a beautiful child!" A voice yells out from the foyer just outside of the living room. It was the voice of Julie Defour, the eighteen-year-old daughter of Mr. and Mrs. Defour. Mrs. Defour and Mrs. Jenkins had now moved from the living room into the kitchen, so Koweena was alone with Samuel in the living room. She had Samuel lying on the end of the sofa while she sat at his feet. Koweena stared at the floor as she spoke. "Yes, ma'am, he is." Julie now entered the living room. She was wearing a gentle smile on her face. "No, I meant you, Sweetheart! What is your name?" The friendly and passionate tone in Julie's voice made Koweena look up at her.

"My first impression of Julie was one of suspicion," Koweena recalled. "After all, she was white, and the only experiences I had with white people were bad ones. But there was just something in the way she looked at me, like she really wanted to know who I was. I could tell right away, she had taken an interest in me, and that peeked my curiousity."

Koweena could see the expression on Julie's face. She had never seen a white person look at her like that. She had seen many a slave look at her with that expression, but never a white person; once again a new experience Koweena was going through that day. What Koweena and Julie didn't realize that afternoon was that their two very different worlds were about to collide. Koweena raised her eyebrows and pointed at herself. "My name!?" Julie approached the sofa. "Yes, Dear, your name." "Koweena, ma'am." Julie was taken back. She took a deep breath and held her chest. "That is the most beautiful name I have ever heard!" She said as she exhaled. "Koweena, wow! That is really beautiful," Julie continued, "you are so precious looking!" Julie just couldn't get over how beautiful Koweena was. Koweena went back to staring at the floor. "Yes, ma'am," she replied. "I bet people tell you how beautiful you are all the time don't they?" "Not really," Koweena was thinking to herself. Koweena, still staring at the floor, spoke up. "Only my mom tells me how pretty I is, ma'am." "Koweena, Koweena," Julie was trying to get her attention but Koweena just kept starring at the floor. "Koweena," finally Koweena looked up at the pretty, long blonde haired, fair skinned Julie right in the eyes. She had reminded herself over and over again never to look white folks in the face; but for the first time in her life, she noticed something different at the face staring back at her. There was no disgusting look glaring back at her. Koweena was thinking to herself that this woman was actually, genuinely interested in who she is and what she had to say. She had never seen that look from a white person before. "You don't have to call me ma'am, okay. You are so pretty, my goodness! You know, you're even more beautiful when you're not looking down at the floor," Julie said with a soft tone in her voice. Koweena had never been talked to like that from a white person. She was somewhat confused by Julie's politeness towards her. The confusion made Koweena scared. If she knew the importance of whom Julie was, she would be even more terrified. Julie walked closer to where Koweena was sitting. "Why do you look down, Koweena? As pretty as you are you need to be looking up and showing that pretty face off!" "Yes, ma'am," Koweena said as she slowly and hesitantly looked up at Julie again. Something about Julie peeked the curiosity in Koweena. Maybe, from Koweena's prospective, it was the strange way in which Julie was talking to her and looking at her. Or maybe it was the nice compliments Julie was giving her. Either way, for the first time in her life, Koweena actually wanted to know a white person; this young woman who had intrigued her. "How old are you, Koweena?" Julie asked. "I don't know, ma'am. I think I is five, but I'm not sure." "Of course," Julie said to herself in a whisper. It broke Julie's heart that Koweena didn't know how old she was. She realized that Koweena called her ma'am again too; she knew it was out of habit and if Julie really wanted her to stop calling her that she realized that she would have to get to know her better. Julie also noticed that Koweena went back to staring at the floor again. "Koweena," this time Julie noticed that Koweena looked up at her right away. Koweena realized it as well, and it scared her; but on the other hand she liked the positive attention Julie was giving her, and the gentle looks she would give her when she would look up at her. Both were surprised at just how quickly Koweena looked up when Julie called out her name. For Julie, it excited her; but for Koweena, looking up at Julie so fast only heightened her fear. Julie continued, "Koweena, I want you to practice looking up for a few minutes instead of looking down at the floor. Can you do that?" Julie couldn't help but notice as she stared at Koweena, something she noticed right away from the beginning; and that was Koweena's light skin and hair. "What happened that caused this?" Julie thought to herself. "Who are her mom and dad?" She continued to wonder. "Koweena, can you do that for me? Can you try to look up at me and show off that pretty face?" Koweena, realizing that she looked up at Julie instantly before, wasn't about to do the same thing again. After a few seconds had passed, and realizing that Koweena was not going to budge her head; Julie took the next step of trying to get Koweena to open up to her. She went around her and sat next to her, on the opposite side of the sofa as Samuel. "Koweena, look at me please?" The soft, gentle voice of Julie really began to work on Koweena. It was beginning to break down the fear that had been growing and growing since her beating. Before now, she had only been used to her mother talking to her like that, with that gentle, soft tone. But now, it was someone different talking to her in that tone; and it was someone white on top of that. "Koweena, I know you're afraid to look at me, and I can't even begin to understand why; but I want you to know that I'm not going to hurt you. It's obvious you've been hurt before." At this point Julie realized that she was trying to break down some heavy barriers that stood in front of Koweena. It was obvious someone had hurt her in the past, Julie thought. Julie could sense the fear in Koweena. She just couldn't imagine a child so little being so afraid. "Koweena, will you look at me, I just want to look into your beautiful eyes?" Koweena started tearing up, she felt like she was going to collapse emotionally. All the pain, all the verbal abuse she had experienced in the past, started surfacing. Maybe it was how sensitive Julie was being towards her that made her get emotional. Or maybe it was listening to Julie telling her that she had been hurt in the past. It made her start thinking about all she had been through. Julie noticed that Koweena's eyes were welling up with tears, and that she was beginning to jerk, trying to hold back from crying. It was breaking Julie's heart to watch this little girl suffering like this. "Koweena, do you want to tell me what makes you so sad? I'm here to help you if you'll let me, Sweetheart, but you must open up to me." Koweena was afraid to open up to Julie, she barely knew her and she was white; she was also afraid that if she started crying in front of Julie that she would get beat. She knew Julie long enough, although be it just a short time, Julie had made such a strong impression on the little five year old in just a short amount of time, part of her knew that Julie wouldn't hit her; but she had been hurt by the white man far too much that the other part of her didn't want to take the chance. So she fought as hard as she could to choke back the tears. "Koweena, I'm here to help you if you'll let me," Julie said. She just couldn't stand to see this shy, pretty little girl fighting back her tears like she was. "I, I," Koweena was trying to talk while jerking, and trying to catch her breath at the same time, "I don't, I don't want to talk about it." Her desire to burst out crying intensified with each passing second. Finally she started crying out loud. Julie wanted so desperately to put her arms around Koweena and hold her tight; but she just sat there and let Koweena cry it all out. "It's okay, Koweena, Dear, you can cry," Julie said in a sensitive voice. That remark only made Koweena cry that much harder. As Julie sat there and watched Koweena cry, she thought back over the last thirty minutes to when she first saw Koweena. From the moment she saw that little girl she took to her right away. She loved everything about her. To how pretty she was, to how shy and reserved she was. She even thought Koweena's name was so pretty that she just loved saying it. It didn't matter to her that Koweena was babysitting the child of the most prominent man on the Plantation; she barely even noticed Samuel lying there. No, it was Koweena, and Koweena only, that drew her attention that day in the living room. Julie gently placed her hand on Koweena's shoulder. "It's okay, Koweena, Baby." She was careful about touching her. Julie could sense that Koweena was a little frightened of her by the way she moved her arm over a bit when Julie stretched out to touch her. Several minutes had passed and Koweena's sobbing had subsided somewhat, but she still wouldn't look up at Julie. Julie still had her hand on Koweena's shoulder. "Koweena, you shouldn't be so sad, you're so young, you still have your whole life ahead of you." Julie had obviously been sheltered from her father's slave business. She didn't realize just how brutal it was out there. She thought that Koweena actually had a future on the Plantation. She was naïve about Koweena's little world.

Julie's mom had walked into the room at this point, along with Mrs. Jenkins. Mrs. Defour quickly glanced over at where Julie and Koweena were sitting and noticed Julie's hand on Koweena's shoulder. Mrs. Defour was angered at what she saw. Mrs. Jenkins went over to pick Samuel up. "Why is my baby wet?" Mrs. Jenkins inquired of Koweena. Koweena thought to herself, "Here comes some more verbal abuse." Mrs. Jenkins noticed that Samuel's diaper was soaked. She glared disgustingly at Koweena. "Why have you not changed my baby's diaper!?" She said in a high pitched voice directed at Koweena. "The little Nigger is falling asleep on the job, Dorothy," Mrs. Defour commented. Julie snapped back. "Mother! Leave Koweena alone, it was my fault, I was talking to her. I must have distracted her. There's no need in calling her names!" Her mother had her hands on her hips as she stood overtop of Julie. "Oh, you distracted her? Since when do you call strange niggers you've never met by their first name Julie?" Mrs. Defour asked her daughter. "Mom, stop it, I mean it!" "Why are you taking up for this little thing, Julie? She's not worth the effort," Mrs. Defour said. Koweena had never had someone take up for her before, especially a white person. This act by Julie quickly caused Koweena to feel protected by Julie a little bit. "I is sorry, ma'am," Koweena told Mrs. Jenkins. "Well, there's no excuse for it. Next time pay more attention to Samuel, you got it!" Mrs. Jenkins demanded. "Dorothy, lets take Samuel to the bedroom down the hall. We can change him there," Mrs. Defour said. Mrs. Defour walked by both Koweena and Julie. "Worthless Nigger," she said under her breath. Her whisper was loud enough to where Koweena and Julie both heard her as she walked by them. "Shut up, mom, you're so mean! It's just a wet diaper!" Julie shouted. Mrs. Defour suddenly stopped from walking out of the living room and turned back to Julie. "Don't you dare talk to me that way, Julie!" "Well, quit talking mean to Koweena then!" Julie shouted back. "You better watch this taking up for the help business Julie, or else." "Or else what, is that a threat, mother?" "I'm just saying, Julie, stop fraternizing with the Nigger okay, Dear, that's all I'm saying." "Don't you see that Koweena is crying, mother, don't you care?" "I don't care, Julie, what that little thing is doing!" "You know that's enough, mom, she doesn't deserve to be talked to that way, just leave, okay?" Mrs. Defour, taking a deep breath and exhaling while staring at both Julie and Koweena, turned and walked out of the living room. Julie began rubbing on Koweena's shoulder. "I'm sorry about that, Koweena." "Not only had Julie taken up for me, but she was now consoling me," Koweena thought to herself. The episode Julie just had with her mother changed Koweena's view of Julie. She was no longer frightened of her. "You stood up for me. Nobody has ever stood up for me before," Koweena said surprisingly. It flattered Julie to hear that, but it also troubled her to hear it as well. She now not only wondered why Koweena looked the way she did, but she also began to wonder just what all Koweena had been through. "Koweena, can I ask you a serious question?" "Okay," Koweena said in a shy, reserved manner. "What has happened to you to make you so sad?" "I don't want to talk about it," Koweena said. "You know, you might not believe this, but it helps to talk things out and get them off your chest. It makes you feel better inside." "I don't want to," Koweena said, this time with tears beginning to form in her eyes once again. Julie realized she was making Koweena uncomfortable, and quickly changed the subject. "Would you like something to drink?" Julie asked. Koweena had never been asked that before by a white person. She had experienced a lot of new things that day in that house and this was just another in a long line of learning new things about white people; from the beautiful things they had in their house, how they acted, how they talked, and now how polite they were, at least one of them anyway. "Yes, ma'am, I would like that." "Okay, I'll be right back."

As Julie was gone, Koweena began to think about this white woman who had defended her as she was getting verbally abused. Koweena was thinking that not only was she consoling her and talking to her nicely; but she was standing up for her as well. "Why?" Koweena thought to herself. Her fear had left her in regards to Julie, but her confusion about Julie was still there. She was white, and she was polite, very confusing, Koweena thought. Julie entered back into the room. "Here you go, Dear." Julie handed her some sweet tea. Koweena looked at it funny. "It looks like muddy water," she said out loud accidentally. Julie laughed. "It's sweet, Koweena, you'll like it." Koweena took a sip. It tasted very different than water. It shocked her taste buds at first, but she loved the sugar. She gulped the entire glass in seconds. She had never been offered anything to drink at Mrs. Jenkins house before, this was a certainly a treat. "Wow, you must have been thirsty! Have you ever had anything to drink but water before?" "No, ma'am, just water." "Koweena, please don't call me ma'am. I know you've done it your whole life, but I'm not like the other white people you've encountered, you don't have to say ma'am to me," Julie insisted. "Do you know how old you is?" Koweena asked Julie. Koweena was trying to divert the conversation away from the pain she was experiencing. Julie realized that Koweena didn't say ma'am to her. Julie removed her hand from Koweena's shoulder once she noticed her sobbing had stopped. "I'm eighteen." "How do you know how old you is?" Koweena replied. "Well, I don't know, I've just always known my birthday." "What's a birthday?" Koweena asked. Julie realized after that remark that Koweena had been deprived of the simple, enjoyable things in life. "A birthday happens once a year. It's a time where you celebrate the day you were born. Sometimes you throw parties and have lots of fun, other times, like when you get my age, you just invite some of your close friends over for lunch or dinner, to celebrate." Koweena looked at Julie's hands which were lying on her lap. "I don't know when my birthday is," Koweena said. Julie instantly formed a frown on her face upon hearing that. "What are friends?" Koweena asked. Julie's hurt was further worsened with each passing comment and question Koweena made. She realized more and more how Koweena had no sense of the enjoyable pleasures in life that she herself had taken for granted her entire life. "Friends are people usually your own age, that you talk to and play with." "I have a friend." "You do, who?" Julie asked, inching a little closer to Koweena. "Josi," Koweena replied. "Do you play with Josi?" "Sometimes," Koweena said, staring Julie right in the eyes, she didn't even realize she was doing it. Julie's eyes were so tender, looking back at Koweena, that Koweena had begun to feel so comfortable with her that she had forgotten what had been etched in her brain for so long, especially the last few months; do not look at white folks, period. "Me and Josi play in the dirt, that's what we do for fun." Once again Julie was crushed by the response. She realized Koweena had nothing to play with, no dolls, no toys, nothing. "It's good that you have a friend, Koweena, everyone needs a friend. You know what, Koweena?" "What?" "I have a great idea."

Meanwhile, Mr. Jenkins had left Mr. Defour's office and was now walking down the hallway approaching the entrance to the living room to go to the front door. He stopped right at the corner of the living room entranceway. He could overhear Julie talking to Koweena. He peeped around the corner and noticed that it was only Julie and Koweena in the living room, all by themselves. Julie and Koweena were so engrossed in their conversation that they didn't hear Mr. Jenkins' loud boots hitting the wooden floor. "Here's my idea, Dear. What do you say to spending the entire weekend with me?" "She's calling that little Nigger dear, and inviting her over for the weekend? This is not good at all," Mr. Jenkins whispered to himself. Julie was overflowing with excitement. "We could play with dolls all weekend?" She said. At this point Julie had made up her mind. She was going to alter Koweena's life and give her the kind of life she thought Koweena deserved. "What do you say, Koweena?" "I don't know, Julie," Koweena said. Julie noticed that not only had Koweena stopped saying ma'am to her; but she was now saying her name. Julie just smiled and clinched her hands together, rubbing them one on top of the other. She was excited. She could now tell that she was successfully breaking down the barriers that were so fortified when they first met. Koweena, on the other hand, was so relaxed around Julie now, that she didn't even realize she had let down her guard. Koweena was a little apprehensive about spending the weekend with Julie however. It was a big step for her. She had had such bad experiences with white folks, and now this white person was asking her to play with her, and for the entire weekend. "I have to work," Koweena said. "Oh, don't worry about that, I'll take care of that, you don't have to worry about a thing there," Julie said in a reassuring voice. To Koweena, it sounded too much like the promise her mom made to her when she said that she didn't have anything to worry about when it came to the overseers. "I'll get in trouble," Koweena said sadly. For the first time in a while, Koweena was now staring at the floor as she said this. Julie realizing this said, "Koweena, look at me." Koweena looked up and stared at Julie. Koweena wanted so desperately to believe in Julie, to believe that she could be happy and have fun, that it showed in her eyes. Julie could sense this as she stared back at Koweena. "I promise you that everything will be alright." "It's just that I is been promised things before, and well, it didn't work out like I is told," Koweena said. Mr. Jenkins had heard enough. "This is disgusting! Julie promising to play with that Nigger. I can't believe this," he said to himself. He walked by the living room entrance, turned and looked at Julie. "Hey, Mr. Jenkins," Julie said in a nice tone. For the first time Mr. Jenkins didn't even acknowledge her. He left the house in a hurry. Julie thought that was strange but didn't think about it long, she was too involved in Koweena to pay it much mind. "I tell you what, wait right here, and I'll prove to you that it will be alright," Julie said. Koweena wondered how Julie had such authority to make such promises. Julie got up from the sofa. "Julie." "Yes, Koweena." For her age Koweena was smart and it was about to show. "Where do you live?" Koweena asked. Julie responded, "Here, Dear." The nightmare Koweena was thinking when she asked that, had come true. "This is the boss man's daughter," Koweena thought to herself. Panic began to settle inside of her. "I will surely get in trouble," she thought as Julie made her way down the hallway toward the room her mother and Mrs. Jenkins was in.

Julie dreaded the walk as she continued down the hallway. She didn't like that room, didn't even like to be anywhere near it; but she entered it anyway. "Mother, I've invited Koweena to come and play, and spend the weekend with me." Her mother took a deep gasp of air, "you what!?" "You heard me." Her mother let out a sarcastic chuckle. "No way, no way, Julie." "I'm serious, mom." Her mother took a deep breath and exhaled as she stood there with her hands on her hips. "Have you lost your mind!?" Her mother yelled. Mrs. Jenkins just stood there silently, holding Samuel. "I don't want that little animal in my house spending time with you!" "Mom, stop talking about her in those terms! She's not an animal! Didn't you notice how beautiful she is?" "I don't care, Julie, she's not spending any time in this house with you this weekend." "You act like you've never had black people in the house before. Look around, mother, their everywhere, all over this house!" "That's different, Julie, they work in this house, they don't play." "Mother, I'm not asking you, I'm telling you." "Julie, this is ridiculous, you've known this little thing what, a few hours, and now you want that thing to spend the entire weekend with you?" "I don't know, mom, there's something about her. I took to her the moment I saw her." "I can't listen to this, you're talking nonsense, girl!" "Mom, she's not a thing, or an animal, she's a beautiful little girl who has been through a lot in her young life.

She has it written all over her face!" "You're talking about her as if she were a human being." "She is a human being!" Julie screamed out. Her mother began shaking her head at Julie. "You always get your way, Julie. That little Nigger is not spending the night, you got it! And she's not going to eat with us, day, or night!" "That's fine, but you're not going to give me any problems about this, mother," Julie said as she quickly left the room; she couldn't stand to be in there one second longer. "One weekend only, Julie!" Her mother yelled out as Julie was walking down the hallway. Koweena could hear them arguing, and she could also hear Julie sticking up for her again. Koweena was nervous about all that was transpiring around her. It was all happening so quickly. She had just met Julie, and now she had just realized that she was the owner's daughter. But oh, the way Julie treated her. She felt loved and wanted by Julie, and she felt so comfortable around her as well. After having some time to think it over, as Julie was talking to her mother, and as she listened to Julie defending her like she was, Koweena decided she was going to do it. As Julie returned to the living room, Koweena could see the big smile Julie had on her face. That made Koweena feel a whole lot better about everything. As it started to gradually become darker outside, Julie sat again on the sofa, this time on the opposite side of Koweena than where she sat before, where Samuel had been laying earlier. "Okay Koweena, it's all set, you're spending the weekend with me." Julie noticed that Koweena's muscles throughout her entire body were tightening and she was breathing heavily. Julie could sense she was panicking. "What's wrong, Koweena?" "I'm scared, Julie." "What are you scared of?" "Your dad; and mom." "Oh, don't worry about them. I do whatever I want around here, Koweena. If I want to invite a friend over, then that's what I'll do, there's nothing they can do about it." "But still. I don't know, I mean, I is a slave, I'm not your friend." "You are my friend, Koweena. Do you hear me? You are my friend. Don't worry; nobody will do anything to you." Still, Julie had no idea what Koweena had been through. Koweena had heard that same line before, and look what happened to her. But once again, children Koweena's age are resilient; and her desire to have some fun, and actually play with toys, thrilled her and made the thoughts of possibly getting beat again take a back seat. "Okay, I'll do it," Koweena said after giving it some more thought. "Perfect! Okay, here's what were going to do. I will have a maid pick you up tomorrow morning. What time do you get up?" "I don't know, we is don't have a clock." "Okay then, well, just to be safe, let's say around nine o'clock. Does that sound good?" "What time is nine?" "Let's just say the sun will be up by then." "Okay," Koweena said. "We will play all day; you don't have to worry about working at all." Was Koweena dreaming? She thought she was. Play all day and no work; it was too good to be true. "And we is gonna to do it the next day?" Koweena asked. "Yes Koweena, two days of nothing but playing, how does that sound?" Koweena got so excited she could hardly contain it. "Great!" She said. Finally, she thought, she was going to enjoy herself and not have to worry about the slave life, at least for a couple of days anyway. "Let's go!" Mrs. Jenkins yelled out to Koweena from the foyer. "Okay, I is see you tomorrow, Julie!" "Okay, Koweena, bye." From the time Julie first saw Koweena to now, she had made such progress with the little child. To Julie, it seemed as though she had broken down all the barriers that Koweena had up. Julie was happy with that as she watched, with her arms folded at her stomach, little Koweena leaving the house. She felt like she really accomplished something that day, and in just a few hours she had become quickly attached to Koweena. And Koweena, walking out the front door with Mrs. Jenkins, felt the same way.

Back at the Jenkins household, Mr. and Mrs. Jenkins were sitting in their living room that night, they had just finished eating dinner, and Mr. Jenkins began to speak. "I don't know, Dorothy, I overheard something today at Mr. Defour's house that really disturbed me. I just can't get it out of my mind. It just keeps playing over and over again in my head." "What is it, Honey?" "Well, I overheard Julie talking to that little Nigger, saying nice things to her, being all lovey-dovey with her; and it just stuck in my craw. I just can't believe that someone in Julie's position would lower herself enough to talk to a thing like that." "What did she say, Donald?" Mrs. Jenkins asked. "She was calling that little spook dear! And you know what else!? "What, Honey?" "She even invited that Nigger to spend the weekend with her! To play with her and stuff! Can you believe that!?" Mr. Jenkins despised Julie for her actions that afternoon, mainly because of the fact that she was Mr. Defour's daughter, and should have known better than to behave around a slave like that. "You know, I did overhear Julie and her mother in their back bedroom today," Mrs. Jenkins said. "Oh yeah," Mr. Jenkins said. "Yeah, it got pretty heated in there. Julie was yelling, Mrs. Defour was yelling, it was just a mess. Hey, how did you overhear Julie talking anyway?" Mrs. Jenkins asked. "Oh, I was walking in the hallway toward the front door and, well it doesn't matter. What matters is that I overheard that sickening conversation, and it angered me greatly. Enough about that, what did you hear Julie saying?" Mr. Jenkins asked. "Well, I was just standing there holding Samuel alongside Mrs. Defour, when all of a sudden Julie comes barging into the bedroom and tells her mother that she had invited that Nigger to spend the weekend with her. My mouth just dropped. She went on to tell Mrs. Defour that there was nothing she could do about it either." "What did Mrs. Defour say?" Mr. Jenkins asked. "She was upset, no doubt about it." "Well, I would be too!" Mr. Jenkins interrupted. Mrs. Jenkins continued. "She told Julie she was out of her mind and that she wasn't going to allow it. But you know Julie, she always gets her way. I just stood there in shock and silence." "I don't like this, Dorothy, one bit! Should I tell Mr. Defour about all of this, I mean, I almost feel obligated to, you know. He is my boss and all." "I don't know, Donald, it definitely is disturbing to say the least." "And what about that Nigger babysitting for us now," Mr. Jenkins said in a concerned voice, "should we continue that?" "Well, she is pretty. You know if we are going to have a slave babysitting for us, I at least want her to be pretty." "I don't know, Dorothy; if this thing escalates, that little wench may start thinking she has a run of the house here. It may get the big head and start thinking it's white or something. That little slave could put Samuel in harm's way!" "I know, Honey. I think we should just see how far this goes with Julie though first. I would wait to tell Mr. Defour, at least wait until we see if this thing does indeed escalate."

Meanwhile Jial, an elderly female slave, the only full time slave maid in the Jenkins' household, was listening intensely to the conversation from the hallway, just around the corner of the living room. "Koweena is gotten herself into some big trouble," Jial says to herself. "I better tell her mother," she continued.

Mr. Jenkins, continuing the conversation in the bedroom, was lying on the bed when he began to speak. "You know, Dorothy, I could just end this thing once and for all by telling Mr. Defour." Mrs. Jenkins spoke out from the bathroom bedroom. "Like I said, let's just see how this all plays out, then we'll talk about you telling Mr. Defour." "Or, I could tell an overseer and have the little slave reprimanded." "She's done nothing wrong, Donald." "She's cozying up to Julie! That's enough!" Mr. Jenkins said. "But she's just a child," Mrs. Jenkins said. "She not a child, she's a slave." "She's too young to discipline, Donald. Anyways, she is a very good babysitter, to be so young." Mr. Jenkins spoke aloud as he was getting under his covers. "Well, I still feel like I need to do something," "Just give it time, Donald," Mrs. Jenkins said while putting moisturizer on her face.

"I's don't like it one bit!" Amitha told Koweena in their shack that night. "But, mom," "but mom nothin," her mother interrupted. "You is don't know these people, Koweena! And what have I told you about the white folks, huh? I mean look at what they did to you!" "But, mom, this girl's different. "How, Koweena, she's still white, that's not goin to change." "But she's different. She's kind and polite. She talks to me like you talk to me, calling me sweetheart and dear and cuddling with me. You know what, mom? She stood up for me today." "What do you is mean she stood up for you?" "Her mom and Mrs. Jenkins were saying bad things about me and talking down to me as all white people have done; but this time, this Julie girl takes up for me and tells them not to talk to me that way. It was the first time I's ever seen that before." "Taking up for you huh." Her mother said. She was so hesitant to give her approval to Koweena that she was careful in what she said; but she was impressed with this Julie girl. From what Koweena was telling her, this white girl seemed like a rare breed. Amitha had never heard of a white person treating a black person like Julie was treating Koweena. Her mother grabbed a hold of Koweena's shoulders. "But, Koweena, she is the slave owner's daughter. Spending the weekend with her is just too dangerous. I mean, you could do any little thing, like just breaking one of their decorations or somethin. Any little thing could set them off; then you don't know what they could do to you!" "But, momma, if you had just been there and seen how Julie treated me and stuck up for me you wouldn't be so upset." "I'm not upset, Dear, it just worries me that you will be around all those powerful white people. What about Mr. Defour? Does he know about this?" "I don't know, momma, but Julie said I had nothing to worry about. She said she's the one in charge there, not her parents." Although Koweena had no formal education, she had a sixth sense about life. When it came to situations concerning her and the people around her, she was way far advanced for her years. She could explain situations that surrounded her with great keenness and understanding. "Momma, I got the feeling after spending just a few moments with Julie, that she loved me." "Loves you! A white girl!" "Yes, momma, she said I was beautiful and had a pretty name," "every person says that Koweena," her mom interrupted. "Yeah, momma, but a white girl? I never felt so comfortable around someone before than I did with Julie, except for you of course." With each statement from her daughter, Amitha grew more and more impressed with Julie. "Maybe this girl does care for my little child," she thought. "But she's still white," she continued thinking. "Koweena, you still have the marks on you that prove what white folks can do to you." "But, momma, I can tell the difference between a white person who has hate in their hearts and a white person who loves and cares for me; and Julie loves and cares for me." "I would feel better, Koweena, if she would bring her toys over here and spend time with you." "In this shack!?" Koweena shouted out.

The time spent in the main house of the Plantation made the shack Koweena was in, a shack she had once thought of as normal, seem insulting and pitiful. That afternoon in the Defour house, with all the new things she had experienced for the first time, it changed Koweena's entire prospective on her little life. There was more to life than living in this disgusting shack and waking up day after day, working in the fields. For her, there were now beautiful large homes, dazzling, colorful, shiny new objects to look at; and a new white friend that made her feel like a person and not an object. She was no longer depressed and hopeless. For the first time she was experiencing what a five year old should be experiencing; and that was a future filled with fun dreams. Julie had given her that hope, and not only had Koweena realized it, but Amitha had as well. Koweena began jumping up and down, pleading with her mom to let her go the next day. "Momma, I like Julie a lot!" Her mother sat down on Koweena's hay bed. "Koweena, I don't know. What if an overseer sees you in that house playing with this Julie; or worse yet, what if Mr. Defour sees you playing in his own house!?" "Momma, her mom knows I'm goin to be there, and she said it was okay!" Amitha didn't like this one bit, but she could see the change in Koweena. She was now talking, she had life back in her eyes, and more importantly, her mom noticed that Koweena was no longer staring at the floor. Amitha couldn't deny the fact, just on appearances alone, that this Julie had changed her daughter for the better; and she was afraid that if she didn't let Koweena go the next morning, that her daughter could possibly shut down again, and this time it could be much worse than before. After giving it some serious thought, and because of this change she had seen in Koweena, Amitha decided to let her go. "Promise me one thing, Koweena, please don't look those white folks in the eyes, okay." Koweena could see the obvious worry in her mother's face. "Don't worry, momma, Julie will be with me." Koweena said that matter of factly, never giving it a second thought; by now she trusted Julie completely and in such a short time. Maybe it was because of her age, little children, especially little children who are treated the way Koweena was treated by Julie, tend to trust easily. Whatever the reason, Koweena just knew that she was safe with Julie by her side. Koweena grabbed a hold of her mother's hand. "Momma, it will be okay." Amitha placed her arm around Koweena's shoulder. "I'm just glad you is better now, Koweena, and not sad." It dawned on Koweena for the first time that day that she was no longer depressed. For the entire evening after leaving the Defour house she did not think once about the abuse she had suffered just months ago. Up until that time it had been on her mind constantly. Her mother realized it as well. Julie had truly impacted her in a life altering manner that afternoon. That night Koweena could hardly sleep; with the possibilities of what the next day would bring, and how much fun she would have, she was just too excited to sleep. The upcoming weekend was all she could think about.

Chapter 5   New Experiences

*I*t was an usually warm, sunny, mid December Saturday morning when Koweena arrived at the Defour house. Julie was at the front door to greet little Koweena. Seeing Julie there waiting on her, relaxed her nerves somewhat; and it made her even more excited than she was the night before, if that were possible. Julie stretched her arm out toward Koweena. "Hey, Dear," Julie said. "Hey, Julie," Koweena said with a big smile. Julie began laughing a bit. "Come on in!" She told Koweena. She was laughing because Koweena had suddenly paused for a second at the front door, with Julie's arm wrapped around her back. For that brief moment Koweena thought of Mr. and Mrs. Defour, and what their reaction would be to her being there. Julie began giving Koweena a slight nudge toward the entranceway. "Come on, Koweena, it's okay," Julie said with a big smile. Finally, after a brief moment of feeling the same feelings she had felt for months, the new feeling Julie had created in her just a day ago came to the forefront; with that feeling inside her she stepped into the house.

"Everything had changed," Koweena recalled. "It was like night and day inside that house. As if the previous day wasn't enough new things for my eyes to absorb there, I had that morning to absorb some more. As soon as I entered the house, I could smell the strong odor of fruit cake baking in the kitchen. What I was gazing upon caused me to take a deep breath. My eyes were opened wide. I had an excited shock sensation about me as I looked upon the new appearance of the house. I quickly noticed, right in front of me, dark green garland wrapped around the long staircase handles on both sides, from top to bottom. It looked like thick grass to me. From there I gazed at the red and white poinsettias that were placed along the bottom of the walls along the wooden floors, with two placed on the small table just to the right of the stairway against the wall. My eyes were barely big enough to contain what I was looking at. My little brain was trying to soak it all in. I was like a kid in a candy store all over again, just like the day before. I glanced over to my right and noticed some more of the beautiful, colorful poinsettias lining the sides of the hallway. I could barely contain my excitement as I looked all around with my mouth open. The smells and visions I was experiencing were all so new to me. Just like the day before, I had that excited feeling inside as I was adventuring new things. I didn't know what I was looking at, or smelling. All I knew is that it was all so new to me. Sure, we celebrated Christmas in my little slave world, but nothing compared to what I was looking at and smelling. I didn't realize plants could be so colorful and eye catching. There were still more new things that awaited my little eyes."

Julie just laughed watching Koweena soaking everything in. "Do you like what you see, Koweena?" She asked. She couldn't help but laugh as she noticed Koweena's amazed expression. Julie realized this was all new for Koweena, and she was happy just to watch her expression as Koweena took it all in. "There's more, Dear, follow me," Julie said as she took a hold of Koweena's hand and lead her into the living room. Koweena thought she was going to burst from her insides as she walked into the living room and saw what was next. She immediately noticed the giant Christmas tree standing in the corner of the room. It had white garland wrapped around it. Koweena thought it was unbelievable. "White grass," she thought to herself as she stared at the garland. She also noticed more of the colorful arraignments of Poinsettias sitting around the floor and tables of the room. Koweena, so curious about the garland, finally asked Julie. "Is that grass?" "What, Dear?" "That stuff on the stairs, and the stuff wrapped around that tree, is that grass?" Julie laughed again. "No, Sweetheart, that's called garland, it's not real, it's fake; looks kind of like grass thought doesn't it?" "Yeah!" Koweena said in complete awe. As she stared at the tree she also noticed the many different ornaments hanging from it, as well as the red velvet bows dangling on the limbs. At the bottom she noticed a railroad track circling the tree with a train on it. Once again this was new to her, she didn't know what she was staring at, but she thought the movement of the train going around the tree was fascinating and breathtaking. Koweena pointed down at the base of the tree. "What's that?" "What, that?" Julie said, pointing at the train. "Yeah." "That's a train," Julie said. "That is the neatest thing I's ever seen," Koweena said with excitement.

Julie so enjoyed showing Koweena all the decorations. Julie almost got as much excitement out of watching Koweena's facial expressions as Koweena did looking at all the various colors, ornaments, and especially the train. "Can I get closer to it," Koweena said, looking up at Julie. "What, the train?" "Yeah!" "Sure, Dear, go ahead." Koweena ran over to the tree and knelt down in front of the toy train. She noticed upon getting closer to it that it was made of all medal. She just sat there in wonder at the little train going around and around the tree. Julie knelt down beside Koweena at the foot of the tree. "Do you want me to stop it, so you can touch it?" "Will you!?" Koweena said as her eyes were fixated on the train. "Sure, let me just unplug it here." As the train came to a stop, Koweena reached out her little hand and touched the cold metal. It was the first time she had ever seen a toy up close, much less touched one. Julie chuckled."Neat huh?" Her enjoyment of watching Koweena made her laugh with joy almost every time she opened her mouth. "Do you want to see an ornament?" Julie asked. "Okay," Koweena said. Julie stood up and grabbed an ornament from the tree. It was a gold colored plastic ball with an insignia of the Defour house on it. Koweena held the ornament in her hand. "Wow, it's beautiful!" She said. "Why do you hang these things on this tree?" She asked. "It's just for decorations, to make it look pretty; it adds color to the tree. Each ornament is different," Julie said as she grabs another one off the tree to show Koweena. "You see this one is a statue of a horse, it's made out of porcelain." Koweena takes the ornament with her other hand, now holding both ornaments together. "Yeah, they is different. And each one is different like these two?" "Yes, each one is unique, there are no two alike," Julie said, now sitting back down with Koweena. "Oh, I see the Nigger is here," Julie's mother said as she walked by the two sitting on the floor by the train. Julie quickly snapped back. "Mother!" "Make sure that little spook doesn't break any of my ornaments, and keep her off the carpets," her mother continued. "Mother, watch your mouth!" It swiftly put a damper on Koweena's mood. Julie could see it written all over her little face too. Julie quickly got up and headed over to where her mom was standing in the dining room. Everything had been going so great up to that point, Koweena was thinking. She was fearful of Mrs. Defour and her downgrading words. Koweena knew that Mrs. Defour would put a damper on things if she came around.

"Mother, she's not a pet or some animal that you have to keep off the carpets! Now, she's a guest in my home and I expect," "my home, Julie," her mom interrupted, "well, she's a guest of mine and I expect you to treat her that way," Julie responded back. "First of all, you invited it over here without consulting me first," "I did consult you," Julie interrupted, "and now," her mother continued, "you have it sitting under my tree touching my valuables." "First of all, mom, she's not an it, and secondly, I live here too. I really like this girl, mom, she's special to me, at least you can respect that." Mrs. Defour pointed to one of the area rugs in the living room. "Just don't let her on the carpet, she's dirty." "She was sitting on the sofa yesterday, and you didn't say anything then about her being dirty," Julie said. "That's different; she had to be here yesterday to babysit Samuel. She doesn't have to be here today." "Oh, so it's okay if she was here because of Mrs. Jenkins, but when she's over here because of me, it suddenly doesn't make things alright." Her mother grabbed one of Julie's hands. "I see where you're going with this, Julie, and I'm not playing that game, just keep her in line, you hear," her mother said. Julie quickly pulls away from her. "You're impossible, you know that!" Julie said while walking away.

Koweena just sat there staring at the little toy train listening to every word that was being said in the dining room. She was hurt, but with what she had seen and experienced so far, and the fact that she was so excited, she was determined that Mrs. Defour was not going to rain on her parade. So her dampened spirits didn't last long. Julie arrived back in the living room and sat next to Koweena once again. That instantly made Koweena feel better. "I'm sorry about that, Koweena, just ignore her, okay?" "I'm starting to learn," Koweena said with a crooked grin. "Hey, do you want to come up to my room?" Julie asked. Koweena had been waiting to hear those words from Julie all morning; she was now more excited than ever. "Yeah!" She said with great anticipation.

As Koweena was walking up the stairs that lead to Julie's room she gently let her hand glide along the garland that covered the hand rails.

"It's so soft, and it tickles," Koweena said. Julie just laughed. As Koweena approached the closed door that led into Julie's bedroom, it was as if she was getting ready to unwrap a gift. She could hardly wait to see what was on the other side. "Are you ready!?" Julie asked with a raised voice and a smile on her face. Koweena was too excited and preoccupied with what awaited her on the other side to say anything. Julie opened the door, Koweena entered Julie's room, it was just as she had dreamed it would be. She quickly glanced over to her left and noticed the white bookcase. Finally, she got to see what she and her child slave friends had only envisioned and talked about. The bookcase was filled with dolls, from top to bottom. Koweena began to open and close her mouth quickly, as if she were tasting something. Her eyes wandered about the room. She noticed the piano in the right corner, and the beautiful bed in the middle of the room. She had never seen a bed before, much less one that looked like this one. It was covered with tiny pillows at the head, with satin light blue sheets neatly folded tightly from head to foot. The sheets flowed from the side of the bed all the way to the floor. She then noticed the light brown oak hope chest at the foot of the bed. Her curiosity was peeked as she stared at the chest. She wondered what was inside it. Julie, noticing that Koweena had been staring at the chest for quite some time, asked, "Do you want to see what's inside of it?" Like the train downstairs, Julie couldn't wait to let Koweena experience new things. Her goal was to spoil her any way she knew how, and so far she was doing an excellent job. "Come, let me show you," Julie said as she walked ahead of Koweena toward the hope chest. She looked back at her as if to wonder why Koweena wasn't moving. For a moment Koweena couldn't move; her eyes had absorbed so many new things in just the last couple of hours that her little brain was trying to process it, which kept her from moving. Julie laughed once again as she spoke. "Koweena, are you alright?" She noticed the stunned look on Koweena's face, and knew it was from all the new and exciting things her little mind was trying to grasp. This made Julie laugh with happiness. She chuckled as she spoke. "Come on, Sweetheart, it's okay." Koweena finally began walking over to the chest; it was a slow walk though. She could barely keep up with all she was observing. Julie opened up the chest and Koweena peered into it, once again her eyes got as big as saucers. By now she had completely forgotten about the scars on her back, the beating, the verbal abuse, and to some degree, even her mother. Her little slave world was a distant memory, at least for the time being. She noticed shiny jewelry in an opened box in the corner of the chest. She didn't even think of asking if she could touch the jewelry, she was so excited that she forgot. She grabbed a handful of necklaces and gold rings and brought them near to her face. Before this, the closest she had ever gotten to jewelry was when she was next to a white person, including Julie. She had always been fascinated by the accessory and wondered how heavy it was, and what it felt like to the touch; but most of all, she wondered what it would look like on her. "Can I try some of these on!?" Koweena asked, she was so excited that her voice was shaking. "Go ahead, Dear, there's a mirror over there." Koweena walked over to the mirror that was in between the bookcase that housed the dolls and Julie's light oak dresser. Koweena just stood there gazing at herself with the jewelry on. She had as much jewelry on, as much as her little hands could carry over to the mirror. She had necklaces, bracelets on both wrists, and rings on both hands. "Your skin color really sets the jewelry off Koweena." "What do you mean, sets the jewelry off?" Koweena asked. "It makes it stand out on you, it makes the jewelry really flashy on your skin," Julie explained in more childlike terms. The jewelry really did stand out on Koweena's butterscotch skin tone. After staring at herself, and touching the jewelry for several minutes, Julie said something that Koweena was not expecting. "Would you like to take some home with you?" "Do you really mean it!?" Koweena said with a shocked ring in her voice. "Yes, pick out what you like, and take it home with you." "But I don't have anything to keep it in," Koweena said sadly. "I have plenty of jewelry boxes; I can let you have one." Koweena could barely believe what she was hearing. "Are you saying I can have some, or just borrow some?" Koweena asked. "No, you can have as much as you want, Koweena. Here's a box, fill it with as much jewelry as you want." Koweena could hardly believe her ears as she went through all of Julie's jewelry, picking out what she wanted.

Meanwhile, as Koweena and Julie were carrying on in the bedroom, Amitha was working out in the field, when Jial approached her from behind. "Amitha." "Jial, what is you doin here? You is shouldn't be out here, you is far away from where you is suppose to be." "I know, but this couldn't wait," Jial said. "Listen," she continued, "I is need to talk as soon as possible." "What about?" Amitha inquired. "I don't have time to tell you right now, it's too dangerous out here in the open. Can we talk tonight, this can't wait." Amitha picked up on the panic in Jial's voice. "What is it, Jial? Just tell me." "Tonight, Amitha, it's about your daughter." "What about her, is she in trouble!?" "Like I said, I can't talk right now, we is get in trouble. Tonight, at your shack, okay?" "Alright," Amitha said hesitantly. She wanted to know right then, especially when Jial said it was about her daughter; but she knew an overseer could spot Jial easily, and then she would never know what Jial knew about her daughter. She would have to go the rest of the day wondering what was wrong with her daughter. As the day grew on, Amitha's thoughts of what could possibly be wrong with Koweena jumped to the worst case scenarios. "Could she have been threatened by one of those white folks? Is her life in jeopardy? Is she dead?" Her thoughts went from bad to worse with each passing second. It was a torturous day for Amitha.

In the meantime, back at the Defour house, Julie was allowing Koweena to play with her doll collection. "Be very careful with them, Koweena, they are fragile, okay?" "Okay," Koweena responded. Finally Koweena got to be a kid. For the first time in her five year life, she was actually playing with toys; and beautiful, expensive toys at that. She spent hours just accessorizing the various dolls, and combing their hair. Julie spent that time reading one of her many books. As she was reading, she glanced up at Koweena and noticed the mark she had above her eye. "Koweena." "Yes, Julie." "Where did you get that mark above your eye?" Julie asked with great concern. That question brought all the bad memories flooding back into Koweena's mind. "I don't know, I think I got it out in the field one day." Koweena instinctively lied; she didn't trust Julie enough to tell her the truth. "I'm sorry," Julie said. "It looks like it hurt however it happened," Julie said. Koweena quickly changed the subject, "What else can we do, Julie?" Although it excited Koweena to play with the dolls, she was too curious about the rest of the room to continue playing with them. "I know, I can play the piano for you!" Julie said with great enthusiasm. Yet again, something Koweena had never experienced before. She glanced over at the big black funny looking thing. She was yet to realize the beautiful sound that object could produce. Julie walked over to the piano, sat down, and began playing. Koweena was amazed at the sounds. It was the first time she had ever heard music. "This is a song, Koweena; I'm going to sing it to you." Koweena, as Julie began to sing, noticed the beautiful sound coming from Julie's voice. She had heard humming before, but never singing. As Julie was singing, Koweena was intensely listening to every word. The song was a simple one to understand, that's why Julie stayed up late the night before writing it just for Koweena. As the sunlight rays streamed through the bedroom window, Julie sang the song which was about a girl saying, "I'll never quit, I'll never give up, nothing can hurt me as long as I keep my head up and continue on," the song continued. Koweena, amazed by Julie's voice, and the fact that it was the first song she had ever heard, quickly memorized the entire song. It was a short song with a few words. Julie's goal in creating that particular song had paid off. She wanted Koweena to understand it, to be able to sing it on her own, and that's exactly what happened. Julie just sat there playing and singing that song over and over again; by about the fifth time, Koweena was now singing it on her own. Julie, noticing that Koweena was singing, stopped playing in order to listen to Koweena sing. It was then that Julie realized just how smart Koweena was to be able to memorize that song so quickly. "You have a beautiful voice, Koweena," Julie said smiling from ear to ear. Koweena stopped singing, "no, you is have the beautiful voice, Julie." Julie placed her hands together in a prayer position. "Continue singing, please!" She begged. Koweena continued singing the song she had just memorized. Julie just sat there listening to Koweena's soft, beautiful voice. They were both having one of the best days of their lives, especially Koweena. As she sang, she made up her mind; Mrs. Defour was not going to spoil this day for her. She also noticed as she continued singing, how unusual it felt not to be working in the middle of the day. "You want to come over here and sit beside me, Koweena?" Without hesitation, Koweena got up from being surrounded by dolls, and made her way over to the piano. She sat next to Julie on the bench, watching her fingers stroke the black and white keys. They both just sat there, singing in harmony, that now familiar song Koweena had just learned. As the room began to get darker, and with the lights now on in Julie's bedroom, Julie, wished this day could go on forever. "I wish we could do this all night, but I think it's time to call it a day, Koweena." Koweena looked down at the ground in disappointment. Julie lifted Koweena's face up with her hand. "Hey, look at me? We have all day to do this tomorrow, Koweena!" That caused Koweena to look at Julie and laugh.

Amitha stood in the shack that night with her arms folded on her stomach, watching Jial pacing back and forth. Amitha took her eyes off of Jial and fixated them on Koweena, who was lying on her hay bead. Amitha sighed; she was so relieved to be looking at her daughter. She had been worried all day that something bad had happened to her; but that night, she had never seen her daughter so happy. It was the happiest she had ever seen Koweena. Amitha knew that Julie played a big role in this extraordinarily happy child of hers. She looked back at Jial, pacing back and forth as she was holding her hand to her mouth. "What is it, Jial!?" Amitha said with a frustrating, yet concerned tone in her voice. "Can we go outside, Amitha?" They stepped outside; it was a cold, clear, moonlit night as they stood on the dirt road that separated the shacks from the fields. Amitha was rubbing her hands together in worry as she spoke. "What is it, Jial? You's had me worried sick, all day!" "Okay, Amitha, promise me you won't panic when I tell you this?" Amitha began shaking her arms at Jial. "Just tell me!" "Okay, Amitha, I accidently overheard Mr. Jenkins the other night," Jial paused. "Saying what!" Amitha demanded. "He was telling his wife how he overheard Julie and your daughter talking at Mr. Defour's house." Amitha began moving her arms in a rotating fashion as if to be saying hurry up with it. "And!" Amitha said. "He was very upset; he didn't like the fact that Julie was talking to your daughter so politely. He said, well, he said that Julie shouldn't be doing that, and that he was goin to tell Mr. Defour about it." Amitha put her hands to her head. "What!? Tell Mr. Defour! What am I goin to do!? Tell Mr. Defour, that's the worst thing that could happen!" Amitha said.

Meanwhile, inside the shack, Koweena could overhear her mother yelling; but she was too busy singing her new song she had learned that day to pay any attention to what her mother was saying. "Lower your voice, Amitha, Koweena will overhear you," Jial said. "What am I goin to do!?" Amitha said now in a strong whisper. "Well, from what I is heard through the grapevine, Julie runs the show at the Defour place." "So what!" Amitha continued in a whisper. "Well, I think Julie would protect Koweena if something were to happen." "Like what!?" "Well, if Mr. Defour found out that Julie was buddying up to Koweena, I think Julie could talk her dad out of doin any harm to your daughter." "Yeah, but you's don't know that for sure! I can't take a chance with my daughter's life just because you *think* Julie will protect my Koweena." "Yeah, but what I's also heard through the grapevine, is that Julie has really fallen for your daughter, treatin her like one of her own." "What do you mean?" Amitha asked. "Julie is crazy about your daughter, Amitha!" Jial continued. "So crazy for her that she wouldn't let anything happen to her," Jial said. "Yeah, but Mr. Jenkins, he's the head overseer, and Mr. Defour, he owns this whole place. That's just too many important people getting involved in my daughter's life. I's got to stop this now." "Think about it, Amitha, this is Koweena's chance." "What do you mean?" "Her chance at happiness, she could actually have a future here if she gets close to Mr. Defour's daughter. I mean think about it, if she gets close to Julie, it could be her ticket out of here." That remark made Amitha think for a while, as her breath was visible in the chilly nighttime sky. "Your right, Jial, it could be her break! It's still too dangerous though. I'm not goin to gamble my daughter's life away for the hopes that she would somehow get out of here." "Would you rather see her goin through what she went through a few months ago?" "No, that's why I'm thinkin about stoppin this before it gets out of hand." "No, I mean if she doesn't get in with Julie at the Defour place, she could be picked on and targeted because of the way she looks for the rest of her life by the overseers. This way, she could have some protection." "What do you think I should do, Jial?" "I think you should let her continue seein Julie. That way she will be protected by Julie. Think of it, having an inside track of connections, and not just any connections, your daughter would be friends with a Defour, and not just any Defour, the only child of Mr. Defour!" "You have a point, Jial." Jial was slowly convincing Amitha to continuing allowing Koweena to see Julie. "And you say this Julie runs the place over there?" Amitha asked. "Yeah, they allow her to do anything she wants!" That convinced Amitha to allow Koweena to continue seeing Julie. As she went back inside, Amitha noticed something different as she stared at Koweena sleeping. She noticed that Koweena was lying on her back for the first time since the beating. Amitha also noticed the peacefulness that Koweena seemed to show in her body language as she lay there. She was no longer tossing and turning, no longer screaming out loud during one of her many nightmares. Seeing the obvious change in Koweena, how happy and peaceful she was that night, caused Amitha to make the decision not to tell Koweena about what Jial had told her.

The next day Koweena continued her playing at the Defour house. Julie actually gave her the opportunity to play on the piano a little bit. She actually went the entire day without encountering Mrs. Defour. Koweena was the happiest she had ever been in her whole existence, and she owed it all to Julie. She soaked up all the attention that Julie was giving her; and Julie was giving her a lot of one on one attention. For two whole days, it was just Koweena and Julie, no one else was involved in their bonding time. With each passing hour, Koweena was growing more and more close to Julie, and more importantly, her trust in Julie was growing. That weekend, they were like two peas in a pod. Julie wouldn't even eat lunch with her parents. She wanted to spend every possible minute with Koweena. Koweena was exhausted at the end of the weekend. She had experienced so many new things, and tried so many new things, that she was give out. But she had played more in those two days than she had played in her previous five years. In a matter of forty eight hours, Koweena's life had turned around for the better; but it was back to reality on Monday.

She was at the Jenkins' residence doing her normal babysitting routine of Samuel that day, when Mrs. Jenkins walked into Samuel's room where Koweena was washing him down with a sponge. "Can you stop that for a minute and put him in his crib, I need to talk to you, meet me in the living room," Mrs. Jenkins said. Koweena's stomach began to churn after hearing the tone in Mrs. Jenkins voice. It was stern and mean sounding, like she was getting ready to verbally abuse Koweena. Koweena, as she laid Samuel in the crib, began to go over and over in her mind all the things she had done that day while at the Jenkins' house. She was trying to recall if she had done anything that might have set Mrs. Jenkins off. Koweena was so nervous she felt like crying. After the weekend she had just experienced, she thought all of this abuse by white folks was behind her. As she walked into the living room where Mrs. Jenkins was sitting in a wood and silk Queen Anne style chair, she quickly noticed the look Mrs. Jenkins had on her face. Her eyes were squinted and her eyebrows were facing in a downward direction. By that expression, Koweena knew she had done something bad. Immediately her eyes began to water up, and her heart began to beat fast. She was getting prepared for another verbal assault at the hands of a white person. "Just stand there, this won't take long," Mrs. Jenkins said in a sharp tone. Koweena stopped, standing about ten feet in front of Mrs. Jenkins. "Where do you get off becoming buddies with Julie?" Mrs. Jenkins said. "You're just a nigger, that's all." Tears were beginning to fall down Koweena's cheeks. "Don't stand there and cry, you know it's true. Stop your crying!" Koweena couldn't stop though, sudden memories of the attack months ago, and the verbal abuse she was now taking, was too much for her to stop the flow of tears. "Do you realize who you're associating with, coon? That's Mr. Defour's daughter, that's not some nigger you work with out in the fields." After a minute of silence, only the jerky breathing of Koweena was the only thing making noise. Mrs. Jenkins continued. "Well, say something, Nigger!" "I'm sorry, ma'am," Koweena hesitated for a second trying to choke back the tears before she spoke up again. "I won't do it again, I promise." Koweena could only think of the beating, she thought she was going to get beaten again, and like the many verbal assaults in the past, she was trying to think of what she had done to deserve this terrible verbal lashing. "You're going to stop hanging around Julie aren't you, Nigger?" "Yes, ma'am." "Alright, I'm done with you, get out of here, you disgust me!" Mrs. Jenkins said. Koweena had suddenly been transformed back into the frame of mind that plagued her before her weekend with Julie. "I'll never get to spend time with Julie and all her wonderful stuff again," Koweena thought. All the hard work Julie had put into brightening Koweena's spirits for two days had vanished in just a matter of minutes. Koweena was back to feeling depressed and worthless. The lifeless look in her eyes had returned, and she was back to starring at the floor. Countless and countless times, her emotions had been shattered by the words of the white folks, and their mean looks as well.

Julie had caught wind of what had happened at the Jenkins' house that afternoon, and decided that she was going to go to Koweena's shack before sundown. Because of her experiences in the past, Julie was afraid to go near the shacks alone and she wasn't about to go at night, so she took two of her slave hands, both males, with her. She knew that if she brought along a couple of overseers, which is exactly what she wanted to do, after all, the overseers would indeed make her feel safer; she knew if she did that, it would only make Koweena more scared, and make things worse on her. So she picked the two male slaves that made her feel safest, and that she trusted the most, to go with her to Koweena's shack. The advantage of having the slaves with her is that they knew exactly where Koweena's shack was located, and that would keep Julie from having to walk around the area any longer than she wanted to. It was late afternoon, and the sun was beginning to set against the backdrop of the pale blue sky. There were some small, puffy, gray clouds throughout the skyline as Julie made off for the trip.

Amitha was standing there with her hands on her hips, staring at Koweena who was sitting on her bed. She knew something had happened to her daughter that day. Koweena was back to no longer talking, and her body seemed lifeless and limp. Amitha also noticed that Koweena was no longer looking up at her. "Koweena, do you want to tell me what happened today, Dear?" Koweena didn't respond. Amitha wondered how much more her daughter could take emotionally. Koweena was going from one extreme to the other. From being at her lowest point for months, to being at the highest point emotionally that she had ever been, to now being back to her lowest point. Amitha was beginning to think that this roller coaster ride was going to kill her child. Suddenly there was a knock on the door. Amitha went to open it. As she did, she noticed a pretty white girl standing there with two very large slaves standing beside her. "Can I help you?" Amitha asked. "Yes, ma'am, my name is Julie." Amitha couldn't believe it. Not only was she staring at the Plantation owner's daughter right in the face, but this very powerful girl had come all the way down here into her slave world. "Miss Defour, ma'am," Amitha said. "Yes, you must be Amitha. Koweena has told me so much about you; it's nice to meet you." Julie extended her arm to Amitha. Amitha, in shock, extended hers back to Julie. Amitha had never experienced a white person talking so politely before. "What can I do for you, ma'am?" Amitha asked. "Actually, I'm here to see Koweena, is she here?" Koweena couldn't believe it either. Just to hear Julie's voice, it was exactly what Koweena needed. She instantly perked up and looked up at the entranceway. "Julie!" Koweena shouted. Amitha turned and looked at Koweena, Koweena's face was lit up like a Christmas tree. It hit her mother like a ton of bricks as she heard her daughter speaking for the first time that day. This Julie girl had taken her place in the role of cheering up her daughter, Amitha thought. Amitha was happy that someone could cheer up Koweena; but she was saddened at the fact that she couldn't do it herself. "Koweena!" Julie shouted from outside. "May I come in?" Julie asked Amitha. "Sure, come in." As Julie entered the shack, Koweena ran up to her and gave her the biggest hug her little body could muster up. Her mother now realized just what an impact this young eighteen-year-old girl had on her child. Julie knelt down, now eye level with Koweena, and placed both her hands on Koweena's shoulders. "Koweena, I know what happened today. And I want you to know that it is unacceptable. You are not to be talked to that way ever, you hear me," Julie said. Amitha was still in shock as she watched and listened to Julie console her daughter. "I want you to forget about what happened today okay? And guess what? I have something for you that I think will make you forget about all this; in fact, I know it will make you forget about what happened today. Are you ready to go with me somewhere?" Koweena could hardly contain her excitement. The success Julie had over the weekend in breaking down the barriers emotionally for Koweena came shining through during those brief few moments in Koweena's shack. Instantly upon hearing and seeing Julie, Koweena broke out of her shell. Julie was now the only person in the whole world who had the power to bring Koweena out of her deep, low emotional state. Amitha realized that fact as well, she also realized at that moment just how much Julie genuinely cared for her daughter. "Where is we goin?" Koweena asked in a soft voice. "It's a surprise, Sweetheart. Come, follow me." She took Koweena by the hand and began leading her out. She paused for a moment and turned to Amitha. "Is it okay, Amitha, that I take her somewhere?" "Sure, it's fine, Miss Defour." Julie didn't want to be down in that area of the Plantation any longer than she had to be, so she quickly led Koweena out of the shack, and with the two slaves walking by her side, she headed for the open pasture to the right just beyond the cotton fields.

As Koweena was walking with Julie through the Plantation for about fifteen minutes now, still holding on tightly to Julie's hand, she noticed that she was in an area she had never been in before. It was a vast sprawled out area with tons of open low grassy fields; it was one giant open area of grass as far as the eye could see. Koweena noticed that there were wooden railed fences all around the field. "Have you ever been here before, Koweena?" Julie asked. "No, I is not," Koweena said, looking amazed at the mammoth field. Koweena suddenly began to notice a smell creeping into her nose as she approached a large wooden building. She easily figured out the one odor, it was hay, sleeping on it night after night, that smell was easy to recognize, but she couldn't figure out the other scent. "I smell hay," she said, "but what's that other smell?" "It's manure." Julie responded. "What's manure?" Koweena asked. "It's what horses poop out," Julie exclaimed. That made Koweena laugh. The barriers had been broken down once again for Koweena. "Horses, what's that?" Koweena asked. "Do you know where we are?" Julie continued, asking Koweena. "No," Koweena replied. Julie stretched out her arm toward the stable while having her other arm around Koweena's shoulder. "This is a stable!" Julie said. Koweena noticed as she neared the stable, the movement of some large animal. As she got closer, entering the barn now, she peered through the wooden gate into the tiny stall and noticed this huge four legged beast. Her mouth dropped as she just stood there for a moment and stared at the animal. Julie stood behind her with a smile and allowed Koweena to soak up the scenery. "What is it!?" Koweena said in amazement. "It's a horse!" Julie responded with a giggle. It was just like the scene when Koweena entered Julie's house that Saturday morning and saw the house busy with holiday decorations. She was experiencing the same type of awe sensation, just as she had on that Saturday morning. Julie was as well, just standing back with a smile, enjoying looking at Koweena's facial expressions. "What do you do with these animals!?" Koweena asked, with her curiosity at a heightened level. "Well, you ride them, you pet them, you feed them, and you give them baths." "You ride them, how?" Koweena interrupted. Julie pointed to the left of the stall, just beside the gate. "You see that leather thing hanging over there?" "What is that?" Koweena asked. "It's a saddle." Julie said as she walked over to it and pulled it off the stake it was hanging on. "It looks heavy," Koweena noticed. "Yes, it's a little heavy. Would you like to get on it?" "What, the saddle?" Julie chuckled. "No, the horse, Dear." "Get on that big thing! Is you serious!" "Sure," Julie said. "I don't know, I'm too small and it seems kind of scary." Koweena was a little frightened by the giant animal, but her excitement had gotten the better of her. "Yeah, I'll get on it." "Great!" Julie said, patting Koweena on the back. "Now, let me just open the gate here." Julie opened the gate. As the gate opened Koweena got a real up close view of the entire body of the horse, without the gate blocking her view this time. Her eyes opened wide and she stepped back a bit as she gazed at the horse. "What's wrong, Koweena?" "It's so big!" Koweena exclaimed. Julie began stroking the horse's back. "Come on up here and pet it?" Once again, Julie was introducing Koweena to some new experiences, and just like before when Koweena felt all of those new sensations at the Defour house, she had completely forgotten about her 'white folks' ordeal she had gone through earlier that day, just like she had forgotten about the beating while spending time with Julie over the weekend. Koweena slowly walked up to the horse. "Where do I pet it?" She asked. "Pet it on the nose like this." Julie showed Koweena how to pet the horse on the nose. Koweena lifted up her little hand and placed it on the horse's nose, and gently began to pet the horse. "If feels funny," Koweena noted. She began laughing. "It's much bigger up close than when I was standing at the gate lookin in!" "Would you like to get on it and ride it?" As Koweena was petting the horse it stuck out its tongue and licked Koweena's hand. "Eewww!" Koweena blurted out. Koweena laughed so hard she could hardly control herself. Julie laughed right along with her. "That felt funny," Koweena said after a few minutes of the both of them laughing. "So would you like to get on it?" Julie asked. "Okay," Koweena responded. As she approached the side of the giant beast, feelings of excitement and anticipation flooded over her. "Go ahead, Baby, step on that strap right there and push your foot on it and wrap your other leg around the horse at the same time." As Koweena got on the saddle, and was now on top of the horse, she thought to herself that she had never been this high up off the ground before. She was a little nervous, but she could barely contain her excitement. With Julie close by, she knew she didn't have to worry about a thing. "Come on, Koweena, are you ready?" Julie grabbed the horse's reigns and began leading it out of the stall. Koweena was now experiencing her body shifting from side to side as the horse began to move. "I love this, Julie!" Julie wasn't about to let go of the horse, she didn't want it to go fast and throw Koweena off. So she walked at a slow pace, allowing for a slow fluid motion from the horse as Koweena sat on the saddle. "Koweena, grab those leather strings right there." "What leather strings?" Koweena asked. "That leather cord on the horse's neck. It' s used to control the horse's head while you ride." Koweena was so excited that she fumbled around trying to grasp the cord. "There you go," Julie said. "Now you're riding a horse, Dear, what do you think of that?" "I love it!"

An overseer was standing at the edge of the barn watching the whole thing. "What is Julie doing?" The overseer said to himself. Two other overseers came up behind him as he said this. It was Ray and Charles. "What is that little bitch doing with Julie," Ray said. He of course was the ring leader behind the beating, the one who spearheaded the entire brutal ordeal, the same one that had the run in with Koweena a year ago at the water station. "I don't know, but this is not good guys," Charles commented. "Should we tell Mr. Jenkins?" The other overseer asked. "Hell yeah we should," Ray strongly blurts out. Ray spits his tobacco juice from his mouth. "That little spook is cozying up to the owner's daughter, that really pisses me off!" He said.

Meanwhile, Julie had pulled the horse, still walking at a slow pace, out of the barn, the opposite side of the barn from where the overseers were standing.

"I knew she needed that," Julie recalled. "I knew she needed to be away from her slave world, and as far away from that Mrs. Jenkins as possible. The horse ride, the fresh air, I knew it would do her some good. I just wanted to brighten her day, that's all I ever wanted to do with her. My goal was simple, to spoil her as much as possible."

Koweena was just soaking this experience up. Out of all the new things she had seen and experienced over the last several days, this by far was the best. Koweena laughed with excitement. "This is so fun, Julie!" "I thought you would like it, Koweena." After about forty five minutes of walking around the field, Julie decided that it was time to call it a day. She walked the horse, with Koweena still on it, back to the stall. Koweena got off the horse. "It feels funny to be standing, after riding the horse for so long." "I'm glad you enjoyed it, Dear. I want you to know, this will not be your last time here; we're going to do this some more in the future." "Yes!" Koweena said, now full of hope from Julie's comment. They were both standing in the barn, in the open walkway between the stalls that were running down both sides of the barn. "Koweena, I want you to know something, okay," Julie said. "I talked to some people today about Mrs. Jenkins, and you babysitting Samuel. You will no longer have to babysit that little boy, and you will no longer have to be around Mrs. Jenkins okay." Koweena took a deep breath and let it out slowly, she was so relieved to hear that. As Julie had done so many times already in just their few days of knowing each other, she had come through for Koweena. "All you have to do now is work in the fields," Julie said. Julie didn't want to say anything now, she didn't want to give Koweena false hope without actually knowing for sure herself; but she was going to try and see if she could keep Koweena from having to work at all. "Does no longer having to babysit sound good?" "Yes, Julie, thank you so much, you is so good to me." After saying that Koweena gave Julie a big hug. Julie was so touched by the words and hug of Koweena that she felt like crying. After composing herself a bit, Julie continued talking. "Okay, Koweena, this slave is going to take you back to your home," Julie hated calling that place Koweena lived at a home; but she used the word home for Koweena's sake, she thought it sounded more humane. "Why don't you come with me?" Koweena asked in a depressed voice while looking down at the ground. It was obvious that Koweena was really attached to Julie now by her reaction. Julie didn't want to tell her about her own past, which was the reason she didn't want to go back to the shack area with Koweena. "I'm late for dinner." Julie said. She was telling her a half truth, she was late for dinner, but she did have time to walk Koweena back to her shack. "Hey, listen," Julie said. She wanted to change the subject so she could get away from the somewhat lie she was telling Koweena; and she wanted to brighten Koweena back up after what she had told her about ending the day, and having the slave man take her back without her. Julie knelt down in front of Koweena, now looking at her right in the eyes. "I'm going to see if I can have you come spend Christmas with me at my house in a couple of weeks." "Really!?" "Yes!" Julie said. "How does that sound?" "Great!" "Okay, I'll see you this weekend, alright?" "You mean we get to spend another weekend together!?" "Yes!" Julie said as she jerked her head in a sideways motion real quickly, wearing a smile. "Wow! Okay," Koweena said in amazement. Julie had to do some serious explaining to her parents about Koweena. Julie had just promised Koweena that she would see her this weekend, something she hadn't talked to her parents about; especially her mother, who thought it was just a one time deal. She also needed to talk to her mother about Koweena spending Christmas with her. Two subjects Julie knew would be a challenge to convince her mother to agree to. "See you later, Koweena!" Julie said as they walked out of the barn. She was now walking in the opposite direction, away from Koweena, with her hand held up in the air waving good bye. "Bye, Julie!" Koweena yelled. Julie turned and walked away while Koweena walked backwards, still staring at Julie walking away. Koweena was obsessed with Julie now. Julie was in a position where if she hurt Koweena, Koweena would be more devastated than all the times that white folks had hurt her in the past combined.

"Mom, Koweena is going to be spending every weekend with me now," Julie said one night while sitting in the living room with her mother at the Defour house. It had been a couple of days now since the horse ride with Koweena, and Julie had worked up enough courage by now to approach her mother on the subject. Her mother, once laid back in her chair, now sat straight up. "Like hell she is, Julie!" "Mother!" Her mother began shaking her head. "Mother me nothing! No way in hell I'm going to allow that, no way!" "Mother, you haven't even given me a chance to explain." "Explain then." "You don't even realize, I had just as much fun last weekend with Koweena as she did. This is just as beneficial for me, as it is for her; for once in my life I'm impacting someone else's life. I feel alive, rejuvenated." "Julie, I can't let you do this." Mrs. Defour did in fact notice however how Julie spending time with Koweena had impacted her daughter's life for the better. And with the past her daughter had gone through, she needed something good to happen to her. "Don't you care that I'm impacting someone else's life, that I'm making a difference." "But, Julie, why does it have to be that little slave; I mean, you saw how she was handling my things when she was here last time, it was disgusting." "Mother, she's just like us." "That little thing is nothing like us!" Her mother interrupted. "She's property; she's your father's property! My God, Julie, you have it walking around here, touching and playing with our stuff like it's one of us. Why didn't you just tell me you wanted to impact someone's life and I could have gone to one of my friends and brought a child of theirs over here for you to play with?" "It wouldn't be the same, mother. There's more to it than just having Koweena around to play with. I really care for this girl. And she needs me, mother, she really needs me, and I've never had that before, someone needing and depending on me." "But, Julie, a slave! Why a slave!?" "It's not like I went out one day and said, 'I'm going to go out and find me a slave to befriend,' it just happened." "But, Julie, you know how you hate to be anywhere near where those niggers live." Her mother was saying that tactic to scare Julie into stopping this whole thing. "Mom, I went down there the other day." "You what!?" "Yes, I went down there the other day; I had two big slaves go with me." "I don't care who you had, Julie! You shouldn't be going down there, period, with or without protection." "It was fine, mother, I mean I was a little scared, but I was fine." "Have you so quickly forgotten what happened to you?" "Of course not, mother." "And you want to go down there amongst them?" "I've been thinking for a while, and I've decided that I also want to educate her. I have all this education that I've been storing up inside me all my life; and I want to give some of it away." "Have you completely lost your mind, girl!?" Her mother yelled. "What's the point in educating her?" Her mother continued. "What can that thing do with an education, she's not going anywhere. It's not like she's going to have a family to rear. What does she need with an education?" "She's smart, mother, I can tell from observing her. I think I could teach her a lot." "I can't believe this, Julie; I thought we raised you better. What if your father heard you talking all this nonsense? He would hit the roof!" "Dad wouldn't care, he lets me do anything I want, and you know that." Her mother rolled her eyes. "Yes, I know." "I also want her to spend Christmas here with us," Julie said. Her mother began pointing her finger at Julie. "Absolutely not! Now you're going too far, Julie." "You can't stop me, mom. She's going to spend weekends with me, and she's going to spend Christmas with me, and that's final." Mrs. Defour allowed Julie to get away with pretty much anything, especially since what had happened to her some years back. "The same rules apply, Julie, that thing will never eat with us at the table, you understand me! And don't tell your father, my goodness, that's the last thing we need on top of all this." "He's going to find out at some point, mom." "Yes, but the later it is the better." "So, it's a go, mother?" "What if my friends find out I'm letting a nigger spend time with you? I'll be disgraced! You wouldn't want that now would you?" "Mother, your guilt trip isn't going to work. Besides, you can just tell them she's part of the maid staff." "Okay, Julie, okay." With her mother's approval Julie thought she would push the envelope a little further. "You know, mom, if I begin to educate her, that means she will have to start coming over on weekdays." "What are you saying, Julie?" "Can she stop working?" "No!" "Please, mom, it's the only chance I'll have to teach her. When will I get a chance to spend some quality time with her?" Julie was really pressing her mom now. "You have the weekends, Julie." Julie went over and knelt down in front of her mom. "But that's not enough time, I need more time," Julie said. "Please!" She begged. "Okay, weekdays, but she's not going to stop working, that's non negotiable." She had pushed her mom far enough she thought. "You know, dad's going to find out sooner or later don't you." "Yes, I know, Julie, I know."

That entire week Koweena couldn't sleep; all she could think about was playing with dolls, listening to Julie's piano, singing, wearing the jewelry Julie had given her, playing with that toy train, riding that horse, and of course, Julie. Julie had literally changed her life. Electrified, dazzled, and turned upside down kind of changing of her life. Julie had managed to change Koweena's thoughts of abuse into thoughts of joy and happiness. Her dreams were now filled with happy things, play filled things, things a child should be dreaming of. The days of her nightmares of abuse were behind her, or so she thought. Little did she know there was a buzz starting around the Plantation with the overseers about Koweena's involvement with Julie. Would it be just a matter of time before Koweena's old abusive life would come back up to the surface? That's what her mother was thinking one night that week as she stood over top of Koweena while she slept. Amitha just simply thought this relationship with Julie was too good to be true. She knew the slave world and all its trappings. "Koweena is just too young to understand how bad it is out there," she thought to herself. Although Koweena had already been beaten, something Amitha had never experienced, as was the case with most women and girls on the Plantation, Koweena still had never experienced years of hard labor and eating the same food day after day. And the years of verbal abuse, Koweena had just started to get a taste of it. It will only get worse for Koweena, Amitha thought. She thought this thing with Julie would only be a phase; that it would come and go; and if that were to be the case, Koweena would really be crushed. But what could she do. She didn't want to intentionally hurt her daughter by ending her relationship with Julie, and she didn't want Koweena to sink into a deep depression again; but at the same time she didn't want her daughter to have to experience false hope, believing that the white folks were good, descent, honest, and kind to her people. She had lived too long to believe that. But she couldn't deny the simple fact that Koweena had changed like she had never seen before; so quickly out of her depression, and happy, happier than she had ever seen her, so happy in fact that the suddenness with which she had changed, made Amitha somewhat hopeful that this Julie was the real deal.

Koweena just sat there with her legs crossed staring at her black cotton socks that were pulled up to her knees, and her shiny patent shoes. She was tugging on her white ruffled blouse. She was nervous wearing such nice clothes at the Defour house that day. She had never worn anything so pretty before. Years of wearing old hammy down overalls all her short life made what she was wearing now seem very uncomfortable. She looked pretty that day, all dressed up. Julie had spent time that morning in her room fixing up Koweena's hair and putting jewelry on her that matched her outfit. Yes, Koweena felt good about herself; but she thought it would make her an easy target for the white folks. She figured it would only invite a verbal onslaught upon her. It was Christmas morning on the Natchez Plantation. Julie had given her the clothes just a few days earlier; Julie thought it was the proper thing to do considering the occasion. She failed to think, however, just how nerve wrecking it would make Koweena as she sat there among all the white folks. Koweena would glance up occasionally at the large swinging pendulum on the giant wall clock in the Defour house living room. With Julie sitting there right next to her on the main sofa, it made her uneasy feelings settle somewhat. There were three overseers in the room along with their families. Koweena wasn't about to look up at any of them, she was afraid that if she did, she might just look right into the eyes of one, or both, of her attackers. The one overseer that was their just happened to be the very same man that was with Ray and Charles at the horse stable when Koweena was riding that horse for the first time. What if her attackers were there in the flesh watching her with hatred in their eyes? It was all she could think about as she continued tugging on her blouse. Her intense nervousness was almost too much for her to bear. "I will surely get beat again," she thought to herself. Her curiosity got the better of her though, and she quickly glanced up at the three overseers. She was relieved that none of them were the men that beat her, and she was also relieved to find that none of them were staring back at her. "You okay, Dear?" Julie said as she patted Koweena on the knee. She noticed Koweena fidgeting a bit with her shirt and realized that she was nervous. "Just relax, it's okay," Julie said, trying to relax the young child. Koweena just didn't feel comfortable; the clothes, all the white folks in the room seemingly surrounding her, and the fact that Mr. and Mrs. Defour hadn't yet arrived in the room, made Koweena's heart pound at a rapid pace. Her heart was pounding so hard that it felt like it was going to jump out of her chest. "Julie, can we go upstairs?" Koweena whispered into Julie's ear.

Koweena didn't like the living room; ever since she first entered that house she had had nothing but bad experiences in there. Playing with that toy train was the only good thing that had happened to her in there; the rest was nothing but verbal abuse. Julie's room was where she felt the most comfortable. "Sweetheart!" "Dad!" Julie blurted out. There he was, standing there like a presidential candidate, in the flesh, Mr. Defour. It was the first time Koweena had run into Mr. Defour since meeting Julie; heck, it was the first time Koweena had ever run into Mr. Defour. Mrs. Defour was standing right there along side her husband. She spread her arms open. "Welcome everyone!" She said. Koweena was under the most intense pressure she had ever been under; she thought she was going to throw up right there in front of Mr. Defour and all the white folks sitting there around her. Koweena really had to get up and leave the room, or she was really going to throw up right then and there. "Julie, we need to go upstairs, I feel like I'm going to throw up." Julie grabbed Koweena's hand. "Okay, Dear." Mr. Defour walked right by the sofa, he said something again to Julie, but Koweena was so nervous about throwing up that she paid no attention to what was said. She did notice however that Mr. Defour didn't even look at her as he walked by. He acted as if she wasn't even there. Koweena couldn't believe she looked Mr. Defour right in the face. Maybe it was all the time spent in that house that made her look up, or maybe it was all the time she had spent with Julie that made Koweena look up at the powerful man walking above her. Whatever made Koweena comfortable and confident enough to look up; one thing is for sure, she looked up without giving it a second thought. "Oh, I see the Nigger is here," Mrs. Defour said in a smart tone. That comment was enough for Julie to want to get out of there. "Let's go, Koweena." Julie said, still holding Koweena's hand as she tugged on it with a quick jerking motion. They got up and walked out. It was none too soon for Koweena; she had to get to a bathroom and quick. "I have to tell Ray and Charles about this," the overseer who was at the stable said to himself in a whisper.

Koweena, now bent over at the toilet in Julie's bathroom, was throwing her guts up. Julie, standing at the entrance to the bathroom, could only watch. "I'm so sorry, Baby; I didn't know you felt that bad. Are you just sick? Or was it because you felt uncomfortable downstairs?" Julie asked. Koweena, still throwing up, couldn't say a word. After several minutes, she ceased the violent convulsing. "It was your dad," Koweena said in a shaky voice. "What about my dad, Dear?" After a momentary pause, Julie continued speaking. "Oh, I get it, you had never met him before and you were afraid of him, right? Is that what made you sick? Here, let me get you a towel." Koweena wiped her mouth with the towel Julie had given her. "Yes, it was your dad." "I'm sorry, Sweetheart, I just didn't know, well, I just didn't realize that it was going to be that hard on you. Do you forgive me?" "It's okay, Julie. Can I look at my hair again in the mirror?" Koweena was so glad to be in Julie's room, although she didn't want to have to throw up to get there, she was still happy to be there. She wanted to look at her long, flowing, curly brown hair that Julie had spent an hour fixing up. Her hair was pretty without it being fixed up; but the fact that she had gotten her first make over in her life, she wanted to take advantage of it by staring at herself in the mirror. Koweena just stood there for what seemed like forever looking at her clothes, jewelry, and hair. "You look so pretty!" Julie said, standing at a distance. Koweena didn't want to tell Julie about how scared she was regarding the overseers downstairs. She just didn't want to tell Julie about the beating she had received just months prior either, she didn't want to tell Julie any of it. "I'm sorry, Julie; I just couldn't stand bein around all those white folks, and especially your dad." "I understand, Koweena, after that comment my mom made about you, I didn't want to be there much either." She went over to Koweena, knelt down, and took her by the arms. "I want you to know something Koweena; I have great plans for you in the future. We are going to spend as much time together as possible. Every weekday, every weekend, will be ours to spend together." That comment made Koweena, for the first time, feel like telling Julie that she loved her; but something held her back.

Part of her still felt like this was too good to be true, and part of her still had those old harboring feelings of distrust for the white person, even though it was Julie she was now dealing with. "Julie, is this goin to end?" "What, Dear?" "This whole thing between us; are you is goin to get tired of me?" "What ever makes you think that, Sweetheart! You are so important to me in my life! You are the most important person in my life, Koweena! As long as you don't want to stop seeing me, nothing is going to end our relationship, nothing!" Julie began shaking Koweena ever so gently as she continued talking. "You never, never, have to worry about me leaving you, okay! Never!" "Okay." Koweena said as she hugged Julie. Their bond was growing tighter with each passing moment.

For weeks leading up to Christmas, and the many months that followed, Koweena and Julie spent every possible moment of their free time with each other.

"After I worked in the fields during the weekdays, I couldn't wait to head straight for Julie's house, and all her toys," Koweena recalled. "Her dolls, and doll clothes accessories, her plastic tea sets, her rocking horse, I loved to play with them all. And then I got to hear Julie sing. Oh, how I loved to hear her sing. She had the most beautiful voice I had ever heard. And of course, the weekends, that was the best part of my week. I never had to work one single minute during those two days. And it was two days completely uninterrupted with Julie. I loved the weekends so much because I mainly got to spend them outside. Outside, without having to worry about any overseers. What freedom I felt on those Saturdays and Sundays. While I was outside, I would ride horses, hop on the various tractors, riding them throughout the Plantation fields. Julie would let me play with the sheep, rabbits, and roosters that were pinned up around the stable area. On the weekdays, I would mainly be in Julie's room, playing with her dolls, and having tea parties. Julie was always so patient with me, playing with me as if I was the only person in the world. Julie's parents had just purchased her a brand new camera, one of the first cameras ever invented, when I first started seeing Julie. I would have a ball taking pictures of my made up dolls, pictures of Julie's room, and Julie herself. Julie would actually allow me to take some of the pictures home with me where I nailed them up on my wall just above my bed. My life had improved dramatically during that year, It was practically drama free. I had had no run ins with any of the overseers, and no run ins with Mrs. Defour or Mrs. Jenkins either. Things were looking up for me, and after the year and a half that I had just had, it was about time. There was no separating me and Julie. I no longer thought about her as one of the white folks. She was my best friend now."

With a year gone by now without any emotional wear and tear on her little body, Koweena had some consistency in her life; and more importantly, she had peace and happiness; and her life would only improve from here.

Chapter 6   The Education

It was a cool, wintry January night on the Defour Plantation, and Koweena was spending one of her customary weekday nights in Julie's room. Koweena had been spending over a year and a half with Julie now on weekday nights and weekends. On one such night, in Julie's bedroom, Julie interrupted Koweena playing with her dolls. "Koweena, I want to ask you something very important, okay. I've been thinking about this for a long time now, and I think you're ready for us to have this conversation." "What is it, Julie?" Koweena, now six and a half years old, responded. "Kowie, I want to start educating you. Do you know what I mean by that?" "Not really," Koweena said, looking puzzled. "I want to start teaching you how to read and write; how to read and play music, just all kinds of stuff. How does that sound?" Koweena went back to playing with her dolls. "Why do I's need to learn any of that?" "Do you realize how smart you are already, Kowie? I mean, if I taught you, well, if you began to learn some basics, I think you would catch on quickly." "But why do I need to learn all that, I'm just a slave." Julie grabbed Koweena by the arm gently. "Don't you say that! Don't you dare say that, Kowie! You are not a slave!" Julie said strongly.

"Julie was living in another world. At least, not the world I was used to living in," Koweena recalled. "Julie was denying the obvious when it came to me. The world I had to live in when I wasn't with her on weeknights and weekends, that's what she was denying. She just didn't want to face reality when it came to me, and what I had to put up with on a daily basis. Julie didn't want to accept the fact that I was nothing more than property to everyone else on that Plantation. I don't

138

know if she was just plain ignorant of my circumstances, or just didn't want to accept the fact that I was nothing more than just a slave. She wasn't accepting reality, or my plight as a slave. She was in her own little world. She just thought of me as the Koweena of the weeknights and weekends. She never saw what I had to go through during the day. Maybe she wanted it that way, I don't know. But one thing I do know. She never gave up on me."

"I had been shielded from the Plantation by my parents," Julie recalled. "The various daily occurrences that went on there, I didn't know anything about it. I didn't know how the slaves were being treated, how they were being beaten, let alone knowing that Koweena had undergone such a barbaric act. Sure, I had a past that involved the slaves on my Plantation, did I ever. But I truly never realized what Koweena's little world consisted of. The conditions, and the toll it took on her, having to live in those shacks, the verbal abuse, the constant looking over her shoulder for an approaching overseer, and the hard back breaking work she had to endure on daily basis. I just didn't know, and I never much asked her about it either. I was just content with the Koweena I saw and played with."

"Kowie, you're a beautiful little girl, you have such a bright future." "Julie, I is just property," Koweena said. She had heard her mother use that term before in describing what she was, she truly hadn't fully comprehended what it meant though, she was too young; but she sure knew how it felt. Even though she didn't understand the reasons as to why she was property, the verbal and physical abuse surely made her understand that she was inferior, a lesser person to the white people. "What do you mean you're property?" Julie asked. The denial about Koweena's situation was apparent. "You're not property, Kowie; no one around here treats you like that." Koweena came close to telling her the truth about her beating at that point, but she restrained herself. "Julie, I's don't understand you, you live on this Plantation, but yet you don't understand." "Understand what, Kowie?" Koweena, at six years old, just couldn't grasp the fact that Julie just didn't understand her little world. "Don't you understand?" Koweena continued. "I is different than you, look at our skin color." "Koweena, I know we're different in looks, but we're the same you and I. I can't stand the way you're talked to by my mother and neither can you. We both love animals, and playing on the tractors. We both love to dress up, we both love music." "That still doesn't change the fact that we is different. You live here, in this beautiful house, and I live in a shack." Julie, ever since she got close to Koweena, wanted to change that fact. She so desperately wanted Koweena to move in with her. She had asked her mom several times about it, but her mom just brushed it off. "I know where you live, Kowie, and I'm going to try and change that, just give me time, okay?" "What do you mean you is going to try and change that?" Koweena asked. "You're going to live with me someday, someday in the near future," Julie responded. Upon hearing that Koweena stopped playing with Julie's dolls. Thinking about what Julie just said, it made Koweena only dream of such a day. She just sat there, and envisioned over and over again in her head, going to sleep and waking up in a real bed, not one made of hay. By now, she had been with Julie for well over a year; and during that time she had grown distant from her mother. Koweena just no longer spent any time with her mother. By the time she got home from Julie's on the weeknights, it was time for bed, and well, of course the weekends, Koweena barely saw her mother. Amitha realized it as well. It hurt Amitha that Koweena had distanced herself from her; but she quickly came to the conclusion that Koweena's happiness was far more important than her own personal feelings of desertion. She actually knew this day would come at some point. Koweena's mother just seemed to fade out of her life altogether. Julie was slowly replacing her mother, and was now becoming Koweena's mother figure, so living with Julie wouldn't be such a huge transition for her.

Koweena pointed up at the roof. "You mean live here?" She said. Julie grabbed a hold of Koweena's arm and shook it gently. "Here, there, somewhere, you're going to live with me, I guarantee it." Koweena grabbed a hold of Julie's arm. "I want that, Julie, I really do." Julie had to be careful here, she didn't want to give Koweena false hope; but she had already made up her mind that one way or another, Koweena was going to live with her.

Mindful of giving Koweena a sense of false hope, she quickly changed the subject back to teaching Koweena. "Koweena, will you let me educate you? It will make you a much happier person. It will open the windows of opportunity for you, it will make the world a much bigger place for you; it will make you dream and hope." "I don't know, Julie, what will I do with an education?" Koweena asked with hesitancy in her voice. "Like I said, Kowie, it will make you so much happier. You will learn about people, places, and events. It will be like you are taking a tour of the world without actually being there, and anyway, what's there to know about, Kowie, you will have so much fun, I promise." "Okay, I guess." Koweena said after giving it some thought. "Great, Kowie, we will get started on Monday. Oh, I have so much planned for you."

"I really didn't understand why I had to be educated," Koweena recalled. "I could think of no reason as to why I would ever need it, much less use it. But Julie seemed so excited by it all that it peeked my curiosity. I wasn't enthused however. I wanted to spend all my time playing, while I was with Julie."

"Will we have to study on weekends?" Koweena asked. Julie chuckled. "No, Dear. Weekends will be just for playing. I will teach you on weeknights only, okay." "Okay." After saying this Koweena went back to playing with Julie's dolls.

Julie was a very educated young woman. She got her start early as a tiny child. Her entire life, from the time she could walk, was spent learning and studying. Her mother pushed her hard when it came to hitting the books. Mrs. Defour got the best tutors from around the state of Mississippi to come and teach Julie. Julie never had to leave the house while learning during her entire upbringing. And Julie loved every minute of it. She absolutely loved reading and writing, learning music, and getting schooled in manners. The tutors would often tell her mother how gifted Julie was when it came to academics. She was like a fish in water when it came to learning. To Julie, being educated was more fun than playing when she was growing up. From the day Julie first received her piano from her parents at age five, she became obsessed with it. She had one of the best music teachers in the state, Mrs. Henry; visit her at home every single day, teaching her piano lessons.

"Okay, Julie, let's take it from the top, one, two, three," Mrs. Henry said. Julie began hitting the keys; the cylinders inside the piano began to turn, hitting the metal teeth in a kind of beautiful musical melody. Julie was a natural, and Mrs. Henry was impressed from the get go. "Mrs. Defour, I've been here several weeks now, and I must say that Julie is a gifted piano player, and I've taught a many a students before" Mrs.

Henry said. She continued, "I've taught her the basics the first few days; scale, and chords, and how to hold her hands, how to read the middle C on the keys, and how to read the notes. She followed the music to perfection." "That's great, Mrs. Henry, that's just great! I knew she could do it," Mrs. Defour responded. "She's just carrying on beautifully," Mrs. Henry continued. "She's going to be a great pianist, Mrs. Defour." Within months Julie was making up her own songs. Mrs. Henry taught her the piano using works like the ones from Irish composer and pianist John Field. Julie was making up songs by mimicking the ones from English composer and song writer George Frederick Handel. His music was designed for the music-loving upper-class wealthy families. She learned secular music songs as well such as the eighteenth century song "The Select Songster or a Collection of Elegant Songs With Music", an upbeat, fast tempo ballet. Mrs. Henry, for two years, came every day teaching her; but mainly to listen to the talented Julie. There wasn't very much teaching going on, on Mrs. Henry's part. She mainly just came to listen. "How am I doing, Mrs. Henry," the young Julie asked. "You are doing great, Julie. You know, the last year, I've just been coming here to hear you play; I've just been sitting back and enjoying it."

To Julie, the piano was the best part of her education. But she loved every aspect of learning. In other parts of her education she read from authors like Jane Austin, and her famous book "Pride and Prejudice". The book taught her the importance of marriage. She read in the book that marriage was "the only honorable provision for a well educated young woman". She also read novels that emphasized marriage, and the relationship between a man and a woman, like books from Marguerite de Lubert, a French novelist who wrote about French fairy tales in the eighteenth century. They were mainly stories about prince and princesses. She read romantic poetry from poets such as Joanna Baillie, who wrote during the early nineteenth century. She also read romanticism novels by John Stuart Mill, Marx, and Dostoevsky. Julie also took manner classes as part of her education. She was taught how to properly walk, how to properly eat at the table, and how to properly talk. She also took weaving, sewing, and pottery classes. Mrs. Defour made sure that her daughter's education was geared toward one thing and one thing only, to become the perfect wife. In the nineteenth century, wealthy women had only one job to do when they became adults, and that was to be the complete wife. Their role was simply to support their husbands and put on social gatherings. They had no say so in the financial affairs of the household, and they certainly had no say so in telling their husbands what to do. They were not allowed to even talk back to their husbands. Nineteenth century upper-class wives had two roles in which they were schooled in; to be responsible for educating their children, especially their daughters in becoming perfect wives, and being supportive of their husbands, no matter what decisions their husbands made. And it didn't matter whether the wives agreed with their husband's decision or not, they had to go along with it.

Even though Mrs. Defour's educational goal for her daughter was simply to make Julie the perfect wife, Julie got so much education growing up, that she started to get a mind of her own, learning more than just what it meant to play the role of an upper-class wife. Julie grew as an independent thinker. Not only did she read works like the one from Émile Zola, which taught her to treat others as equals; but she also read works from Mary Shelley. Mary Shelley was the Eighteenth century novelist who wrote the novel "A Vindication of the Rights of Women". This book was about a woman getting an education to not only make her a better wife and mother; but also to be social equals to men. These writers like Zola and Shelley believed in "self", the preservation of maintaining one's own identity. She got her view of treating slaves humanely in large part by reading Zola, who published his letter entitled "J'accuse!...", which attempted to touch on the very natural "brutish and animalistic" tendencies of the human nature. His letter taught Julie that people, regardless of their stature in society or what color their skin was, should be treated as equals; and never to treat them barbarically. The education Julie was receiving was in deep contrast to the reality in which she was living in. She was being taught early feminism, which taught that a woman should think like a man. She began reading on her own the works of early feminism. Mrs. Defour didn't realize it, but Julie was getting so much education, that she began to educate herself in her early teenage years. She was learning things that Mrs. Defour had no idea about. Julie had become smarter than her mother, and her mother just couldn't keep up with all that Julie was learning, and self teaching herself. Mrs. Defour didn't realize that her daughter, whom she pushed to get properly educated, was in fact, becoming too educated. Julie was becoming more evolved than many of her contemporary friends, and her thinking was more along the lines of Twentieth century thinking than the thinking her mother had been taught. As a result, Mrs. Defour's obsession with getting Julie educated had backfired on her. At the beginning of Julie's life she was just getting the basics to becoming a proper wife; but as the years went on, and the books began to add up, Julie was reading things that were contrary to her own mother's beliefs. Mrs. Defour was hiring so many tutors to educate Julie, that at some point, some of them were giving her books that, according to Mrs. Defour's way of thinking, were corrupt.

Mrs. Defour never caught on to Julie's advanced learning. She just figured the more books she read, the better off she would be as a wife, not realizing that Julie, while educating herself, had therefore separated herself from her family, and the Plantation lifestyle that her father had worked so hard to build. There is no doubt, without her education, Julie would have become just another bigoted white woman of her time. But she was a nineteenth century young woman, with a twentieth century mind. A mindset that created in her the fact that she was her own person, and didn't need to depend on anyone, especially a husband, to get by.

Julie was determined to pass this same education on to Koweena; and she thought Koweena was at the perfect age to begin. Her goal was different than that of her mother, in educating Koweena. She wanted Koweena to be independent, not to direct her education toward making her the perfect wife, as her mother had done her. Once again, Julie was in denial at the fact that Koweena was a slave, and would never be able to use her education, much less to raise a family. Julie wasn't completely blind or stupid to who Koweena was; sure, the idea of Koweena never being able to use her education entered her mind on occasion, she wasn't completely oblivious to Koweena's circumstances; but she knew she could make Koweena's life a better one with an education. But no matter how much education Koweena would receive from Julie, it would never change the fact that Koweena was stuck on that Plantation with no future of ever getting off it, no future of ever raising a family to share that education with. But that didn't stop Julie.

Sunday night at the Defour house, just days after Julie convinced Koweena to allow her to educate her; Julie was sitting in the living room with her mother. The one coffee table lamp that was on, was bouncing its light off of the walls, creating small shadows on the light yellow walls throughout the room. "Mom, you know I'm about to start educating Koweena, don't you?" "I guess," her mother said in disgust. "And I need your help in doing it." "You're not going to get my help, Julie; you know I'm disgusted by this whole thing, I'm not helping you one bit." "Just listen to me, mother." "Okay, I'm listening." "I need for Koweena to get off work at three every afternoon." "No way," her mother interrupted. "Just listen to me, mother. She must get off at three, otherwise I won't have much time to teach her; and time is of the essence here." "Why?" Her mother asked. "Because it's vital that I spend quality time with her during this process; especially in getting started." "Julie, I don't care about that little Nigger getting educated, it's just a waste of time, don't you see that?" "No, mother, I don't, I can't believe you! I just want to help this little girl, can't you see that!?" Her mother was sipping on some tea. "What do you want me to do?" She asked. "I want you to arrange it so that she can get off at three, that's all I'm asking." "Okay, when?" "Tomorrow." "Tomorrow! I can't do that, Julie, tomorrow is too soon. You have to give me more time." "Mother, you can do it tomorrow." "Julie," "Mom," "Julie," "Mom," her mother takes a big deep breath and lets it out slowly. "Please, mother." "Okay, I'll do it tomorrow," her mother said after giving it some thought. Mrs. Defour hated African-Americans; that was apparent, but her desire to please her daughter was much greater than her deep resentment for the slaves. "What are your plans for this little endeavor anyway?" Her mother continued. "Just let me worry about that. I have all the resources I need for years of educating her." "Years!" Her mother just about choked on her tea as she said that. "Yes, years! Is there a problem?" "I thought you were only going to do this for a little while, Julie, I didn't know it would turn into years all of a sudden!" "Yes, mother, it will take years for me to properly educate her. I want to do this right." "You need to be thinking about a husband at this point in your life, Julie, not about educating that little Nigger." "I wish you wouldn't call her that." "Well, that's what she is, Julie. You need to wake up and start realizing that." "You need to wake up, mother, and start realizing that she's a beautiful little girl who deserves to be treated with respect. I mean, don't you wonder why she looks the way she does?" Her mother remained silent. After hearing that question she just stared down at her tea, stirring it with her spoon. She had a look on her face like she was keeping something from Julie. "What is it, mother?" Julie noticed the strange silence from her mother, and the expression on her face. Mrs. Defour's eyebrows were raised, and her mouth was stuck in a crooked fashion. "Is there something you're not telling me?" Julie asked. "No, Dear, I was just thinking about your education that's all." Her mother was trying to quickly change the subject. "You were so into learning, and reading, and playing that piano. It seems like just yesterday that you were getting your first piano lessons. I'm proud of you, Julie, I know I don't tell you that enough; but I'm proud of the way you became educated. You will make the perfect wife." Julie just rolled her eyes at that comment. "Mother, you've told me all my life that I'll make the perfect wife. There's more to life than being a wife." "I've worked hard all my life, Julie, making sure that you are ready for that day when you finally become a wife. It's the only important thing, besides being a mother, that you will ever do with your life." "Know it's not, mom, I want to do more than just nod in agreement at my husband all my life." "What else is there to do, Julie?" "All you've done, mother, your entire life, is just sit there and nod in agreement with dad, whether you agreed with him or not. I don't want to be that way. That's why I want to educate Koweena. I want to impact another person's life for the better." "You can do that when you become a mother. Don't you realize that?" "I'm kind of doing that now, mother; I mean, Koweena is like family to me." Once again her mother just looked down at her tea with that same expression on her face. "I mean, I kind of feel like I'm already playing the role of a mother, and why do you have that same expression on your face? Was it something I said?" "Alright, Julie, that's enough of that talk like she's white. You've got to stop treating her like an equal," Mrs. Defour said, once again trying to change the subject. "You're like a brick wall, mother, you know that? I can't penetrate you, and get it through to you that Koweena is just like us. Her skin tone is the only thing that's different." "No, it's not, Julie, she's not wealthy, she doesn't live in a nice house." "I've been meaning to talk to you about that," Julie interrupts. "I want Koweena to live here with us." Her mother instantly sat up in her chair upon hearing Julie say that, as she sat the tea on the table next to her. "Absolutely not, that's out of the question!" "When I move out, she's going to live with me, and there's nothing you can do about it." "You have to get married first, Julie. Speaking of which, there's a nice man I would like you to meet." Julie rolled her eyes. "Oh God, here we go again." "Mrs. Jenkins told me about him the other day." "Mother, another man you're trying to set me up with. I'm tired of that." "Julie, how else are you going to find your husband if I don't try and work to set you up with these suitable men. Mr. Jenkins approves of him highly, can't say enough good things about him." Julie rolled her eyes once again. "Really," she said sarcastacly. "His name is Thomas; he's a land surveyor here in town. He surveys land all over Mississippi; very successful man, Julie! From what I hear he's really a catch!" "Okay, I'll meet him on one condition." "What?" Her mother said. "You allow me to teach Koweena, uninterrupted, for as long as I want." The fact that Julie was agreeing to meet this man was enough for her mother to agree to just about anything. Her mother slaps the arm of her chair. "Done," she said. "You promise, now, you'll meet him?" "Yes, mother, I'll meet him; just keep your end of the bargain."

The next day, Julie went right into to teaching Koweena. Koweena, during the first few months, spent time learning English, music, math, and science. Julie was Koweena's very own personal teacher. Koweena was thrilled about getting off of work so early in the day, she wasn't thrilled, however, with the fact that she was getting off of work early for the purpose of learning. "Thanks for getting me off of work early today, Julie; but I is gotta tell you that I'm not too thrilled at the fact that it's for this." "Alright, Kowie, I know you're not thrilled about doing this to start off with; but give it some time, you'll enjoy it eventually, I promise. Okay let's start off with some basic reading." Julie was so excited that first day that she already had all of her children's books laid out all over her bedroom floor early that morning, just waiting for three o'clock to roll around. She had paper, and pencils, and markers, and a glass of tea, spread out right in front of Koweena. "Let's start with this book okay. Start reading this sentence." After reading for several hours Julie noticed that Koweena was catching on quick. "This little girl is going to be brilliant," Julie thought to herself. "And she got up fff, fff, fff," "from" Julie interrupted, helping Koweena along. "From," Koweena continued, "from the ch, ch, ch," "chair" Julie said, continuing to assist Koweena, "chair" Koweena continued. "This is too hard, Julie!" Julie was stroking Koweena's long, thick, curly hair. "I know it is, Kowie, it's hard when you first start; but it will get easier. I promise." Koweena threw the book at Julie. "I know, but it's just too hard!" She yelled. "Koweena, come on now. Okay, Dear, let's try it this way." Julie had written some words on some index cards earlier that day that spelled out the word as it should be, and underneath it she wrote some letters that helped her sound out how it was suppose to be pronounced. "I will hand you one index card at a time, try and pronounce the words that you see." Koweena quickly caught on. By the time their first night was at a close, Koweena was pronouncing and reading each word. Julie began gathering up the books and index cards, cleaning up for the next day of school work. "Koweena, you truly are bright. You are learning so quickly, faster than I thought. Okay, Koweena, Julias will take you home now."

Julias was one of the male slaves that worked at the Defour house. He was a giant of a man; the main reason Julie used him to take Koweena home. He was responsible for bringing and taking Koweena from her shack to Julie's house and back. "I'm proud of what you learned today, Kowie, you did a great job," Julie said, trying to encourage little Koweena. Julie knew that Koweena felt like giving up a lot during their first night, and was trying to reassure her that she had made great progress that night.

It was a cold, moonlit night as Julias was walking Koweena home. "I heard you is did a great job in there tonight, Koweena," Julias said. "I guess," Koweena said, sounding kind of down. "You know, you is very lucky to have someone like Miss Defour helpin you, and bein on your side. We is slaves are not all that lucky when it comes to havin someone like that on our side." Julias' words were making Koweena realize just how fortunate she was. Although she wanted to live in the big house with Julie, she began to wrap her little brain around just how lucky she was to have Julie as a friend. To have someone like her, who was such an important figure, to take such an interest in her future. "Julias, do you think I have a chance?" "What do you mean, Koweena?" "I mean, with Julie helping and all, do you think I have a chance of gettin out of this slavery thing?" "I don't know, Koweena. We is kind of stuck in this situation here, you know. I don't know if it matters that Julie is on your side or not." "So you think I'll be stuck as a slave for the rest of my life." "We all is stuck, Koweena, that's just the way it is. But I think with you is bein close to Julie, gives you a chance that the rest of us don't have." That brightened Koweena's mood a bit as she walked along the open field with Julias, as the moon shined on the dewy grass leading to the cotton fields, where just on the other side was her shack. "So you think I have a chance then?" "I don't know, Koweena, I don't want to get your hopes up or anything, but yeah, I think you have a chance. I mean she's educatin you ain't she, that's got to count for somethin." Koweena's spirits had picked up somewhat as they continued walking, but she was still a little down. Why? Like everything else in Koweena's life, this venture of being taught by Julie was something that was being forced upon her, as something she would have to put up with without any say so in the matter. Like working in the fields, or babysitting, or even getting beaten, although it wasn't degrading, and Julie definitely was the opposite of any slave-hating white person on the Plantation, still, Koweena's hand was being bound to doing it without her input on the matter. Sure it wasn't as severe as being beaten, or as harsh or forced, she still felt trapped. Like everything else in her young life, she was doing something she really didn't want to do. "Julias," "yes, Koweena," "would you do it?" Koweena asked. "Do what?" Julias replied. "Would you allow Julie to teach you?" "Heck yeah I would. To have such a pretty lady giving her attention to me all the time like she does you, you is lucky." "Yeah, but when will I ever use this stuff she's teachin me, why do I have to learn how to read?" "I don't know, Koweena, I don't know. You know from observing the way she treats you, I think she thinks of you as her own." "Really?" Koweena said with a big smile. "Yes, really. Okay, we is here."

When Julias told Koweena that Julie may just think of her as her own, it was all Koweena could think about, even later on that night as she lay in bed. The talk she had with Julias really got her to thinking as she lay there, "I just might have a chance!" She whispered to herself in bed. Although the education part was a downer for her, the fact that she still got to spend time with Julie, and the fact that she thought, if people like Julias was observing Julie treating her as her very own, then other people must be observing the very same thing. It gave her a warm feeling that night in the cold shack. Her emotions were mixed that night as she went to sleep. She was a little down because of having to learn, but she was excited at the same time about her and Julie's relationship.

As the months passed, Koweena's outlook on her education changed. Julie's educating of her meant much more to the both of them than just books and music. Julie became a mentor for Koweena; and more importantly, a sister figure, and also at the same time, a mother figure for Koweena. From Julie's standpoint, Koweena was her very own little sister, and she consistently treated her that way. For Koweena, she truly felt wanted and needed. She no longer felt like a tool used by Mr. Defour, but a human being who was loved and cared for by her master's daughter. Yes, she still had to sleep and live with the other slaves, that didn't change. However, for those weeknights and weekends spent with Julie, she would understand what it meant to love and respect another human being.

Julie's parents stayed out of the education process of Koweena. Because Julie was an only child, this privilege entitled her to do pretty much whatever she wanted. Julie was spoiled, and the Defours didn't want to disrupt that, so no attempt was made to stop the ongoing relationship with Koweena. It was her mom that knew what was going on, her dad was so busy with the Plantation, that he never knew what activities Julie was doing, especially with Koweena.

"As time went on, I was seven now, and I began to figure out, that unlike the other things I was required to do in my life, this time spent with Julie, being educated by her, was suddenly making me feel good about myself," Koweena recalled. "I was accomplishing something that I could tangibly put my finger on, something I was successfully doing for myself, not for someone else. Like picking cotton day after day, which was now my full time job during the weekdays. Doing that type of thing didn't make me feel accomplished. I wasn't getting any self gratification out of it. With this whole education thing, I was getting self gratified. I could see my hard work and efforts turning me into a better person. I was experiencing what it was like to be successful at something. Hard work equaled pleasure, not just more hard work, which the fields brought me. As a result, I really applied myself to learning. Julie said I reminded her a lot of herself when she was my age, when it came to academics. I was quick on the draw at comprehending things, intelligent, smart, quick witted, and a natural at learning, just like Julie. I soaked up what I was learning like a dry sponge being put to water. I quickly caught on to everything Julie was teaching me. After almost a year had past, I had advanced beyond what even Julie could have ever imagined. I was at the top of the mountain emotionally. I was feeling better about things on the Plantation, about myself, better than I had ever felt before. It had been almost two years since my last real encounter with an overseer. Sure, I would run into an overseer every now and again in the cotton fields, but it was nothing major, just a little 'work harder' comments every once in a while. After the verbal comments of my past, those words just rolled off my back. Because of my education, I had so much self confidence. Julie was constantly telling me how great I was doing. Sure, my mom had told me that in the past, but coming from Julie, it really resonated with me. It made a bigger impact on me. I guess it was due to the fact that it was coming from a white person, but it was more than that. It was coming from Julie, the person I admired the most. I began to think that my slave world was becoming more tolerable. I began thinking back to my conversations I had had with Julias, about how I might just have a chance at getting out of this place. My relationship with Julie had caused all this newfound postiveness that I was now experiencing. I was becoming totally dependant on her for my happiness. That was scary for me."

One weeknight, in Julie's bedroom, Julie pointed to the various books that were spread out around Koweena on the floor. "Koweena, I believe we have moved past this right here, and that. And I know we have moved past that. So we don't we start with some more advanced stuff, okay." Julie began to pull out some of her favorite books, books from female authors of the eighteenth century. That night, in Julie's room, Koweena began reading about fairy tales from authors Julie had read, like the one from French novelist Lubert. Her little mind became fascinated with stories about prince and princesses. She also read a little English poetry from the works of Anna Laetitia Barbauld. Julie let Koweena read some of her romantic poetry as well, like works from Baillie. Julie didn't think Koweena was too young to be reading such works, after all she was almost turning eight, and Koweena was far more advanced than her age academically. "Do you like it, Koweena?" Julie said, biting her nails. She was nervous that Koweena would become uninterested in learning once she began trying to grasp the more advanced stuff. Julie was taking a chance introducing Koweena to this stuff so soon after grasping some of Julie's basic child books. "I love it, Julie!" Koweena said with a big smile on her face. Julie gave a deep sigh of relief. Julie had noticed how quickly Koweena was growing up, and maturing, since she had begun educating her. Her speaking had improved greatly, and she noticed her growing stronger emotionally as well. Koweena was growing up right before Julie's very eyes, and at such a rapid pace.

That night, Koweena was walking home with Julias, and about halfway into their journey to Koweena's shack, Koweena spoke up. "You know, Julias, do you remember that conversation we had a while back about me having a chance?" "Havin a chance? What is you mean havin a chance?" Julias responded. "You know, having a chance to make it out of this slave world we're in." "You is thinkin that you will not be a slave any longer?" Julias asked. "I don't know, part of me is thinking that. I mean things are really going good for me now, Julias. There's more to this world than picking cotton, or doing what the white man says." It was apparent that her education was broadening her horizons, and giving her a different perspective on her little world. Reading some of Julie's books on early feminism was beginning to shine through. "I don't know, Koweena; you is talkin like you is gettin out of here. I don't think that is goin to happen." "But you told me that since I was so close to Julie, the slave owner's very own daughter, that I had a chance of getting out of here." "I said *might*, Koweena, I didn't say you actually would. There's a big difference there you know." "Yes, I know, but you still said might, and the way things are going for me I might just have a chance." "Don't you is goin and gettin all confident on me now; slaves like us don't get chances to get out of here, education or no education." "I don't know, Julias, I just have a feeling, I have a feeling that things are really turning around for me here. I think Julie could actually get me out of being a slave." "Hold on now little one, don't you goin and thinkin you have a road out. It's impossible for people like us, we is nothin but cattle in the eyes of these white folks." "Not to Julie I'm not," Koweena interrupted. "One person isn't goin to get you out of here," Julias continued, "I don't care how important she is, or who she's related to." "Yes, but, Julias, she's the Plantation owner's daughter, with that being the case, I couldn't have a better chance." It almost appeared in listening to Koweena, that she was using Julie, but of course that wasn't the case. "Koweena, all I is a sayin is don't let all this education business go to your head. You is still just a slave." It didn't matter what Julias was saying to her, Koweena was growing more and more confident by the day. With each passing minute, dreams of one day no longer being a slave, surmounted in her head.

That night as she went to bed, she could only daydream of princes and princesses, beautiful stories about love, and about people overcoming obstacles to have bright futures. This was building the stage for molding Koweena into her own person, with the kinds of dreams her slave peers never had, or could ever dream of having. Her education was expanding her mind beyond her little slave world, into a world filled with ideas of palaces and beautiful romantic relationships, little boys and girls growing up to be great influential people as adults. Her education was planting seeds in her mind of what life outside the Plantation would be like.

"Hey, Koweena, I's heard you is gettin all smart and stuff, is that true?" Josi asked one day as the both of them were working in the cotton field. "Not now, Josi, I'm working," Koweena responded. "I can tell, ya know. You language is different all of a sudden. You is talkin different and stuff," Josi exclaimed. "Josi, I am getting educated, and it's the best thing that ever happened to me. If you could just read some of the books that I'm reading, it would change your life for the better." "What is you reading?" Josi asked. "I'm reading lots of things, books about love stories, books about being your own person, and not letting others run all over you. You know, Josi, you can have a mind of your own, you can be somebody someday. You don't have to stay in these cotton fields forever." "I's can't even read, Koweena, and you is telling me I can get educated. Who is you kiddin?" "Maybe I can teach you some day, how would you like that?" Koweena asked. "Would you is really do that Koweena, for me?" "Sure, Josi, we'll figure it out one day, I'll teach you." "I's always wanted to be able to read, Koweena." "Well, maybe you will get your chance someday, Josi."

Meanwhile, on that same day, around mid-morning, not long after Koweena began reading those advanced books Julie allowed her to read, Julie was standing in the downstairs hallway below the stairs just beyond the foyer of her house. "Hey, Julias!" She shouted. Julias was standing just outside the kitchen area with his giant, muscular body between the kitchen and the hallway. He was polishing some silverware when he heard Julie's voice. "Yes, ma'am!" Julias shouted back. "Can you come here for just a minute; I have a project for you!" "Yes, ma'am, just let me put up this silverware, and I is be right there!" After several minutes had passed Julias made his way down the hallway toward Julie, "Yes, ma'am," Julias said standing at attention in front of Julie. "Julias, I have a project for you. I want you to go to Koweena's house." Julie always called Koweena's home a house and not a shack. She was the only white person on the plantation that referred to the shacks in that manner. "Koweena's house, ma'am?" "Yes, I want you to go there, there won't be anybody inside, you'll have the whole place to yourself. I want you to take some measurements for me." "Measurements, ma'am?" "Yes measurements, Julias. I want you to measure the space between Koweena's bed, and the bed next to hers. Now there's an open space between the two, but I have no idea how far apart they are. That's where you come in." "Yes, ma'am," Julias responded with some eagerness. He was just happy to be doing something else different from his normal daily routine he performed each day. "I want to put a desk, and a bookcase, next to Julie's bed, up against the wall, and I need your help, okay." "Yes, ma'am." "Once you walk into the house you will see a bed in the very far right hand corner. The bed in the very corner is hers, got it?" "Yes, ma'am." "Okay, Julias, using the wall as a guide, I want you to measure how wide the wall is between the beds, and then I want you to measure how tall the wall is from the floor all the way up to the ceiling. Do you think you can do that?" "Yes, ma'am, I can do it." "This is very important to me that you do this right, and get the exact measurements of the entire space. Can I count on you?" "Ma'am, I's have one question." "Of course, what is it, Julias?" "What do I say if an overseer stops me and asks me what I is doin?" "Just tell them you're running an errand for Miss Defour, they will leave you alone." "Yes, ma'am." "When you get the measurements, Julias, come back to the house and find me. I will then have another project for you along the same lines as what you are doing now." "Yes, ma'am."

Julias went off toward the shack with a pencil, a small piece of paper, and a tape measure in hand. As he approached the shack and began to open the door a loud voice rang out, "what the hell do you think you're doing, Nigger?" It was Ray. Ray knew the shack Julias was going into all too well. Because beating a child was never practiced on the Plantation, he quickly knew that it was the place where he led the beating of Koweena, and he also knew it was where Koweena still lived. "I, I, I," "spit it out Coon," "I is doin an errand for Miss Defour, sir." "Are you doing something for that little half breed?" Ray asked, referring to Koweena. "Yes, yes, yes sir." Julias really didn't know what Ray was referring to, he just agreed to whatever Ray was saying in order to get him off his back. Ray walked away irate as he spit his tobacco juice on the ground. "I'm going to finish that half breed off if it's the last thing I do," he grumbled to himself. Charles approached the disgusted looking Ray. "What is it, Ray?" "It's that little nigger child we beat a couple of years ago, you know the one, the one that's been buddying up to Mr. Defour's daughter." "That was such a long time ago, Ray, why don't you let that go?" "Let it go! We have a nigger who is befriending the boss man's daughter. That's a disgrace. That little Nigger has been under my skin from the day I encountered it. I hate everything about that little wench, especially the way she looks." "I think she's a pretty little girl, Ray." "Shut up, Charles! You keep talking like that and I'll have you out there picking cotton with the rest of them spooks." There was no doubt, Ray was bias toward Koweena, and his hatred of her, simply because she was the prettiest slave on the Plantation, and he just couldn't stand that. "Do you want to do something about it, Ray?" Charles asked. Ray spoke up with a menacing grin. "No, no, let's not do anything right now. I have a plan for a later date. Patience my boy, patience."

Julias returned to the Defour house with measurements in hand. He found Julie in one of the upstairs guest bedrooms, busy writing with zeal on a note pad, stepping around the room in a circular motion gazing up at the walls talking to herself. She was so into whatever she was doing that she didn't notice Julias entering the room. "Excuse me, ma'am!" Julias said in a soft tone. Julie quickly turned around and noticed Julias standing there with the measurements. She instantly got excited. "Great, you got them!" "Yes, ma'am." "Okay, Julias, I have something else for you to do." She reached into her dress pocket and pulled out a sheet of folded paper. "Okay, Julias, I want you to take this to the lumber factory. It has the desk and bookcase descriptions on it. In case they don't understand, I want you to explain to them that I want both the desk, and bookcase, to be made out of nothing but solid oak. The best oak they have. I want the bookcase to reach up to the ceiling with two feet to spare at the top, with four shelves. I want the desk to have two drawers on each side. I want the chair to be made out of oak as well, with straps of wood interwoven together to make the seat, and back of the chair. Can you remember all of that, Julias?" "I think so, ma'am." "It's okay if you can't; I have it all written down here." Julie hands the folded paper to Julias. "Take this piece of paper to the lumber factory. Do you know where the lumber factory is located?" "Yes, ma'am, it's a far piece off in the distance though." "I know, it is quite a distance," Julie said. "It will take you the rest of the day to make it there and back; but I need for you to do it today. I want to get this done as soon as possible." "Yes, ma'am." "Oh yeah, Julias!" Julie yelled out as Julias was walking out of the room. Julias peered back into the room. "Yes, ma'am?" "Did an overseer see you?" She asked. "Yes, ma'am." "What did he say?" Julie said with concern as she began biting her nails. "He said something about a half breed, and if what I was doin had somethin to do with this half breed person." "Thanks, Julias, that will be all." "Yes, ma'am," Julias said as he walked out of the room.

Julie continued biting her nails. She began to wonder if an overseer was catching on to her close relationship to Koweena; and if so, what did that mean. Could Koweena get in trouble? She thought. "My dad knows about it, and he hasn't said anything to me," she whispered to herself. She began to get really nervous. "Oh, I'm just over reacting, there's nothing a little overseer can do to Koweena, even if they knew she was spending time with me," she said to herself. She quickly quit biting her nails and went back to writing and studying the room. Once again, she was oblivious to what was actually going on outside the four walls of her home.

Several nights later, Koweena was studying, as she usually did, in Julie's bedroom, when Julie got up from sitting in front of Koweena. Julie became enthused. "Okay, Kowie, now we're going to learn music!" Julie had been waiting for this moment. For Julie, this would be the most exciting part of teaching Koweena. Julie had been playing for Koweena, various songs she had learned growing up, since they first started their studies; but this would be the first time Koweena would begin to learn music on her own. Julie was concerned however that Koweena would not like it nearly as much as she did. She recalled back though, to the day when she played Koweena that song she had written for her, and how Koweena took so quickly to the song; and how excited Koweena was at seeing and hearing the piano when Julie played it. She was hoping for that same reaction on this night. She and Koweena sat at the piano with Julie playing a few notes from her works she had collected over the years. She began with works from composer John Field. There was no doubt in Julie's mind, after playing for a few hours, and observing Koweena intensely listening to her every stroke on the piano, that Koweena loved music. Koweena learned music that night from other song writers like the Hutchinson family. The Hutchinson family wrote songs that were anti-slavery, pro abolitionist's songs. Koweena now had songs to go with how she had been feeling all along. She loved learning these kinds of songs with Julie, there was no doubt about that; but learning these Hutchinson songs about anti-slavery made those times spent in the fields, coupled with all the abuse she had received as a young child, and her slave life, and all that accompanied it, seem despicable. Now, for the first time, she realized there were others who despised it as well. What an uplifting moment for her to know that others outside her little Plantation agreed with her. "Are these songs you're playing right now," she was referring to the Hutchinson songs, "are these from white people?" "Yes, Dear, why?" Koweena's heart leaped for joy. She had now learned that there were some white people who hated what she was currently going through on a daily basis. "White folks hate slavery?" She asked with curious enthusiasm. "Yes, Kowie, not everyone is for slavery. Did you not realize that? Do you love your little world that much?" Koweena couldn't believe Julie said that. Once again Julie was oblivious to Koweena's circumstances, or maybe she just didn't realize how insensitive she was being. Nonetheless, before being educated, Koweena was the one who was oblivious to what the world was thinking about her little world. Koweena and Julie were at polar opposites at this moment in time as they sat at the piano together. Julie, who was sheltered from slavery in her own back yard; was very educated, but lacked knowledge of the slave world, and it was all around her. Quite the opposite for Koweena. She was sheltered from anti-slavery views outside her slave world; she still lacked being sufficiently educated, and yet she knew slavery all too well. There they sat, beside each other, sitting on opposite ends of the spectrum when it came to slavery. One didn't know much about it with a plethora of education, while the other knew it first hand with very little education. "Why do white people hate slavery?" Koweena asked. "Well, slavery is mainly down here in the south. They don't have slavery up north," Julie responded. "Wow, I wished I lived up north," Koweena said in a disheartened fashion. That comment by Koweena hurt Julie. She suddenly began to feel like Koweena no longer wanted to be around her. At that moment, Julie could only think of herself. She didn't think, when Koweena was making that statement, that Koweena was thinking of the hard labor she had to endure daily, and the harsh living conditions she had to undergo while living in her shack. Part of it could also be seen as ignorance on Julie's part, and part of it could also be that Julie just didn't understand the severity of Koweena's life apart from the time spent with her on weeknights and weekends. Koweena and Julie were very close, but when it came to slavery, Julie's lack of knowledge on the subject caused her to be insensitive toward Koweena. Her insensitivity however, was not purposeful.

After Julie had taught Koweena a few notes, Koweena began to play a little on the piano. "You know, Kowie, when I first started playing the piano, I picked up on it right away. That same first day I was playing advanced notes. Let's see how you do." Julie didn't mean to place undue pressure on Koweena, and luckily for Julie, Koweena didn't see it that way. As Koweena was playing, she didn't pick up the piano as quickly as Julie did, it just didn't seem to come natural to her as it did Julie. Yet she loved to play this big, black beautiful machinery. Julie was thrilled that Koweena was taking to it, although not as gifted as Julie was when she was at that point in her life, Julie was still thrilled that Koweena enjoyed it. "It's only been one night of learning, she'll get better," Julie thought to herself. There was no doubt that Julie, in her subconscious mind, was putting pressure on Koweena. Julie thought that she would pick it up as quickly as she did when she first started; but that was putting some unrealistic expectations on Koweena. Julie was a prodigy when it came to the piano; she was trying not to put undo pressure on Koweena to pick it up as fast as she did; but it was hard for Julie not to. "Koweena, you have to be more fluid when you hit the keys! Now try it again, and this time concentrate!" "I'm trying, Julie, gosh, it's my first time. Give me a chance!"

Julie realized she was pushing Koweena too hard that night. She couldn't believe she was being so harsh. She felt like crying when she realized what she was doing to Koweena. She quickly snapped out of it. "I'm sorry about what I just said there, Kowie, I didn't mean to push you like that. Hey, let's take a break, okay." "I really enjoy it, Julie, I'm just not picking it up as fast as you did." "It's okay, Kowie, Sweetheart; at least you enjoy it right?" "Yeah!" Koweena said. "Okay, that's what is important." Julie got up from her piano bench and began walking toward the entranceway to the room. Julie looked back at Koweena as she was walking out of the room. "I'll be right back, Kowie, okay." "What are we having tonight, Julie?" Koweena asked. This made Julie stop right at the entrance of the room and turn back around. "Roast beef, I think." "Yummm!" Koweena blurted out. As Julie exited the room she quickly stopped right at the corner of the entranceway and leaned against the wall. She was breathing heavily as she looked up to the ceiling. "Goodness, I put too much pressure on her," she said in a whisper. "I just got in a zone as she was playing, thinking back to me playing, and how quickly I picked it up when I first started." Her eyes began tearing up. "My God, I almost ruined it for her, she could have stopped playing all together and began hating music," she said to herself still in a whisper. "I'm glad I stopped when I did, or else it could have gotten bad in there."

After composing herself, she tippy toed down the stairs. When she got to the bottom she stopped. She was listening intensely to try and locate where her parents were at that moment. She could hear them in the living room. "Their having their usual nightcap," Julie whispered to herself. Julie could hear her parents laughing and carrying on as they drank their brandy. This was her parent's nightly ritual after dinner. They would go from the dining room into the living room and sit for hours, talking and drinking, enjoying their nightcaps. Julie, slowly and gently, turned to her right, and began walking down the hallway toward the kitchen. "Here it is, Miss Defour, ma'am," Martha told Julie. Martha was one of the many cooks assigned to the Defour house. It was her job every day to prepare Koweena's meals. "Thanks, Martha, you're a gem," Julie said as she winked at Martha. Julie, with plate in hand, snuck back upstairs to her room. "Here you go, Dear, roast beef with gravy, mash potatoes, and green beans."

This was Julie's nightly ritual. Koweena would remain upstairs while Julie would sneak downstairs to the kitchen and get Koweena's dinner from Martha. Julie had it down to a science. She never, not once, got caught by her parents. With the help of Martha, Koweena was fed on a daily basis, even on weekends. Julie would come downstairs for dinner with her parents, while Koweena remained in Julie's room studying or playing. After Julie finished eating with her parents she would go back upstairs, after an hour or so, she would then make her move back downstairs to get Koweena's food. When Koweena had finished her studies, or playing, she would eat. Koweena could never quite get used to the fine food she was eating. She would always gobble it down in such a hurry. Each time she would eat, she thought to herself, that was the best meal she had ever eaten. Every time she put her mouth to the tasty daily dishes she would get a new sensation to her taste buds. Julie would just sit on the bed and watch Koweena eat her meals right below the bed on the area rug spread out on the floor. Koweena didn't mind when she would occasionally glance up at Julie staring at her with a grin on her face, she enjoyed the attention. Julie seemed to get more pleasure out of watching Koweena eat than Koweena got out of actually eating the flavorsome meals. Julie spoiled Koweena, the best she could do under the circumstances anyway. After eating, Julie would take Koweena by the hand and quietly walk with her down the stairs to the front door, first making sure that her parents were no longer in the living room. Julias would be waiting for her across the driveway in the well manicured front lawn. Koweena and Julias would take the same route every night. A diagonal path through the front yard, about thirty yards, where they would enter a tall weeded field. They would continually walk diagonally through the weeded field right into a cotton field, where they would then end up at the road separating the fields from Koweena's wooden shack.

The next several nights Koweena began studying the works of Mary Shelley. During those nights, Julie would read her the novel by Shelley "A vindication of the Rights of Women". Koweena was learning something that would change the rest of her life. She was learning how a free woman lived. After listening to the novel, Koweena's mind was dancing with ideas of how to live free. She had always wondered how a white person lived; and now she was getting first hand instructions on not only how they lived, but what they did while living free. Koweena started experiencing conflicting emotions as she studied with Julie on the novel. She was learning how to behave as a free woman by night, and living in a controlled, restricted environment by day. Her eight year old mind was having a hard time learning one way of living, while experiencing another. She was laboring in the fields of the Defour Plantation during the day, and entering an entirely different world by night. Not only was she being treated like a free person while spending time with Julie, but she was learning about the free world as well. Learning that stuff only made her days even more depressing working under the watchful eyes of the overseers. As she picked cotton under the hot sun, she couldn't help but notice the other slaves around her, and the overseers standing over them with rifles in hand, and how trapped they were now that she knew how free a free person could really be. And as the overseer that stood over her yelled comments of "work harder" at her, she realized that she was just like the rest of them, trapped and tied down. She was living in two different worlds. The more educated she got; the more she realized just how hopeless her life truly was. What had once given her hope; was now causing her to realize just how bad her life was. Was educating Koweena really benefiting her? Or was it making her life worse? Julie thought that it only benefited her, while Koweena was beginning to think it was only making her life a living hell.

"Julie, I can't do this any longer," Koweena told Julie one night as they studied in Julie's bedroom. "Can't do what, Sweetheart?" "I can't go on living like this. Studying and listening to you about one thing at night, and then living a totally different life during the day. I just can't do it." Julie noticed Koweena was looking down at the floor with a deflated look on her face. It had been a long time since she saw that look on Koweena. It crushed Julie to see that expression. The last time she saw that was years ago; of course Julie didn't know it then, but that was the time just after the beating, when Koweena was so depressed. Julie was speechless; she didn't know how to respond to what Koweena was telling her. "Do you understand what I'm saying, Julie?" Julie remained silent. She thought things were going so well. She thought she was making Koweena's life better. She thought she was spoiling Koweena enough, and giving her enough attention, that somehow it made everything alright. "I um," Julie just couldn't think of the right words to say, her mind was frozen. "Julie, I'm so confused right now, I'm living in two different worlds. Don't get me wrong, I appreciate everything you've done for me up to this point; but you're teaching me one thing, and I'm living another. It's just too much." As Julie was listening she couldn't help but notice just how well Koweena was talking, the progress she had made from just a couple of years ago; but she also noticed the pain in Koweena's voice. She had to think of something to say that would not only calm Koweena's fears, but would convince her to continue her education. Julie knelt down in front of the standing Koweena as she placed her hands on Koweena's cheeks. "Koweena, I know what you're saying, and I know you're hurting, and I completely understand where you're coming from; but things are going to get better for you. You just have to give me time. You just have to give me a chance. I've been seeing this man, and he's great. If it leads to marriage, then that will be my chance to have you come live with me? It will get you out of this!" "What do you mean you're seeing someone, how, when?" Koweena's eyebrows were in a downward position, she was now mad. "I've been seeing him on Saturday and Sunday nights for several months now. I see him after you leave, that's why you've never seen him before." "Why didn't you tell me?" Koweena insisted. "I was going to, I just couldn't find the right time to." Koweena was jealous, she had been getting all the attention up to this point, and she wasn't about to relinquish it to some guy. "Does that mean you're not going to see me anymore, Julie?" "No, Dear, quite the opposite actually, like I said, if things keep going the way they're going, you will get to move in with me for good. Aren't you excited about that?" Koweena was too mad and jealous to be excited. Julie picked up on it. "Kowie, I promise you, if you just hang in there a little longer, things will get better for you, it will be alright, you just have to trust me, okay." Koweena's mind instantly flashbacked to the time when her mother had promised her that very same thing, that everything was going to be alright; and look what happened to her then. "No offense, Julie, but I've been promised things before, and it didn't get me very far." Koweena began thinking to herself. Julie is white, and she does have some authority in this place, maybe, just maybe, she has the power to carry out her promise. "My mom had no authority," she was thinking. "Kowie, I don't mean to be teaching you things that confuse you. I just want you to know that it's a big world out there, more than just what's on this property." "But when am I ever going to get off this property, Julie!" Koweena yells out frustratingly. "I just told you, Kowie, if things work out with this man you can move in with me!" "*If*, Julie, *if*, I need more than just an *if*." Julie took a hold of Koweena's hands. "I promise you, Kowie, at some point you're going to move in with me. I'm just asking you to hang in there a little while longer until that day comes!" "But what if that day never comes?" "It will, Baby, it will." "I thought it would just be the two of us, Julie?" Once again, Julie noticed that Koweena was mad that she was seeing this man. Julie clutched onto Koweena's hands, shaking them gently. "Listen to me, Kowie. Nobody, and I mean nobody, will ever come between you and I. That will never happen. You mean too much to me to allow anyone to come in between us. Do you understand me?" After a brief moment of silence, Koweena finally spoke up. "Okay, Julie, okay, I'll hang in there just for you." "Great, Kowie!" Julie gave her a big hug upon saying that. "That desk, bookcase, and necklace, will make up for all of this," Julie thought to herself. "Listen, I have a surprise for you waiting for you when you get home." "Really!?" Koweena said with excitement and anticipation. That made the negative feelings Koweena was experiencing instantly go away.

When Koweena arrived back at her shack that evening she could hardly believe her eyes. There they were, sitting up against the wooden wall next to her bed. Two beautiful pieces of furniture, the desk and the bookcase, side by side. Along with it was a beautiful handcrafted chair. It was the first and only pieces of furniture in the entire shack, besides an old wooden split chair and her little wooden box that housed her jewelry. Koweena slowly walked up to it with her eyes wide open and touched the desk with one hand. She could still smell the fresh scent of oak and varnish on the two beautiful pieces of furniture as she stared at both of them. She quickly noticed the dolls on the bookcase, along with some books she had read. There was paper and pencils lying on the desk. She also noticed a gold necklace hanging on one of the dolls hands that was within reach of her arm. It was a necklace with a black heart locket on it. There was a note attached to it. As she reached up and grabbed the note and opened it, it said, "To my dear Kowie from your Julie." Koweena immediately opened up the locket. She gave a big laugh, and then started crying out of happiness. She quickly closed the locket and put the necklace around her neck. She held onto the heart shaped locket tightly for several minutes. "What is it, Dear?" Her mother asked. "It's a necklace, mom! I'm never going to take it off!" Koweena lied there that night in bed just staring at the desk and bookcase, holding onto the locket of her new necklace. Those pieces of furniture were the nicest things she had ever gotten, except for that necklace of course.

Koweena awoke the next morning, and her eyes immediately went to her necklace and the new furniture. Her nose instantly picked up on the fresh smell of oak and varnish, just like the night before. She felt like a kid on Christmas morning. Everything was brand new to her all over again. The way her sleepy, swollen eyes were observing everything around her, it was like that morning at the Defour house when she noticed all those new decorations for Christmas. Except this time, it was her own shack that was amazing her eyes. She was so proud that morning to actually be in that shack. That was a first for her.

That same day, Ray and Charles were walking by Koweena's shack. "Wait a minute, Charles?" "What is it, Ray?" Ray stooped down and stared at Koweena's shack. "I'm just curious about something." "Curious about what, Ray?" "That little bitch has been spending a lot of time with Julie, right?" "I guess," Charles responded. "I just wonder if there's anything in that shack that is a result of their time spent together?" "What are you going to do, Ray?" Charles asked in a concerned voice. Ray just continued to stare at the shack. Charles tugged on Ray's overalls. "Come on man, let' just go." "No, wait a minute, Charles. I have to see for myself if there's anything in that shack that's not supposed to be there. Something just doesn't feel right." "Ray, man, let's go!" "Come with me, Charles." They entered the shack; Ray's eyes went immediately to the desk and bookcase. Ray began laughing out loud. "We're going to have ourselves a bonfire, Charles!" "Ray, come on man, let's just get out of here." "That little bitch doesn't deserve anything that nice!" Ray said emphatically as he spit his tobacco. Ray walked up to the bookcase and noticed the pictures of Julie on the wall above Koweena's bed. Ray began gritting his teeth as he stared at the pictures. "You've got to be kidding me! This is an outrage! I'm so mad right now." Ray went and grabbed a gasoline container full of gas from a nearby shed. He arrived back at the shack with container in hand. "Come on, Charles; help me get all of this stuff out of here!" They violently jerked the desk and bookcase from the wall, so violently in fact that it scattered all of Koweena's dolls and books all over the dirt floor. "Come on, Charles, let's go back in there and pick up all those dolls and books and throw them on top of this stuff." They grabbed the books and dolls, and threw them on the desk and bookcase, both of which by now were lying on the road separating the shacks from the fields. They were ripped into little pieces. "Let's light this shit up, Charles!" Charles threw gasoline all over Koweena's once beautiful dolls, books, and furniture. Ray lit the match and threw it on the pile. With the varnish, combined with the oak, mixed in the now dirty rubbish; it made the pile go up in flames in no time. Ray looked on with an evil grin. "Hah, look at that, Charles, the little bitches beautiful stuff, going up in flames!"

Koweena was devastated when she arrived home that night from Julie's to find her furniture and dolls missing. She hadn't even had them twenty four hours. She didn't even get a chance to enjoy them, and just like that, they were gone. She saw the burnt ashes outside her shack and quickly put two and two together. "Someone has burned all my valuable stuff," she thought to herself. She was actually looking forward to coming home to her sickly wooden shack for the first time in her life because of the new stuff that she thought was awaiting her there. She clutched on tightly to her necklace. "Thank goodness, I have my necklace." She knew it was an overseer, but was it that guy she thought. The man who first started verbally abusing her, the same man who was responsible for her beating, these thoughts raced through her mind as she stared at the open space next to her bed. "Could it have been him?" She wondered. She suddenly became frightened as she just stood there at the entranceway. "Is this man out to kill me?" She continued thinking. She began crying. Her mother came over to where she was. She put her arm around Koweena's shoulders. "What is it, Sweetheart? Is it your missing furniture and dolls? Do you know anything about this?" Amitha asked. Koweena began crying. "Every time something starts going good for me, mom, the rug gets pulled right out from under me, and I feel like I'm right back where I started!" Koweena said. "I know, Baby, it's like you take two steps forward, only to take one step back." "Exactly, mom!" "What do you think happened here?" Her mother asked. "Well, I noticed the ashes outside the shack, so I guess they burnt everything up." "Who did, Koweena?" "I'm guessing the overseers, mom, I don't know." "The overseers, yes, that makes sense. But why?" Her mother wondered to herself. "I think one of them is out to get me," Koweena said as she began crying even harder. "What!? An overseer is out to get you. Who, Baby? The one that beat you?" "I don't know." "Shhh, come over here, Dear," Amitha was trying to calm her down; she took Koweena by the hand and led her over to her own bed which was three beds over from Koweena's. She gently sat Koweena down, and then sat alongside her, now holding both her hands. "Koweena, that was such a long time ago, how could the same men that beat you still remember you? They're too busy to worry about one little slave girl out of this whole Plantation." Now, like Julie, it was her mother that was in denial. "I don't know, mom." "You know, it could have been one of the slaves, even one of the slaves that lives here," her mother continued. At that moment, there were no other slaves in the shack, just Koweena and her mother. "What do you mean, it could have been one of the other slaves, who?" Koweena's crying had subsided somewhat, she was now down to a sobbing, slow cry. "I don't know, a slave could is seen you here with all of this nice stuff and got jealous. You is gotta remember, Dear, you is the only slave here, on this huge Plantation, among the hundreds of slaves, that is buddies with the owner's daughter. That could make for some pretty jealous slaves." "That's a possibility, but now I have to worry about slaves in addition to overseers, mom!" Koweena yelled out. "What if someone is trying to send me a message!?" She continued. "Koweena, I think you is overreacting a little bit. Anyway, I don't think those men who were responsible for your beating even remember it any longer. I don't want to have to tell you this, but overseers beat slaves all the time." "I knew that, mom." "I'm just saying, Baby, there's no way they still remember you, no overseer has it out for you, I promise." Once again, another promise Koweena thought. From her past experience, Koweena couldn't believe her mother when she said those words "I promise." Koweena was still frightened, despite what her mother was telling her. "Can I sleep with you tonight, momma?" "Sure, Baby."

That night while lying in her mother's bed, Koweena couldn't help but feel frustrated and scared. She had gone almost three years without anything bad happening to her, and now this. "When will this all stop?" She wondered to herself. "Don't I deserve to be happy?" She asked herself. "Do I tell Julie what happened here today?" She continued thinking. "No, I don't think that's such a good idea," she whispered to herself while lying there next to her mother. She was always against the idea of telling Julie anything bad that had happened to her in her little slave world. For one thing, she didn't want Mr. or Mrs. Defour to find out, and for another, she knew that if she did tell Julie, Julie would cause a scene, and that could possibly get to the ears of an overseer and really make her life miserable. No, she had made up her mind; she wasn't going to tell Julie about any of this. She reached down to grab her heart locket, when she did, she opened it. The moon that was shining through the only window in the shack was bright enough to where she could see inside the locket. She stared at what was inside it, and gave a quick smile. It was the only thing that helped her sleep that night.

The next morning, Koweena didn't want to get up out of bed, she was too depressed as she stared at the wall where her new things had been sitting just a day ago. She was experiencing the opposite effect of what she had experienced the previous morning. Instead of her sleepy, swollen eyes gazing wide open at the brand new objects that she could freshly smell, stunned and amazed and overly excited at what she was looking at, she was now looking at the vacant wall with her sleepy, swollen eyes, gloomy and sad, only thinking of the memory of it. She tried her hardest to smell, to smell any kind of the same scent from the previous morning, the same scent of fresh oak and varnish. Her shack, which just twenty four hours ago had started looking like a real home, was now back to looking like a shattered old dump. Koweena had gone from two different emotional extremes, in two different back to back mornings. After staring at the wall for a moment, she planted her face back down on the bed, burying her face in the hay. "Come on ,Koweena, it's time to get up!" Her mother yelled. "I'm not going to work today, mom." "You is not what!? Now, Koweena, you is know that slaves don't have a chance to stay in sick and take the day off. We is always gotta work, rain or shine." "I'm not going, momma." Amitha walks over to the bed where Koweena is lying. "Koweena, I know you is depressed, and I'm sorry, but we is slaves, we don't have a choice as to whether we go into work or not. We go to work no matter what. Now get up, let's go." Amitha was trying to pull Koweena's lifeless body up off the bed, but to no avail. "Koweena, you is goin to get in a whole lot of trouble if you don't get up!" "What else is new, mom?

I get in trouble even when I don't do anything wrong." "Come on, Koweena, stop feeling sorry for yourself, let's go, get up! I'm tired of all this emotional nonsense from you!" "Is this the same mom from last night? Doesn't she realize all that I've been through?" Koweena thought. This was a new side of her mother that she had never seen before. "My mom has always been consoling and understanding when things bad happen to me, but today she's different," Koweena thought to herself. "Her tone seems more harsh and she appears to be just plain mad," she continued thinking. "Why don't you understand all I've been through, mom?" Koweena asked her mother. "Koweena, we all have it rough, we is all slaves here, no exceptions!" "Yes, but, mom, I'm just a child." Koweena's eyes starting watering up. "You quit being a child when you stepped out onto that field, Koweena." Koweena could hardly believe her ears. She couldn't believe how insensitive her mother was being that morning. Maybe Amitha had cracked under all the pressure that Koweena's life had put on her. From the beating, to having to worry about Koweena spending time with Julie, and now this latest thing, the destroying of Koweena's property, and who might be behind it. Or could it be that she was jealous of Julie. Jealous of such an influential person, giving things to Koweena and watching her receiving all of that material stuff from Julie; knowing that she couldn't get those things for her herself."Mom, is something wrong?" "I'll tell you what's wrong. I'll sure tell you what's wrong. Being a slave is what's wrong. Doing this day in and day out is what's wrong. Some of us don't have the opportunities you have, Koweena, the education, the cozying up to one of the most powerful people on the Plantation." "Mom, you're scaring me," Koweena interrupted. "Listen, Koweena, you get out of that bed or else. You need to face facts, slavery is hard, and we is in a hard business. There is no hope for us, do you understand that? Now get out of bed!" Koweena rolled out with tears rolling down her cheeks. It was the first time her mother had hurt her, and she did it at such an inopportune time. Koweena made the decision then and there, Julie would be her only family from here on out.

That whole day Koweena spent working in the fields, seemed like a dream to her; her body was there, but her mind was somewhere else. She was thinking about that overseer who beat her. Was he indeed after her? She thought. She was thinking about how her mother, who just turned on her that morning. "I have Julie now, I'm not going to let my mom bother me," she thought. Koweena was tough. After all she had been through, she just kept right on working, despite her depressed mood. But most of her day was spent thinking about what had happened the day before to her desk and bookcase. She was trying to figure out who could have been behind it all. She felt violated, similar to how she felt after her beating. "That damn shack, first I'm beaten in it, and now all my stuff is destroyed in it, was nothing safe anymore, not even in my own home?" She wondered. She had noticed that morning as she was getting ready for work that there was something jutting out from beneath the hay under her bed; she was so confused and upset by her mother's actions, that she forgot to check it out. That was just another thing in the long line of things that were occupying her mind that day as she worked. She was so curious about that object she saw that morning that her curiosity grew as the day wore on. "I have to see what's under my bed," she thought.

Normally, Julias would come and pick her up from the fields and take her directly to the Defour house. Today however, Koweena had decided that she was going to make a run for it after three o'clock. She was going to run to her shack and see what was sticking out from under her bed. There was a problem however, she didn't know when three o'clock was, the only way she would now it was three, was when she would see Julias waiting for her. Without Julias showing up, she wouldn't have a clue what time it was. She would have to wait on Julias, she had no choice. Three o'clock came and Julias was there ready to take Koweena to Julie's house. "Julias?" "Yes, Koweena." "We need to go back to my place for a minute, just for a minute." "I don't know, Koweena; you know how Julie worries about you if you is not there on time." "I know, but this will only take a second." Julias agrees to go with her on one condition; that she goes in that shack for just a brief second. "One second, Koweena." "One second, Julias, that's all I need." As Koweena entered the shack, with Julias waiting outside, she noticed Delco, one of the male slaves she lived with, standing next to Koweena's bed. "What are you doing standing there, Delco!" Koweena yelled out. "Did you have something to do with this you little," "wait just a minute little child," Delco interrupts. "You're here because you knew no one would be here, just like yesterday, right? You did this didn't you?" Koweena said as she ran over and pushed Delco in the chest. "Did what?" Delco looked around and finally rested his eyes on the wall next to Koweena's bed. "Oh you mean your furniture?" Delco said, pointing to the wall. Koweena began pushing up against Delco. "Yeah, tell me why you did it, Delco!?" "I didn't do anything, I wasn't here yesterday, at all, the whole day, I promise!" Julias, hearing the yelling, came in to investigate. "What's going on in here, Koweena?" Julias asked. Koweena stared at Delco for a minute. "Nothing, Julias, it's nothing, go back outside please," Koweena said. Delco held his chest with both hands. "Koweena, I is sorry this happened to you, but I promise, I had nothing to do with it." "I know you didn't, Delco. I'm just a little stressed; I didn't mean to overreact like that." Julias became concerned. "Koweena, what's going on? You said you would only be a second." "It's nothing, Julias, it's nothing, just go back outside, I'll be there in a minute," Koweena said. She wasn't about to let Julias catch wind of what was going on, Julie would surely find out then. "Excuse me, Delco; I need for you to move over just a bit." As Delco moved, Koweena could see the corner of the object poking out a bit from under the hay. Koweena reached down and grabbed a hold of it. It was a tiny children's book. "This is the first book Julie ever read to me, and the first book I ever read," she whispered to herself. Delco could overhear her. "What is the first book you is ever read?" "Nothing, Delco, just go back to what you were doing, okay." Koweena smiled as she rubbed the book with her hands. She needed at least something good to go her way that day, and finding that book was the ticket. "Koweena, come on!" Julias yelled from outside the shack. "Coming, Julias!" Koweena yelled back.

As Koweena entered Julie's room that day, and noticed Julie writing something down as she sat at her; and what was now, Koweena's desk, she couldn't help but smile. Upon looking at Julie's back, everything that had happened to her over the last twenty four hours just seemed to fade away. Just the mere sight of Julie calmed Koweena down. "Hey, Julie," Koweena said with a smile as she clutched her book with one hand and held on tightly to her necklace with the other. Julie turned around to look at Koweena. "Hey, Sweetheart! How's my girl!" Julie's expression said it all.

"Every time she would look at me, it was as if she was looking at me for the first time," Koweena recalled. "Like that afternoon I was babysitting Samuel at the Defour house, and Julie walked in and we made eye contact for the first time. It was like that everytime she looked upon me. It made me feel like the only person in the entire universe. I needed that look on that day more than ever."

Julie noticed Koweena holding on tight to the necklace she had given her, it made her feel warm inside. "What book do you have there?" Julie asked. "Oh, this is just something I grabbed this morning." "You mean you worked all day with that book by your side?" Koweena hated lying to Julie, and she was about to get caught in one. "Well, it wasn't hard; I just laid it by my side one the ground as I worked. Will you do me a favor, Julie?" Koweena wanted to get off the subject of her lie. "Sure, what is it, Dear?" "Will you read this book to me, I mean, I know I can read it; but I've had such a hard day. It would make things a whole lot better if I could just hear your voice as you read it to me." "Sure, Dear, say you had a rough day? Do you want to talk about it?" Koweena desperately wanted to tell Julie all that had happened, but she was just too scared to. "No, I just want you to read me this book." "Oh," Julie said as she put her hand to her chest, "this is the first book I ever read to you. Do you remember that?" Tears began to well up in Koweena's eyes. "I'll never forget it, Julie." Julie could notice in Koweena's eyes that she had had a tough time of it since they last met; but she wasn't going to pry. Koweena said she didn't want to talk about it, and that's exactly where Julie was going to leave it. Koweena's memories of her day; and what she went through the previous night, just faded in the distance with each word from the book that Julie spoke. It wasn't the book; and the contents therein, that soothed and healed Koweena's emotions; it was listening to Julie's voice, and the fact that it was the first book Julie had ever read to her, that did the trick. It actually had nothing to do with the story, it was the sentimental value the book had, the place in the history of Koweena's life, is why the book found such importance. As Julie was reading the book, Koweena couldn't help but notice sounds of hammering and wood cutting going on in the adjacent guest bedroom. "What is that, Julie?" "What's what, Kowie?" "That sound of some kind of building going on in the other room." "Oh, that's nothing, Dear." Julie didn't want to give away her secret to Koweena, not until things were completed anyway.

As Koweena was back in her shack, lying in her bed that night, she felt much better than she did the previous night, or that morning for that matter. All was not lost; her relationship with Julie was stronger than ever, she had her necklace around her neck, and she managed to find her favorite book when she thought she had lost everything from the burning the previous day. Yes, Koweena felt fortunate, even though she didn't want to be there, not just because of the normal reason, the fact that the shack was repulsive, she didn't want to be there for another reason, a new reason, she no longer wanted to be around her mother.

The next day, as Mrs. Defour was walking through the foyer, she could hear the ruckus in one of the upstairs guest bedrooms. "What in the hell is going on up there?" She wondered as she gazed upward in the direction of the sounds. As she walked up the stairs, stepping up each and every step, the clanging and banging got louder. As she got to the top, she could pin point the exact bedroom the sound was coming from. As she turned in the direction of the sound, she noticed Julie standing at the entranceway to the bedroom with a note pad in her hand. "What is she up to now?" Mrs. Defour said to herself. "Julie, what in the hell is going on up here?" Mrs. Defour asked as she was approaching Julie. "Hey, mother! I'm redecorating, what do you think!?" "What the hell? What do you think you're doing!?" "You always tell me we have too many guest bedrooms, so I thought I would turn one of the rooms into a play and study room for Koweena. What do you think?" "Yes, Dear, I told you we had too many guest bedrooms, but that didn't mean you could just go and do whatever you wanted to, to one of them; and doing it all for that Nigger, come on Julie. Where's your head? Is it screwed on straight?" "Yes, mother, my head is screwed on straight. My room was too cramped, I didn't want her to have to sit on the floor all the time to try and learn. I want her to have her own desk to write on; and her own chair, and couch to read off of, an area here in the corner where she can do her own painting. She's so into learning that I want her to have her own place to spread her wings and learn away." "I knew when I agreed to this," her mother continued, "that educating that little thing would be nothing but a headache. What if your dad finds out?" "Mother, I've been doing this now for years, and neither he, nor you, have run into any problems with Koweena. Am I right, or am I right?" Mrs. Defour stretched her arm into the bedroom. "Yes, but this is carrying it a little too far don't you think?" "Mother, it's too late for any of your shenanigans. It's about an hour from being fully completed, so there's nothing you can do about it. And anyway, didn't we make a promise a while back before I started this whole thing with educating Koweena, that if I agreed to see that man you wanted me to see that you would keep your nose out of my business when it came to teaching her?" "Yes, and it seems to me, Dear, that that's working out just fine as far as I can tell. You're still seeing that man to this day aren't you?" "You won't stop reminding me, that's not the point, mother; the point is, you promised me you wouldn't interfere if I did that." The fact that it was working out between Julie and that man made her mother realize that she had no grounds to get in the way. "Julie, don't think for one minute that she's going to live here by you doing all of this." "I know, mother, you've made that very clear from the beginning, she won't be living here." "Okay, now that that's settled, see to it that this is all you do for that little Nigger, nothing more is to be done to this house for her, understood!" "Yes, ma'am, my goodness!" Julie said as her mother was walking away. Julie was staring at her mother getting ready to go down the stairs. "Tight ass!" She said. "I heard that, Julie!" Her mom yelled back as she was going down the stairs.

That afternoon, as Koweena was walking with Julias up the driveway to the Defour house, as she normally did every afternoon, Koweena noticed something unusual. Julie was waiting for her at the foot of the front porch steps. "What is it, Julie? What's wrong?" Koweena asked as she approached the base step where Julie was standing. "Nothing's wrong, Kowie, I have a surprise for you! Follow me!" Julie takes Koweena by the hand and leads her into the house. As they were walking into the house, Koweena could see the excitement written all over Julie's face. Koweena looked up at Julie who was still holding her hand. "Is this surprise for me, Julie?" "Yes, Sweetheart, it is, and I think you're going to love it." Koweena suddenly began to get that same feeling she got that night she saw the desk and bookcase inside her shack. A feeling of stunning wonder began to flood her mind, thinking about what it could be. Her heart began to beat faster with each step she took up the stairs. An overwhelming since of excitement was overtaking her as she made her way to the top of the stairs. She noticed as she reached the top that they were not headed in the normal direction, toward Julie's bedroom.

Koweena looked up at Julie and noticed Julie smiling back down at her. Koweena could hardly contain her excited emotions. She let out a little laugh by accident as they approached the guest bedroom. As they came to the entranceway, Koweena could hardly believe her eyes. She first noticed the walls. They were painted light blue with small hand painted designs of little books, papers, and pencils in various green, yellow, and white colors scattered throughout the walls of the room. She then noticed the leather couch to her left; and the beautiful bronze crafted metal chair in front of the white painted oak desk, the chair was actually made out of iron, but to her, it looked like metal. She then noticed the beautiful art easel in the corner. She noticed the bookcase full of dolls, and a rocking horse on the other side of the room. "Is this all for me!?" "All for you, Dear, you like it!?" "It's the most beautiful thing I've ever seen, Julie!" "I painted the little books, pencils, and papers that you see on the walls myself." "You did all of this for me!?" This had more than made up for Koweena losing her desk, bookcase, books, and dolls. "Go ahead, Kowie, sit on the couch, sit in the chair, get a feel for the desk, go ahead."

Koweena, with her mouth wide open, walked slowly into the room. "My very own room!" She said to herself. Although she wasn't going to be living there, this was the next best thing. "Everything that you see here, Kowie, is yours. Everything in here can easily be transferred to my house when we move, and we can put it all in your room." "Are we moving now!?" Koweena said in excitement. Julie laughed at Koweena's excitement. "No, Dear," Julie said. "I'm just saying, when the time comes for me to move, you will get all of this stuff when you come live with me." "Oh!" Koweena exclaimed. "From now on you'll be studying and learning in here, instead of having to be cramped on the floor in my room," Julie said. "This will also be your playing room as well." For the next several months Koweena became obsessed with that room. Each day she couldn't wait to get off of work in order to spend time in that room, learning and studying. It made her hit the books even harder. She began to really excel in her studies. And on weekends, she spent all of her time in there. She just couldn't get enough of that room. Once again, Julie had come through for her. Since she was five, Koweena had been going through one emotional roller coaster after another, and this time, she was at the peak once again. She was having the best time of her life.

Chapter 7   Cuddle Time

*I*t was a clear, sunny, autumn day throughout the Defour Plantation. The Plantation was hustling and bustling with slave activity, as it normally is on a weekday such as this. The slaves, by the hundreds, were working like an army of ants, tirelessly, non stop, throughout the cotton and apple fields, as well as in the lumber yard. The overseers were pacing up and down the fields, making sure the slaves were marching to their every beat. Sounds of them yelling out orders rang throughout the Plantation. All of the overseers were supervising their own plot of ground in the fields, and their own assigned slaves, all except one, that is. Ray was standing in one of the open rows of a particular cotton field section with rifle in hand. He wasn't barking orders that day as he normally did like his peers, no, he thought his job was not to stare, observe, and bark orders at the slaves on that day, in his particular slice of the Plantation. No, Ray had made up his mind on that certain day that he was going to stare only at Koweena. He had been staring at Koweena for several hours now. Koweena was some twenty yards away picking cotton, minding her own business. None of the other overseers dared ask Ray why he wasn't pacing up and down his row barking orders at the other slaves. Ray was a big man, and the other overseers, most of them anyway, were intimidated by this mountain of a man. Ray just stood there, his feet now permanently dug into the dry, parched ground, not budging an inch. He was like a statue, with one hand in his overall pocket, and the other wrapped around his rifle. Koweena never even noticed Ray staring at her; she was too engrossed in her hard labor to even recognize the eerie staring Ray, glaring at her every move. Why was he focusing his attention on Koweena that day? Whatever the reason, it wasn't good, and Koweena, though she was too busy to realize it, was already the target of a diabolical plan from an evil man. Like the many times before, she had done nothing wrong to draw the attention of this mammoth overseer. She was simply an easy target. Maybe it was just simply because of her looks, or maybe it was because she was so close to Julie. Whatever the reason, Koweena had a bull's eye on her back with Ray eyeing in on the target.

"Hey, Josi." Koweena called out to Josi who was working next to her on the other side of the row. "Yeah, Koweena, what is it?" "Do you want to come over and play with me at Julie's house this weekend; I can show you my new room?" "Can you is do that, Koweena?" "Sure, I just have to ask Julie first." They both were talking while they had their heads down toward the ground picking the cotton. "I can show you all of my dolls, we can spend time accessorizing them, and I can read you some of my books, and you know what? I can teach you how to read. How does that sound?" "Great, Koweena!" Josi replied with a smile on her face. "Hey, keep it down over there niggers!" One of the overseers yelled out at both Koweena and Josi. Koweena had been picking cotton now for quite some time in her assigned row. And yet, she still hadn't looked up to notice Ray glaring at her with some type of devious plan written all over his face.

Meanwhile, over at the Defour house, Julie was in her bedroom getting ready for her afternoon out with Thomas. She and Thomas had been seeing each other now for almost two years, they were hot and heavy over each other, and no one could have been more pleased about that than her mother. Her mother walked into Julie's room and noticed Julie standing in front of her mirror. "You look pretty, Dear! That's a pretty dress." "Thanks, mom," Julie responded. "Are you going out with Thomas today?" "Yes, were going into town for some lunch at the Restaurant." "You know, Julie, I couldn't be happier that things between you and Thomas are working out so well. I told you that Mr. Jenkins said he was a great guy, didn't I?" Julie didn't like the fact that Mr. Jenkins spoke so highly of Thomas, she didn't care for Mr. Jenkins one bit. "You know, mother, I don't like Thomas because of Mr. Jenkins, I could care less what that man has to say. I would rather you not mention the fact that Mr. Jenkins said anything nice about Thomas at all."

"Julie, remember now, it was the Jenkins' that recommended Thomas to me in the first place. Without them, you two wouldn't be together." "Don't remind me, mother." "What do you have against the Jenkins' anyway?" Her mother questioned. "I don't have anything against Mrs. Jenkins; it's that Mr. Jenkins that I can't stand." "Why, Dear, what did he do to you?" "He's done nothing to me; it's just the way he stares at Koweena, looking all repelled when he sees her." "Well, you can't blame him, Julie, he is the head overseer, it's his job to look down on people like that." "What do you mean when you say people like that, mother? You mean people who are black like Koweena, don't you?" "Well, she is a nigger, Julie." "Alright, mom, not today, please." "Well, I'm just saying, Dear." "Well, say it somewhere else, okay? You always start in with that nigger stuff; you know how uncomfortable that makes me feel. You also know how close I am to Koweena, and yet you say those things just to get under my skin." "Well, speaking of things that we know, you know, Julie, that it bothers me that you are so close to that little thing." "You can say her name, mother, her name is Koweena, she's not that little thing, and she's not a nigger." "I just call them like I see them, Dear, and that little thing is not white. So if it's not white, it can only be one other thing." "Don't say it, mother, I know what you're going to say, just save your breath. You know, I'm really happy with the way things are in my life right now, and you've failed to even notice it. Things are going well with Koweena, very well, and you haven't even said one thing about that. Yes, things between me and Thomas are going well, but that's all you've noticed. Don't you care that I'm making a big difference in a young girl's life. I mean, I've invested a lot of time into her, and she's really happy." "Julie, it's just a waste of time. Nothing will come of it; you're just spinning your wheels." Julie began flapping her arms against her dress. "Can't you say that you're at least proud of me? I mean, my God, mother, Koweena and I have been close for years now. I spend all my time with her." "You need to be spending all that time with Thomas," her mother interrupted. "I don't know why I bother talking to you about this," Julie continued. "I mean all you do is belittle Koweena and my relationship with her. Things couldn't be going any better for me right now, and for Koweena for that matter; and I'm not about to let you ruin that." "Honey, I'm not trying to ruin it, I just wish you would realize how futile helping a nigger like that is." "Just leave, mother. Just get out!" Julie yelled as her eyes began to tear up. She wasn't all that upset at the fact that her mother didn't agree with what she was doing. She was upset at the fact that her mother constantly disgraced Koweena and disparaged her.

As Julie and her mother were upstairs talking, Mr. Jenkins had arrived at the house to meet with Mr. Defour. After several minutes of going over some business, Mr. Jenkins thought it would be a good idea to get personal with Mr. Defour. He realized he was taking a chance at bringing up personal things to his boss, especially things concerning his own daughter; but Mr. Jenkins had been bottling this situation with Julie and Koweena up for such a long time that he just couldn't take keeping it inside any longer. "Okay, Donald, that concludes our business for today," Mr. Defour said as he closed up his financial books on his desk. "Mr. Defour, sir," "yes, Donald," "you know I think the world of your daughter, and I hope you don't think I'm being too straight forward here; but I think she's getting involved with some stuff that's not, well, that's not suitable for a young woman such as herself, and with her stature, to be getting involved with, sir." "What do you mean, Donald, involved in what? "Well, sir, I hope you don't think I'm interfering in your family's business, and I don't mean to pry." "Out with it, Donald," Mr. Defour interrupted. "Sir, your daughter is cozying up to a nigger." Mr. Defour, who was always busy with work and had no time to keep up with his daughter's life, was shocked at Mr. Jenkins' statement. "Donald, I um, I don't know what to say. I mean, I must say it's very brave of you to come in here, into my office, and talk about my daughter's life like this, as if I don't know what's going on in my own family." "I know, sir, and I realize that, and like I said, I don't mean to get into your family affairs, and I know you're way too busy to keep track of little things like what goes on in your daughter's life; but I just thought you should know." "Donald, you're beginning to offend me here a little bit. I know I'm a busy man, but I do love my daughter, and I do try my best to follow what goes on in her life." "I know, sir, and I'm not implying that you're too busy to be a good father, I know you're a good father, it's just I also know how busy you are, and, well, I just didn't know if you knew that. You know, that your daughter is getting so close to a nigger." "Well, now that you mention it, Donald, I have noticed a little nigger walking around my home quite a bit, but

I have lots of niggers walking about my home working. But like you so obviously noted and pointed out to me, I am rather busy, so I haven't been paying that much attention to it. But please go on, tell me more." "Well, sir, I'm afraid to have to tell you this, but I think it has been going on for several years now." Mr. Defour slapped both his hands on his desk. "Years!" He yelled out. "Yes, sir, years. I noticed one day as I was leaving your office; your daughter was talking to the little nigger in your living room. Your daughter was telling it how she was going to allow it to spend time with her, and how she was going to play with it, and how she was going to allow it to well, spend time in this house. I then later found out that it was going much deeper than that." "Go on," Mr. Defour interrupted. "Well, sir, your daughter is educating that little nigger now." Mr. Defour leaned back in his chair and put his finger to his mouth as if to be thinking intensely. "Well, I must say this is uncomfortable, Donald, for you to come in here and tell me things about my own daughter's life. Especially things I was unaware of." "I understand that, sir, I feel real uneasy about having to do this, but it was just bubbling up inside me. It caused me a many sleepless nights. Well, I just figured you should know." "Well thank you, Donald, for bringing that to my attention, I'll surely address this to my daughter."

As Mr. Jenkins walked by the stairs and through the foyer toward the front door, Julie was coming down the stairs all fixed up pretty and ready to go on her afternoon adventure with Thomas. As Mr. Jenkins grabbed a hold of the front door he quickly turned around and noticed Julie approaching the bottom step. "Good afternoon, Julie," Mr. Jenkins said. "Hey," Julie quickly said in a snobbish tone. Mr. Jenkins was about to say something else but Julie quickly turned her head and body away from him in a sharp, quick like manner, and headed toward the kitchen in the opposite direction. "Jerk," she said to herself under her breath.

"Julie!" Mr. Defour yelled from his office which was at the end of the hallway past the kitchen. "Yes, dad!" Julie yelled back. "Can you come in here for a minute, Dear; I need to talk to you about something!" "Okay, dad, I'll be right there!" Julie stopped at the closet adjacent to one of the two kitchen entrances to grab her scarf. She then walked into her father's office. "Yes, dad, you wanted to see me?" "Yes, Dear, have a seat." Julie grabbed a seat that was directly in front of Mr. Defour's desk. "Julie, it has been brought to my attention that you are, well, spending a significant amount of your time with one of my slaves. Is that correct? Please tell me it's not." "Daddy," Julie said as she rolled her head, turning it away from her father. "Julie, just be honest with me. I really hope this is not the case, but if it is, just let me know, just come right out and tell me, are you getting close to one of my niggers?" "Who told you this, Mr. Jenkins!?" "Yes, as a matter of fact it was." "Dad, you can't listen to that bigot fool!" "Julie, I will not have you disrespecting one of my top employees, now just tell me the truth." "Yes, dad, I am seeing someone you so disgracefully called a nigger, her name is Koweena. I call her Kowie," Julie said with a smile. Her father leaned back in his chair with a grimace look on his face. "Julie, no!" "Dad, she's a bright, intelligent, beautiful young girl." "I don't care what she is!" "Just listen for a second, dad, before you go getting all upset. When I first saw her, she was the most depressed thing I had ever seen; but I fell for her the minute I saw her. There was just something about her, we had an instant connection, and it's only grown from there. Yes, I'm close to her, very close to her." "Okay, I've heard enough, Julie. You know, this sickens me to know this about you. I thought you would have better sense than this." "Dad, don't be like mom on this." "Like what?" Her father questioned. "All the negativity and name calling, putting Koweena down, telling me what a waste of time it is." "Julie, do you realize what a position I'm in here? You can't go befriending my property. That's not what these people are on my land for. These niggers are here for one reason, to keep us rich. I don't care about being nice to them, I own them." "See, dad, this is what I'm talking about, you don't think of these people as human beings." "Julie, do I need to remind you of what happened to you back when you were just a child?" "Dad, you didn't have to go there." "Well, Julie, I'm just trying to get you to see that these niggers are animals, not human beings. You just can't go around educating them and playing with them. Don't you care how that looks on me. You're disgracing me by doing that." "Oh, so that's what this is about huh, me disgracing you. Well, what about my life, dad, I'm my own person you know." "Is that why you're doing this, Julie, to prove that you are your own person. Are you not getting enough attention from your mother and me?" "Dad, please, I'm not talking about getting attention from you, I'm talking about doing what I want to do, with my life." "Julie, how do you think that made me feel to have one of my own men come in here and tell me that my own daughter is friends with a piece of my property. It was a slap in my face, it made me look incompetent and worse, it made me look like a bad father." "How does the fact that I'm friends with Koweena make you look like a bad father?" "A lady doesn't carry on with a slave. It is unseemly," her father said. Julie tightened her jaw. "I don't care what people think, and I don't care what you think. It's my life." "It's not just your life," her father said. "It reflects poorly on the family as a whole." "And slavery doesn't," Julie said. "Slaver is ordained by God," her father said. Julie snorted. Her father's face turned red. "I forbid you to ever see that nigger again. Do you hear me?" Oh, she heard him all right. She just couldn't believe what he had said. How dare he use that word? How dare he tell her what she could or couldn't do? She opened her mouth to say something, but thought better. She'd bide her time. Once she was married, she'd do as she pleased. As Julie began walking out of the office, her father spoke up. "I can ship her away!" He yelled. Julie suddenly stopped at the entranceway to the office, the comment from her father stunned her a bit. After composing herself for a moment, she turned back around and faced her father. "Are you threatening me, dad?" "Take it as you see it," her father replied. "If you do that, dad, if you do that, you will no longer have me in your life. I will cease from being your daughter. I will leave, and you will never see me again." "So that little thing means more to you than I do?" "Yes, dad, she does." After saying that Julie walked out of the room. Mr. Defour threw a brass paperweight shaped like a boat up against the wall in anger. "There's no way I'm allowing that nigger to get a foothold in this family," he said to himself.

Upon hearing the sound, Mrs. Defour came rushing into the office. "What is going on, Dear!?" She said to Mr. Defour. "That daughter of ours is what's going on; she's completely out of control. If she thinks I'm going to allow her to continue her relationship with that little bitch, she's sorely mistaken." "So you know," Mrs. Defour said. "How long have you known?" Mr. Defour asked. "I've known pretty much since it started." "Why didn't you tell me?" "You're just so busy all the time. I didn't want to get in the way of what you were doing. I thought I could handle it," Mrs. Defour said. "Well, now I'm stepping into the situation. Julie's got another thought coming if she thinks I'm going to sit idly by and watch her make a mockery of this family." "How's she making a mockery of the family, Dear?" "By letting that little nigger within striking distance of my office, not to mention allowing her to wander freely about this house like she owns the place." "There's kind of something I need to tell you," Mrs. Defour said while biting her bottom lip. "What is it? You look nervous," Mr. Defour said, noticing the expression on Mrs. Defour's face. "I um, kind of made a bargain with Julie a while back, and I didn't tell you about it." "What is it?" Mr. Defour asked. "I basically told Julie that if she would go out with Thomas and give him a chance that I would allow her to continue seeing that nigger without interfering. It really wasn't that bad of a deal now that you look at it; she's now involved with a suitable man because of it." "I see you're point, but that still doesn't give her the excuse of acting like some anti-slavery activist. I thought we raised her better than that. I'm going to have to do something." Mrs. Defour, now sitting on the corner of her husband's desk, asked. "What are you going to do, Honey?" "I'm going to do something to that nigger of course." "You better be careful, Dear," Mrs. Defour commented. "You better not let Julie find out you're going to do something to that little spook." "I know, she threatened me today by telling me that she would no longer be my daughter if I did anything about this situation," Mr. Defour said. "Yes I know, she's told me similar things in the past too," Mrs. Defour added.

"I don't know, Thomas, I mean I love my parents, but the way they're carrying on about my relationship to Kowie, it's like they're two different people, you know." Julie, who was visibly upset, was talking to Thomas at the table of the finest Restaurant in town, The Jublié, a fine French cuisine establishment. Her boyfriend, Thomas Callahan, was a well to do gentlemen. He, like Julie, was born and raised and currently lives in Natchez. His work is based in Natchez, but he travels throughout Mississippi surveying land, a very respectable and well paying job. He was not born into money like Julie, he became well off by working hard in his job. Julie was impressed with him from the outset, with his hard working nature, he very much appealed to her, and his looks didn't hurt much either. But Julie was even more impressed by his attitude toward Koweena. He had no background of slave owning or of having any part in slavery. His business didn't depend on slavery either, so he had no hatred in his heart toward African-Americans. He was so crazy for Julie and so in love with her that it didn't matter who was in her life, if Julie cared for that person, than he was going to care for that person, regardless of who that person was. He always went along with her and agreed with her in whatever she was talking about, regardless of the subject. It was the kind of relationship that whatever she said went. If she said jump, Thomas would yell how high. "I hate seeing you so upset, Julie, I wish there was something I could do." "Maybe there is, Thomas." "Name it, Sweetheart." "You could talk to Mr. Jenkins for me." "And say what?" "Tell him to back off of me and my relationship with Koweena." "I don't know, Julie, will he listen to me?" "He thinks the world of you right? Maybe you could talk some sense into him." "Okay, I'll give it a try." "That way," Julie continued, "maybe my dad will give it a rest." "Okay, Baby, I'll give it a try, anything for you," Thomas said.

Meanwhile, back at the Defour Plantation, Koweena was just about to wrap up her day on the cotton field. She was on her final row of the day. Ray had followed her all day, from one row to the other, and yet Koweena still hadn't noticed him. Koweena had worked hard that day, never looking up for one minute. Ray had kept his distance from Koweena the entire day, still standing some twenty yards from her, when all of a sudden another overseer came up to him and whispered something in his ear. Koweena, with her thoughts this late in the day now geared toward playing and studying in her new room at the Defour house, noticed a piece of cotton located at the bottom of one of the stalks near the ground. As she reached down to pick it off, suddenly, out of nowhere, she was violently jerked up off her feet, she gave an instinctive squeal. As she was being carried off she tried to scream but a large, grimy hand quickly covered her mouth.

When three o'clock came, Julias arrived at the field to pick up Koweena. There was something strange that day during his daily pick up of Koweena, she was no where to be found. That was unlike Koweena to be absent. Julias looked all over, yelling out her name. He asked the other slaves where she might have gone, but none of them had seen her. Julias knew something was wrong. Koweena was always there. She was always there with a big smile on her face, looking forward to the evening that she would spend in her room. "I'll go back and report this to Julie," he thought to himself. When he got back to the house, Julie, like Koweena in the field, was no where to be found. Julias felt helpless, he knew something wasn't right. He had a feeling deep down in his gut that something bad had happened to Koweena. As he stood there trying to rationalize what had just happened, he began to think. "She's out with Julie I bet," he said to himself. After convincing himself of that, he went back into the house and continued with his chores, yet he was still concerned about Koweena's whereabouts.

Later on that afternoon, Koweena was sitting on the floor in the middle of her play and study room at the Defour house. She had been sitting there for an hour now in complete silence when she heard Julie entering the house from the downstairs front door. For the first time since their relationship began some two and a half years ago, Koweena was waiting on Julie this time. Julie had always been the one that was waiting on Koweena to either come from the fields on the weekdays, or come from her shack on the weekends; but this time it was the other way around. This time, Koweena was the one waiting at the Defour house. "Bye, Thomas!" Julie yelled from the front door out into the driveway. By now it was five o'clock; Julie was late because her afternoon with Thomas had stretched well into the early evening. Something Julie never allowed to happen in the past because she always wanted to be there when Koweena arrived at the house. She always wanted Koweena to see how happy she was to see her, so Koweena could see that look on her face, that look Koweena loved so much. While Koweena waited she did nothing in the room. She just stared down at the throw rug, picking at it as she sat there. "I'll run up there and apologize to her and make it up to her," Julie thought to herself as she ran up the stairs in great anticipation of seeing Koweena. "Koweena, Sweetheart, I'm so sorry I was," Julie paused for a moment as she stood there at the entrance to the room. She was getting ready to explain how sorry she was at being so late, but then, she noticed something that took her breath away.

"Koweena, my God, girl, what's that on your arms!" Julie said with her eyes and mouth wide open with a nervous tone in her voice. Julie, glancing at both of Koweena's arms, noticed red, bloody stripes going from her wrists all the way up past her elbows. Julie walked a little further into the room, this time, with a slight panic in her voice. "Kowie! How did you get those stripes on your arms!?" Koweena did nothing to respond, she just continued picking at the carpet. In a panic, Julie marched over to where Koweena was sitting and grabbed both of her hands. "How did you get these!?" Julie demanded as she shook Koweena's hands. Fearing the worst, Julie turned Koweena around and lifted up her shirt. The mere sight of Koweena's back caused Julie to hit her knees. Koweena's back was a disgusting sight. Bloody stripes were all up and down Koweena's back. Julie impulsively and without thinking began to run to her bathroom crying uncontrollably where there, she threw up. It was a combination of things that made Julie vomit, the fact at how bad Koweena's back looked, and the fact that someone had done this to her precious Kowie, brought on the instant nausea. After throwing up several times, Julie quickly closed the door to her bathroom so Koweena wouldn't be able to hear her cry. Julie cried so hard she could hardly catch her breath. "Oh my God! Oh my God! They hurt my innocent little Baby!" Julie kept wailing these words out over and over again as she continued to cry all the more harder. Julie had never ached like this before. For those few brief moments in the bathroom, Julie painfully realized for the first time the realities of slavery. Now it finally hit home with Julie, slavery was real to her, and it took this beating of Koweena for her to wake up to the reality about what actually went on on her own property. After years of being sheltered from it by her parents, and not knowing hardly a thing about it, even though it was all around her, she now had been hit like a brick to the face with what life on her property was like. Thoughts began to flood Julie's mind. "Did I go too far by having that furniture, dolls, and books put in her home? Should I have sent Julias to her house that day to take measurements? Should I have been more secretive in keeping my relationship with Koweena a private matter? Should I have kept it more hidden? I know I caused an overseer to know about our relationship by doing something." She was trying her best to blame herself for what she had just seen on Koweena's body as she just laid there against the vanity cabinet of her bathroom, motionless. Little did she know that an overseer, Ray, had had it in for Koweena long before she even met her. "I must get Koweena into my room," Julie thought to herself. "I know she loves that play and study room, but if I don't get her to my room, and quickly, things could get much worse. My room is where she feels the safest," Julie said, talking to herself. After crying for several more minutes, she composed herself and got a sponge from her bathroom cabinet, soaked it in cold water, opened the door and walked into the guest bedroom now turned into a play and study room for Koweena. As she approached Koweena, she noticed that she had tears slowly falling down her cheeks. Julie struggled to hold back tears of her own. She thought she was going to lose it again, this time right in front of Koweena, and ever since seeing the stripes all over Koweena's body, it was something she was determined not to do. She was not about to make things worse on Koweena by having a breakdown right in front of her. As Julie tried to choke back the tears, her throat tightened and her heart pounded. By this time she was behind Koweena. As soon as she lifted up her shirt again, the tears began to flow once again for Julie. With every ounce of strength she could muster, she fought back the urge to cry out loud. She just knelt there as Koweena sat humped over slightly, her body worn out from what she had just endured. Julie applied gentle pressure on Koweena's ripped flesh with the cold sponge. She then applied some ointment onto her freshly scarred wounds. Both of them were quiet at that point, but tears flowed down both of their faces.

As a few minutes passed, Julie felt that she was able to talk without crying. "Kowie, Sweetheart, we need to get you into my room, okay."

"I didn't say a word," Koweena recalled. "All I could think about was how great things had been going. How much fun I had started having. How I really started to enjoy life for the first time. I could remember Julie reading to me the Shelley novel, listening to how a free woman should live, and what free people did. I remembered the promise Julie made to me just months prior about us moving in together, and how everything would be better. She said I just had to trust her. Something I could still rememeber my mom saying years ago. I remember the promise of her telling me that no white man would hurt me. They both promised me something that was a hoax, at least to me it was. I didn't need my mom this time after this beating, I needed Julie, and Julie only. I no longer needed my mom for comfort, I had Julie for that now. And oh, how I needed her on that day."

"Kowie, dear, can you get up so we can go into my bedroom, wouldn't that be better?" Julie knew she had to get her into her room, but actually getting it done was another matter. "It hurts to move," Koweena finally spoke up as she said that in pain. It was obvious by looking at her, with the beating prevalent all down her arms and the way her back looked, that this beating was much more severe than the one she received when she was five. "How about I carry you?" "You will have to touch my back and arms though," Koweena said in a soft, shaky voice. "How about this, if you can stand up, I'll pick you up by your legs and put you up over my shoulders, that way I won't have to touch your back or your arms." This would be no easy task for Julie, Julie was five foot nine, but of average build, she was not muscular by any means; and Koweena was tall for her age, so she would be heavy. Koweena slowly got up, moaning and wincing in pain the entire time. Julie lifted her up onto her shoulders, her knees buckled a bit; at this point however, Julie was going on pure adrenaline. She carried Koweena from the play and study room into her bedroom. Koweena grunted in pain the entire way. "Don't lay me down on the bed, Julie, it will hurt too much." "Okay, Dear." Julie carefully laid her down on the throw rug beside her bed in a fashion so that Koweena's bottom would be resting on the rug. Julie sat next to Koweena with her legs overlapping one another so that she could look Koweena in the eyes. "When did this happen to you, Sweetheart?" "This afternoon," Koweena replied. "Is this the only time this has happened, or has it happened before?" Julie braced herself for the answer. "It's happened before." "How many times, Kowie?" "One time before this one." Koweena was so young already, how could this have happened before? Julie thought. "Was it because of the way I look, Julie?" "No, no, Sweetheart, you are the most beautiful thing I have ever seen, it wasn't because of the way you look, don't even think that." Julie didn't know for sure, it could have been for all she knew; she was just trying to console her precious Kowie. "What did I do wrong? Why did they hurt me?" Koweena softly asked. The words from Koweena were breaking Julie's heart. "I don't know, Sweetheart, but everything is going to be okay." Julie felt helpless by saying those words to Koweena. The pain and abuse had already been inflicted, and yet she was telling her that everything was going to be alright. She felt like there was nothing she could do or say to make things better for Koweena. As Julie began to ask the next question, she began to get nervous, her throat tightened once more because she knew that this next answer might cause her to have another outburst of crying, and she didn't want to do it in front of Koweena. With a shaky voice she asked. "Kowie, when was the last time this happened?" "When I was five." Julie wasn't prepared for that answer, without realizing it she had let out a loud gasp of air which permeated the room. She quickly put her hand to her mouth and once again began crying so hard that she could hardly breathe. "Five years old! How could someone do that to a five year old?" Julie was thinking as she cried. Somehow she was able to keep it quiet and hide her emotions from Koweena. After a few minutes of crying, Julie composed herself, she began to ask two gut wrenching questions. Questions she dreaded to know the answer to, but she had to know. "Was it worse than this one?" "No," Koweena answered in a shaky voice. Even though the first one was not as bad as this one, the answer didn't make Julie feel any less sorrowful. Now, the second gut wrenching question for Julie. "Was it before or after you met me?" "Before," Koweena replied. It seemed selfish for Julie to be thinking of herself under these circumstances, but once again the answer didn't make Julie feel any less heavy-hearted; but she knew at that point that it was not all completely her fault. "Both times," Koweena began saying, "I just kept saying 'I'll be good,' 'I'll be good, please stop,' but they would only hit me even harder every time I spoke up." Koweena began sobbing once again. Julie just couldn't believe the brutality on this innocent little child's body with which she was witnessing. It was tearing her up inside just to look at Koweena's bloody body. "How many times did they hit you, Kowie?" "When, this time or the last?" "Both times?" Julie asked. "I don't know, I lost count after about the sixth time." "Were you the only one being hit?" "Yeah, this time they tied my hands up with a rope and made me lay across a bench. Both times they ripped my shirt off and that's when the stinging and burning started on my back, and this time on my arms. Both times I wasn't doing anything wrong; I was just minding my own business. What did I do to deserve this?" Koweena asked, sobbing once again. "I don't know, Sweetheart, I don't know." Tears began freely falling down Julie's face as well. She was trying to grasp what she was looking at. "Do you know who did this, Kowie?" "I kept hearing the name Ray, I recognized it because it was the same name I heard the first time I was beaten." It was impossible for Julie to wrap her brain around the fact that someone her father had hired could have beaten a little child, not once, but twice. Julie carefully lifted up Koweena's shirt again, this time to get a closer look at her back. Through the fresh bloody strips from this beating she could see welled up scars that had formed from her previous beating. She counted the fresh lashes on her back. At that point, Julie went from feeling sad, to feeling irate. Julie stroked Koweena's hair. "I'll be right back, Dear." Julie said as she quickly left the room.

Julie immediately rushed downstairs to her father's office. "What the hell did you do!? How could you do it!?" Julie was standing just inside her father's office, shaking from head to toe she was so infuriated. "Julie, I don't know what you're talking about, just calm down." "Oh, don't play dumb with me, dad! A mere child!? An innocent helpless child!? Eight years old! I saw with my own eyes, dad! Fifteen lashes on her back, not to mention her arms! Fifteen! Who would do something like that to a little girl!? His name is Ray, you find this man, dad, you find this man and you make him pay, and you make sure that he can never do this to a child again!" Her father immediately looked down at his desk. Neither of them spoke again for what seemed like hours. The silence was deafening. To Julie it seemed like forever before her father finally looked up at her. "Don't worry about it, Dear, it's none of your concern." Her father's response made Julie lose control. "Kowie is my concern, when she hurts I hurt! You might as well have beaten me, you bastard! I can't stand to even look at you right now!" "I have a certain reputation to uphold, Julie." "What the hell does that mean, huh?" Julie interrupted, "what the hell does that mean!?" Julie was yelling so hard that her entire body was convulsing. Julie didn't realize it at the time because she was so uncontrollably irate, but she was actually making things worse on Koweena. Koweena could clearly hear the yelling. It was only making her hurt even more. She was afraid now that Mr. Defour would come up there and hit her. Before this, she had been able to stop her sobbing, but this caused her to begin crying out loud for the first time since being in the house that day. The shaking of her body from the crying made her shirt rub against her scars, only making the pain worse, which in turn only caused her to cry that much harder. "You're a jackass, you know that, dad! If you're responsible for this, I swear I'll not only never speak to you again, but I'll remove myself from your life completely!" "Don't talk to your father like that!" Julie's mother interrupted as she came into the office. She could hear the yelling from the living room and came to investigate. "What's going on in here, Julie? Why are you talking to your father like that?" "He beat Koweena, mother," Julie was so exhausted after what had transpired over the last hour that she didn't have the strength to yell at her mother. Her father stood up from his desk chair. "That's not true, Julie," he said. "Don't talk to me, dad!" Julie was back to yelling. "Dear, just calm down, your father did no such of a thing." Her mother, while saying this, tried to put her hand on Julie's shoulder. "Get your hand off of me, mother!" Julie shouted out. "Did you know she's been beaten twice, that's right, twice!?" Julie continued. "A little child, mother, has already been beaten twice! Not only that, mother, but she believes that the same man did it both times! Now I told dad that he better deal with this man, or else!" "Or else what, Julie?" Her mother asked. "Or else you guys will never see me again, I'll take Koweena and we'll go live with Thomas, and you can kiss that great wedding you have planned and your relationship with me goodbye!" "Don't you think you're overreacting, Dear," her father said. "Overreacting! You should look at her, dad, she's covered in blood!" It would be hard for Julie to just get up and leave her parents, she was too dependant on her parent's wealth. "Julie, you need to quite yelling, especially at your father, that's very disrespectful, and besides your cheeks are starting to flush, and you're starting to sweat," her mother said. "Stop it, mother. Is any of what I'm saying even getting through to you guys!?"

Julie's mother was the typical plantation owner's wife. She conducted strict tea and brunch schedules with the other top elite socialite wives of the area. She was many times the hostess of social parties and gatherings for the upper-class business men and their families. Mrs. Defour was a perfectionists, and she pushed the envelope of perfection onto her daughter. Mrs. Defour not only pushed Julie to the limit when it came to her education, but with Julie being the only child, it made the nitpicking, perfect-tweaking mother almost intolerable. Mrs. Defour's childhood was spent being pushed at being the perfect wife and mother. The problem was that not only did she aim for perfection from herself, but she pushed it onto her daughter. During this time she lacked one important element in her life, feelings. Mrs. Defour was void of any feelings, and her lack of compassion only drove Julie farther apart from her as she grew older. The same could be said of Mr. Defour. Although he didn't push Julie to be perfect, he was distant from her. Despite this, Julie was indeed spoiled, spoiled in the sense that she got anything she wanted. That is if defining being spoiled is getting a lot of material things and getting your way every time, while at the same time lacking the affection from either parent. Pacifying Julie is what it could be better defined as. Despite this kind of treatment by her parents, Julie was the opposite of her parents. Opposite in that instead of perfection taking precedence over feelings and compassion, Julie's life was ruled not by perfection, but by compassion. She showed it by respecting the slaves that she came into contact with, and she showed it especially in her affection toward Koweena.

Julie stormed out of the office; she wanted nothing to do with her parents. Could Mr. Defour have been the mastermind behind this much more brutal beating of Koweena? It's important to note here that Mr. Defour was over the control of three hundred slaves and around seventy five overseers on a roughly nine square mile piece of land, almost half the size of the town in which he lived, not to mention being responsible for the entire operation of the success financially of the Plantation. He had no contact whatsoever with his slaves. He depended heavily on delegating authority; there was no way one man could control that big of an operation by himself. He also depended heavily on the overseers to watch over the slaves to make sure they did as they were told so Mr. Defour could focus all his time on his successful financial operation. Remember though, it would be impossible for one slave owner to know the goings on of every slave at every minute of the day, especially in such a large plantation as the one Mr. Defour owned. However, he was very upset that day at finding out about Julie's relationship to Koweena; but would he have had enough time to orchestrate the beating just moments after his talk with Julie? Could it have been Mr. Jenkins that ordered the assault on Koweena? His hatred of Julie's relationship with Koweena had been building for years. One thing is for sure, they both had the motive. And let's not forget about Ray. He had had it in for Koweena from day one, without anyone instigating it either. Sure he brought Charles along for the ride a time or two, but Ray and Ray only, was the one who hated Koweena, except of course for Mr. Jenkins and now, after this day, Mr. Defour himself. One thing is a definite, they all hated Koweena, and what had she done to deserve such hatred? Absolutely nothing. Who was really behind the beating of Koweena that day? And would Julie ever really know if her time spent with Koweena was the real reason behind her beating?

"Honey, did you have that little Nigger beaten today?" Mrs. Defour asked her husband after Julie left the office. Mr. Defour sat back down in his chair. "Close the door, Sweetheart, we need to talk."

Meanwhile, Julie was slowly walking back up the stairs toward her bedroom. Her face was enshrouded with emotions. She only got up to the third step when she collapsed onto the stairs beneath her; she was bombarded with feelings of despair. As she sat there on the steps, she cried for what seemed like hours during that late autumn afternoon. The late afternoon sunlight streamed from the semi-circle window above the front door, permeating onto the staircase as Julie sat there wondering what to do next. The racing thoughts of Koweena's beating, and visualizing her stretched over a board taking the lashes, echoed in her head. Yet, she still had to compose herself, she did not want Koweena to see her upset, worsening her already fragile state. After several minutes of hard crying, Julie was calm now, yet the pain of her precious Kowie being so brutally beaten was still there, like a knife penetrating her heart. After giving it some serious thought in the quietness of the moment on those stairs, Julie knew before she entered the room what she was going to do to try and ease Koweena's pain. How though? Reversing the psychological damage that had been done to this eight year old little girl, now her second time at being beaten; seemed impossible. Her nightmares, the not understanding what she had done to deserve such pain, the crushing blow to her fragile self-esteem, the repetitious question that would play over and over in her mind, "What did I do?", something that took her a long time to overcome when she was just five. Yet this child would have to overcome it again. Could she do it again? What could Julie possibly have in mind to ease her pain? Julie was ready to make her move. She slowly got up from the steps and began to proceed up toward her room. She knew what awaited her there; a shattered and battered little girl who needed her desperately.

As Julie entered the room she knew she had to be as delicate with Koweena as possible. She went over to her. Koweena was lying on the floor in a fetal position. The mere sight of her in that position broke Julie's heart even further. She noticed Koweena was holding on tightly to the necklace Julie gave her which was around her neck. Julie's heart was breaking more and more with every step she took toward the broken, crushed, and devastated Koweena. As Julie stared at her as she continued walking closer to her she couldn't help but think back to the last couple of years, especially the months after Koweena got her play and study room. How happy and excited she was about life, how motivated she was at studying and learning. All of that work Julie had put into making sure she was no longer that depressed little girl she first saw in her downstairs living room when Koweena was five, had seemed to fade. All of that progress seemed lost now as Koweena laid there sucking her thumb and holding onto the necklace. Julie was crushed as she stared upon the girl she thought of as her very own. She was no longer thinking of her happy afternoon with Thomas, that moment was long gone, in the here and now of the moment. Julie, now standing over Koweena, bent over and with her left hand she gently touched Koweena's shoulder and whispered in her right ear. "You did nothing to deserve this, Sweetheart. I'm here for you now and I'm not going to leave your side." It was the only thing Julie could say at that moment, the only thing she could think of to try and lift Koweena's spirits. Julie would try something else to sooth Koweena, she had it all planned out, planning it all out on the steps just moments earlier of how to make Koweena's situation better. Julie walked over to the piano, sat down on the bench; Koweena was still lying in a fetal position on the floor as Julie began playing. She was just playing a melody, but it wasn't just any melody, it was the melody to the first song Koweena had ever learned. It was not only the first song she had ever heard, but it was the first song she ever learned to sing. Julie didn't sing on that terrible afternoon, she just wanted Koweena to hear the music. Koweena, quietly sobbing, listened to the melody, suddenly the words came flooding into her mind as she laid there thinking to herself, "Why did those men hurt me again?" After playing and looking at Koweena for several minutes, Julie noticed that her sobbing wasn't stopping. "I know what she needs," thought Julie, "she needs to be held." Julie got up from the piano and walked up to Koweena. "I'll be back, Kowie, just one second." Julie walked over to the play and study room and immediately saw what she was looking for. It was lying on the leather couch, the first book Julie ever read to Koweena. It was worn and tattered due to Koweena's use of it so much in the past; Koweena read the book almost daily. She had especially grown close to it since it survived the burning of her furniture and other books at her shack just months prior. Julie grabbed a hold of the well handled book and walked back into her room. She walked over to Koweena and again bent over her, this time she reached over with her arm and held the book in front of Koweena at an angle so that Koweena's eyes would be able to glance at it. Julie knelt down now with the book still stretched out in front of Koweena. She just knelt there waiting for Koweena to move. "Look, Dear, it's okay," Julie said. Koweena didn't move, she was still frightened that Mr. Defour was going to come up there and start the nightmare all over again. "Why won't you look, Sweetheart?" Finally Koweena spoke up. "I'm afraid your dad is going to come up here and hit me." "No, no, no, my Precious, that's not going to happen. Kowie, I'm right here, no one is going to hurt you." Julie suddenly had thoughts of Koweena going back to her shack and living in that terrible place. Julie knew from past experiences in her own life, that that place was not a good area of the plantation, but she now realized just how bad of a place it truly was. She just wished she hadn't learned it at Koweena's expense. "She's not going back there," Julie thought to herself. As Julie continued to hold Koweena's favorite book out in front of her, and after several minutes had passed, Koweena finally looked up at Julie as she still clutched onto her necklace tightly in that same fetal position. "Can I hold you?" Julie asked in a soft, gentle voice. "It will hurt." "I will be gentle, Kowie." After a couple of minutes had passed Koweena began to get up from a position she had been in for quite some time. Julie walked over to her closet and grabbed a blanket. She took Koweena by the hand and gently sat her upright. Koweena was careful not to touch the bed and risk rubbing her scars against it. Julie wrapped her arm around Koweena with the blanket in hand, carefully and gently, so as to not aggravate her wounds. She put Koweena's head on her shoulder and slowly leaned back against the bed. "Did the sponge and ointment make it feel any better?" Julie asked. "A little," Koweena responded. Koweena enjoyed being in the safe arms of Julie. After several minutes of silence, and Julie kissing on Koweena's head, Julie opened up the book and began reading to Koweena. After reading for a little while Koweena's sobbing started up again. "I know what you need, Dear," Julie said. She closed the book, put it to her side and began singing to her. She was singing that song; that very same first song, the song Julie had played on the piano just moments ago, the song Koweena had learned two and a half years ago in this very same room.

The sunlight, which just moments ago was bouncing off the walls of the bedroom, had now gone behind the trees. The light that was on in the room began to saturate the room throughout. For Koweena, the room began to look like it did that night Julie first taught her that song. For the first time that day, it brought her comfort. Between the familiar scenery in the bedroom, and the song Julie was softly singing to her, and being in the clutches of Julie's arms, Koweena began to feel safe. Julie just sat there singing with her beautiful voice over and over again the words to the song, words that rang out again and again in that room that evening, "I'll never quit, I'll never give up, nothing can hurt me as long as I keep my head up and continue on," the song said. After about fifteen minutes of singing, the sobbing stopped. Julie just kept right on singing that song and cuddling Koweena until finally the day had completely turned into night. "I bet you're hungry aren't you?" Julie asked. "Yeah," Koweena responded. "I have something in addition to your regular supper." "What?" Koweena asked with curiosity. "Apple pie!" Julie said with enthusiasm while gently squeezing Koweena. "How does that sound!?" "Okay," Koweena said with a smile. When Julie saw that smile it melted her heart. It had been a long emotional day for the both of them and that smile helped them both. "I'll be right back." Julie said as she got up and went into Koweena's play and study room and grabbed a couple of Koweena's favorite dolls from the book case. She then grabbed a few doll clothes and accessories and went back into her bedroom. "Here you go, Sweetheart. I'll be right back with your food." As Julie was making her way out of the bedroom, Koweena began to take the focus off of her pain and onto her dolls, playing with them quietly. As Julie was walking toward the kitchen she ran into her mother. "Mother, you scared me; I wasn't expecting to run into you." "Julie, I want to talk about what happened today. "Mother." "Julie, you're going to listen. I will not tolerate you taking sides with that Nigger over your father, do you hear me?" That set Julie off. "Well, mother, you are going to listen to me, and I don't want you to talk back. Koweena is going to stay with me tonight, and not just tonight, but from here on out." "Julie." "Mother." "Julie." "Mother." "Julie, you know what your father can do." "What does that mean!?" Julie asked, visibly upset by the comment of her mother. "I'm just saying, Julie, your father," "no, mother, you listen," Julie interrupted, "I've had a very long day, and I'm not about to stand here and argue with you on this, Koweena is staying. After what she has been through she at least deserves that." "I'm through talking with you," her mother said as she stormed off into the living room.

"You tell me what I can do to make things better for you, Kowie," Julie said as she does her nightly ritual of watching Koweena eat. "Will you play dress up with my dolls and dress up like they do?" "Absolutely," Julie said. Watching Julie dress up like Koweena's dolls was the most fun and most enjoyable thing for Koweena. She enjoyed that more than any other thing her and Julie would do together. She would get such enjoyment out of watching Julie dress up. Julie enjoyed it too; she enjoyed getting a kick out of watching Koweena's facial expressions as she dressed up in different attire, matching what the dolls were wearing. They both loved it, and that night, they both needed the enjoyment desperately. "How does this look, Kowie," Julie said with a smile. "I love it, Julie, try something else on," Koweena said laughing. The activity was beginning to work for the both of them. Although Koweena was still hurting physically, emotionally she was improving. Accessorizing her dolls and watching Julie get all dressed up caused Koweena to come out of her catatonic state. It was just what the doctor ordered.

So ultimately after staring, gazing, and curiously wondering what it would be like to stay the night at the beautiful Defour house for the last two and a half years, Koweena finally got her chance. That night, as the moon shown through the window next to Julie's bed, Koweena laid there, cuddled right up next to Julie. There was no other place she would rather be at that particular moment in time, heck, no place she would rather be ever. Julie's bed was the most comfortable thing she had ever lain on in her entire life. She couldn't believe she was about to go to sleep on such a warm, soothing piece of material. Even though her back was hurting, the bed was so soft that she was able to lie on her back. Although she was broken in spirit, saddened, and scared, at the same time, she was living a dream. Despite her obvious troubled feelings, being next to Julie as she was on that bed, made her feel safer than she had ever felt. For a brief moment in time, as Julie lay there sound asleep, Koweena felt like those princesses she had read about in all of those books. She fought back the sleep that was trying to overtake her because she just simply did not want this night, this moment, this feeling, to end. Did anyone else deserve to experience what Koweena was experiencing that night more than Koweena? Consider the day she had had and the life she had lived up to that point; and the fact that the pajamas Julie lent her were rubbing against the sores on her back and arms. No one deserved it more. Koweena was about to say something she was scared to say. After all, she had only said these words to her mother; she had never said them to anyone else before. She had always been fearful of the response she might get out of Julie if she said it, so she thought she would say it while Julie was asleep, thinking Julie wouldn't hear her. As Koweena was drifting off to sleep she whispered out loud, "I love you, Julie." She had refrained from telling Julie that for such a long time even though Koweena loved Julie for years now, after the hurt she had been through she was just afraid to express her feelings to Julie, or to anyone for that matter. It was a big step for her to say that to someone out loud, especially to Julie. Thinking Julie was asleep she thought she wouldn't hear a response. But to Koweena's surprise she heard a response from the other side of the bed. "I love you too, Kowie," Julie said as she rolled over and wrapped her arm around Koweena and cuddled her tightly to her. Koweena's mouth and eyes opened wide. After that, Koweena just simply gave a big smile from ear to ear. Julie had just told her that she loved her; it didn't get any better than that she thought. She then drifted off to sleep. It was the best sleep she had experienced in her entire life.

Chapter 8   Gaining Confidence

Koweena had been living and sleeping at the Defour house, in Julie's bed, with Julie right alongside her, for several months now without being detected by Mr. Defour. The house was so large, and had so many rooms, not to mention the large number of servants busily going about the house, that it was easy to lose Koweena in the sheer size and activity that the house brought. It was quite easy to sneak Koweena out of the house early in the morning in order for her to go do her daily chores out in the fields. Julias would just simply wait at the front door for her, when she arrived from Julie's upstairs bedroom to the front door, he would then walk her to her assigned row for the day. Julie's mother knew that Koweena was staying in the house, but she kept it from her husband. With Mr. Defour engrossed in his business, he never suspected a thing. After receiving her second beating in three years, living in the big house was exactly what Koweena needed to heal emotionally, especially sleeping next to Julie each and every night. She couldn't ask for anything better. During her time staying there, especially at night and early in the morning, she actually felt like a white person. One, because Julie treated her like one, and two, she was constantly surrounded by all the material things white people enjoyed most. It made her feel like one of them, except of course when she would spend her day out in the fields, it was then that she was brought back to reality.

"Julie, come in here for just a minute!?" Mr. Defour yelled from the living room one night as he caught Julie sneaking downstairs toward the kitchen during her nightly ritual of getting Koweena her dinner.

"Coming, dad!" Julie yelled back from the hallway where she almost made it to Martha in the kitchen who had Koweena's meal ready and waiting. Julie walked into the living room. "What is it, dad?" "Come in here and sit on the sofa for a minute," her father said. Julie's mind began to race as she made her way over to the sofa. "Does he know about Koweena?" She thought. As Julie sat down, Mr. Defour began to talk. "Julie, is that Nigger still walking the halls of this house?" Julie spoke up with a nervous giggle. "What makes you think that, daddy? Why, have you seen her?" "No, I haven't seen her, Julie, but I just have a funny feeling that you're keeping something from me." "What could I possibly be keeping from you, dad?" Meanwhile, Mrs. Defour was just sitting in her chair opposite of Mr. Defour, drinking her nightly brandy in silence. She was giving Julie a stern look as if to be saying "keep quiet." Julie glanced over at her mother and noticed the look. "Dad, if you haven't seen her then what's the problem?" "Julie, I don't want to see that Nigger around here. It would be a terrible embarrassment to me if you were still hanging around that wench. My reputation would be ruined. You wouldn't want that now would you?" "Dad, first of all watch your language." Mrs. Defour cleared her throat as she looked at Julie. She was trying to give her a clear signal not to upset her father. Julie quickly got the picture from her mother and changed the subject. "Dad, just relax, you worry too much. You have this big Plantation to worry about. Everything is hunky-dory, just worry about your business, okay, dad." Julie looked over at her mother; Mrs. Defour gave an approving smile. "Can I go now, dad?" "Sure, Honey, I didn't mean to disrupt your evening, go ahead." Julie wanted desperately to ask her father if he had done anything to that overseer she had mention to him about, the overseer that Koweena had told her about several months back, and the one who may have beaten her twice. During that time she threatened her father that if he didn't do anything about that man that she was going to pack her things and leave, but she didn't mention it to him that night. She thought she would leave well enough alone.

"Julie, I want to teach Josi like you have been teaching me," Koweena said that night as she was eating her dinner. That brought a big smile on Julie's face. Julie could clearly see the results her efforts were making on Koweena. "That sounds like a great idea, Kowie." "I was hoping she could come over this weekend and I could teach her how to read. Would that be okay?" "Absolutely, Dear, just have her ready when Julias comes to pick you up on Saturday morning."

The next day in the cotton fields Josi was working alongside of Koweena. "Josi, I have some good news for you." "What is it, Koweena?" "I talked to Julie and she said it would be alright for you to come over to her house Saturday." "Wow, is you serious?" "Sure, and I'll get to teach you how to read and everything. We can play with my dolls and stuff." "That sounds awesome, Koweena!" "Shut up over there!" An overseer yelled out. "You shut up!" Koweena yelled out. "What is you doin, Koweena, my goodness, we is both goin to get in a lot of trouble with you yellin back at an overseer like that!" "Don't worry about it, Josi." What had got into Koweena? Had living at the Defour's made her think she had the right to yell back like that? Or maybe she had been beaten so much that she just didn't care. Whatever the reason it was a new side of Koweena, a brave side. The overseer walked over to where Koweena was. She was kneeling down picking cotton as he stood over top of her. "What did you say to me, you little bitch!" "I said, you, shut up!" Josi couldn't believe her own ears. "I have a mind to stick you in that pit, you little Nigger, for talking to me like that!" The overseer said, now leaning over, right on top of Koweena. "Your words and your rifle don't scare me. Go ahead and do that if it makes you feel any better." Something had definitely got into Koweena that day. She was becoming her own person; she was standing up for herself. Maybe it was because she knew deep down that Julie would protect her. Koweena, now nine, was growing up. It could be due to all that education she was receiving. Whatever caused her to talk back, one thing was for sure, Koweena was no longer that timid, frightened little girl she had once been. The overseer was taken back a bit by her bravery, it stunned him somewhat. "Now, if you're not going to do anything to me, I suggest you get back to your post," Koweena said sternly. The overseer was so completely stunned that he actually began to respect Koweena for her bravery. He stood up from leaning over Koweena and walked back over to where he had been standing before. "Wow, if that's what bein educated and livin with Julie is all about, I want some of that!" Josi stunningly said. "I will give you some of that, Josi, this Saturday." "Will it be for just one day?" Josi asked. "No, I'll arrange it so that you can come over, not every weekend, but most every weekend." Koweena didn't want to go too far, she didn't want to share Julie with Josi that much. Julie was very protective of Koweena, but Koweena was just the same way. She wanted Julie all to herself. That is why she didn't care much for Thomas. Even though Thomas was very good to Koweena, she still didn't have much use for him. Thomas would spend many an evening helping Koweena with her homework, and even playing with Koweena; but Koweena would never say thank you or smile at Thomas. She was always jealous of him because he took Julie away from her.

"Koweena, you're doing very well," Thomas told Koweena as he was helping Koweena study math one night in her play and study room. Thomas was especially good at math with his job as a land surveyor, he had to be good at it, he used it all the time while on the job. "How are things going in here, you two?" Julie asked as she walked into the play and study room. "Fine, Dear," Thomas replied. "Kowie, how are things going?" Julie asked Koweena. "Fine, I guess," Koweena said snobbishly. She didn't want Thomas in there with her. For years Thomas stayed out of Koweena's time spent with Julie, but more increasingly, over the last eight months, Thomas had been spending time with both Koweena and Julie. What used to be just Koweena and Julie's time spent together on weeknights and weekends; was now being invaded by Thomas. He had now begun spending that time with them during what Koweena thought was sacred time with Julie. Koweena didn't like it one bit. That night after Thomas left Koweena approached Julie on the subject in Julie's, and now Koweena's bedroom. Koweena approached Julie and grabbed her hand. "Julie, I don't like Thomas." "Kowie, he's been spending all this time with you, what, about eight or nine months now, and I've been with him for years, and you're just now telling me this." "I didn't want to interfere," Koweena said. "You still could have told me a while back, Kowie; you know I wouldn't think you were interfering. You're the biggest part of my life, how you feel affects my life in a big way, don't you realize that by now?" "I guess, I know how much you like him, or love him by now, and well, I just didn't want to get in the way of that." Julie was stroking Koweena's hair. "You know, I didn't want to tell you this, but I picked up on the fact that you didn't like me seeing him a long time ago," Julie said. "You did!" Koweena said, sounding surprised. "Yeah, I should have said something back then, but I didn't. Listen, Koweena, there's something important I need to tell you. Here, have a seat on my bed." Koweena sat on the bed while Julie sat beside her. Koweena had a serious look on her face. "What is it, Julie?" "Kowie, Thomas and I are going to get married." "What? When?" Koweena asked with an upset expression. "Well, it's November right now, so next April is when it's going to happen." "So just five months from now!" Koweena said, still visibly upset. "Koweena, I know you're not happy about this, but it's actually great news. You will get to live with me and have your very own room with your own bed!" That changed Koweena's prospective a bit. She was no longer upset. All she could think about was having her own room. "There's a catch though, Kowie, and I'm so sorry to have to tell you this, it really pains me to tell you, but the house will still be on this property." Julie's attachment to her parent's wealth was too great for her to turn down the idea of still living on her parent's property. "This means you will still have to work in the fields. There was nothing I could do about that." Koweena quickly went back to being upset. "But, Julie, I thought that, well, I thought we were going to move away from here." "I know it, Kowie, and I'm sorry. Just look at it this way, no more sneaking around. What do you think about that!?" "Yeah, but I'll still have to work. I'll still have to worry about those damned overseers." "Kowie, I don't know if you're going to understand this or not, but sometimes you have to compromise on things." Koweena was puzzled. "What do you mean, compromise?" "That's a big word I know. Basically what it means is that you can't always get your way all the time. Sometimes you have to take the good with the bad. You have good things and you have bad things, both in your life, and sometimes you have to give up the good things. That's what compromising means." "I understand," Koweena said as she looked down at the floor. "At least I'll still be with you," Koweena said. That made Julie's eyes tear up. Julie hated breaking the news to her that she would still have to work, but she could see in Koweena's eyes that having her own room made up for the disappointment. Julie was enthusiastic. "Hey, I know what will make things better for you!" She said. "What?" Koweena asked. "You can sit in front of the mirror and I can fix you up, dress your long, curly hair up and everything. How does that sound?" "Okay!" Koweena said with excitement. She loved for Julie to play with her hair and twirl and twist it all up into a fancy design.

Christmas was coming up soon and it always made Koweena nervous during that time, mainly because she didn't want to run into the Defours. It would be her fifth Christmas spent with Julie at the Defour house. The first year was the nightmare Christmas, when she almost threw up all over the sofa with all those white folks sitting around her when she first saw Mr. Defour in the living room. Unbelievably, after all these years, it was still the only time Koweena had a close encounter with the Plantation owner. The other four Christmases, Koweena had spent them in Julie's room, the entire day. On this special day, as she did every weeknight and weekend, Julie would sneak downstairs to get Martha to prepare Koweena a meal and she would sneak it back upstairs for Koweena to enjoy, this time though, as in Christmases past, it would be a special holiday meal.

"Merry Christmas, Koweena!" Julie told Koweena as they were sitting up in Julie's bedroom that Christmas morning in front of Julie's big mirror, while Julie was fixing up Koweena to look extra pretty for the day. Koweena was wearing a velveteen green dress with white cuffs attached at the end of the sleeves around her wrists. The dress buttoned up from her backside. She wore white tights and black patent shoes to go with the dress. "Julie, why do you fix me up so? All I do is stay in your room all day." "I thought you liked it when I dressed you up?" Koweena was touching her primped up, long, flowing, curly hair. "I do, I love it, but I guess I just don't see the point, that's all." "Tonight we are going to do something different than we have in the past Christmases, Kowie." "What, Julie?" "Well, after everyone leaves and my parents go to bed for the evening, were going to sneak downstairs and have Christmas with Martha, Julias, and the other slaves from the household, in the kitchen. How does that sound?" Koweena was enthusiastic. "I love that idea!" She said. Julie was putting the final touches on Koweena's hair. "I thought you would. You look so pretty, Kowie," "You look pretty too, Julie," Koweena said. Julie was wearing a red velveteen vest with a plaid skirt and black socks with black, suede high heeled shoes. Julie spoke up as she was stroking Koweena's hair. "Let me go downstairs for a minute and make my yearly appearance in the living room, and I'll be right back, I have a special gift I want to give you, I think you'll like it." "Awesome!" Koweena said with great anticipation.

Koweena glanced over at Julie's dresser as she was sitting in front of the mirror, while Julie was downstairs, and noticed a tiny wrapped square box with a bow on top. She became very curious and wanted desperately to open it. Her excitement was about to get the best of her. "That has to be the gift Julie's talking about," she thought to herself. "No, I'll wait for Julie to come back up and give it to me," Koweena said to herself. Julie usually only stayed downstairs for an hour during Christmas, but on this day, an hour came and went. It had now been two hours, and two hours turned into four hours, and still no sign of Julie. Koweena was starting to get upset, after all, this day belonged to her and Julie. After Julie had been gone now for five hours, the slow build up of Koweena wanting to cry came to the forefront, she began crying out loud. She was crying so hard that her mascara was beginning to run. Julie could faintly hear her crying from downstairs. She quickly became disturbed. "Well, good day everybody, I think I'm just going to go back upstairs and retire for the day. Mom, dad, Merry Christmas, I'll see you tomorrow." "Merry Christmas, Sweetheart," Mrs. Defour told Julie as Julie left the living room and headed upstairs. As Julie entered the room she noticed Koweena sitting on the throw rug by their bed sobbing. "Koweena, Dear, I brought you something to eat." Koweena pointed to Thomas who was standing next to Julie. "What is he doing here!? He doesn't belong here!" Koweena shouted. "Koweena!" Julie said abruptly. "Well, he doesn't!" Koweena said sternly. "Honey, why don't you go back downstairs, just tell my parents I wasn't feeling well as to the reason why you went back down there alone," Julie said to Thomas. "Sure, Sweetheart," Thomas said. "Koweena, I didn't mean to upset you," Thomas continued, "I thought you would be use to me by now." "Just get out!" Koweena shouted. "Okay, Koweena, that's enough," Julie calmly said. "Thomas, I'll see you later, okay," Julie continued. Thomas gave Julie a kiss on the lips and left the room and headed for the stairs. "Koweena, I'm sorry I didn't come back up sooner, I just lost track of time." Thomas ran back in Julie's room and planted another kiss on Julie's lips. Koweena could only roll her eyes at, what she thought, was a disgusting scene. "I just had to give you one more kiss, Julie, before I left." "Thank you, Thomas, Dear, good night." "Good night, my Angel," Thomas said as he left the room and closed the door behind him. "You know how important these days are for us to spend together, Julie, and yet I had to sit up here all alone," Koweena said, still sobbing. "Here, let me get a towel and wipe your face off," Julie said. "Save it, Julie, why don't you just leave so I can be alone for the rest of the day." "Okay, Kowie, that's enough of that, I said I was sorry, it was just a few extra hours, that's all." "Five hours, Julie, time you spent with Thomas instead of me!" "Look, Kowie, I'm trying to do the best I can with spending time with you while also spending some time with Thomas. I'm trying not to leave the both of you out in the cold. Thomas is a part of my life; you have to accept that fact." "You left *me* out in the cold today, Julie, today of all days!" "Kowie, I said I was sorry. Look, I have something for you!" Julie decided not to get a towel to clean Koweena up, her face still had makeup running down both cheeks as Julie, wanting to change the subject, went over to the dresser to get that little wrapped box Koweena had been staring at all day long. "I don't want it!" Koweena said forcefully. Julie stopped on her way to the dresser after Koweena said that and turned to face Koweena. "Look, Koweena, I said I was sorry. Listen, I spend more time with you than I do Thomas, you know that. What more do you want from me?" "When it's Christmas time, I want you to spend it with me, is that too much to ask?" Koweena asked. "I'm here, Baby, I'm right here," Julie said. "We're going to spend the rest of the evening together. We have that party to go to down in the kitchen tonight, we're going to have a good time alright, just relax," Julie said. Julie was feeling the strain of trying to share her time with both Koweena and Thomas. She felt bad at what she had done to Koweena, but she had to spend some time with Thomas; she hurt Koweena unintentionally of course in doing that. "Kowie, do you forgive me? I'm really sorry. Just try to understand that I'm trying to make you and Thomas both happy. Can you see it from my prospective?" "I don't want you to make Thomas happy," Koweena said in a mean tone. "Listen, Koweena, Thomas is going to be my husband in just a few months. Now you need to get used to that or we're in for a tough road. It's been years now that he's been in my life, you need to start accepting him by now." Koweena had gone quite a while resenting Thomas, even though he was very good to her. "Has Thomas done anything to hurt you?" Julie asked. "No," Koweena responded. "And has he been good to you?" Julie continued asking. "Yes," Koweena said. "Okay then, there's no need in you being so upset at him. You need to understand that he is a part of my life, and in turn, that means that he is a part of your life as well." "I know," Koweena said as she stared down at the floor. "Please don't look down at the floor, it breaks my heart when you look down with that long face," Julie said in a tense voice. Ever since Julie saw her that very first day they met in her downstairs living room, looking down at the floor so depressingly, she hated seeing Koweena with that long face staring at the floor. "Will you look at me?" Julie asked Koweena. Koweena looked up with mascara running down both her cheeks. "I promise," Julie continued, "I don't mean to hurt you. The last thing I ever want to do is hurt you. Let's just forget about this, okay?" After Koweena stared at Julie in the eyes for a moment she finally spoke up. "Okay, Julie, I'm sorry." "Will you open your gift now?" Julie asked. "Okay," Koweena responded in a low, soft tone. Julie picked up the wrapped box from on top of her dresser and walked over to Koweena and sat down on the rug right in front of her. Julie was gripped with excitement. "Open it!" She said. Koweena quickly opened up the box, the eagerness to see what was inside caused her to forget about her feelings of abandonment by Julie, and her anger towards Thomas. As she opened up the top of the box her eyes got as big as saucers. "I had it hand crafted just for you, Kowie," Julie said as she began to get emotional due to all the hard work she had put into the gift and watching Koweena's reaction to it. Koweena glanced upon the object with her mouth open. It was a ring with a giant, pink sapphire stone set in a gold band. "Go ahead, Kowie, try it on!" Julie said, choking back the tears. Koweena put it on her right ring finger. "It looks so beautiful on you," Julie said. "Of course anything would look beautiful on you, but this ring, wow!" Julie continued. Koweena, now, also began choking back the tears. "I love it, Julie. How did you, I mean, how did you know that?" "I knew pink was your favorite color," Julie interrupted, "and well." "How did you know pink was my favorite color?" Koweena interrupted right back. "I notice the little things about you, Kowie. Little things that I observe when you don't think I notice." "But how?" "Well, I noticed one day when we were out planting flowers in the garden, you asked me why I didn't have any pink roses with me instead of just white and red. And when we were talking about what you wanted your new room to look like at my new home, you said you wanted pink curtains. I was also making a pink dress for you one night while you were studying and I noticed your eyes lit up like a Christmas tree when you saw it. So I put two and two together and realized that pink was your favorite color." "You really do love me!" Koweena said with a surprised tone in her voice. "Yes, Kowie, more than you know."

In the meantime, downstairs in the living room, Thomas approached Mr. Jenkins as everyone was getting ready to leave the Christmas party. "Mr. Jenkins?" "Yes, Thomas, my boy, what can I do for you?" "I was wondering if I could walk with you as you made your way home tonight. I would like to talk to you about something. Would that be alright?" "Sure, let's go," Mr. Jenkins said. As they were walking down the Defour's rocky driveway toward Mr. Jenkins' house, the sun had begun to set. Thomas and Mr. Jenkins were walking alone with Mrs. Jenkins and Samuel walking a few yards behind them. "So, Thomas, what is it?" "Well, Mr. Jenkins," "hold on there a minute, Thomas, now I don't call you Mr. Callahan do I?" Mr. Jenkins interrupted. "No, sir." "Okay then, don't refer to me as Mr. Jenkins, call me Donald, please." "Okay, Donald, I wanted to talk to you about Julie." "Sure, I hear things between you and her are going great, you and Julie sure make a great couple." "Well that's really not what I want to talk to you about, Donald." "Oh yeah, well tell me then, Thomas, what did you want to speak to me about Julie for?" "Well, sir, it's about Julie and Koweena." "You mean, hold on just one minute, Thomas." Mr. Jenkins stopped the conversation for just a minute to open the front door of his house to let Thomas and his family in. "Have a seat, Thomas; I'll be in there in just a minute." As Mrs. Jenkins and Samuel went into Samuel's room, Mr. Jenkins followed behind them. "Dorothy, do you have a moment?" Mr. Jenkins asked his wife. "Sure, Dear, what is it?" "Samuel, wait right there for just a minute while me and your mommy talk, okay," Mr. Jenkins told Samuel. Mr. and Mrs. Jenkins walked out of Samuel's room and into the hallway. "Dorothy, Thomas wants to talk to me about that little Nigger," Mr. Jenkins said. "What Nigger, Dear?" "That little Nigger Julie's been hanging around." "Why?" Mrs. Jenkins asked. "I don't know, that's what I'm about to find out." "Well, do you think he's on your side on this matter?" "I sure hope so, Dorothy. I don't know though, that boy really has fallen for Julie, maybe he's come over here on behalf of that Nigger." "Surely not," Mrs. Jenkins replied. "I don't know, Dorothy, Julie could have sent him over here to try and smooth things over with me and that whole situation." "Well, just go talk to him and see what he has to say," Mrs. Jenkins said.

As Mr. Jenkins made his way into the living room he asked Thomas. "So, Thomas, would you like some scotch or some tea perhaps?" "No, sir, I'm fine thanks." "Well, I think I'm going to have me some scotch, you sure you don't want any?" "Yes, Donald, I'm fine." "Okay, I'll be right back." "Yes, sir." Thomas began rubbing his pant legs with his hands trying to dry the perspiration that had been forming on both his hands. He was getting nervous and it was beginning to show. Mr. Jenkins made his way back into the living room and sat down in the chair next to the sofa where Thomas was sitting. By now it was getting dark and the lights were on in the room. "So, Thomas, talk to me about Julie. I believe you were saying it had something to do with her and that little Nigger," Mr. Jenkins said as he sipped his scotch. "Yes, sir, Koweena," Thomas said. "Whatever her name is, Thomas, it doesn't matter. What about Julie?" "Well, Donald, Julie is upset because she believes you went to Mr. Defour about her seeing Koweena behind her back." "That Nigger you mean, Thomas?" "Koweena, sir," Thomas replied. "Whatever," Mr. Jenkins responded. "Well, sir, she would just like it if you stayed out of her family affairs. She loves that little girl." "And what about you, Thomas, have you grown attached to that little bitch?" Thomas went from being nervous to becoming angry. "Sir, I didn't come here to talk about me." "Thomas, call me Donald alright." "Okay, Donald, Julie just doesn't want you to interfere in her business." "Thomas, let me let you in on a little secret; I don't give a damn what Julie thinks! I'm the head overseer here, I'm in charge of not only seventy five overseers, but I'm in charge of all three hundred of those niggers out there. Now, I don't expect you to understand this, but anything that goes on with any of my spooks is, in fact, my business. Do you understand what I'm telling you?" Now they both were getting a little heated towards one another. "Donald, I don't think it's any of your business what Julie does with her life." "Is a nigger involved or what?" Mr. Jenkins asked. "Well, yes but," "okay if a nigger is involved, then it becomes my responsibility to make sure that nigger stays in line. Is that clear enough for you?" Mr. Jenkins interrupted. "Donald, I just don't think," "that's right you don't think, Thomas," Mr. Jenkins interrupted again. "There are procedures that go on on this Plantation. I wouldn't expect you to understand with you not coming from a slave background, so just keep to your little world and I'll keep to mine," Mr. Jenkins said. "Donald, please, just stay out of Julie's business." "Thomas, I have nothing but the utmost respect for you, you know that; but please don't sit there and tell me how to run my business. I wouldn't begin to tell you how to run your land surveying business, so don't sit here in my home and tell me how things should be done around here."

Thomas could clearly see he wasn't getting anywhere with Mr. Jenkins, so he left. He went back over to the Defour house. He was upset and he had to see Julie. He, like Koweena, only needed one person when upset; and that was Julie. "Julie, can I talk to you for just a minute, it will only take a minute, Koweena, I promise," Thomas said as he peeked his head into Julie's room. "Julie!" Koweena said frustratingly. "Koweena, we talked about this remember? Now, it will only take a minute, I'll be right back." Julie made her way to the hallway just outside the entranceway to her bedroom. "What is it, Thomas?" "I talked to Mr. Jenkins just now." "And." "And, well, it didn't go well. I don't think I got my point across to him very well." "What happened?" "Well, things got kind of heated between us. I was telling him not to interfere in your business." "You said that!" Julie interrupted. "Yes, I said that, and he just kept saying how Koweena, in no uncertain terms, was his business." Julie snapped her fingers. "God, that bastard," she said. "Well, anyway, Dear, I tried." "Thank you, Sweetheart, I know you did. Well, maybe you got to him anyway, even if it didn't seem like it," Julie said. "Well, I hope so. I just want you to know that I defended Koweena in there." "You did!" "Yes, he kept calling her a nigger and I kept saying that her name was Koweena," Thomas responded. "Oh, thank you, Honey!" Julie gave him a big kiss. That is what Thomas needed, that is why he went back to see her that night, to get that affection from her, the affection he now craved. "Okay, Sweetheart, I'll see you tomorrow," Thomas said. "Okay, Dear, bye!" Julie yelled as Thomas was walking down the stairs. Julie went back into her room where Koweena was playing with her new ring, twirling it on her finger. "What was it, Julie?" "Nothing, Dear, don't worry about it."

"Okay, Sweetheart, you ready to go downstairs?" Julie asked Koweena. "Yeah, I've been waiting on this the entire day. I can't wait to show my ring off to everyone in the kitchen." "Hold on, Koweena, there's something I want to tell you," Julie said. Koweena was so eager to go downstairs and start the party with the other slaves that she was about to leave Julie behind as she darted for the hallway toward the stairs. "Koweena, come back!" Julie yelled. Koweena stopped in the hallway and turned back toward the bedroom. As she entered the room Julie began to speak. "You know, I just want to tell you how proud I am of you. The way you are speaking is wonderful. Your grammar has improved so much. I can tell just by listening to you talk that you have really worked hard at learning, and I just want to say that I'm very proud of you and that I love you so much." "Thank you, Julie, I'm really glad you noticed how well I'm speaking. I can tell that my education is paying off as well. You have really changed my life and I just want to say that I'm sorry about today. I just thought that you forgot about me. I didn't mean to get upset at Thomas. I'll learn to get use to him, I promise." "That makes me feel good to hear you say that, Kowie, it really does. You know, Thomas really cares about you." "I know, Julie, I know." "Okay, let's go downstairs and have some fun," Julie said. "Oh, I can't wait!" Koweena said excitingly as she began to skip through the bedroom and into the hallway.

As they made their way down the stairs both of them were laughing and carrying on. They both were talking and laughing as they were looking down at Koweena's ring. Suddenly, as they got to the bottom of the stairs, they bumped right into Mr. Defour, who was standing at the foot of the steps. "Julie, what are you doing this late at night?" Mr. Defour asked. "Daddy, you startled me!" Julie said in a nervous tone. She called her father daddy when she was nervous around him. "Julie, what are you doing?" Her father continued to ask. "Well uh, daddy, you see, uh, here's the thing." Julie was fumbling, trying to think of something to say. Koweena was petrified as she stared up at the infamous man. But there was something different about her. Yes, she was scared, but she was now self-confident. Like that time in the field when she talked back to that overseer, she had grown so brave over the last year that looking Mr. Defour in the eyes was not a problem for her, and she wasn't getting nauseous either. "Julie, you were saying. Hey wait a minute." Mr. Defour's eyes went from fixating them on Julie to now fixating them on Koweena. For a moment the two were now staring each other right in the eyes. Koweena just stood there staring at him for a few seconds.

"Are you this little Nigger that's been running around my house?" Mr. Defour asked. Koweena just stood there, staring at him eye to eye. She had definitely grown up. Maybe it was the quick growth spurt she had undergone over the last year that made her stand up so tall to Mr. Defour; to her he didn't look as tall as he once had in the past when they first met five years to the day. Mr. Defour chuckled as he stared at Koweena. "Look at you," he said. He was glaring at her skin tone on her face and arms. "What are you?" He asked. Koweena was instantly becoming a little intimidated as Mr. Defour checked her out from head to toe. She also began to feel humiliated. "You're pretty," Mr. Defour continued, "but you're still a nigger. I mean look at you, are you some kind of mixture or something? You sure as hell don't look like my other slaves. You look like," Mr. Defour quickly stopped in mid sentence. He realized what he was about to slip up and say. From that moment on he just kept his mouth shut. The silence seemed to go on forever. "Excuse me, daddy," Julie said as she grabbed a hold of Koweena's hand and went around her father through the foyer and toward the front door. She quickly opened it and walked out onto the front porch still holding Koweena's hand. "Stay right here, okay; don't move until I come back out. Don't move!" Julie went back inside, shut the door, and approached her father. "Julie, what's going on?" Her father asked. Julie had to think of something to say, and think quickly. "Oh that, daddy, she is one of our maids' daughters, that's all." "What were you doing holding her hand?" Her father asked. "I don't know, daddy, I was just guiding her outside that's all." "Okay, well, good night, Dear." "Good night, daddy." Her father proceeded down the hallway to his bedroom. Julie watched him go all the way down the hall until he disappeared into his bedroom. Julie quickly went back to the front door, opened it, stepped out onto the porch and grabbed a hold of Koweena's hands. "Are you alright, Kowie?" "Yeah, I wasn't nauseous or anything that entire time, and I stared him in the face." "That's great, Kowie, that's great, I just about had a heart attack." Julie was breathing heavily from being so nervous. "Okay, let's go in the kitchen and forget about this whole thing," Julie continued. Julie was frightened by the entire ordeal, while Koweena on the other hand, was excited at the fact that she wasn't hurt by the remarks of Mr. Defour. For so long she had been conscious about her looks, but with years of Julie telling her how beautiful she looked, she no longer worried about her appearance. With the combination of living with Julie, being educated, and just plain maturing into a preteen adolescent, Koweena had moved beyond the insults and intimidation of the white folks, she was becoming tougher, more confident, and Julie of course played a large role in that.

"Running into my dad scared the hell out of me," Julie recalled. "I thought I had placed Koweena in a precarious; and dangerous situation. But I was so proud of my Angel. She really stood her ground that evening. It dawned on me that night as I stared at her looking eye to eye with my father, she had really matured. I also realized just how tough she had become. I knew I was doing what I was called to do, and that was playing the role of aiding in helping to grow a young girl into a confident person, a person who could stand on her own two feet. I realized, later on, just how important my aiding her in growing up truly was. She would need it for what she was going to have to endure in the future."

Chapter 9   Fatherly Confrontation

*I*t was April, and it was now just days from Julie's big wedding day. It was a weekday, and Koweena was studying in her play and study room when Julie entered. "Koweena, I have something to ask you." "What is it, Julie?" Julie walked over to where Koweena was lying on the leather couch, and knelt down to ask. "Kowie, I want you to be my ring bearer." Koweena was puzzled. "What's that?" She asked. "A ring bearer is someone who stands in between the bride and groom, and holds the wedding rings on a pillow during the wedding." "What's a wedding ring?" Koweena asked. "It's kind of like the ring you have on now. It's just a symbol of the fact that the man and woman are married to each other. It shows everybody that 'hey look, I'm married.' Do you mind doing that? I have your dress all made and everything." "You made a dress for me to wear in your wedding!?" Koweena was very excited about that, but then she thought about Julie's father. "What about your dad?" Koweena asked. "For all he knows, you could just be one of the servant's girls. Don't worry about that." "Okay, I'll do it." "Great! You know it wouldn't be truly my wedding unless you were in it, Kowie." "It's on Saturday, right?" Koweena asked. "Yes, two o'clock."

Josi was in the room, studying with Koweena, and listening to every word. As Julie left the room, Josi spoke up. "Wow, Koweena, you is truly lucky. You get to be in a big white person's wedding. I is never even seen a wedding before," Josi said. "I haven't either, Josi." "And you is get to wear a fancy dress, and stand up there in front of everybody and everything. Is you goin to get nervous?" Josi asked. Koweena smiled. "No, I won't get nervous. It should be a lot of fun though." "Koweena, what's that on your finger, and around your neck?" Josi asked. "Oh, this? That's a ring Julie got for me for Christmas." "Can I is see it?" Koweena held out her right hand, right up to Josi's face. "Sure," Koweena said. "Wow, look at that big shiny thing, it's huge!" Josi stretched out her hand and touched the stone. Her fingers just glided along the round, smooth shape of the stone. "What's it called?" Josi asked. "It's called a sapphire stone." "Why is it pink?" "That's my favorite color," Koweena said. "It's beautiful, Koweena. What's that black thing hangin around your neck?" Josi asked. "It's a heart shaped locket. You can't touch this though." "Why not?" "Because this is very important to me, and I don't want to take the chance of you breaking it, or tearing it off my neck." Unlike the ring, Koweena wouldn't allow Josi to get anywhere near the necklace, she was way too protective of it. Koweena even held on tight to it for several minutes, after telling Josi that she couldn't touch it.

The following day, the both of them were working in the fields, picking cotton together, when an overseer approached them. The overseer pointed to Koweena. "Do you know this little bitch?" He asked Josi. Koweena quickly recognized the voice as she glanced up at the overseer. From Koweena's standpoint, he was standing just to the right of the sun, so when she looked up at him, the sun was right in her face; but Koweena was able to make out the face through the sunlight, it was Ray. Koweena began to panic; her fist instinct was to protect Josi. "No, she doesn't know me," Koweena said. Josi was getting ready to speak up and tell Ray that she did know Koweena. "Um," Josi was getting ready to speak, but Koweena was waving her arms at Josi to get her attention. "Psst," Koweena made a noise, trying desperately to get her attention. "Psst," she continued. Josi finally looked up at Koweena. Koweena was shaking her head back and forth saying no with her mouth vehemently at Josi. Koweena actually wasn't speaking; she was just simply moving her mouth. Koweena had her eyebrows raised, and she was shaking her head at Josi. "Say no you don't," Koweena was motioning to Josi with her mouth without any words coming out. Ray was looking at Josi the entire time, so he wasn't noticing Koweena's head jerking motions, arm waving, and mouth moving. Finally, after several seconds, Josi picked up on what Koweena was so desperately trying to tell her. "No, sir, I is don't know her." "Are you sure, you were looking over at her for a long time like you did know her," Ray said. "No, sir, don't know her," Josi continued. This time Koweena kept silent, she didn't look up at Ray. If it had been anyone but him, she would have looked up and probably said something, but with it being Ray, she was too scared. Her muscles tightened and her airways seemed to constrict as she knelt there, now returning back to picking cotton. Ray just stood there over her in silence, to Koweena, the silence seemed like hours. She was expecting to get grabbed at any second. Suddenly, out of the blue, that mature, brave, grown up, almost ten year old Koweena, came to the forefront. "If you touch me, you will have to deal with Julie," she told Ray. For a second there, she couldn't believe she had just spoken up to the man that had beaten her twice. Ray leaned over Koweena. "What did you say to me, you little bitch!?" "Like I said, if you touch me, the boss man's daughter will be all over you like white on rice." Koweena was turning over a new chapter in her life. She was fearless now, undaunted by the man who had crushed her spirits so many times in the past. The beatings, the education, the spending time with Julie, all of this had toughened the young Koweena. Ray, for whatever reason, left her alone that day. "I'll deal with you later, bitch," he said as he just continued on walking past them after Koweena spoke up. Koweena took a deep breath after he left. "What in the world was that all about, Koweena?" Josi asked. "He beat me, Josi." "He what!?" "He beat me, and I think he did it more than once." "You is been beaten twice!?" "Yes," Koweena replied. "Oh my God, Koweena, we have to tell somebody!" "Julie already knows about it," Koweena said. "Is she goin to do somethin about it?" "I don't know, as you can see, he's still out here, walking around like he owns the place. I overheard her tell Mr. Defour to deal with him or she was going to leave and never come back; but I don't think he's done anything about it." "I can't believe you is been beaten, Koweena. I couldn't imagine how that must have felt." "It was a nightmare, Josi, an absolute nightmare." "Hey, shut the hell up over there!" An overseer hollered out from behind them. Koweena turned as if she was going to say something, but then thought better of it and quickly turned back around and went back to working. No sooner had she began working again than she glanced back up at Josi. "Hey, Josi." "Yeah, Koweena." "I have an idea about you and the wedding coming up in a couple of days." "What is you have in mind?" "Wait until our shift is over and I'll tell you." "Do I get to be in it?" "Something like that, Josi."

The day had arrived, the wedding day of Julie and Thomas. It was a beautiful sunny, warm day, not too hot and not too breezy either, just a perfect day weather wise. The servants were busy in the wedding area cleaning the white chairs and doing any last minute manicuring of the lawn and the stage area. Koweena and Julie were up in Julie's room getting ready for the event. Julie was dressing Koweena in a peach cotton dress that went all the way from her neckline to her ankles. "Do you have your ring on, Kowie?" Koweena lifted up her hand to show Julie. "Yes, it's right here," she said. "What about your necklace?" "I never take it off Julie," Koweena responded. "Are you nervous, Julie?" Koweena asked. "Yes, how can you tell?" "You seem all fidgety," Koweena said. "Well, it's a big day, Kowie," Julie said in a nervous tone. "Ray talked to me the other day in the fields!" Koweena blurted out as Julie was on the other side of the room looking at herself in the closet mirror. Julie was dressed in an all white satin dress, with a white organza overlay, and a train that stretched all the way down trailing from her backside about ten feet. She was holding her laced veil, which when put on, would cover her face. When Koweena told her that, those words made Julie stop what she was doing and turn and stare at Koweena with eyes wide open. "He what!?" "He approached me while I was picking cotton, like he had done before, and well; I was scared at first, but then something inside me came alive and I spoke up to him." "What did you tell him?" Julie asked. "I basically said that if he didn't leave me alone that you would deal with him." What a day to be telling Julie this. With all that Julie was trying to do to get ready for her big day, she now had to worry about what Ray could do to Koweena. Koweena really didn't mean to tell Julie that, it just sort of slipped out. Koweena got enthusiastic. "Don't think about it today Julie, today is your big day!" Koweena didn't know much about weddings, nothing in fact, but she could tell it was a big day for Julie, and she didn't want Julie worrying about her. But Julie's thoughts ran back to that conversation she had with her father about how she would have nothing to do with him if he didn't do something about Ray. She had to protect Koweena she thought, and Ray was definitely jeopardizing that. "Is the fact that I'm staying on my parent's property keeping my dad from doing anything about Ray," Julie thought to herself. She would have to eventually approach her father about the subject, but not today. Today was all about her, despite that; Julie couldn't help but worry about Koweena. Koweena was her life, and even on her biggest day, Julie was thinking about Koweena, and her safety. "Maybe when Koweena settles into my home things will improve in the fields for her," Julie thought. "You know what, Koweena, tonight you get to move into your new home, isn't that exciting!" "Yeah! I can't wait! My very own room! Hey, Julie, would it be alright if Josi comes over and spends the night some in the future?" "Sure, Dear, that would be alright. Just let me know in advance okay." "Okay," Koweena said.

Facing the front of the Defour house, the wedding was being conducted directly to the left of the house, in the open lawn area. The entire wedding area outdoors, from the stage area where Julie and Thomas would be standing, to the seats stretched out down through the lawn, with only the peach colored carpeted aisle separating them, was about seventy yards in length. It was a massive size wedding. As the crowds gathered, Koweena could see the spectacle from Julie's upstairs bedroom. Koweena was amazed. "Wow, now that's a crowd of people," she said. As she peered through the crowd, she noticed that they were all very well to do white people, wearing fine dresses and suits. This intimidated Koweena greatly. "Now I'm the one getting nervous Julie." Julie laughed out loud. "It's okay, Dear. It will be a quick ceremony. It will be over before you know it." "Do you know all of those people?" Koweena asked. "Only a few, most of them are my parent's friends." "Your parents sure have a lot of friends." "Most of them are not really friends of my parents, they're all just rich, so it's the money that my parents have that makes them known to them. If my parents didn't have money, that crowd you're looking at wouldn't even be half that size." "Can I go downstairs a minute, Julie?" "Sure, but don't be gone long, it's just about time."

As Koweena walked down the stairs, her hair, which is pulled back in the front and on the sides into a pony tail, with a peach ribbon slightly behind the top of her head, with the rest of her curly hair flowing in the back, was bouncing up and down with each move she made down each step. As she reached the front door, she opened it and found Julias standing to the left, at the bottom of the steps, holding Josi's hand. "Josi!" Koweena yelled out. Josi got excited. "Koweena!" She yelled. Koweena ran down to the bottom of the stairs. Koweena smiled at Josi. "So, I see you made it, and you're wearing my dress, it looks good on you," Koweena said. "You think so, Koweena?" "Yes, it looks good on you." "Wow, this is the first time I is ever seen a wedding before! So, what do you want me to do?" Josi asked. "Julias here will take you to the back of the house. From there, you will be able to see the entire wedding. The stage area might block your view a little, but you'll get to see most of it." "Thank you, Koweena, for this opportunity, it really means a lot that you went out of your way to do this for me." "Not a problem, Josi, you said you had never seen a wedding, so I thought I would rectify that by bringing you here and letting you watch it from a distance." "Are you nervous?" Josi asked. "You look real beautiful," she continued. "Thanks, yes I'm a little nervous, especially after seeing all of those white folks in the audience." "Oh, don't worry about them, Koweena, they will ignore you completely," Julias told her. "Are you sure?" Koweena asked with some doubt in her voice. "Trust me, they won't even know you're there," Julias responded.

Meanwhile, there was a knock on Julie's bedroom door. "Who is it?" Julie asked while she sat at her mirror next to her dresser conducting last minute touch ups on her face. "It's Thomas." Julie quickly got up from her chair and rushed over to the door. "Thomas, you know you're not supposed to see me until I go down the aisle! What are you doing here!?" "I just couldn't wait to tell you something." Julie let out a nervous chuckle. "Well, tell me, and then leave, don't open the door." "I just want to tell you that I love you more than anything in this whole wide world, Julie Defour. You are my soul mate, Jules; and I don't know where my life would be right now if you weren't in it. Without you, I'm only half a man, you make me whole. You're my Spring Queen! Do you hear me, my Beautiful Rose Pedal?" "Yes, Sweetheart, I hear you." "Well, I guess that's all I wanted to say." "I love you, Thomas. Now get out of here!" "Okay, see you down there, oh, I can't wait!" "Go!" Julie yelled. She walked back to her chair laughing and shaking her head.

The time had come. The packed house crowd was now standing to their feet, the piano was playing "Here Comes the Bride" as Julie stood there, arm and arm with her father. Her veil, now draped over her face, was covering her beautiful fair skin, as well as her blond hair, which was pulled back into a knot with tiny strands of curly hair stringing down the sides of her face. Koweena was standing there behind her and her father, with her hands under the small aqua pillow that held the two rings. Julie began to walk slowly down the aisle. She was walking toward her future life mate who was standing in front of a giant, white wooden arched trellis with white and pink carnations, and pink rambling roses covering it all around. As Koweena was walking behind them down the aisle, she could hear whispers coming from both sides of the aisle. "Look at that Nigger, who does she think she is," one woman said. "Look at that filthy Nigger ruining this wedding," another woman said. She would hear these whispers all the way down the aisle. A few years ago that would have crushed her spirit. It would have definitely made her start crying. But not with this new and much tougher Koweena; she just smiled as she continued hearing the insults hurled at her. She did think of Julias at that moment, who told her that she didn't have to worry about a thing from those white folks, and how they wouldn't even notice her. It was amazing how Koweena had changed since she was eight when she had received that second beating. Had living with Julie, and no longer having to live with the slaves in those shacks for almost two years, have made that much of a difference in Koweena? It certainly was one of the leading factors in Koweena's new approach to those who thought they were above her.

"Thomas Callahan," the preacher said, standing confidently straight up, "do you take Julie Defour to be your lawfully wedded wife, to love and to hold, to cherish and protect, in sickness and in health, for as long as you both shall live?" The preacher continued. "I do," Thomas said.

"This was all new to me," Koweena recalled. "For the first time, I was experiencing, as I listened to the preacher's words, what loving someone was all about. I suddenly began to desire that same kind of love for myself. I began having visions of meeting that special someone someday in my future. As I looked upon Julie, I wanted to wear that same kind of dress. I wanted to be in that same kind of ceremony, with all the attention centered on me, just like it was with Julie on that day. I became determined as I stood there on that sunny afternoon in front of the backdrop of hundreds of people on that beautiful lawn; I was going to experience this same kind of day that Julie was experiencing. All eyes were going to be on me someday. This caused me, for the first time since living on that Plantation, to start thinking about escaping.

The word escape had never entered my mind until that moment. Yes, I thought about escaping as I stood there holding that little pillow."

"I now present to you Mr. and Mrs. Thomas Callahan," the preacher proudly said. Julie and Thomas proceeded down the aisle arm and arm as the crowd was throwing rice on them. As Koweena was walking down the aisle in front of them she was laughing out loud, enjoying the spectacle of the rice throwing, as rice fell on her.

As Koweena walked into her new room, she could smell the fresh paint permeate the room. The walls were pink of course; and everything that had been in the play and study room at the Defour house was now in her room. She quickly noticed her very own bed located against the wall in the very middle of the room. She jumped on it and just laid there for a moment. Her dreams had come true. "Why would I want to escape?" She thought to herself this time. "Maybe I can have a wedding like Julie's right here." She said to herself out loud. But deep down, she was educated enough to where she knew that that was a far fetched idea. But for now, she was enjoying her new bed. She couldn't believe it as she lay there, that this entire queen mattress was going to be all to herself. She stretched her body out as far as she could and she still couldn't touch the ends. Her happiness had reached an all time peak that day. She just couldn't believe that she had made it this far, from that tiny little shack from whence she came, to now lying in her own bed in her own room.

For several years, Koweena lived in peace at Julie's home. She got to eat at the table with Julie and Thomas every day for morning breakfast and evening dinners, that is, when Thomas wasn't on the road surveying land. During those days it would be just Koweena and Julie eating together. There was no more sneaking around, she came and went as she pleased. That was the biggest difference, no more secrecy. She felt like for the first time that she was part of a family. Her self-confidence surmounted during those years. Koweena was changing into a beautiful teenage girl, whose stature, at least in Julie's household, was equal to that of a wealthy white girl. Josi would come over at least once or twice every week to spend the night and get educated by Koweena. The sisters really grew close during this period. Koweena and Julie did as well, if that were even possible. She had also grown closer to Thomas as well. During those years, Koweena had a nucleus of people in her life that were a constant, Julie of course, Josi, and Thomas. She really began to grow attached to all three over the next several years. She and Julie, and sometimes Thomas, when he was home, would sit in the living room at night and read books to each other and play cards, just like a real family.

For four solid years, it was a time of peace for Koweena in her life, that was, until Mr. Defour showed up one night. Koweena, Julie, and Thomas were in the living room playing cards when the doorbell rang. "I'll get it," Thomas said as he made his way from the living room into the foyer area toward the front door. The living room and foyer were not separated by any walls; they just blended together into one giant living space. Thomas opened the front door. "Mr. Defour, sir, what a pleasant surprise, you don't come here much, what brings the successful man of the land to our home?" Mr. Defour never visited Julie; this was only the second time since they moved in over three years that he actually came over. "Hello, Thomas, I actually came to see Julie, is she home?" "Yes, sir, she's in the living room." "Yes, I can see her from here," Mr. Defour said as he peered into the house and noticed Julie and Koweena sitting together in the living room. "Please, come in," Thomas said as he directed his arms toward the living room. Mr. Defour slowly walked into the living room. "Dad." "Julie. Can you excuse us for a moment," he told Koweena as he gave her a disgusted look. Koweena had seen that look all too many times in the past; she was used to it by now. "Kowie, why don't you go upstairs and do some reading for your History assignment tomorrow while dad and I talk for a moment." "Okay," Koweena said as she got up from the sofa and walked over to the foyer where the stairs were located, and began walking upstairs to her room.

As Koweena entered her room, she sat at her desk and began reading, with her desk lamp on, the book by the eighteenth century English novelist Daniel Defoe; she could suddenly hear voices coming from downstairs. She knew it was a heated conversation because she couldn't hear any voices before, until now. With her curiosity peeked, she got up and went over to the door and opened it just a bit to get a better earshot of what was being said. She could now tell that there was some kind of arguing going on, but she was still too far away to make out just what was being said. She tippy-toed outside her room, to the banister just at

the top of the stairs to get a closer look. "Are they arguing about me?"
She whispered to herself.

"That slave upstairs is my property!" Mr. Defour yelled at Julie.
"Her name is Kowie, daddy." "I don't care what her name is, she is my
property, and I can do with her what I damn well please! She may live
under your roof, but she is still my slave!" "But," "I'm not finished yet,"
Mr. Defour interrupted Julie. "She is a slave, and she will act like a slave.
She will do the same amount of work as my other slaves!" "Has mom
talked to you, because it sounds like she has?" "Leave your mother out
of this; this has nothing to do with her. This has to do with me and
that slave your harboring here like some kind of wealthy white girl!"
"But what about her studying?" Julie asked. "Why does a slave need
to study? That little wench will never leave my property, what good is
an education going to do it?" "You haven't done anything about that
Ray guy have you?" Julie asked. "What Ray guy?" "The guy that beat
Koweena." "I don't care about this Ray guy you're talking about, all I
care about right now is treating that little bitch you have up there like
a real slave, education or no education." "She gets off at three, daddy,
every afternoon, that's the deal we made." "That's the deal who made?
You didn't make that deal with me!" "I made it with mom, and she
swore to it." "Before three, after three, it doesn't matter, she's still just a
slave, and she's my property!" "She's a teenage girl, daddy, not just one
of your farm machinery!"

At that moment, as Koweena was intensely listening, she began to
feel trapped. At fourteen years old, she suddenly began to feel like she
was eight all over again. She was listening to Mr. Defour calling her
property, and her heart sunk. She began to feel like all this hard work
she had put into bettering her life, was for nothing. In just a matter of
minutes, she was back to feeling like a helpless slave, just like she felt
when she was little. Things had been going so well for her up to this
point. And now, with just a few words from Mr. Defour, that was all
shot. After being reminded, once again, that she was just property, and
not a human being like Julie, her self-confidence was taking a nose
dive. She didn't resent Julie for her upper-class status, she never did;
quite the opposite in fact, her goal was to be like Julie in every possible
way. She wanted the husband, she wanted the house of her own, and
more importantly, she didn't want to be someone else's property. If one

thing at least was coming out of living with Julie and being educated by her it was this, you can be and do anything you set your mind to. Julie instilled that in her from the very beginning. As long as she could remember, she had been learning about important female figures of the eighteenth century, who not only taught her to be independent, but who were also successful women of their time in their own right.

"Daddy, get out!" Julie yelled, at this point she had had enough of her father's ranting. "Remember this, Julie, while you're playing sister or mother or whatever the hell you think your role is with this little bitch, I can have her shipped out of here in a heartbeat, before you even knew she was gone!" Julie said nothing, her dad was right and she knew it. Her father did in fact own Koweena, and he did in fact have the right to ship her to any plantation he pleased. As Koweena continued to listen, emotionally she felt like she had been beaten all over again. "Thomas, don't you have any say so in this marriage?" Mr. Defour asked. "I mean, you're the man of the house, and you're letting this little Nigger run around here like she owns the place. Why don't you get some back bone about you and set your wife straight?" Thomas said nothing as he just stared at the floor. He loved Julie too much, and he cared for Koweena as well to disagree with Julie. "Daddy, he stands with me on this issue." "Is that true, Thomas?" Mr. Defour asked. "Yes, sir, I stand by my wife." "Why don't you be a husband, Thomas, and control your wife!" Mr. Defour demanded. "Remember, Julie, I could have her shipped out of here and all your hard work would be meaningless. You couldn't stop me!" Julie, again, just remained silent. She just stared at the floor upon hearing that, and she didn't look up until her father had walked out the front door.

Koweena came storming down the stairs toward Julie and Thomas who were still standing in the living room after Mr. Defour left the house. Koweena was yelling as she was running down the stairs. "Why didn't you say something, Julie!? Why didn't you say something!? You just kept silent!" She approached Julie and Thomas, who were standing beside the sofa. "What are you talking about, Kowie?" Julie asked. Koweena began flailing her arm up and down, while her other arm was on her hip. "I was up there, and I listened to the whole thing! You just stood there and said nothing when your father mentioned to you that he could ship me off. You just said nothing!" Koweena said. "Koweena," "no Julie," Koweena interrupted, "you just kept silent when he brought that up! You could have threatened him when he started talking about shipping me away, but you didn't!" Koweena continued yelling. "You didn't!" She yelled, as she began crying out loud as she ran back up the stairs and slammed her bedroom door. She ran over to her bed and plopped down on it face first where she just laid there crying hysterically. She was just lying there crying, holding on to her locket that was attached to the necklace that was around her neck. She felt abandoned by Julie. She felt Julie could have stood up for her more. "I have no control over my life," she said out loud as she was trying to catch her breath from crying so hard. "I could be shipped away, and my life would be destroyed. I'm nothing but a piece of worthless meat," she continued telling herself. After several minutes of hard crying, it was now quiet sobbing. "Mr. Defour owns me; I'm not my own person. God, get me out of here!" It was then, like that time at the wedding, that she began thinking of a possible escape; but she just couldn't think of a way to do it. She felt so trapped that she began to feel claustrophobic. "I'm only fourteen, where would I go, how would I survive on my own? This Plantation is the only world I know, I've never even been off of it," she whispered to herself. The hopelessness she felt was overwhelming. She didn't know how to escape this terrible plantation life, and she couldn't control her own destiny. "Things were going so well for me up to this point," she thought to herself. "I don't want to be shipped away, I do like my life here with Julie in this house; but I feel like I have no control over my future here," she whispered. She just laid there thinking. She was going over the pros and cons of staying on the plantation, compared to trying to escape it.

After an hour had gone by, there was a quiet, gentle knock on her bedroom door. "Who is it!?" Koweena yelled out in a mean tone. "It's Julie, can I come in?" "No!" Koweena yelled back. "Kowie, please let me come in, I really want to talk to you." After thinking about it for a while, Koweena slowly got up and went to the door, she opened it. "What!?" She said in a quick, sharp tone. "Listen, Baby, I know you're upset, but will you give me a chance to explain." Koweena, with her head down, stretched out her arm toward the inside of the room. "Come in," she said. "Can we sit down on your bed?" Julie asked. Koweena walked over to her bed and sat down with her arms crossed at her chest. "May I sit down?" Julie asked. Koweena shook her head in an up and down fashion with her eyes closed as if to say "go ahead if you have to." Julie sat next to her on the bed. "Why didn't you say no when your father threatened to ship me off? You could have said something, but you didn't." Koweena said. "It may be hard for you to understand right now, Kowie, but my father is right." "Right about what?" Koweena asked. "This is hard for me to say, Kowie." "Try, Julie," Koweena interrupted. "Okay, to me, you are my very own flesh and blood, my sister. That's how I think of you. Ever since you were five, I have tried to take care of you the best way I know how. I'm educating you, you are now a part of my home and family, I love you more than anything." "Yeah, but Julie, where is that going to get me when your father decides to ship me off, it will get me nowhere," Koweena responded. "As much as I try not to accept this fact about you," Julie continued, "the point is is that it's true, you are my father's property." Wow, at fourteen years old, hearing those words from Julie's own lips, it hit her and hit her hard. Koweena was indeed just property, and not only that, listening to Julie say those words, she now realized that there was nothing Julie could do to change that fact. The one person that never treated her like a slave; and the one person that she could always turn to when things got rough on the Plantation, was now telling her that she was indeed the property of someone else, and not just anyone, but property of the father of the person she relied on most. It pained Julie to admit that to Koweena. Julie hated slavery and everything associated with it. She was in a tough spot though, she wouldn't be where she was today without her father's slaves, she knew that. But watching her father's system of business that brought her peace, wealth, and security, at least security for most of her life, and material possessions, slowly eat away and deteriorate what dignity and life her precious Kowie had left, made her even more bitter at the thought of slavery. Like Koweena, who felt trapped because she had no control over her future, Julie was now also feeling trapped, because she was benefiting from slavery, the very thing that was making Koweena suffer so.

"I realized that night sitting next to Julie, I have no rights," Koweena recalled. "I had no control over anything. I felt helpless. Depression had got its ugly grip on me once again because of these feelings. My innocence had been stripped from me a long time ago, but with what happened to me that night, my optimism and hope had been stripped from me as well. Characteristics that are a teenage girl's best friend. I had no future, I thought. The education that I worked so hard to attain now seemed futile. What did I have to look forward to?"

Julie grabbed a hold of Koweena's hand. "Kowie, I promise you, I will do everything in my power to keep you here. I've protected you up to this point, and I'm not about to stop doing that, do you understand me? I will allow nothing to happen to you. I love you more than anything. You are my whole world, and I'm not going to give you up." That all too familiar innate protective tone came out in Julie's voice as she said those words, that same tone that Koweena had heard so many times in her past when she needed Julie the most. Koweena had been depressed so many times in her past, and each time that protective tone would seem to come to the forefront from Julie when Koweena was desperate for it. This was no exception. Once again, hearing Julie's voice helped to relieve some of the anxiety that was building up in Koweena. She suddenly felt at ease. Like so many times before, Julie had come through when Koweena needed her most. The trust Koweena had for Julie, which was shaky just moments ago, was now back. It wasn't as strong as it had been for so many years in the past, too much damage had been done by Mr. Defour's words, and Julie's lack of response to those words, and now hearing Julie tell her that she was indeed property, made the trust in her weaken.

It was sad, Koweena had been broken in spirit that night, her world had collapsed all around her, and although Julie was making it a little better on that bed that night, she just couldn't trust Julie like she had in the past. Maybe it was Koweena's age that kept her from fully trusting Julie again. Koweena was just years away from becoming an adult, she was no longer that little child who trusted so easily, she had grown and matured, words were just simply not enough, like they had been in the past. Julie's actions spoke louder than her words that night according to Koweena. But Julie had never let her down in the past, and that's what Koweena was thinking as she sat there on her bed next to Julie. "I believe you, Julie, I really do. I know you'll try to protect me and try your best to keep me here; but that still doesn't change the fact that it could happen at any moment, me being shipped off." "Kowie, I panicked down there tonight. I got nervous around my father, I couldn't think of the right words to say at that point in time. If he does attempt to ship you off, I will threaten him again just like I have before, and tell him that he will no longer see me again." "Do you mean it; you won't let anything happen to me?" Koweena asked. "I promise, Kowie. He will have to kill me before I let him do anything to you." Julie's comforting words were helping to reassure Koweena's faith in her. And although Koweena's trust in her had weakened that night, she still believed that Julie wouldn't allow anything to happen to her. It was that belief on this night that Koweena clung to. With solid reassurance from Julie, Koweena grabbed a hold of that trust Julie had built during Koweena's childhood, and used it that night to convince herself that everything was going to be alright.

Julie went to bed that night torn between slavery and her own Plantation. Thoughts of what slavery was doing to her precious Kowie were racing through her mind. "What is it, Dear?" Thomas asked while lying alongside Julie. "I hate slavery, Thomas, yet I'm reaping the benefits of the slave's hard labor." Julie was struggling with her own little world, the world of the slaves and her father's Plantation. "I never wanted Kowie to be a slave," she continued telling Thomas. "Ever since Koweena was five, I've been planning ways to get her out of this slave business. The planning escalated when I saw with my own eyes her beating when she was eight. And now, that same guy that beat her might still be after her. If I can't change dad's plantation, Thomas, at least I can try to change Kowie's situation, I thought to myself years ago. I just didn't realize how difficult that task would be. I can't help but blame myself for the way Kowie feels tonight." "You have to stop blaming yourself, Jules. You're trying your best; I mean you've given her a home and everything. You're doing the best you can." "I can't change my father's Plantation though, no matter how hard I try to think of a way to. My father is just too far gone on the subject of Kowie and slavery compared to my own belief system," Julie said. Julie had made up her mind that night; she was going to get Koweena off that Plantation. But no more did she think that, than suddenly the thought raced through her mind that cut her to the core. "I will have to let Kowie go!" She blurted out by accident; she didn't mean to be so loud. "What, Dear?" Thomas asked. "Thomas, I want to get Kowie off this Plantation, but I don't want to lose her though. I mean, Thomas, so many nights I've lied awake thinking about how great mine and Kowie's life would be together on this Plantation, but the more the years go by, the more unrealistic that seems to be." "Julie, there's something I need to tell you," Thomas said. "What is it, Thomas?" "I really don't want to do this, but I think it's something you need to know." Upon hearing that Julie reached over and turned on the lamp that was next to the bed. "Thomas, tell me, whatever it is, I can handle it." "Okay, here it goes. Your dad called you some pretty terrible names one day while I was over at his house grabbing some of your things." "What did he say, Thomas?" "I really don't want to tell you, Jules." "Tell me, Thomas." Thomas took a deep breath and started to speak. "He called you a nigger lover, a white slave, things such as that. Listen I really don't want to talk about this." Thomas, by now, was starting to get upset just thinking about it, he didn't like saying those words, period, much less to Julie. He hated hurting Julie, under any circumstances. "What did you say back to him?" Julie inquired. "I didn't say anything, Jules, he's your father, what was I suppose to say?" "What else did that jerk say, Thomas?" "I don't know, Jules; I tried to block it out of my mind." "Well try unblocking," Julie steadfastly persisted. "He said you," Thomas paused for a second to gather himself for what he was about to say next. "There has to be a way out of telling her this, I don't want to hurt her," he thought to himself. But deep down he knew Julie wouldn't rest until he told her, he felt like he had no choice. "Jules, he said," once again he paused. He then continued, "he said you were a slutty little slave girl." Although this was more than she could bear to hear, Julie loved her father, despite the name calling. Julie's love for her father was misguided though. She coupled love with how many material possessions she possessed from him. Julie's love for her father was based on the gifts he gave her. She never once stopped to think, "Does my dad love me for me." Mr. Defour did spoil her, but not emotionally. Giving her stuff kept her at a distance, but Julie didn't see it that way. Her and her father rarely talked, nonetheless Julie loved him. It was a blind love for her father. As Julie heard those bad names from Thomas, she quickly turned from him so that she was lying with her back to him. Julie choked back the tears as she spoke. "Do you feel the same as my father, Thomas?" Thomas reached over and placed his hand on Julie's back. "Jules, how could you say that? You know that I am yours, I am totally and completely yours; and you are mine. If pouring your soul into Koweena makes you happy, then I'm happy, do you understand what I'm saying, Dear? Julie, Koweena is a big part of your life; I see it in your eyes every day. You spoil her like crazy, Jules. You're crazy about that little girl; it's obvious to everyone around you, even to your father. And, Julie, I genuinely care for that little girl too, maybe not as much as you do, but I care for her." Julie turned off the light. "I love you, Thomas."

As the night turned into the wee hours of the morning, Koweena was still lying awake in her bed. As the moonlight shone through her window, she was thinking that she was at least assured of one thing that night; that everything was going to be alright, at least for the time being. But thoughts of escaping still entered her mind. She began to think of a plan. "Maybe I could get some slaves together, and we could try and escape in one big group, stick together as a team. I could get Julias, Josi, Delco, and some others," she thought. "But that means I would have to leave Julie, oh, how I would miss her. I don't know if I could stand to be away from her," she continued thinking as she lay there that night in bed trying to go to sleep.

Chapter 10   The Plan

"*O*ver the years I had spent with Julie, my twenty-nine-year-old beautiful wife, and thus, time I also spent with Koweena," Thomas later recalled. "I grew to love and adore the sixteen-year-old-girl who had lived such a tough life. What were my views however, on the business that had so affected Koweena's life since the day she was born? Had Koweena influenced me enough to sway me toward the side of being like a northern abolitionist? Or had she not influenced me in the least on the subject? Unlike Julie, I was indifferent to slavery when I first met Julie. My business didn't depend on it; I had nothing to do with the operation that dominated the South. I hadn't grown up around the lifestyle either. So I was never forced, during my entire life, to make a decision as to whether or not I agreed or disagreed with the practice. Hell, my parents never even brought up the subject to me. Even after I had been seeing Julie for such a long time, my viewpoint on slavery continued to be indifferent. Yet, as time went on, time I would share with Koweena, she really began to influence me, so much so, that I really began to not necessarily agree with the barbaric behavior. As the years passed, I found myself caught in the middle. Living with Koweena made me think hard on the subject, and with years of watching my Lovely Julie agonizing over Koweena's plight, watching her in constant torment, I suddenly became influenced to a degree to where I felt pressured, mainly by Julie, to come up with a decision on the subject."

Thomas and Julie were sitting on the living room sofa of their house one Thursday night, when Thomas spoke up. "Julie, I need to talk to you for a minute." Koweena had been teaching Josi. Josi had just left the house from Koweena's room moments earlier. Julie could see the intense pressure on Thomas' face, a look like he had been agonizing over something for quite a while. "Sure, Thomas, what is it? You look stressed, Dear, what's wrong?" Julie asked. "You know I love you right?" "Sure I do, Dear." "And you know I wouldn't do anything to hurt you, or Koweena for that matter. And you know me by now, meeting you was the best thing that ever happened to me in my whole life." "Thomas, you're starting to scare me, what's wrong?" "I need to talk to you about your father's business." "What part of my father's business?" Julie asked. "The part about him owning slaves." "I've been waiting for you to tell me how you feel about this for a long time, go ahead, Baby." "Well, until I met you, I knew nothing about slavery, heck; I had never even been around a slave. I mean I wasn't completely ignorant about the whole thing, I knew slavery went on, but I truly never knew what it was all about, that is, until I met you. All this time spent with you, watching you hurt over Koweena, and the things that have happened to her, watching you have to sneak her in and out of your father's house all those years, just watching you anguish over your father's views of Koweena, it just has me thinking. I really never realized that slavery was such a hurtful thing, until I got involved with you. I just feel like I need to take a stand on the subject. You know, I stand by you on everything, there's nothing I wouldn't do to defend you, no matter the subject. And there's no one out there to whom I wouldn't defend you to, even your father." "Thomas, you're really worrying me, where are you going with this?" "Hold on, Sweetheart, just let me finish and you'll understand. I've also observed your father all these years. He really works hard for a living, he's wealthy, he's provided for you very well, he's taken good care of his wife and made sure you both always had what you needed." "Tell me you don't support him, Thomas." "Well, Julie, if it wasn't for his business, there's no telling where you would be." "But, Thomas, you're just as successful as he is, and you did it without any slaves." "Yeah, but I had to struggle growing up, I didn't have it easy, Jules, we weren't wealthy like your family. I had to do without a lot." Julie began stroking Thomas' short, black hair. "And that's why you work so hard, Sweetheart," Julie said. "I know, that *is* why I work so hard; but the point I'm trying to make is that slavery can't be that bad of a thing if your father is so wealthy; and you guys have benefited from it so well." Julie became emphatic. "Thomas, how could you say that. You've seen what it has done to Kowie, how it has damaged her. Slavery is barbaric!" She said. She continued, "You know, Dear, I didn't know a lot about my father's business growing up, I was sheltered from what slaves actually went through." "But what about when you were little?" Thomas interrupted. "I thought when I told you what happened to me, that one time, that we weren't going to bring that subject up again, not ever," Julie replied. "I know, I'm sorry, Dear." Julie suddenly looked down at the floor in discouragement. Thomas took a hold of her, and cuddled her up to him. "I didn't mean to bring it up, Jules, I'm so sorry." After several moments, she pulled away and began talking again. "Thomas, I've seen first hand how bad slavery is. Like I said, I was sheltered from it growing up, that was until I met Kowie. Watching all that she has gone through, seeing the devastation on her little body like I have, it's brutal Thomas; I wouldn't wish what I've seen on Koweena's body, not to mention her emotions, on my worst enemy. Do you want me to bring Koweena down here and let her tell you, first hand, how bad it is?" "No, Sweetheart, I get what you're saying. I don't want you to think that I haven't grown attached to Koweena, because I have. At first, I liked her only because she was important to you; but since I've been spending time with her, and since she's been living in this house for a number of years, and how we've spent time every night in this living room having fun, playing games together, just the three of us, I don't know, there's just something about her, she's so sweet and humble, you can't help but fall in love with her," Thomas said. Julie smiled. "She's something isn't she?" She asked. "She truly is, Julie, she's something special. I wasn't going to tell you that I agreed with slavery, no, just the opposite, because of you and Koweena, I disagree with the whole thing. It's created a soft spot in my heart for the slaves around here." Koweena's charm and appeal had rubbed off on Thomas, it was evident. "I'm really glad to hear you say that, Thomas. I don't want you to disagree with it because you just want to go along with me. I want you to disagree with it because you know in your heart that it's wrong, and because you know Koweena, and how special she truly is, not just because she's special to me, but because of her personality, her smile, her sense of humor, how beautiful she is, both inside and out." "Don't you wonder why she looks the way she does though," Thomas asked. "I mean, don't get me wrong, she's a very beautiful girl, but don't you just wonder?" He continued asking. "Sure, I wonder, but she doesn't know why she looks the way she does, and she's very self-conscious about it, so I don't mention it in front of her, but sure, I wonder." "What do you think it's all about?" Thomas asked. "I don't know, Thomas. Like I said, I just don't bring it up."

"I know you've thought about getting her off of this Plantation." That statement by Thomas cut Julie to her core. Just the mere thought of it saddened Julie greatly. Julie just sat there for a moment, trying to catch her composure. She began chocking back the tears. Thomas could see that he hit a spot in Julie that was a very sensitive one. "Are you alright, Dear?" Thomas asked. "I didn't mean to upset you," he added. "No, it's okay. Just thinking about it makes me come all unglued," Julie said. "Should I change the subject?" "No, Thomas, we need to talk about it at some point. I've been wrestling with this for a long time now. I think we should talk about it." "So, what do you think?" Thomas asked. After several minutes of silence, and with Julie still chocking back the tears, Thomas spoke up. "Maybe we just shouldn't talk about it right now." "No, we need to talk about it, it's time," Julie said. After Julie composed herself a bit more she continued. "Thomas I think we need to get her off this place. She just simply has no future here. I've been educating her almost her entire life now, and if she gets off this Plantation she can use that education for some good, you know." "Yeah," Thomas said. "I'm not shaping and molding her into a young woman, so she could just stay here and feel trapped the rest of her life. And ever since my father threatened me by saying that he was going to ship her off, I can't stop thinking about what if she does get shipped off. I know he told me that several years ago, and he hasn't done anything since then, but he could, and at any moment. Then she won't have any chance at a life." Tears began flowing down Julie's face as she continued. "It hurts me, Thomas, to talk about this subject, because I don't want to lose her." Thomas wiped away her tears. "I know, Dear, I know," he said. "So, you're saying you want to do this?" He asked. Julie grabbed Thomas' hands to help wipe away her tears. "Yes, yes, I want to do this," she said.

"Koweena!" Thomas yelled in the direction of Koweena's upstairs bedroom. "What are you doing, Thomas? You're not going to ask her about her looks are you, or what we were just talking about?" "Of course not, Dear, I just want to tell her something. Koweena! Koweena!" He continued yelling. Finally, Koweena walked out of her room and stood at the banister at the top of the stairs. "Is someone yelling for me!?" Koweena shouted. "Yes, Koweena, it's me!" Thomas yelled back. "Can you come down here for a minute!?" He continued. "I'll be right there!" Koweena yelled back. She wondered what Thomas wanted. It was unusual for him to want to speak to Koweena with such intensity as he was expressing by yelling at her like he was. "I wonder what's on his mind?" Koweena questioned to herself. As Koweena made her way down the stairs and into the living room, Thomas spoke up. "Sit right here, Koweena," Thomas said as he pointed to the space on the sofa in between Julie and him. "Right there?" Koweena asked. Koweena was surprised that Thomas was so eager for her to sit right next to him. "Sure, come sit here for a moment, I just want to talk to you for a second, and then you can go back upstairs and study," Thomas said. As Koweena uncomfortably sat in between the two, she looked at Thomas and noticed that he was staring at her right in the eyes. Koweena then looked over at Julie and noticed that she had a smile on her face, and that she was nodding her head in the direction of Thomas as if to say "go ahead, look at him." Koweena then looked back at Thomas with a puzzled look on her face. "Koweena, I called you down here because I just want to tell you how proud I am of you, and how much you mean to me." Koweena raised her eyebrows in surprise. She had spent a lot of time with Thomas, but when they talked it was just mainly small talk, things about her toys, or how her studying was going, or about Julie. "Koweena, I know you've been through a lot," Thomas continued. "And I know you've had a rough life. Well, I just want to tell you that I love you, and care deeply for you." Julie just sat there on the other side of Koweena with her head down, smiling, with very happy emotions inside over what Thomas was doing. "You inspire me, Koweena. Your work ethic, how resilient you are, how much you love Julie, and how you've allowed me to come into your life." Koweena chuckled. "Thank you, Thomas," she said. "If you ever need anything, you can count on me, okay," Thomas said. Thomas brought the three of them together, scrunching them tightly on the couch. "Alright, Thomas, thank you," Koweena said. "Koweena, what I think Thomas is trying to say is that we're both here for you, and we will do whatever it takes to make your life better for you." "I know you would, Julie, and thank you, Thomas, for telling me that. It means a lot. Can I go back upstairs now; I'm reading an awesome novel about a woman who has overcome tremendous obstacles in her life, and is becoming a successful woman and making a difference in the world." "Is that the one from Fanny Burney, the English novelist that I asked you to read?" Julie asked. "Yeah, can I go back upstairs and finish it now?" "Sure, Dear, go ahead," Julie said. As Koweena made her way up the stairs, Julie began crying. "Come here, Dear," Thomas said as he gently grabbed Julie, and once again cuddled her to him. "See, Thomas," Julie said while continuing to cry, "She's reading beautiful novels about women overcoming great obstacles. That's why we need to give her a chance at a better life. We need to get her off of this Plantation." Thomas leaned back on the sofa, continuing to cuddle Julie. "I know it hurts you to say that, Sweetheart, but I think you're making the right decision," he said. They leaned back on the sofa for several hours, both of them thinking about what they had just said.

A few weeks later, as Thomas was surveying some land in the western part of the state, just north of Natchez, about fifty miles from the town, he ran into a black man at the local store there. Thomas was buying some surveying supplies for his current land project. As the black man studied Thomas inside the store from a distance, he must have picked up on Thomas' six foot two frame standing by the compasses looking them over, and noticed that Thomas had a gentle, trusting, sympathetic look about him. Either that; or the black man was feeling extremely bold as he approached Thomas. The black man had been looking at some cowhide gloves, getting ready to purchase them before Thomas walked in. "Sir, excuse me, I is don't mean to be abrupt with you, but I thought I would introduce myself. My name is Joe." Joe said as he extended his hand out to Thomas. Joe had a motive behind meeting Thomas, he was on the hunt to find some more slaves to take back north with him, and he needed all the help he could find, even if that meant approaching a white man in a southern store. Joe was taking a chance, but once again, there was something about Thomas' demeanor that Joe picked up on right away, that made him feel like he could trust this white man. Thomas extended his hand right back to Joe's, and shook it. "Hi, Joe, I'm Thomas Callahan." That move by Thomas made Joe take a deep sigh of relief. With the fact that Thomas was even speaking to him at all gave Joe hope that he had found the right man. Joe began talking to Thomas, taking to him right away. "So, Thomas, what do you do for a livin?" Joe asked.

Joe was a fugitive slave. He had run away from a plantation and made his way up north one time, and was looking to make his second trip. During his first trip, along his journey, and while up north, he had been schooled by abolitionists, and other blacks, on how to scout out white people down south who would be sympathetic to his cause, and he was also taught the art of once finding that white person, how to actually get them to assist him in his cause. Joe had lived on one of the plantations in Natchez before his escape, and had just returned from up north when he met Thomas. Joe had been part of the Underground Railroad movement where he travelled from Natchez to as far north as central Indiana.

"I'm a land surveyor, Joe. I survey land all over Mississippi." "Sounds like an important job," Joe said. "It is, and it pays well, so the hard work is worth it." Joe relaxed a little; it appeared that he had found the right man. Joe didn't know much about land surveying, but one thing he did know, it had nothing to do with slavery, unless he was scouting out new plantations. That crossed Joe's mind, so he asked. "Do you live on a plantation, Thomas?" Joe had been taught just what questions to ask in this situation. "Yes, as a matter of fact I do, Joe." That response by Thomas caused Joe to back up a little from Thomas and start walking away. Joe thought he had the right man, but now it appeared that he was gravely mistaken. One wrong move by Joe down here in the south, and his freedom could be snatched away in an instance. Joe had to get out of there, and out of there in a hurry. He didn't know Thomas' situation, and how he was actually very close and cared deeply for a slave, neither did he know Thomas' viewpoint on slavery. If he had, he wouldn't have been so eager to disappear. "Wait a minute, Joe, where are you going to so quickly?" Thomas realized that when he said he lived on a plantation that he scared Joe away by saying that. "Joe, I have nothing to do with slavery!" Thomas yelled out to Joe as Joe was walking away in a hurry. That comment by Thomas caused Joe to stop dead in his tracks. That was the last thing Joe was expecting to hear at that moment. He thought he was dreaming when he heard Thomas say that. He had to make sure that he wasn't indeed dreaming it up, so he asked Thomas. "What did you say, sir?" "I said, I have nothing to do with slavery." Thomas didn't know for sure at this point, but deep down in his gut, he got a sixth sense that this man, who he noticed was walking about the southern streets alone, just might be Koweena's ticket out. "Come here, Joe, I'm not going to hurt you." As Joe slowly made his way back up to Thomas, Thomas continued. He had to know more about this black man, to see if indeed his instincts were right.

"I must say, Joe, you are very brave and have a lot of nerve to come up to a white man and introduce yourself like you did, especially down here in the south. What's that all about?" Joe nervously checked over Thomas from head to toe. "You seemed like a nice man, sir," Joe said. Joe had one goal in mind in approaching and talking to Thomas, to free more slaves. The Underground Railroad movement was full of people like Joe, who came back down south to risk their lives in order to rescue slaves, slaves he considered to be like his own brothers and sisters. According to him, he wasn't merely rescuing more slaves, the men, women, and children that he came back for, risking his life on the treacherous journey back to hostile territory, were family to him. "So, is there something I can help you with, Joe?" Thomas was asking the question in hopes that Joe would say that he was an escaped slave, and therefore, in turn, would be able to help Koweena. "Do you hate slaves, Thomas?" The question by Joe made Thomas feel like his instincts were right about this man. "He wants to know my view on slaves, to see if he can trust me," Thomas thought to himself. "No, Joe, quite the opposite. I feel that what is being done to blacks is horrific." Both men were tying to feel each other out. Thomas was trying to see if this man was indeed a slave, or an escaped slave, and Joe was trying to see if Thomas would be sentimental toward his cause. That statement by Thomas was the clincher for Joe, he knew now that it was time to open up to this white man. "Thomas, I is an escaped slave." That is just what Thomas wanted to hear, his intuition had paid off. He was right about this black man. "Where was the plantation you escaped from located, Joe?" Thomas asked. "Natchez, Mr. Callahan." Thomas got very excited once he heard that. It couldn't get any more perfect than that, he thought. Thomas became excited. "I'm from Natchez, Joe!" "What plantation do you live on?" Joe asked. "The Defour Plantation," Thomas responded. Joe took a deep breath and shook his head in an up and down fashion. He had heard of that plantation, as had most everybody else in the state. It was the largest plantation in Mississippi. "A lot of slaves on that Plantation, sir," Joe said. "Yes, it's quite large, have you heard of it?" "Oh yeah, I is heard of it alright." Joe felt like he had hit the jackpot, he could definitely get some slaves there, he thought. "So, if you escaped, Joe, what are you still doing down here in the south, did you just escape? Like I said, it's pretty brave of you to be walking these streets if you did." "No, I escaped several years ago. I is been up north and everything." "How did you get up north? And why are you back down here?" "Well, Mr. Callahan," "Please, Joe, call me Thomas." "Well, Thomas, as I was goin to say. While I was on my Plantation, I is heard one day of an escape route already mapped out for slaves to travel up north. I is heard that there was people, even white people, who would help me if I went on this route." Thomas became greatly enthused. "Really!" Thomas said. With each word Joe spoke, Thomas was getting more and more excited for Koweena. He began to think back to that conversation he and Julie had had about Koweena getting off the Plantation, that his and Julie's plan could work after all, and even better, there were routes, he had now learned, that Koweena could take to escape. "Yeah ,Thomas, actual routes that would lead all the way up north. I could hardly believe my ears when I heard it. And not just routes, but white people that would help me get up there. I thought it was too good to be true." "So with you actually being up north and all, was it true? You know, everything that you heard, was it all true?" Thomas asked. "Yeah, it's actually true, I is experienced for myself." "So why risk your life and come back down here?" "With what I experienced, Thomas, I just felt like I had to come back down and share it with other slaves. You know, help them get out of their situation. I felt I could do it, so here I am."

Joe talked, and Thomas listened, for what seemed like hours. Joe spilled the beans about everything. From the exact route he took from Natchez to Indiana, to the safe houses he stayed in along the way there and back. "The uh, uh, ultimate goal is to get to Canada, Mr. Callahan." "Joe, call me Thomas." "Yes, sir." "How old are you, Joe?" "Don't know, sir, mid-twenties I suppose." "I bet you've never celebrated a birthday have you?" Thomas asked. Joe immediately dropped his head and slightly slumped over, as if the wind had been knocked out of him. "No, sir; never tasted a birthday my whole life." "What a shame," Thomas exclaimed. "Now, you is see why I do what I do, sir," referring to the reason as to why he's back down south. "I admire your courage, Joe. It takes a lot of guts to do what you're doing. You're out there risking your life, not thinking of yourself, really, you're a hero." Once again, Koweena's influence was shining through on Thomas, and it was exemplified in his treatment of Joe. He had grown to have sympathy and respect for slaves, not just Koweena, but all slaves in general. Thomas had watched Koweena mature and blossom into a smart, intelligent, young girl over the last ten years, and she truly had changed his life and his prospective of people, especially black people.

As Thomas and Joe were talking, a farmer by the name of John Chandler was shopping just on the other side of the aisle from where Thomas and Joe were standing, and could overhear the two talking. John knew Thomas, but more importantly he knew Mr. Defour. As John stood there wondering how much the plow he was staring at would cost him, his thoughts went from the plow, to now trying to get closer to where Thomas was standing. He had heard half the conversation already, but wanted to get a closer shot of the two, and what they were saying. He peered over the plows that were stacked in front of him to get a peek of just exactly where Thomas and Joe were located on the other side of the aisle. He thought it was a black man Thomas was talking to, but now he knew for sure as he looked at the back of Joe's neck. Joe was wearing a light brown straw farmer's hat to help disguise himself. At first, when John heard Thomas' voice, he wanted to walk over there and talk to Thomas, but as he heard more and more of the contents of what was being said between Thomas and Joe, he suddenly felt the urge to eaves drop. He humped over slightly as he walked down his aisle, so that his head wouldn't be seen through the openings in the tools that stretched down the entire aisle. He came to the corner of the aisle and abruptly stopped. The end cap of the aisle was now the only thing that was separating John, from Thomas and Joe. As John slowly peeked around the corner, he could see the left side of Thomas' face. If Thomas glanced slightly to his left, he could easily see John looking at him, but Thomas was too engrossed in the conversation to pay any attention to who, or what, was around him.

"Where are you headed next, Joe?" Joe had learned from being trained by abolitionists along his journey to be hesitant of questions like that from curious white folks, so he hesitated a bit when Thomas asked him that. He began to trust Thomas, but when Thomas asked him that question, his trust of him began to waver somewhat. But there was just something about Thomas that eased Joe's fears. From the time Joe first saw him, he knew there was something different about this man. It was in Thomas' facial expressions, a sincere, gentleness about his face as he was talking to him. It was in his voice as well, the tone was not rough or harsh, something Joe had been used to by white folks his entire life. Thomas reminded Joe of those white anti-slavery activists he had met along his journey up north and back. Meanwhile, John, hidden by the end cap, was keenly listening to every word. Joe declined to answer Thomas' question about where he was headed next, he just didn't trust him enough yet. Thomas, realizing Joe wasn't going to answer his question, fired off another one at him. "Help me figure something out, Joe? If you're this fugitive slave, why then be so bold as to walk around in public like you are?" "Must take chances sir, comes along with the territory. It comes along with tryin to rescue more slaves. To get where you goin, you goin to get seen, one way or another, sir. Anyways, the way I is seen it, it's worth it, you know freedom and all, I is tasted it, this freedom, and it's worth it, sir." "Do you have much education, Joe?" "A little I picked up from white folks in safe houses up north that I stayed in." "Well, your English is actually pretty good." "Thank you, sir." "I've been thinking, Joe, I want to help. My wife and I take care of this slave girl, Koweena, quite a charming young girl, she actually lives with us. I was wondering, that is, if you want to, maybe you could sit down with her and talk to her, you know, about some of the things you've been telling me about, and some of the things you've gone through on your journeys up north. Come to think of it, it would be a perfect way to further your cause." "How's that, sir."

In the meantime, John, now engrossed in the conversation, was thinking to himself out loud, "Thomas is a dead man."

"I live on the Defour Plantation," Thomas continued, "and you know exactly where that is, right?" "Yes, sir." "Well, I have an idea; my work here will be over in a couple of days." "You want me to help your slaves, right?" Joe interrupted. "No, Joe, I want you to help Koweena.

My main concern is her." Thomas would go to the ends of the earth for Julie, and thus, would do the same for Koweena. "Okay, I'll do it Thomas," Joe said. "Great, Joe, can you stay here for a couple of days and go back with me to Natchez?" "Sure." "Okay, let's meet up right back here in two days, say around noon, and we'll make the trip together. I want you to meet my wife, and of course Koweena." Thomas was bursting at the seams; he couldn't wait to tell Julie the good news, and to introduce Joe to her.

Meanwhile, as Thomas and Joe were winding down their conversation, John made his way to the back of his aisle. "I've got to tell Mr. Defour about this," he whispered to himself.

Two days later, Thomas had arrived back at his house. It was dark now, and the lights were on in the house. As Thomas approached the front door, with Joe alongside him, he could see through the window in the front door, Julie and Koweena sitting on the living room sofa reading a book together. His heart melted. He missed Julie something awful when he would go on his many trips, and he loved seeing her for the first time when he arrived back; and Koweena for that matter. As Thomas opened the front door and walked in, Julie and Koweena looked around and noticed that it was Thomas. "Thomas!" They both said aloud in harmony. The talk Thomas had had with Koweena in the living room several weeks back had really changed her perspective of Thomas. With him telling her how much he cared for her, it really made her more easily show her care toward Thomas. "Hey guys!" Thomas said. "Who do you have with you there?" Julie asked. "Guys, I would like you to meet Joe. I meet him in Stanton a couple of days ago while shopping for supplies." Joe tipped his hat toward Koweena and Julie. "Ladies," he said. "Hi, Joe, welcome," Julie said. "Joe, make yourself at home, go ahead and sit on the sofa there," Thomas said. He stretched his arm out toward Koweena. "This is Koweena," Thomas said. "Hi, Koweena, nice to meet you." "Hi," Koweena said. Koweena was very shy around people she would first meet. As Joe made his way to the sofa, Thomas motioned for Julie to get up. Julie stood up from where she and Koweena had been sitting, so that Joe could sit in her spot, right next to Koweena. Thomas wanted it set up that way so Koweena and Joe could talk more easily with one another. "Julie, Dear, can you come with me into the kitchen for a moment?" Thomas asked. Once again he was trying to set up the situation for Koweena to get to know Joe as they both sat on the couch.

As Julie and Thomas entered the kitchen, no more had they walked inside, than Thomas grabbed her by the arms and said emphatically. "You're not going to believe this!" Julie laughed at Thomas' excitement. "What, Thomas, calm down?" Thomas began shaking Julie by the arms. "This guy can get Koweena out of here!" He told Julie. "Calm down, Thomas, what do you mean?" "He's an escaped slave who has already been up north!" "What!?" "Yes, he's escaped, and he's been successful at it too!" As Thomas said those words Julie became upset and frightened. It suddenly hit her, this could actually happen, Koweena could leave her. Thomas placed his arm around Julie's shoulders. "What's wrong, Dear, I thought you would be happy," he said. "I don't know, Thomas, she could die out there." The reality of that statement made the both of them drop their heads in silence.

Meanwhile, in the living room, Joe started up the conversation with Koweena. Koweena wasn't about to say any words to Joe without Joe saying something first. "So, Koweena, I understand you is a slave here?" "Yeah." "You know I was once a slave," Joe said. That instantly peeked Koweena's curiosity. A black man who had once been a slave, she had never heard of such a thing, and now she was staring at someone who was in fact just that. "What do you mean you were once a slave?" Koweena asked. "I escaped from a plantation not far from here." Koweena's eyes opened wide. "Escaped!" She said.

Back in the kitchen, after a moment of silence, Thomas spoke up. "Just let the two of them talk, Jules. Let Koweena learn that there are people like her out there who have successfully escaped." "I don't know, Thomas, I'm scared for her." "I know, Sweetheart, but just let her get a taste of what it's like to see a black person actually being free. It will be a new experience for her, and then we'll see how she reacts to the whole thing." "How did this man make it all the way up north?" Julie asked. "There's actually a system set up for slaves to escape! They don't have to do it on their own, Jules!" "What do you mean a system?" "They actually have routes out there that lead all the way up to Canada, and not only that, but there are white people who help them along the way." "So it really is a well thought out plan, a designed system huh?" Julie asked. "Yes, Jules; and we have a man in our own living room, actually talking to Koweena, who has successfully made the journey." The thought of this designed route system eased Julie's mind a bit, and relieved the tension she had been feeling upon hearing about it. But it still didn't change the fact for Julie that this thing had gone from just talking about it weeks ago, to now maybe actually happening. She began to think, even though she had been thinking about it for a long time now, since this man was here, in her own living room talking to Koweena, she really began thinking hard about the fact, could she truly live without Koweena in her life? It scared her to death; it took her breath away to even think about it actually happening for real.

"How did you escape?" Koweena asked Joe as they continued talking in the living room. "Well, I heard one day, from some of the other slaves, that there were some escape routes designed to help slaves get all the way up north, and not only that Koweena, but there are actually white people who help you get up there along the way." "You mean you get help from white folks?" "Yeah, there are actually white folks out there that believe like us, that slavery is a bad thing." Koweena, from her studies, already knew that. "What do you mean they help you?" Koweena asked. "They help you in a lot of ways. There's white folks who live in houses that allow you to stay there and rest, and eat, and sleep, until you is ready to go on further. These houses are called safe houses. There's also places in addition to the safe houses where you stop and rest, and meet up with other slaves who are making the same journeys. These places are called Depots." "So this thing is very well thought out I take it." "Yes, Koweena, very well thought out. These people that help us along the way, have special codes, and special languages they use with one another to tell one another when we is coming through. There is markers in front of the safe houses to alert us as to whether or not the house is safe to enter." Koweena was no longer shy towards Joe, she was too intrigued by what she was hearing to worry about being shy, she was just sitting there taking it all in. She could hardly believe what she was hearing. Not only was there a chance of getting out of this place she thought, but there was a devised plan already set up to make it a successful trip. "Is it hard?" She asked. "Well, it's not easy, Koweena, I can tell you that much. But is it worth it? Most definitely. To get that first taste of freedom, there's nothing like it in the world." "What are you doing back down here? I mean, aren't you scared about being on this Plantation?" "Well, it's not my favorite place to be, but it's why I came back down here." "I don't understand," Koweena said. "I came back down to free people like you, Koweena. I've been through it, I've tasted freedom, and now I just want to make sure others, like yourself, get to experience what I've experienced." Koweena looked downward while biting her nails. "What makes you think I want to leave?" She said. "I can tell by your reaction to what I'm saying that you want to. And I can tell by your body language, like when you just said that, your whole expression changed. I can just tell."

"I'm going back in there, Thomas," Julie said while standing on the other side, opposite Thomas, at the oak bar, situated in the middle of the kitchen. "Let them talk it out, Jules, just let Koweena learn about it." "It's been enough time, Thomas." Julie, deep down inside, didn't want Koweena learning about any escape plan. "Julie, come back!" Thomas yelled out as Julie opened the swinging kitchen door to go into the dining room that separated the kitchen from the living room. "So what's going on in here, guys?" Julie asked as she made her way into the living room. "Julie, you're not going to believe this!" Koweena said with excitement. "I know, Kowie, I heard all about it from Thomas. Why don't you say good night to Joe here and go to bed, it's about your bed time." "Okay, good night, Joe, it was nice meeting you." "Nice meetin you, Koweena."

As Koweena made her way upstairs to her room, Thomas made his way into the living room. "Joe, I have a great idea." "What, Mr. Callahan?" "Why don't you stay here with my wife and I?" "Oh, I couldn't impose, sir." "Where else are you going to go, Joe? Come on now, stay here with us." "Well, if you insist." "I insist, Joe," Thomas said. "Okay," Joe said. Julie got up from the chair next to the sofa. "Joe, come upstairs with me and I'll show you to your room," Julie said.

As she came back downstairs, Thomas was sitting on the sofa drinking some tea. "Julie, I really like the way this is going, you know. I like where this is headed. It's a perfect situation for Koweena." "I don't know, Thomas, it doesn't feel right." "Jules, you can't allow your personal emotions to get in the way of this. We've talked about getting Koweena off this Plantation, you agreed to it, you said it was time, and now this opportunity basically just fell into our laps." "I know, Thomas, I know. But I just can't stand the thought of not having Kowie around.

It would break me. I wouldn't be able to go on. It would be as if she died, and I couldn't take that." "Jules, think about it. When she gets up north, she can write us from wherever she winds up. We can go visit her. Doesn't that sound like a great idea?" "*If* she makes it, Thomas, *if* she makes it. There's no guarantee she will make it." "Look at Joe, Jules, he made it, and he made it back down without getting injured." "Yes, but he's a man, Koweena is just a shy little girl, so many things can happen, so many bad things. It's just too risky, Thomas." "Julie, Koweena is sixteen years old, she's almost an adult, you're just caught up in the emotions right now of the fact that this thing could really happen. You need some time to think." "She's still just a child, Thomas, and anyway how long is enough time; I'll never be ready for her to leave. It crushes me just to think about it."

Meanwhile, Koweena was thinking about what Joe had said that night as she lay there in her bed with the moonlight streaming through her room. "I can actually do this," she whispered to herself. "I can get Josi, and we can actually pull this thing off," she continued to whisper. "Joe will help us!" She got so excited she began tossing and turning. But then she thought. "What about Julie? I would miss her so. How would she get along without me, and how would I get along without her?" She continued weighing out the options until she fell asleep.

The following night, Koweena, Julie, and Thomas were in the living room playing cards as they normally do, while Joe was upstairs in the guest bedroom. "Do you think Joe's for real, Julie?" Koweena asked. "What do you mean, Kowie?" Julie responded. "I mean, do you think he really made it up north, or was he just saying that stuff?" "Of course he has, Koweena," Thomas interrupted. "You don't think he's just some black man roaming the streets down here in the south all alone, do you?" Thomas continued. "I mean, look at him," Thomas said, "he's by himself, he has no white man around him, he's tied down to nothing, he belongs to no plantation, and I've heard his stories about his journey, he's for real," Thomas said. "Are you planning on having any kids, Julie?" Koweena asked. "I wonder what it would be like to have a family," she continued. It was apparent, Koweena had been thinking of escaping. She was thinking of having kids of her own some day, and Julie could sense it.

"Thomas, can you give us a minute?" Julie asked. "Sure, Dear, I'll be in the kitchen if you need me." "Great, Dear, thanks." As Thomas made his way into the kitchen Julie began to speak. "Kowie, Thomas and I have been talking about having kids for several months now, why do you ask?" "Well, hearing Joe yesterday talking about how great things were up north, I was just thinking about starting my own family one day." Koweena was at the age where she was thinking about a husband now, and thinking about that, in turn, lead her to begin thinking about having her own family at some point in the next few years. "You've really been thinking about this haven't you?" Julie asked. Koweena became emphatic. "Yeah, a lot!" She said. Julie knew that if Koweena stayed on this Plantation that there would be no way she could have a family. Julie knew the consequences of keeping Koweena here just for her own selfish desires. She was hoping that this subject wouldn't have come up so soon, but she knew with Joe here at the house, Koweena's thoughts would begin to wonder toward living free, and that, in turn, would lead Koweena to begin thinking of the possibilities of having her own family. Ever since Koweena was a child, because Julie knew how bright Koweena was, Julie knew at some point that Koweena would reach the age to where she would be ready to spread her wings. And now, as she sat there staring at Koweena, she knew that Joe now provided the air beneath her to where she could do just that. Julie had a choice to make, the same choice that had kept her up all night the night before, the same choice that had caused her to nervously pace her bedroom floor over and over again for the last several months. And that choice was to either try and keep her on the Plantation, or let her go and try to live the life that she herself was living, a life Julie had taken for granted, until now. Julie realized as she sat there that Koweena was fighting an uphill battle to claim a life of her own. Julie realized, right then and there, just how fortunate she had it herself. Julie's heart was breaking as she knew she had to make the decision here and now, but she knew she couldn't be alone with Koweena to make that choice. She needed support to tell Koweena what she had decided.

"Thomas, can you come in here please!?" Julie shouted into the kitchen. She needed some moral support for what she was about to tell Koweena. As Thomas made his way from the kitchen into the living room, Julie's thoughts began to race. She began thinking about the pros and cons of letting Koweena go. She began to think about the pros first. "If Koweena stays here with me, I'll be happy for the rest of my life. She can still have a baby by a slave, and she can raise it right here in this house. We can be one big happy family," she thought to herself. Julie's desire to keep Koweena there with her was causing her thoughts to become erratic and unrealistic. Then she began thinking of the cons. "She could be shipped off at any time, without notice, and if she did have a baby, she could lose it and have it stripped away from her in an instant. That kind of pain would be unbearable. She would never have the chance to have a husband. She would never truly have a family." As much as this was going to break her heart into pieces, she had come to a decision. Koweena was puzzled staring at Julie sitting there thinking. "Julie, what are you thinking? You've been sitting there with that look on your face like your seriously contemplating something," She didn't realize the pain Julie was going through at that moment. She didn't realize what Julie was going through on the inside, nor the seriousness of the situation. "Okay, Dear, I'm here, what's going on? You sounded stressed when you yelled out to me," Thomas said. "Yeah, Julie, you're beginning to scare me, what's wrong?" Koweena asked. Julie had been staring at Koweena for several minutes now, motionless, just staring into Koweena's eyes. Finally, Julie spoke up. "Thomas, I'm ready to talk to Koweena about what we've been talking about." Koweena began to get even more worried when she heard Julie say that. "Julie, you're really scaring me, what is it?" Koweena asked. "Julie, are you sure?" Thomas asked. "Thomas, this is my decision, we agreed on that a while back." Koweena was getting really nervous. "What decision, what's going on?" She asked. "Koweena, if you want to escape, if that is truly what you want to do, then I, I mean, we, Thomas and I, will not stop you." Koweena was in shock as she looked at Thomas who was smiling at her. She then looked at Julie. She could see the pain Julie was feeling, written all over her face. "But, Julie, I um, I mean I, what about you?" Julie's eyes began welling up with tears. "Koweena, don't think about me in making this decision," she said. "Julie, I can tell by the way you're reacting, you don't want me to go, I know you don't, right!? You're about to cry." Part of Koweena wanted Julie to try and stop her, she wanted Julie to put her arms around her and tell her not to go. But she realized as she sat there staring at the pain on Julie's face, that she was an adult now, no longer a child who years ago would get that hug from Julie. Koweena became emphatic as tears started welling up in her eyes. "Julie, I don't want to hurt you!" Julie sensed that it was too much for Koweena to handle right now to come to a decision right away. Thomas, as he observed both of them, realized that they were both going through a lot of pain. He knew, at that moment, that the both of them were experiencing the same kind of pain. Neither of them wanted to let each other go. Thomas walked over to where Koweena was sitting on the sofa, and sat down beside her. He put his arms around her, this made Koweena's tears start flowing. Julie, upon seeing Koweena, began to let the tears flow freely as well. "Come here, Julie," Thomas told Julie as he had one arm around Koweena and the other stretched out in the direction of Julie. Julie walked over to where Thomas and Koweena were sitting and sat down and cuddled in Thomas' arms. Thomas just leaned back against the sofa, Koweena and Julie leaned back with him. Thomas just sat there cuddling the two as they cried. "I don't want to lose you, Koweena," Julie said. That statement by Julie caused herself to begin an all out full blown cry, Koweena soon followed with the same crying. "Shhh, it's okay you two, it's going to be alright," Thomas said, trying to console them both. After a few moments of crying, Julie composed herself and continued speaking. "I don't want to lose you, but I want you to be happy, Kowie. I want you to have the same kind of life that I have. I want you to grow up and get married, have a husband, have children." Koweena, still crying, spoke up. "I want that too, Julie, but I don't want to lose you!" As Thomas was holding them both close to him, he was patting both their upper arms with his hands. "Kowie, you're going to have to let me go, it's the only way," Julie said. "Listen you two," Thomas spoke up. "It's not the end of the two of you, and your relationship to each other. Koweena, when you get up north, you can write us and we will come visit you. It's not the end." "It sure feels like it, Thomas," Koweena said. "Thomas is right, Kowie, you can write us anytime while you're making your journey." Julie was desperately trying to convince herself that everything was going to be alright. They both pulled away from the arms of Thomas and sat straight up and stared at one another. Julie placed her hand gently on Koweena's cheek. "Kowie, you know I love you, and you know I wouldn't put you in harm's way, but with you staying here, that's exactly what I'm doing. My father could have you shipped off at any time, you heard him say that from his own lips a while back, and if that happened, I would never see you again. At least this way you can have your freedom, and we can stay in touch with each other," Julie said. Koweena became emphatic. "But why don't you guys move far away with me, will you!?" Koweena said as she began crying all over again. "Kowie, listen to me, you are legally my father's property, there's nothing I can do about that. He has legal papers and everything. You're stuck on this property. That's one of the reasons Thomas and I decided to live on this land, so I could be close to you." It agonized Julie to have to tell her that, but it convinced her at the same time that Koweena needed to escape. They both lay back down on Thomas' chest. Both Koweena and Julie knew that there was only one option in this scenario, and that was for Koweena to escape, it was a surreal moment in the living room that night as they all three just sat there on the sofa in silence.

The next day there was a knock on the front door of the Defour house. Martha opened the door and saw a man standing there with dirty, grimy hands, dirty work boots, and wearing overalls with holes throughout. "Yes, is Mr. Defour here?" The man said. "Do you is have an appointment?" Martha asked. "Listen, I really need to speak with Mr. Defour, it's very urgent that I do so." Mrs. Defour just happened to be walking by at the time the man was speaking, and she recognized the voice. "John Chandler, how are you!?" She said as she approached the front door to welcome him in. "Please, come in. Martha that will be all, you're excused. So, John, how have you been?" "Very well, ma'am, and yourself?" "Oh, just fine, just fine. What brings you down here to Natchez?" "Well, ma'am, I need to speak with your husband."

John didn't look like the kind of man that would know the Defours on a personal level. He wasn't well kept, he looked poor and grungy. But in fact, he was the wealthiest man back in his town. He was one of the most successful farmers in the state of Mississippi. And although he didn't dress like it, he was very well off. "Wait right here, John, I'll see if my husband has anyone in his office with him, and I'll be right back out." "Yes, ma'am." John stood there in the foyer, he had his farmer's straw hat at his waist, holding it with both hands, he was rubbing it with his fingers. He was extremely nervous about being there, after all, he was about to tell one of the most powerful men in the state that his son-in-law was not only harboring a slave, but that he was planning some type of escape for Mr. Defour's slaves. "John, he's ready to see you," Mrs. Defour said as she walked back out into the foyer. "It's the last door on the right," she told John. "Thank you, Mrs. Defour." "Sure, John, it was good seeing you." "Good seeing you too, ma'am."

As John made his way down the long hallway, he was going over in his mind what he was, in fact, going to say to Mr. Defour. He didn't want to insult the powerful plantation owner with his words, so he had to be meticulous in his approach. John made his way to the entranceway of Mr. Defour's office. "John, my boy! What brings you all the way down here from Stanton town? How's the farming business up there?" "Fine, Mr. Defour, just fine." Mr. Defour took a puff on his dark oak pipe. "Have a seat, John. So, what can I do you for, John? I know it must be important for you to come fifty miles to see me like this." "Yes, sir, it is. It's of a grave matter concerning your business." That made Mr. Defour sit straight up in his swiveling chair that he normally leaned back on. "My business, John? You don't have one of my slaves up there now do you?" Mr. Defour said as he laughed in a joking manner. "No, sir, but I might soon unless something is done." That comment by John made Mr. Defour take his pipe out of his mouth and place it on his desk. "What do you mean, John?" "Well, sir, I just happened to be shopping last week at the local store there in Stanton, and your son-in-law was in there." "So you talked to Thomas did you?" "No, sir, not exactly, I overheard him talking to a nigger. "Uh huh, you did, did you?" "Yes, sir, and what he had to say to that Nigger I think you need to hear, and well, that's why I made this trip all the way down here to see you." "Go on, John." "Well, sir, the Nigger was telling Thomas how he had escaped from his plantation right here in Natchez, and how he had made it all the way up north." "An escaped slave huh, right here in Natchez?" "Yes, sir." "Okay, go on." "Well, he was telling Thomas how he made it up there and back using some kind of system of routes and special codes used by white people along the way, and how those white people helped him along his journey." "A system? Routes? Codes?" Mr. Defour questioned. "Yes, sir, a kind of designed highway for niggers to travel on to get up north." Mr. Defour became very concerned at this point; it was news he dreaded to hear, but it had always been in the back of his mind, something he was fearful would someday come true, and now, for the first time in his career as a plantation owner, it seemed like it had indeed come true. "Tell me more, John." "Mr. Defour, what I'm about to tell you next is the real reason I'm down here talking to you right now." Mr. Defour grabbed a hold of the desk, bracing himself for what John was about to say next. "Thomas has that Nigger here, on your Plantation." Mr. Defour slammed the side of his fist against his desk. "What!?" He yelled. "Yes, sir, he's here." "Did you get his name, John?" "Yes, sir, it's Joe. He told Thomas that his job was to come back down here from the north and free more niggers from plantations, and, sir, I think he's targeting yours right now." "Damn it, those niggers!" Mr. Defour yelled. "That's not all, sir. Thomas told him to come back with him here to your plantation to help some nigger slave named Koweena." Mr. Defour became infuriated. "My own daughter, stabbing me in the back," he whispered to himself. "Is that it, John?" "Yes, sir, that's pretty much it." "Well, I owe you one, John, for coming down here and telling me this. It certainly is alarming to say the least." "I figured it would be, sir, but I thought you needed to know." "Yes, most definitely. Well, it seems like my worst nightmare has come true, John. Thank you for letting me know all of this." "Yes, sir." "Have a good day, John." "You too, sir." John got up from his chair and left the office. As he was walking through the foyer, Mrs. Defour was there to greet him. "Is everything alright, John, I heard yelling and slamming in there from my husband." "Maybe you should let your husband tell you, ma'am, good day." "Good bye, John, take care, say hello to your wife for me."

"Honey! Honey! Get in here!" Mr. Defour was yelling so loud that Mrs. Defour could here him from the foyer. She quickly ran into his office. "What is it, Dear!?" Mr. Defour was now standing at the giant window that stretched almost the entire length of the side of his office. Mrs. Defour was nervous standing there staring at her husband. She could tell he was upset. "Dear, what is it!?" She asked. It was obvious Mr. Defour was deep in thought. After several minutes, Mr. Defour turned around and looked at Mrs. Defour. Mrs. Defour could clearly see the worrisome concern on her husband's face. "What's wrong?" She again asked. "Not only do we now have a threat of my slaves escaping, but our daughter has turned against us," Mr. Defour said in an agitated tone. Mrs. Defour began to panic. "Julie, what has Julie done!?" She asked. "And Thomas, Thomas of all people, he's on Julie's side," Mr.

Defour said. "Tell me, Sweetheart, what are you talking about!?" "Their conspiring, the both of them." "Conspiring to do what?" "Their conspiring to help my slaves escape." "What!? Julie! Thomas! How do you know!?" "John told me everything. They're hiding a nigger here, right here, in my own backyard. His job is to help slaves escape. I just learned that there is a plan, designed by niggers and white people to help slaves make it up north." "What!? How!?" "I don't know, but something tells me that going to Julie's house will nip this thing in the bud." "I told you, Dear, that you should have remained close to Julie after she moved out of this house. Visiting her just a couple of times was not going to do the trick. You should have kept a closer eye on her," Mrs. Defour said. "And you shouldn't have let that little Nigger into our home in the first place. You're the one that started this by letting Julie see that little coon. And you say it was all worth it because it brought Thomas into the family. Thomas is the very one who brought that Nigger, who is trying to free my slaves, onto this Plantation, damn it! "Surely not dear!" "Yes, it was Thomas! I knew that man didn't have a backbone; he does whatever Julie tells him. I know what I'm going to do now; I'm going to ship that Koweena nigger off this Plantation. That's what I'm going to do!" As Mr. Defour said this he punched the glass with his elbow, cracking the window. "Get Donald in here right now, immediately!" He yelled out to Mrs. Defour. She quickly left the office and made her way to one the servants. "Quickly, I need for you to get Mr. Jenkins, hurry go!" She said in a sharp tone to Julias. She began snapping her fingers. "Go!" She yelled.

After just a few minutes, Mr. Jenkins made his way to the house, and into Mr. Defour's office. "What is it, sir, your wife said it was an emergency." Mr. Jenkins noticed the cracked window to his right as he entered the office. Mr. Defour was now back sitting in his chair behind his desk. "Donald, we have a Code Blue." "A Code Blue!" Mr. Jenkins knew that that was the code word used on the Plantation for a possible slave escape, but he couldn't believe his ears. They had never used those words before in all the years of the Plantation's existence. "Yes, Donald, a Code Blue. Here's what were going to do, were going to plan a raid tonight on a suspected hide out, where an escaped slave may be staying at." "Where sir?" Mr. Jenkins was expecting a shack, or the lumber yard, or one of the supply barns, or maybe somewhere in the fields. What he was about to hear would floor him. Mr. Defour looked down at his desk, shaking his head in obvious disgust. "We're going to raid my daughter's house," he said. Mr. Jenkins just stood there with his mouth open; he couldn't believe what he just heard. "His own daughter's house!" Mr. Jenkins whispered emphatically to himself. After thinking about it for a second, he realized that it really wasn't that big of a shock, after all, from what he heard from Julie, and the fact that Thomas had come over to his house to talk about Julie and Koweena, it really didn't surprise him. "We do it tonight, Donald. Gather four of your best overseers, and have them meet me here at seven o'clock, in my office." "Yes, sir."

Even though Mr. Jenkins wasn't surprised by what was transpiring, Mr. Defour, on the other hand, was taken back by what his daughter and son-in-law had done to him. He just sat there behind his desk in shock, not only at the fact that his daughter may be harboring a fugitive slave, but also the fact that he was about to do a Code Blue raid on her house. Mr. Defour was crushed as he sat there thinking back to his daughter, and the moments he witnessed her growing up, and how proud he was of her back then, even though he never told her that. He just sat there for hours, feeling betrayed by his own child.

That night, Koweena and Julie were upstairs in the guest bedroom that Joe was staying in, talking to Joe, listening to all his tales about his journey up north and back. They both were learning a lot from Joe, things like what the journey was like, what some of the snares and traps were along the way, how Joe would protect Koweena, if indeed she went along with him on his next journey. Julie felt better about Koweena's safety, if indeed Koweena was going to make the trek with Joe. She felt more at ease that Koweena would be going with someone who had done this before, and knew the pitfalls and dangers that could occur along the way. Yet, she still just couldn't bear the thought of losing the one she thought of as her own flesh and blood. The one she cried with, laughed with, played with, and helped to educate and broaden her horizons about the world. Julie knew, with what she had taught Koweena, and what Koweena had learned in her books about the world, that if she was going to go, she was ready. Julie tried to get herself mentally prepared for life without Koweena, as Joe continued telling his tales to them both. But each time she tried, it was just too much of a nightmare to even think about. Koweena noticed that Julie had drifted off to some other place while Joe was talking. "Julie, are you alright?" Koweena asked. "Yes, Sweetheart, I was just thinking, that's all." "About what?" "About you, of course." Koweena just smiled. This time it hit Koweena hard, she was really going to miss Julie. "How am I going to do this without Julie by my side, if I indeed decide to do this," she wondered. "She's been my emotional support for so long, when I was down, she knew just what to do to lift my spirits, she is the only one that can do that when I need it. If I get down on this journey, she won't be there to brighten my mood, what will I do," she continued wondering.

"Boom! Pop!" A sudden loud crash came from downstairs. Koweena eyes opened wide and her jaw dropped. "What in the world was that?" She asked Julie. "You two stay right here, don't move!" Julie said as she got up from the bed and rushed out onto the banister overlooking the foyer. She quickly noticed her father, Mr. Jenkins, and four very large white men. The four white men were standing on top of what used to be the front door. Julie quickly ran back into the guest bedroom. Julie began to panic as she grabbed a hold of Joe's arm. "Hurry, we have to hide you, Joe!" She said. Thomas wasn't there; he was out of town on business. Koweena stood up from the bed. "Julie, I'm scared. What's going on?" "Kowie, just stay there, don't move!" Koweena was standing there rubbing her hands, rocking back and forth. "Quick, Joe, out this window!" Julie said as she opened the one window that was in the guest bedroom. "There's a ledge out here. I need you to stand on it about five feet from the window, right at this point. Can you do that?" Julie asked. Joe was used to these situations; he wasn't panicking in the least. He stepped out onto the ledge. Julie quickly ran over to Koweena. She was standing in front of her now. "Kowie, get in your room and shut the door! Go! Now!" "Julie!" Koweena said in a distraught, upset tone. Koweena started crying as she ran to her room and shut the door. As Koweena stood there in the darkness of her room, thoughts began to race through her mind. "Are they here to ship me off!?" She whispered to herself. "Maybe I should hide too," she thought as she was still crying. She quickly got under her bed. She had never panicked like this before. She thought her life was over. Thoughts of never seeing Julie again, thoughts of never seeing Josi again, being in a brand new place where she would have to live in a shack again, not getting the privileges, like she had on the Defour Plantation. All of that was running through her mind as she lay there under her bed. She could hardly breathe; she was having a panic attack.

Julie raced down the stairs where the overseers were flipping over her furniture and turning her dining room upside down. They were destroying the place. "Daddy, this is my home!" "Julie, as you can plainly see this is not your home, it's on my land, it's my home!" "Daddy, they're tearing up all of my valuables! What are you doing!?" "Julie, you're harboring a slave, and as you can plainly see, we're here to find him!" "I'm not harboring a slave, daddy!" "He's not here, Boss," one of the overseers said to Mr. Jenkins after they wrecked the entire downstairs. Koweena could hear the slamming and banging going on downstairs. She laid there crying so hard she could hardly catch her breath. "There coming to take me away! There going to take me away!" She hysterically whispered to herself. "Tear the place apart upstairs!" Mr. Jenkins barked the order to the overseers. "Daddy, their tearing my house apart, stop them!" "Julie, I'm very disappointed in you! Go ahead men, don't stop until you find that Nigger!" Mr. Defour said pointing toward the upstairs area.

As Koweena was lying there, she could suddenly hear the sounds of loud pounding boots coming closer and closer to her room. Upon instantly hearing that, her door flew open. She put her hand over her mouth so that the men wouldn't hear her panicky breathing. Koweena thought this was it, it was over for her. One of the men peeled the cover from the side of her bed and bent down. Suddenly, Koweena was staring right in the face of one of the mean ugly men, staring directly in his eyes. She thought her heart was going to stop. "We have a live one here, boys!" The overseer said. The man violently jerked Koweena by the shoulders, almost pulling them out of her socket. Koweena was too scared to say a word. When Julie noticed the men going into Koweena's room, she quickly ran upstairs. "Leave her alone! She's not the one you're looking for!" Julie yelled out. Mr. Jenkins was close behind Julie going up the stairs, and was now in Koweena's room. "Tear up this room, from top to bottom, he's got to be around here somewhere!" He yelled out to the overseers. "Leave her room alone!" Julie yelled out. She swiftly went over to where Koweena was standing. Koweena was bent over with her hands on her knees trying to compose herself. The overseers had let her go once Mr. Jenkins gave them the orders to tear the room apart. "Are you okay, Sweetheart!" Julie asked. "Julie, I'm terrified!" Julie grabbed a hold of Koweena by the shoulders as Koweena remained bent over. "It's going to be okay, I'm here, nothing is going to happen to you," she told Koweena. "He's not in here, Boss." "Try the guest bedroom!" Mr. Jenkins hollered out. Julie could only take a deep breath as they went into the guest bedroom. She knew that if Joe was captured, there would go any chance that Koweena might have at a future, and thus, she could still be shipped off.

The men tore the room apart. Mr. Defour was now standing at the entranceway of the guest bedroom. "Check the window!" He yelled out. Two of the men opened up the window to peer out. Even though Joe had been through similar situations like this on his journey, he truly thought when he heard that window being raised, that he was done in for. He could barely see one of the men's heads, slightly sticking out of the window. "Here we go, it's over for me," Joe thought. "Wait a minute, he's not sticking his head out far enough," Joe said to himself. "I might have a chance here." The man brought his head back inside. "Nothing there!" He shouted. Julie could hear the man from Koweena's room, and gave a deep sigh of relief upon hearing that. After tearing the rest of the upstairs apart, the men proceeded to go back downstairs. As Mr. Defour walked by Koweena's room to go downstairs, he noticed Julie sitting on the bed holding Koweena. He walked up to his daughter. He stood there just waiting for Julie to look up at him. Once Julie finally did, he said. "I'm shipping her off as soon as possible." "Dad, no!" "It will be just a matter of days, Julie; I have to get all the paperwork done, and then she's gone." "Dad, please!" Julie shouted. Koweena started crying hysterically. Mr. Defour just turned and walked out of the room and back downstairs, and out of the house with the rest of the men.

The house had been ransacked. It looked as if someone had broken in. But Julie wasn't concerned with that. She realized right then and there, emotions aside, that she had to get Koweena off this Plantation, and off now. Julie spent the night that evening in Koweena's room. With everything either destroyed or turned upside down, the only thing Julie could do was to get a couple of thick blankets and lay them across Koweena's floor. Julie was lying on her back with Koweena lying on Julie's upper chest. Julie had her arm wrapped around Koweena. Both of them were churning inside emotionally. They both knew that this would probably be one of their last nights together. Koweena's mind flashed back to the first night she spent with Julie. How unbelievable it was, and how she felt like a princess lying there next to Julie. She smelled that same scent of perfume from Julie, the same smell she had smelled during her first night they spent together. "Kowie, I want you to know something. I think, no, I know you're ready for this journey. From the time you were five, I've been training you for this very moment. Remember this, Kowie, as you go along on your journey, it's not what people say about you, it's how you react to what those people say about you, that's the difference, that's what you can control, and that's the most important thing. Don't let what people say about you hurt you, or affect you negatively, respond positively. You can't control people, but you can control how you respond to those people. Don't ever forget that, Kowie, okay." "Okay, Julie. Julie, my heart is breaking inside." "I know, Kowie, mine is too." Koweena wanted so badly to ask her to go with her, but she knew how unrealistic that would be. Her father would surely track them down if that happened. Koweena began to cry. "Shhh, don't cry, my little Angel, don't cry. You're going to do just fine without me." Now, Julie was choking back the tears. Similar to the beating Koweena had when she was eight; Julie did not want Koweena to see her lose it here. She had to be strong and sound confident, to ease Koweena's fears. But it was tough, Julie kept from crying out loud, but tears just streamed down her face. "You're going to make it, Kowie; you know that, you're going to make it." Koweena, still crying, spoke up. "I want you there with me though." "Shhh, I know, Baby, I know. I will be with you though, in spirit, and in your locket." When Julie said that, Koweena quickly grabbed her locket that was around her neck. "I won't let this necklace go, Julie; I will never let it go." "I know you won't, Baby." "I love you, Julie." "And I love you so much it hurts, Kowie, you are my everything, you know that." "Will you forget about me?" Koweena asked. "Kowie, don't even think that. I'll be waiting for that letter every day. I'll *never* stop thinking about you! I will miss you so much, Sweetheart!" "I know, Julie, I'll miss you too." This made Koweena cry so hard she could barely breathe. Julie just laid there stroking Koweena's beautiful, long, curly hair as Koweena continued to cry out loud.

The next day, around mid morning, Julie called Julias, and about five other male slaves, to meet her at her house. Julie never used slaves in her own home, so she had to go herself to her parent's home, without being detected, and tell Julias to gather up the other slaves. She had to worry about overseers seeing the slaves meeting at her house. She thought, after last night, that her father would surely have someone staking out the place, but time was not on her side, she couldn't worry about that now, she had to take the chance. The plan was simple; Koweena wanted Josi to be the only one to go with her, along with Joe of course. So Julie and the other slaves devised a plan to sneak Josi into the house that night, and the three of them would leave before sun up the next morning. Julie's heart was breaking, and feelings of anguish came flooding inside her as she was making the plans, but she had to put those feelings behind her now. She was no longer thinking of herself, and how her life would be turned upside down with Koweena leaving, she was only thinking of Koweena and her future now. But deep down, Julie was slowly dying.

Joe told Julie to tell the slaves to gather as much supplies as they could get their hands on. Certain types of food; mainly dry rations that were canned, such as beans, and corn, and apples, nuts, and cornmeal, and he also specified two gallons of water. Julias arrived back at Julie's house that night with Josi and the supplies. "Were you seen, Julias?" Julie asked. "I is don't think so, ma'am." "But you're not sure are you?" "Ma'am, I is pretty sure I wasn't seen." "Okay, thanks, Julias." "Ma'am, if you don't mind me asking, is Koweena goin to be alright?" Julie's heart was ripping into pieces that night, and that question by Julias didn't help matters any. She tried to stay calm the entire day, for Koweena's sake. "Yes, Julias, Koweena is going to be fine." "You know, ma'am, I think this is a good time to tell you this." "What, Julias?" "I think Koweena has been dreamin of this day for a long time. When I used to take her home after she would spend her time with you at your parent's place, she used to tell me how one day she was goin to get off this Plantation. How you had given her hope to one day do it." Julie's eyes began tearing up. Her eyes were swollen from all the crying she had done over the last several days. Ever since she had thought about Koweena leaving the Plantation, she had been in an emotional turmoil inside, and it had come to a head that night. After staring at Julias for a moment, Julie began to cry. "I'm sorry, ma'am; I didn't mean to make you cry." "It's okay, Julias, it wasn't you. I've been crying all day. I'm getting ready to lose the most precious thing to me, and it's just breaking my heart. Oh, I've got to pull it together." "I'll go now, ma'am." "Yes, Julias, thank you." A slight pause ensued, and then Julie spoke up again. "Julias!" Julie yelled out from the living room as Julias was walking out the make shift front door. Julias stopped dead in his tracks and turned around. "Yes, ma'am!" Julie began to smile as she was sobbing. "Thank you! Thank you for being there for my Kowie all these years!" "No problem, ma'am, it was a pleasure!" Julias turned and walked away.

Suddenly, Julie found herself standing in the living room alone. Koweena and Josi were upstairs in Koweena's bedroom, and Joe was in the guest bedroom. Julie felt completely alone. It was just her and her agonizing thoughts as she stood there. She had been through so many unmanageable emotions during the last month that she was exhausted. She plopped herself down on the sofa. She began crying once again. "What if something bad happens to Kowie out there in this big world, she's such a sweet and gentle person, what if she can't handle the tough terrain," Julie whispered to herself. Julie had never been out of Natchez, much less out into the world, and now her Kowie was about to embark on a journey that would take her clear across the country. She pounded her fist against the sofa. "Oh, I need Thomas with me!" She said.

"She had bounced back from some horrific incidences," Julie recalled, referring to Koweena. "I knew she was tough. Deep down, I knew she would be able to handle the emotional wear and tear the journey would put on her. I knew so many people would be trying to track her down though. Her life would be in constant danger, and that thought brought about a fear in me that I cannot explain. A fear that stirred deep within the pit of my stomach. Oh, I thought, Joe better take good care of her. I had to trust Joe now, I had no other choice. Would he take care of her like I had taken care of her for so long? Would he truly be there for her? I was in agony that night, drowning in worry."

Her intense worry that night led her up to Joe's room. She knocked on the door, "Joe, it's Julie." "Come in, Julie!" Joe yelled out from the other side of the door. Julie opened the door and closed it behind her so that Koweena wouldn't be able to hear what she was going to tell Joe. She observed Joe studying a map intensely on the bed as she walked in. "So, Joe, where are you guys heading off to first, what direction?" "Were goin to make our way down the hill, to the Mississippi river, and catch one of the steamboats docking there." "Joe, I know you've been through this before, and I know you're a tough person because of it; but Koweena has never even been off this Plantation. She's really fragile, you know what I mean." "Julie, I is spent time with Koweena, and the impression I got from spending time with her is that she's not fragile. She told me all she's been through, and I think she's a very tough young girl." "Well, Joe, I know her a whole lot better than you do, and you have to understand, she's a very sensitive girl. I mean she takes what people say to her, and do to her, to heart, she's very delicate. I don't know how she's going to take to roughing it out on those waters, roads, and woods." "Julie, she's been roughing it all her life. I think you is just seeing the side of Koweena that you want to see, she's a very tough girl. She will do just fine." "What are you implying, Joe?" Julie felt offended by what Joe had just told her. "I'm just saying, she's had it rough all her life, that's all, Julie." "For your information, Koweena is very happy here, she loves living here." Julie had been around Koweena for eleven years, she knew Koweena better than Joe did, who had just spent a couple of nights with her. But once again, like she had done so many times in the past, she was, well, not forgetting, but she was choosing not to think about the life Koweena had lived up to this point. She was only thinking about the Koweena she had spent time with. Sure, her beating at age eight woke Julie up to the reality of what Koweena had to go through; but Julie had always thought of Koweena as not a slave, but a family member. Yet, she never spent any time with her out in the fields, or in the shack where Koweena once lived, to get a real perspective of what exactly Koweena had to go through on a daily basis. At the same time, like certain times in the past, Julie was not completely oblivious to Koweena's life as a slave, she knew she had it rough; but a part of Julie just didn't want to embrace that. Probably because she wanted Koweena so desperately not to be a slave, it just made her at times not think about that side of Koweena's life. But over the last several years, Julie had succumbed to the realities of Koweena's situation. "You're right, Joe, I'm sorry, she is a tough girl, she has had it rough I know; but I've tried my best to spoil her so much that it would make her slave life pale in comparison." "There is no way you could make slave life pale in comparison to anything, Julie. You know, she's told me how good you are to her. She's told me how special you is made her feel and how you is made her feel like one of those princesses in the books she's read. She said she's really goin to miss that." That made Julie's eyes began to water once again.

Meanwhile, in Koweena's room, Koweena and Josi were talking about the escape. "I'm scared, Koweena. I don't want to be running out there just to get killed. I have a sense that things are going to get pretty rough out there." It was obvious from listening to Josi talk that Koweena had made significant progress in educating Josi. Her grammar had improved so much. "It's not going to be easy, Josi, but we have Joe with us, he knows what he's doing." "I know he knows what he's doing, but still, I can't help but have this feeling inside me that something could go wrong." "You're my sister, Josi; I wouldn't have you go with me on this trip if I thought something bad was going to happen to you." "But something could go bad, Koweena; you don't know for sure, you're just going on pure feelings and speculation." "Listen, Josi, you're going to spend the night with me in this bed here, and we're going to get a good nights sleep, and then in the morning we're going to get up and start our new lives." The slaves had earlier that day turned Koweena's bed back upright, as they had done with most of the furniture that the overseers had turned over the previous night. "But aren't you going to miss Julie?" Josi asked. "Yes! I'm going to miss her like crazy! But, Josi, I don't want to get shipped off, and if I don't go now, that is exactly what will happen, and I don't have much time." "Part of me is excited, Koweena, a chance to finally get off this Plantation and go to places we've only read about in our books, I can't wait." "Okay, let's go to bed so we will be well rested in the morning, we'll need our strength," Koweena said as they both got in bed.

It was two in the morning, and everyone was asleep, except for Julie. She had been pacing back and forth for hours in the living room. She thought she was going to lose her mind as she just kept pacing back and forth on the throw rug wearing out a path in the carpet. She finally stopped, and went over to the hallway closet and grabbed a blanket. She went upstairs with blanket in hand and quietly opened Koweena's door. She peered in and saw Koweena and Josi sound asleep. She tippy-toed into the room and went over to the wall opposite the bed. She sat down against the wall with her knees against her chest, and put the blanket over her. As tears began rolling down her face yet again, she began to sing that song that she had written for Koweena when she was five. She knew as she sat there rocking back and forth and singing that song, that she was spending the last moments, maybe of her life, with Koweena, watching her sleep. She knew Koweena needed her sleep, but the urge was too strong for Julie, she got up and went over to Koweena's bed and gently shook Koweena. All those years growing up, Koweena was the one who needed Julie so desperately, and now, in the last moments possibly of their relationship, it was Julie who was the one who desperately needed Koweena. Julie began shaking Koweena. "Kowie, Kowie, are you awake?" Koweena lifted her head and shook it back and forth, rubbing her nose against her pillow as she groaned. "Yes, Julie, I'm awake, what's wrong?" "Nothings wrong, Dear. Will you lay with me down here on the floor for a while?" "Sure, Julie."

Julie and Koweena laid down on the throw rug at the foot of the bed, with Julie clutching on tightly to Koweena, cuddling her closely. As the blanket was stretched out over them, Julie began talking aloud to Koweena about all the things they used to love to do together over the years. "I loved waking up every morning and seeing that sleepy look you had on your face, and how your curly hair was all over the place in wild disarray. That always made me smile and laugh. I loved dressing you up, and putting make up on you, and fixing your beautiful hair. I loved seeing you grow into becoming a great horse rider. I loved watching you get smarter and smarter with each passing day. And when you didn't realize I was watching, I loved watching you in your room here, pretend like you were a wife and you were talking to your husband." "You watched me do that, Julie?" "Yes, I did, Sweetheart, and it was one of the thrills of my day. I'm with you wherever you go, Kowie, it doesn't matter where you find yourself on this journey, I'll be right there alongside you. If you find yourself in trouble, just call out to me, just say my name." "I will, Julie." "Kowie, a woman's heart is full of secrets." "What do you mean, Julie?" "I mean, a woman's heart is an ocean of undiscovered pearls that haven't been found yet. Experiences a woman has her entire life are kept inside her heart. From her memories growing up, to her memories as a young adult, and then memories of being a mother and wife, they're all locked in tight inside her heart. She keeps them in her heart, because she's the only one that will truly cherish those memories the way they should be cherished." "Because she wants them to be private?" Koweena asked. "Women love hard, Sweetheart, they hold nothing back, they pour all their emotions into it, that's why they treasure those moments. They don't want anyone inside their heart to mess it up, not a man, not anyone. They want those memories to remain untainted. That's why a woman will hide those experiences, to keep them pure, even from her husband." "Why?" Koweena asked. "It makes those moments sweeter when she has them tucked away in her heart. They become a part of her, and sometimes she just doesn't want to share them with anyone." "I understand I think," Koweena said. Koweena drifted off to sleep. Julie, realizing she was asleep, began singing that song again, holding Koweena tightly to her. She wanted to soak up these last few moments, moments she may never spend again with Koweena. She didn't sleep that entire night; she just laid there cuddling Koweena tightly to her.

Chapter 11   The Journey Begins

The following morning, Koweena said her final goodbyes to Julie. Koweena noticed, as she stood there in front of Julie in the foyer area, that Julie had a look about her that she had never seen before, and that look surprised her somewhat. She was taken back at just how fragile Julie looked. Her face was pale, paler than her fair skin normally was, her eyes were swollen, and there were two streaks of dried black mascara running down both sides of her cheeks. After all these years it still amazed Koweena, especially after looking at Julie the way she was that morning, just how much Julie loved her. "Good bye, my Love," Julie said as she hugged Koweena for the final time with tears running down her face. Koweena was caught in the middle emotionally as she stood there hugging Julie. She was upset at Julie's appearance, and she really wanted to take in this final moment with her, but at the same time she was also thinking about what lie ahead for her and her two other escapees. Julie could clearly see the strain on Koweena's face as a result. Julie placed her hands on Koweena's cheeks. "Don't stress, Sweetheart," she told Koweena. "I'll never forget you, Julie." "Hey, hey, this isn't good bye, you have my address in your pocket, let me see," Julie said. Koweena pulls out a yellow folded piece of paper out of her pocket and showed it to Julie. Julie wiped away the tears from Koweena's face. "Now promise me you won't lose it, Kowie." "I'll hold on to it for dear life, Julie." "Write me whenever you get the chance, okay?" "Okay, Julie." "And you have your necklace and ring?" "Yes, they're right here," Koweena grabs a hold of her necklace, and shows Julie her hand that held the ring. "Now remember, keep your head up at all times and be aware of your surroundings." "Okay, Julie." This was the moment, they were parting ways. "Bye, Baby," Julie said as she gave Koweena a gentle kiss on the cheek. Koweena gives her one final long look. All the memories she had with Julie came flooding back to her as she stood there staring at the emotionally worn Julie. Tears began to flow down Koweena's face. Now, for that brief moment, the escape was no longer fresh on her mind, Koweena was finally taking in her last moments with Julie. "How am I going to make it without you," Koweena said as she gave Julie a big hug. "You can do it, Sweetheart, you're strong and resilient. Remember all the tough times you went through growing up, and how you battled your way through those times, you're tough, you can do it." "Koweena, we's a have to go!" Joe said sternly. "Okay, Julie, bye, I love you." Koweena's mind instantly flashbacked to the first time she ever told Julie those words that night in Julie's bed when she was eight. "I love you too, Sweetheart," Julie said as she covered her mouth after she said that to keep from crying uncontrollably. Koweena just couldn't let go of Julie's hand as she was holding her clothes that was in a sackcloth bag with her other hand. "Koweena, you have to go now," Julie said. "I know, but I can't, it's like something has a hold on me." "It's called love," Julie said, as tears flowed down both their faces. Joe was emphatic this time. "Koweena, come on!" he said. "Okay, Joe," Koweena said. She let go of Julie's hand. Would that be the last time she would ever touch Julie? As Koweena walked out the front door with Joe and Josi, she continued to look back at Julie with raised eyebrows. Julie just stood there with her hand raised high, waving good bye to Koweena. As Julie watched her disappear into the darkness, she suddenly fell to the floor and wailed out in agony and heartache. She just laid there for hours, crying hysterically.

It was a humid, August summer morning as Koweena, Joe, and Josi made their way through the cotton fields, it was around five a.m. There was a light fog that had formed from the previous night, and the morning dew was prevalent as their boots were getting soaked by the tall cotton stalks. "Shhh, stop!" Joe whispered. The three stopped dead in their tracks. "We have to be careful here, this is when the overseers start sturrin about," Joe said. "Did you hear one of them?" Koweena asked. Joe held his arm out, holding back Koweena and Josi from moving any further. "I don't know, just be quiet for a moment," Joe said. He didn't hear any dogs, and he didn't see any lights, so they proceeded. "Where are we headed?" Josi asked. "We is goin to go through what is called the Natchez Road. It's a carved out road that leads all the way up to Nashville, Tennessee." "I thought you told Julie that we were going to take a boat up the Mississippi River," Koweena said. "Do you think I would actually tell someone where we were really going to go? Is you crazy!? I said that to throw her off." "Joe, Julie wouldn't have said anything, you should have told her the truth," Koweena said. Joe chuckled. "And risk our entire escape, no way," he said. As they made their way through the cotton fields, Koweena suddenly stopped. "Joe, we have to go somewhere." "Is you crazy, Koweena, we can't afford to get sidetracked now, we can't lose any time." "It will only take a second." "Where is you want to go?" Joe asked. "Josi and I need to say goodbye to an old acquaintance." "Where do you want to go?" Josi asked. "Just follow me, guys," Koweena said as she turned to her right and proceeded in the direction of the shacks.

As they approached the shacks, Koweena knew the exact shack she wanted to go to. "Come on, guys, it's this shack right here," Koweena said. Joe became emphatic. "Koweena, we have to hurry, don't take long!" He said. Koweena knocked on the door to the shack she had approached. "Koweena, we could caught here," Josi exclaimed. "Don't worry, Josi; you will be happy with this." They waited outside the entranceway to the shack for several moments. Finally, a woman opened the door. "Yes, can I help you?" The woman said. She just stared at the two girls, and Joe who was standing alongside them. "Mom, it's me, Koweena." "Koweena? Is that you?" "Yes, mom, and here's Josi also." "You look so different, Koweena and Josi; you guys is all grown up." "Momma, we're escaping," Koweena said. "Escaping the Plantation?" "Yes," Koweena replied. "I always knew you would do something like that, Dear, someday. Are you leaving now?" "Yes, we're on our way to the horse stable; we're going to use some horses to get away. You should see me on a horse mom, I'm very good." Joe was impatient. "Koweena, we have to go!" He yelled in a strong whisper. "Koweena, I always knew you would be successful in whatever you did, and I always knew you wouldn't stay on this Plantation your whole life. I'm just so happy you is takin your sister with you. You both look so pretty," Amitha said with a smile. "Thanks, mom," Josi said. "Well, mom, I just came here to say goodbye," Koweena said. As Koweena said that she reached over and gave her mother a kiss on the cheek, Josi did likewise. "Be careful, girls." "We will, momma," Koweena said as she wrapped her arm around Josi. "Goodbye, mom," Koweena said. Amitha pulled Koweena up close to her. "Come here, Koweena," she said. Amitha whispered in her ear. "Remember, God made you a star." "I know, momma, I remember you telling me that when I was little," Koweena said. "Goodbye, girls," Amitha said. "Okay, can we go now!?" Joe asked in a stern voice.

As they made their way to the horse stable, Koweena asked. "How do we know which way is North?" Joe pointed up to the sky. "Look up there, guys." "It's just a bunch of stars," Koweena noted. "No, it's more than stars, it's our map. Look closely up there, to the right of where you is lookin now. You see that group of stars that form an L shaped curve. Look right there, it looks like an opposite J." Josi got excited upon finally finding it. "I see it!" She said. "Oh I see it now," Koweena said. "That's called the Big Dipper. Okay, now look to the right of that, at the top of the Big Dipper. You see that bright star all by its lonesome up there?" "Okay, I see it," Koweena said as she pointed skyward. "That's the North Star, that star is our guide. We will follow that star all the way to the north." "I got it now, Joe," Koweena said.

"You said you knew how to ride these things, Koweena, you better be right," Joe said with a nervous tone. "Don't worry, Joe, I've ridden these things almost my entire life, I know what I'm doing. Are you ready for a crash course?" Koweena asked Joe. Joe was unenthusiastic at the thought. "I guess," he said. Koweena gave Joe a quick crash course on how to ride a horse. They didn't have much time; the overseers would be out and about at any moment. "Do you think you got it, Joe?" Koweena asked. "I think so, Koweena." "Okay, let's mount up and go," Koweena said as she and Josi got on one horse and Joe got on another one. As the click-click of the horses shoes echoed throughout the stable, Joe suddenly heard what sounded like a rifle being cocked back. He turned and saw the figure of a tall, giant man standing there with his rifle pointed in the direction of Joe and the two girls. "Go! Go! Now! Hurry!" Joe shouted. Koweena turned back, "what is it Joe?" "Go! We is goin to be shot at, right now!" "Kick your heels against the horse's sides and pull on the reigns, Joe, to get the horse moving fast!" Koweena shouted out. Joe did as Koweena instructed, and the horse took off. He was having trouble though keeping up with Koweena and her horse. "Come back here, you niggers!" The overseer yelled out, it was Ray. Ray went running through the stable, zipping past the stalls one after the other. As the horses made their way out of the stable Joe yelled out, "Follow that North Star!" "Boom!" A shot rang out. Joe's horse immediately slammed to the ground, throwing Joe off some five yards so violently that he skidded along the grass face first. Koweena, upon hearing the loud bang, riding some ten yards ahead, abruptly stopped the horse. Koweena could see Joe lying on the grass face first and noticed that he was stiff as a board. "Joe! Joe! Are you alright!?" Koweena hollered out. Joe didn't respond, he just laid there motionless. She could hear the footsteps of a man, it sounded like he was running through the stable, the noise was getting closer and closer. "Josi, we don't have much time, we have to get Joe. He's our only way out of here." Josi panicked. "I know we need him, or this whole thing is over!" She said. Koweena steered the horse back to where Joe was lying. As she approached , she could see movement coming from him. Koweena became emphatic. "He's moving, Josi!" She could also see movement from the stable. She could faintly make out a large man running with a rifle in his hand. Koweena panicked. "Josi, we've got to hurry! Now!" She yelled. "Joe, get up!" She screamed. Joe stammered to his feet, shook his head back and forth, stumbled a bit, and slowly made his way over to Koweena's horse. "Hurry, Joe, hurry! We don't have much time!" Koweena frantically yelled out. Once Joe came to, and got his bearings about him, he remembered the man, and the shot he fired that got him into this situation. "Hop on, Joe, it won't be easy with three of us riding on this horse, but we'll have to make do," Koweena said. Joe struggled a bit, trying to get on behind Josi, but he finally was able to mount. "Boom!" Another shot rang out; this time it grazed Koweena's horse on the front right leg. Koweena was now put to the test. With all of her training by Julie in the art of riding a horse, it was time for her to put that practice into good use. The horse was jumping and kicking around as a result from the shot it had just received. Koweena, with a combination of tugging on the reings and stroking the horse's neck and saying, "hold it, hold it, hold it now, big fellah," she was able to calm it down. "Where did you learn to control a horse like that?" Joe asked as he continued to get situated on the horse. "I had a lot of years of training," Koweena said as she snapped the reigns of the horse and yelled, "Ha, Ha." The horse took off. "Hold on, Joe, this is a very unconventional way to ride a horse, we don't want you falling off!" Koweena yelled. Another shot rang out; the shot sounded like it was right behind them. The horse slowed to a trot. "We're going to die!" Josi yelled out. "Not if I have anything to say about it. Come on big fella, I've ridden you fast so many times in the past, don't let me down now. Ha! Ha!" Koweena yelled out as she kicked the horse's sides and tugged on the reigns, the horse took off like a bolt of lightning into the partial daylight sky. Joe was barely hanging on, grabbing onto Josi with everything he had. "Come here, you niggers!" Ray yelled out as he was running toward the three with his rifled cocked and ready for another shot. Another shot rang out; this time the three could hear the bullet skim off of the tree they were zipping by. "He barely missed us!" Koweena yelled out as she was sitting up a little, with her butt up in the air while jerking on the horse's reigns. "Come on!" She yelled at the horse. "I think we is far enough away now!" Joe yelled out to Koweena after several minutes of riding. Koweena was too busy directing the horse. "Josi, tell Koweena to slow down, we is in the clear!" "Koweena, Joe said to slow down. He says we're in the clear!" They had to yell at one another because of the horses loud stomping and the wind rushing through their ears, it made it hard to hear. "Whoa! Whoa, big fella!" Koweena shouted out to the horse as the horse began to slow down. Josi wiped her forehead. "That was too close for comfort!" She said. "We is not out of it just yet," Joe said. "What do you mean?" Koweena asked. "We is still have the overseer watchtower to go through now," Joe responded. "Watchtower, what watchtower?" Koweena asked. "It's a large tower that the overseers use to guard against escaping slaves. They have an overseer standing on top of it around the clock." "Great, just great, how do you suppose we get past that?" Koweena asked. "The same way we got passed this last overseer. We is goin to use this horse of yours and run right through it." "That's your plan," Koweena said, "that's your plan. Just run right by it. Don't you think the overseer will have a clean shot at us?" "Not if you do some of your good riding he won't," Joe replied. "What do you mean?" Koweena asked. "Do some of your fancy zigzagging, like you did back there, just now," Joe said. "Yeah, Koweena, you can do it," Josi remarked. "What choice do we have," Koweena said to herself.

They were approaching the watchtower. "I can see it," Josi remarked as she peered through the cluster of trees that separated them from the tower. "Let's stop right here among these trees and wait for just a moment," Koweena said. "We is don't have time to wait, Koweena, we is got to go now, it's almost daybreak," Joe said. Koweena once again got in her riding stance, with her butt in the air. "Okay here we go! Ha! Ha!" She yelled out. Once again the horse took off like a bolt of lightning. They were now in the open field, the only thing that separated them from the wooden fence, and what awaited them on the other side, freedom, was that watchtower. "Code Blue! Code Blue!" The overseer, standing guard on the tower, yelled out. He began shooting. Once Koweena heard the shooting, she began whipping the horse to the left and right in a zigzag pattern. Her heart was about to leap out of her chest as she heard the bullets zipping by her, as was Josi's and Joe's. As they were racing by the tower, they could see the fence just up ahead. Suddenly, there was a yell. "Owe!" Koweena and Josi both clearly heard it, but they couldn't stop to notice what had happened. As Koweena was dodging the bullets with the horse, they finally came upon the fence. Without hesitation, Koweena instinctively jerked the horse into the air, Julie taught her how to do it, and the horse went air born over the fence. They continued riding through the woods for several miles until they stopped. Upon stopping, both Koweena and Josi looked over their shoulders and noticed blood running down Joe's arm. "Oh my God, you've been hit!" Koweena yelled out. "Oh, damn it hurts!" Joe said, squinting in pain. Koweena and Josi quickly dismounted from the horse. Koweena was frantic. "Hurry, Josi, get me a towel from the bag!" She said. "Here you go," Josi said, handing the towel to Koweena. Koweena quickly began wrapping Joe's arm with the towel. As she was doing so, she suddenly stopped. She found herself lost in Joe's eyes as they stared at each other in silence for several seconds. "Guys, come on!" Josi said impatiently. Koweena, after looking at Joe, looked at the ground while biting her bottom lip with a sideways grin. She had to catch her breath because of that look. After a moment of this, she looked back up and began wrapping his arm once again, this time noticing as she was wrapping, that the bullet was lodged in Joe's arm. "We have to get to a doctor," Joe said. "I'm bleeding too much, owe, damn it hurts!" "We're out here in the middle of nowhere, where are we going to find a doctor?" Koweena asked. "There's one about ten miles that way," Joe said as he pointed to an open road just to the right of the woods. As they approached the doctor's house Joe had lost so much blood, and was so weak, that he was slumped over on top of Josi's back, almost unconscious. "Joe, how's it going?" Koweena asked. She got no response. "Hang in there for me, Joe, don't give up on me now, we need you too much to give up on us now," Koweena continued. She had grown attached somewhat to Joe over the last several days. When she said "*we* need you" she meant herself.

They finally approached the doctor's house. Koweena noticed that the lights were on. "He's awake!" Koweena shouted. She dismounted and walked up to the front door. She knocked. After several minutes, an old gray headed man answered the door. "Hello, sir, my name is Koweena, we desperately need your help." "Hi, Koweena, I'm Doctor Wilson. What seems to be the problem? What can I do for you?" "My friend, he's been shot in the arm, and he's lost a lot of blood. Can you help?" "Sure, bring him in." It took the doctor, Koweena, and Josi, all three, to drag Joe into the house and lay him down on the living room floor. "Let me get my equipment," Doctor Wilson said as he walked into his office which was adjacent to the living room.

"Now, Joe, here's a leather belt, put this in your mouth and bite down on it. Here's some scotch as well," the doctor said. "Why the belt and scotch?" Joe asked. "You'll need it. You'll need something to bite down on for the pain when I start extracting this bullet, and the alcohol will help you to endure the pain." "Oh God!" Joe yelled out as he downed the scotch and began to bite down on the belt, while the doctor operated on him and extracted the bullet from his arm.

"He'll need to rest here for at least a day," Doctor Wilson said as Joe lied there on the floor asleep, exhausted from the pain he had just endured. "He's lost too much blood to move anywhere today," Doctor Wilson continued. "Come in here to the dining room, and let me get you two something to eat," Doctor Wilson said. As Koweena and Josi made their way over to the dining room, the doctor brought out a plate of bacon and eggs for them both. "So, what plantation did you girls escape from?" Doctor Wilson asked as the girls sat there eating. Koweena instantly looked up at Josi when the doctor asked them that. Koweena was shaking her head with her eyebrows down motioning to

Josi not to say a word. "The Defour Plantation," Josi said. All Koweena could do was flail her arms up in the air after Josi said that. "The Defour Plantation huh. I had an interesting experience there once," Doctor Wilson said. "Oh, yeah, what?" Koweena asked. "It involved the birth of a baby, terrible situation, very unfortunate." As Koweena was eating, the doctor couldn't help but notice Koweena's mixed race look. Koweena noticed that the doctor was staring at her intensely, and she became very uncomfortable. Although she no longer allowed her looks to bother her, she was still somewhat self-conscious about it, especially when someone was looking at her the way the doctor was gazing at her. "How old are you, Koweena?" Doctor Wilson asked. "Sixteen, sir." At one point in her life, when she was five, Koweena had no idea how old she was; but when Julie brought it up when they first met, she went to her mother and asked. She then knew at that point how old she was. "Sixteen, sixteen, interesting," Doctor Wilson said as he put his finger to his mouth as if to be in deep thought. Koweena was now, at this point, feeling very uncomfortable, especially since she noticed after she said how old she was to the doctor, that her comment had put him in deep thought. "What, doctor?" "What?" Doctor Wilson replied. "When I said how old I was, you got quiet and began to think hard about something. Was it something I said?" Koweena asked.

Could it be? Doctor Wilson thought. He was trying to think back just how many years ago it had been when he delivered that baby at the Defour house. "So you say you're sixteen, are you?" "Yes, Doc, sixteen, is there something strange about that?" The doctor instantly had a surprised look on his face. "No, no," Doctor Wilson said. "It's got to be just a coincidence, there's no way," the doctor thought to himself. "Josi, can I speak with you privately in the living room, excuse us for a moment, Doc." "Surely," Doctor Wilson said.

"What if he tells!?" Koweena strongly whispered to Josi as they stood over Joe in the living room. "He's not going to tell. He seems like a nice person," Josi said. "A nice person, he's been interrogating me the entire time he's been sitting there with us. I think he's going to report us. Why did you have to say what plantation we came from!? I told you not to say anything, couldn't you understand my motioning to you at the table when he asked that!?" "Relax, Koweena; he's not going to say anything. Besides, he wouldn't have helped Joe like he did if he wasn't sympathetic to our cause." "He's a doctor, Josi; it's his job to help. That doesn't mean he's not going to go to Mr. Defour." "Koweena, just relax and rest here for a day. We're going to need our rest for the journey," Josi said. "We've just barely made it out, and already one of us is hurt," Koweena said. "I need to go check on my horse and make sure its leg is okay," Koweena said as she made her way to the front door.

Meanwhile, back at the Defour house, Mr. Defour was carrying on about his business as he normally did in his office when Mr. Jenkins suddenly showed up out of the clear blue. "They've escaped!" Mr. Jenkins yelled out as he was trying to catch his breath from all the running he had just done, running from the fields into Mr. Defour's office. "Catch your breath, Donald, now say it again." "One male nigger and two nigger girls escaped, it happened early this morning." "Escaped! On my Plantation!" "Yes, sir, they used your horses to do it. One of my men had to shoot down one of your horses; he did it by accident meaning to hit the slave." "I don't care about my horses, Donald, what I care about are those damned niggers who escaped. If the other niggers here catch wind of this, we could have a mutiny on our hands." "I know, sir, that's why when I found out I quickly rushed over here to tell you." "We need to catch those slaves, Donald, there's no ifs ands or buts about that. If they're on horse, they could be some thirty miles or more away by now." "Sir, I have a man on my crew who would eagerly like to go after those slaves. He got a good look at one of them and quickly recognized the nigger. He said she was some kind of half-breed or something. It will make her easy to detect out there once we put out the bulletin." Mr. Defour put his hand to his mouth. "A mixed girl huh?" He asked. "Yes, sir." "Damn it Julie!" "Excuse me, sir?" "Nothing, Donald, tell me more about this man you're in charge of. Say he wants to go after them?" "Yes, sir, like I said, he told me he knows the little half-breed that escaped." "What's this overseer's name, Donald?" "Ray, sir." "That's not the same Ray," Mr. Defour paused for a second, thinking back to what Julie had said after Koweena had got beaten at age eight about an overseer named Ray. "What is it, sir?" Mr. Jenkins asked. "Nothing, Donald, is this Ray a good overseer, is he dependable?" "One of the best, sir, if anyone can track them down it will be him, most definitely. He says he can definitely catch that little Nigger girl because he says he knows exactly what she looks like." "That definitely is an advantage, an overseer who knows the escapee first hand. I know it's only a couple of slaves, Donald, but like I said, if we don't catch them and rumor gets out that we didn't go after them, there's no telling how many slaves would try to escape. We *must* send a message that this will not be tolerated. Bring this Ray in and let me talk to him first hand before we send him out." "Yes, sir."

An hour later, Mr. Jenkins brought Ray into Mr. Defour's office. "Sir, this is the man I told you about. This is Ray." "Sir, pleasure to meet you," Ray said. "So, Ray, I understand you know one of the slaves that escaped pretty well." "Yes, sir, I've had a few run- ins with her in the past, real attitude problem." "Well, Ray, the big question I have is can you find them?" "Yes, sir, I believe I can. Give me one other overseer, and I'll bring them back. I do have one question though." "What's that, Ray?" Mr. Defour asked. "Do you want them brought back dead, or alive?" Mr. Defour began laughing out loud. "Does it matter, Ray?" He said. That made Mr. Jenkins and Ray both join in on the laughing. "Just bring them back, Ray, we need to make an example out of those niggers for all the other niggers to see. Donald, give him whatever he needs to get the job done." "Yes, sir." "And, Donald," "yes, sir," "send someone over to the Sherriff's office and have them send the Sherriff over here immediately. We need flyers sent out, and we need the U. S. Marshals involved." "Yes, sir."

As Mr. Jenkins and Ray were walking out of Mr. Defour's office and into the hallway, Mr. Jenkins asked Ray point blank. "Ray, what do you need to bring those niggers back?" "Give me one other overseer, allow me to choose him though, two horses, and plenty of ammunition, and I'll get the job done." "We have no time to waste, Ray, the sooner you get going the better." "Yes, I must go now," Ray said.

In the meantime, Mr. Defour was standing by the window in his office, something he did regularly when he was distraught about something. "I'm going to get that damn Julie. I'm going over there right now and end this thing once and for all."

"Bang! Bang! Bang!" Mr. Defour pounded on the front door of his daughter's house with both sides of his fists. "Julie, let me in now!" Mr. Defour shouted. Julie could hear her father's banging as she lay in her upstairs bedroom, sobbing away at the fact that Koweena had been ripped from her heart that very morning. Julie had not slept in days, she was an emotional wreck. "Go away, dad!" Julie yelled from upstairs, but her father couldn't hear her. The banging on the door got louder. It sounded like the door was going to come down once again, like it had several nights back when her father, Mr. Jenkins, and the four overseers knocked it down. The slaves had repaired it when they fixed her furniture, but they didn't repair it nearly well enough. After several more poundings by Mr. Defour's fists, the door came crashing down. Upon hearing it, Julie just turned over in her bed with her back to the bedroom door. "Julie, where are you!?" Mr. Defour screamed out as he stepped over the door. He looked all around the downstairs area, no sign of Julie. He then walked to the stairs, looked up, and noticed Julie's bedroom door shut. "Julie, are you up there!?" There was no response. He walked up the stairs with his boots slamming against the steps with each step he took. Julie could clearly hear, by the sounds of her father's boots, that he was very upset as the banging got closer to Julie's room. "I can't deal with this now," Julie said as she pulled the sheets over her head. Mr. Defour got right up to Julie's door. "Julie, I'm coming in!" Mr. Defour yelled as he opened the door; he quickly noticed the outline of Julie's body underneath the sheets as he stared at her bed, fuming inside. "Julie, come out from under there! We need to talk about that little Nigger you're cozying up to, Kolee, Koree," "Koweena, dad," Julie said from under the sheets. "Whatever the damn little thing's name is, we need to talk. Now, I demand that you get up and speak to me now!" "Dad, I can't deal with this right now." "Where is she, Julie!?" "She's in the fields working like she always is," Julie continued saying underneath the sheets. "Bullshit, Julie! Don't you lie to me! I know she's escaped, and I know you helped her!" "Dad, I don't know what you're talking about." Mr. Defour could distinctly hear Julie sobbing underneath the covers. "Julie, I came here to tell you that I'm disowning you as my daughter. I want you to pack your things and leave my property as soon as possible. I don't even want to look at you any longer!" That instantly made Julie's sobbing that had gone on for hours suddenly stop. With the covers still over her she spoke. "You can't kick me off this Plantation, dad. I have to stay here." "Why, Julie? Tell me why I should allow a nigger lover to stay on my property." The harsh words and tone her father was using just rolled off Julie's back. She was too upset over losing Koweena to worry about what her father was calling her. Julie wasn't about to tell him the real reason she wanted to stay there. Koweena had her address, moving would mean she would lose all contact with Koweena, and she could be assured of never hearing from her again. So she lied. "Dad, I want to be close to you and mom." "Well, Julie, I don't want you anywhere near me or your mother." The words Mr. Defour was using toward his daughter were extremely harsh. Julie began crying out loud. Her father's words were beginning to affect her. "Julie, get out from under the covers, now!" Julie lifted the covers from her face and sat up and stared at her father. The mere look of Julie's face caused her father's heart to sink. Her face was swollen, her hair was a mess, she had dark circles around her eyes, and her mascara was all over her face, and she was extremely pale. She had the appearance as if she had been beaten. For the first time since becoming a father, Mr. Defour had compassion for his daughter. It was the side of her father that she had never seen, but always wanted. "Julie, are you alright?" Her father's tone had suddenly gone from being harsh to being concerned. "My God, look at you. You look like you're hurting so bad." His voice was now gentle and soft. He had always seen Julie fixed up and pretty when she lived with him, never this side of his daughter. Looking at Julie look the way she did caused Mr. Defour to forget about his anger. That was his child who was staring back at him in obvious pain and suffering, a look of pain from his daughter that he had never seen before. Mr. Defour and Julie had had a rocky and distant relationship Julie's entire life; but now, seeing Julie like she was, hurting like she was, brought about a new dynamic into the relationship for Mr. Defour, one of genuine feelings of love and sympathy for his daughter. Mr. Defour sat on the bed wiping Julie's tears from her face. "Julie, I'm so sorry for telling you those things that I just told you, I didn't mean to hurt you." Julie just stared down at the floor. The same Julie that had been so strong for Koweena over the last eleven years; was now the same Julie that she herself found herself needing someone to be strong for her. Could her father be that someone? Mr. Defour thought about it for a while and quickly came to the realization; he knew she was hurting over Koweena. He had to tell her, with the look she had on her face as she just sat there staring at the floor, he felt he had no choice. "Julie, look at me?" Julie looked up at her father with that same blind love she had had for him all her life. "Julie, there's something your mother and I need to tell you. It's been a long time coming, but you need to know. Will you come to the house now, so that we can tell you face to face, just the three of us?" Julie struggled to get out of bed, but once she did she got dressed and made the trip over to her parent's house. Her father tried to be the one to bring her out of her funk, if only temporarily, but not even Thomas, if he were there, could brighten her mood. She would remain miserable until Koweena either returned, or made her way to freedom.

"Donald, thank you for coming in here so quickly." "What is it, sir, it sounded urgent?" Mr. Jenkins asked as he stood there opposite Mr. Defour in Mr. Defour's office. "Donald, I don't want those slaves killed, I just want them captured alive." "But, sir, Ray and the other overseer are already on their way with their orders to kill. The U.S. Marshals have been called in with the same message. We have hired bounty hunters, and even hit men. We now have fliers made out, and they've already been distributed with the flier saying "Dead or Alive," it's too late, sir." "Well, send out another overseer with the orders to capture those slaves alive, and tell him to track Ray and the other overseer down before they get to the slaves. And get a hold of the U. S. Marshals and tell them that the plan has changed." "But, sir, that's impossible, it's just too late." "Just do it, Donald!" Mr. Defour yelled out in a demanding tone.

Meanwhile, back at Doctor Wilson's house, Koweena had just come back inside from checking on the condition of the horse. "How is it?" Josi asked. "It got hit on the leg pretty bad, I need to get the Doc to work on it with his supplies. Hey, Doc?" "Yes, Koweena." "Listen, Doc, my horse has been hit pretty badly by a bullet in the leg; do you think you could work on it?" "Well, animals are not my specialty, Koweena, but I can get my supplies and see what I can do." "Thank you, Doctor. How's Joe doing?" Koweena asked Josi. "He's still out of it." "I hope he wakes up by tonight, we need to get moving," Koweena said. "Even if he does come to," Josi continued, "is he going to be able to continue on so soon?" "He better, we are just too close to the Plantation for comfort. We need to get further away, we should have been long gone by now." As the day turned into night, Joe continued to lie there on the floor of Doctor Wilson's living room.

In the meantime, Koweena and Josi were sitting on the sofa, opposite of Joe, with Doctor Wilson sitting in the chair adjacent to them. After some time had passed, Koweena noticed out of the corner of her eye that Doctor Wilson was still staring at her. She noticed he had a sympathetic look about him as he just sat there staring at her. Finally, after an hour of silence, and the constant staring by Doctor Wilson, Koweena spoke up. "How's the horse, Doc?" She was trying to think of something to say to break the weirdness of the Doctor's staring. "Well, I tried to patch the wound; the bullet grazed his leg pretty bad, I really couldn't stop the bleeding. I'm no horse expert, but from the looks of it, I don't think you'll be riding that horse for very much longer." "Damn!" Koweena yelled out. "There goes our chance at a quick travel," she continued. "We's a have white folks who will help us," Joe suddenly blurted out. He had finally come to. "Joe!" Koweena shouted out as she quickly got up from the sofa and ran over to Joe. "How do you feel?" Koweena asked. "I is a little weak and tired, but I think I'll make it." "Joe, the North Star is out so we need to get moving," Koweena said. "We's a really don't need the North Star right now, Koweena, we have the Natchez Road." "Let me check him over real good one time before you go, just to make sure he's fit for travel," Doctor Wilson said. "Hey, Doc, can I speak with you for a moment?" Koweena asked. "Sure, Joe, I'll be right back," Doctor Wilson said. "Doctor, while you're checking Joe over, I would like to write someone a letter. Could you help me send it?" "Sure, I'll help you guys any way I can. Let me show you where my office is located. You can write your letter on my desk." "Great, Doc, thanks."

As Koweena sat there at the Doctor's desk, with the desk lamp on, she began to write:

> My Dearest Julie,
>
> I don't know when I'm going to get another chance to write you, I have a great opportunity right now, so I wanted to take advantage of it and tell you how things are going. Without giving too much information out about our journey, I don't know who might get a hold of this letter; I just want to tell you that I'm fine. As you can obviously tell, we made it off the Plantation with great success. Your horse lessons really paid off, you should have seen me, I rode my horse like a pro Julie. I hope you're doing okay. Just sitting here writing you this letter makes me miss you all the more. I miss your smile, your voice, the way you reassure me that

everything is going to be okay. You helped me become very brave Julie; I owe it all to you! I can't tell you who I ran into, but he's a very strange man. He keeps staring at me; he just won't stop staring at me. I should be used to it by now, I know, but there's just something about the way this man is staring at me. It's like he has something on me, like he's keeping some deep, dark secret from me. He just keeps talking about how old I am, and what a shame it is every time he finishes saying how old I am, very strange. Anyway, I just wanted to let you know that I'm fine, and to put your mind at ease by letting you know that I indeed will try and write you along the journey. I miss you terribly, but it sure feels good to no longer have to worry about being shipped off to some unknown place. I had a many sleepless nights worrying about that, and it feels good to have that off my shoulders. Soon Julie, you will be visiting me at my new home, with my new family. I love you very much!

Your everything,

Koweena

Koweena's eyes began to well up with tears as she folded the piece of paper and put it in an envelope. She really had no time since her escape to truly think about missing Julie; but writing that letter made all those feelings of abandoning her best friend, come flooding back. She composed herself after addressing the envelope, and went back into the living room with envelope in hand. "Doc, here is the letter; I need for you to wait a week before delivering it. It's very important for you to do that, it will ensure our safety." Koweena felt like she could trust the doctor, despite the weird looks he had been giving her all day. He had helped them so much that day, and was so polite; she couldn't help but trust him. "Will you promise me you'll do that, Doc?" "Sure, Koweena, I'll wait a week, just like you said." "Great, thanks."

It was around midnight now, and Joe was up and about, feeling much better, with his bandage wrapped tightly around his arm in a sling. "Okay, guys, let's go," Joe said. "Doctor, thank you so much for all you've done for us today," Koweena said. "My pleasure, Koweena, do you have all your supplies, the ham and water?" "Yes, sir, right here," Koweena said as she pointed to Josi who lifted up the sack that contained the food and water. "Okay, good bye, Doc!" Koweena said as the three of them walked out the front door. As Koweena was walking through the threshold, she stopped for a second, turned around toward the doctor, who was standing directly behind her, and leaned into to him as if she was getting ready to whisper something to him. "Doctor, I can't leave without asking you this." "What is it, Koweena?" "Why were you so intensely staring at me all day with that sympathetic look on your face? Is there something you need to tell me?" The silence was deafening as the two of them just stood there staring at each other. The doctor was in deep thought, trying to figure out if he should tell Koweena what he knew or not. He knew that if he did, it would change everything, their trip, everything, it would turn Koweena's life upside down. He decided it wasn't his place to mess with fate. "No, Koweena, there's nothing I need to tell you. I've just never seen such a pretty slave before, that's all." Koweena felt creeped out by that statement. "Pervert," she whispered to herself as she walked out the door.

"Joe, I have some bad news about our horse," Koweena said. "What is it?" Joe asked. "It's not going to make it very far." "Damn it!" Joe remarked. "That's what I said when the doctor told me that." "He's a people doctor, what does he know about animals?" Joe asked. "Well, look for yourself?" Koweena asked. Joe noticed that the horse was standing with its hurt leg in the air. "Can he even put any pressure on it, Koweena?" Joe asked. "I don't know, but we're going to find out right now, Joe." As they mounted the horse and placed the supplies on its back, the horse began to shake its head violently and gave out a loud bray. "Whoa, big fellah," Koweena said as she stroked the horse's neck. "Come on now, you can do it big guy." Koweena softly said to the horse. She had learned from Julie that talking to a horse actually works. As they started off, the horse buckled a bit when it immediately put pressure on its hurt leg. "How did we make it this far on it?" Josi asked. "It must have been riding on adrenaline earlier today," Koweena noted. "I don't think we're going to make it very far, if any distance at all on this horse, Koweena," Joe said. "Yeah, it'll make it, we're going to ride it as far as it will take us," Koweena said as she snapped the reigns.

The horse began to slowly gallop along. They were now on the Natchez Road. "This road is full of Choctaw and Chickasaw Indians, guys," Joe noted. "Is that good or bad, Joe?" Koweena asked. "It's a good thing, Koweena, their very sympathetic to our cause."

They had been riding for several hours, when all of a sudden, the horse buckled again, this time sending it crashing to the ground on its side. The three slammed to the ground along with the horse. "God! My leg!" Josi shouted out in intense pain. "Hurry, Joe, she's trapped beneath the horse!" Koweena shouted. There wasn't much Joe could do with his arm in the condition it was in. Joe strained to lift the horse with one arm. "Koweena, I can't lift it with one hand," he said. "You're goin to have to try and lift it on your own," he continued. "What!? I can't do this on my own!" "You're goin to have to try," Joe said. "Hurry, please, someone, my leg!" Josi hollered out, wincing in pain. With the pressure of the situation, and the severity of it resting on Koweena's shoulders, her adrenaline began to flow. She wasn't about to lose her sister, not like this. She gave it all she had as she squatted down and placed her arms underneath the horse. She strained and she groaned as she pushed with all her might. Finally, after several minutes, Josi was able to pull her leg out. "Oh, my back!" Koweena yelled out in pain. After just one day, and just several hours of travelling, all three were now hurt. "Josi, is you alright?" Joe asked. "It's my knee, I think I twisted it." "Koweena, is you alright?" Joe asked. "Yeah, I'll be fine, I just strained my back a bit, I'll be alright." "Josi, can you stand?" Koweena asked. "No." "Okay, Joe, we're going to have to carry her, grab her other arm." Koweena and Joe lifted Josi up, and situated her, with her arms around both of them. "Koweena, can you carry the supplies with one arm?" Joe asked. "I can't carry all of it, maybe some of it." Koweena grabbed a bag and put one ham and one gallon of water in it and proceeded to carry Josi, while carrying the bag with one hand. "We can't just leave the horse here alive, only to die of hunger," Koweena said. Joe became emphatic. "Koweena, now is not the time to worry about a damn horse. We is got to get movin!" He said. "Don't worry, guys, there's a depot just up ahead. We can rest there," Joe continued. Koweena was very interested in seeing what an actual depot was like. With that thought in her mind it gave her enough strength to carry both Josi and the bag far enough to the depot.

Looking at the three of them, it would appear to someone passing by, that they had been in a war, and that's exactly what the station master was thinking when the three arrived at the depot. The station master was asleep when the three arrived at about four in the morning. As they approached the small brick building, not much larger than the shacks back at the Defour Plantation, Joe knocked on the wooden door. The building had an awning in the front, about seven feet in length, with a small wooden bench to the side of the front door. A man dressed in overalls answered the door. "Joe!" He shouted with excitement. "Mr. Lampton, how is you sir?" "Fine Joe, and you?" "Just fine sir, can we come in?" "Sure, sure, come right in." "Wow, I guess it really does pay to be going on this journey with someone who has been through it before," Koweena whispered to Josi, speaking about Joe. "So, Joe, I see you're on another trip." "Yes, Mr. Lampton, I have two other slaves here with me, this is Koweena, and this is Josi." "Ladies, nice to meet you." "Nice to meet you, Mr. Lampton," the girls said in unison. "You guys look like you've been through hell." "Yes, sir, a lot has happened to us in just a short amount of time," Joe said. "Well, as you can see, I have beds and food, so help yourself. I also have some medical supplies for that young girl's leg there." Koweena grabbed a hold of the rubber, elastic knee brace, and placed it on Josi. "How does that feel, Josi?" Koweena asked. Josi stood up, with the flickering lantern in the background, and limped her way around the building. "It's fine, I mean I have to limp somewhat, but at least I can walk on my own." Koweena snapped her arm up and down quickly in excitement, with her hand in a fisted position. "Great!" She yelled. The three called it a night and went to bed, along with Mr. Lampton. Koweena and Josi had to share a bed. They didn't mind though, lying in bed together, being so close to one another, gave them piece of mind and a sense of security.

The next day, the three of them were eating breakfast on the wooden bench outside under the awning, when a black man approached them. He was dressed very well. He was wearing brown slacks, a plaid blue and brown button up shirt, and leather brown dress shoes. "Good day everyone, I'm Nias," he said as he stretched out his arm to Joe. Joe stretched out his arm and shook Nias' hand. "Hey, I'm Joe." "This is Koweena and Josi," Joe continued. "Hi, Koweena, hi, Josi. So, where did you three escape from?" Nias asked. Once again, like with Thomas at the store in Stanton that day, Joe was hesitant to answer that question. "Is you an escaped slave?" Joe asked Nias. "Yes I am. I've come back down here from the north to gather more slaves. I'm preparing to head back up north alone." "That's where we're headed," Josi said. Koweena elbowed Josi in the side as she said that. "I can't believe you told him that!" Koweena whispered loudly in Josi's ear. Joe looked over and gave Josi a disgusted look. Josi bit her bottom lip and looked down at the ground. "So, you're headed up north are you? Great! I can go along with you, would that be alright?" Nias asked. "Um, um," Joe was stuttering as he was trying to think of an answer. Suddenly Koweena spoke up and interrupted Joe. "No, it wouldn't be alright." "Why not, Koweena, it is Koweena right?" Nias asked. Koweena didn't respond. "It would be perfect, you would have someone who has already navigated this area, and I know this area very well." "We already have someone." Koweena said sharply. "Oh yes, who?" "Me," Joe said. "You've been up north?" Nias asked. "Yes, one time." Joe replied. "Well, I've made several trips; I know this area like the back of my hand. How far up north did you make it?" "Indiana," Joe said. "Well, I made it all the way up to Canada, guys." "Can you is excuse us for a moment, Nias?" Joe asked. "Sure, go ahead." Joe pointed to the side of the building. "Koweena, can I talk to you over here?" He said. Koweena and Joe went over to the spot where Joe pointed. "I like this man, Koweena. He's made several trips, and he knows this area better than I do. He could be a valuable asset to us." "Well, I don't like him. For one thing, he dresses too nice to be a slave. Don't you think that's weird? And secondly, he talks too proper to be a slave. He's too well educated sounding." "Need I remind you, Koweena, that you talk very well too, and you is well educated and you is a slave also." "There's just something about this man that doesn't feel right, Joe. I don't know, he gives me the creeps. Besides, we have you!" "But, Koweena, I is only been as far north as Indiana. I is never been all the way up to Canada." "Well, Joe, I trust your judgment, but I still don't like it. There's just something off about him, I can't put my finger on it." "So, you go along with me in agreeing to bring this guy along?" "Well, like I said, I trust your judgment. So if you think he's legit, then I'll go along with you." "Okay, Koweena, I'll let him know." "You better be right about this Joe," Koweena said as she followed behind Joe back toward the wooden bench.

"Well, Nias, it's settled, you is goin along with us," Joe said as he stuck his arm out to shake Nias' hand. Nias reached out to shake Joe's hand. "Great!" Nias said. Meanwhile, Koweena just walked by the newly introduced slave and gave him a mean, suspicious look. She didn't have a good feeling at all about this man. "Josi, you shouldn't have spoken up!" Koweena said sharply. "I didn't mean to, it just slipped out." "Well, help me keep an eye on this man." "Why?" Josi asked. "He just gives me a weird feeling, just stay clear of him as much as you can." "Okay, Koweena."

It was approaching evening now, and it was time to once again follow the Natchez Road. "Well, Mr. Lampton, thank you for having us, you come through like always." "Your welcome, Joe, now you have all your supplies, food, medical supplies, all of that." "Yes, sir," Joe said. "Now, Joe, there's a safe house about a night's journey up the road, I sent word that you're coming, so they'll be expecting you." "Yes, sir, once again thank you, Mr. Lampton." "Take care, Joe." "Take care, sir."

As the four went on through the Natchez Road in the darkness of the night, following the North Star just to be safe, Joe suddenly stopped. "Stop, everyone!" Joe said in a loud whisper. "What is it?" Koweena and Nias both asked. Suddenly there was a loud crack of a branch to their right in the thick woods. "Don't move," Joe whispered again. "I'll go check it out," Nias said. "Is you crazy!" Joe said. "We can't just stand here in the open like this, we'll be sitting ducks," Nias said. Koweena was holding Josi's mouth; keeping her from letting out a loud scream. As Nias walked toward the woods, Joe whispered out. "Take my knife with you, Nias!" "Oh, don't worry, I have one," Nias said as he lifted his knife into the air. Joe was surprised at just how big the knife was. The blade was shining in the moonlight as Nias had it lifted up; it was the biggest knife Joe had ever seen, it was much larger than a butcher knife. "If it's Indians, Nias, they won't hurt you!" Joe whispered. "I know!" Nias whispered back. As Nias made his way into the woods, Koweena, after making sure Josi was going to be quiet, made her way over to Joe. "Did you see how big that knife was?" She asked Joe. "Yeah, it was huge!" Joe blurted out. "That doesn't make me feel any better about him, Joe." "Would you please quit worrying about it, Koweena. He's legit, he's alright." "I trust you, Joe, if you say so." After several minutes had passed, Nias made his way back to the road and walked up to Joe. "It was just a varmint, guys, that's all. Let's keep walking."

As night turned into morning, they could see the safe house off into the distance. "There it is!" Josi shouted out. As they approached the house, Nias spoke up. "Let me handle this, guys." Nias went up to the front door and knocked. A woman answered the door. She was disheveled looking and wearing a white gown, it appeared as if she had just gotten out of bed. "Good morning, ma'am, we are friends of a friend," Nias told her. "Yes, please come in, we've been expecting you." Their nighttime trip had taken them to Ridgeland, a small town just north of Jackson, Mississippi. The house was about seven hundred square feet; it was a one story house with three bedrooms, with a small living room and kitchen. As the four made their way into the house, the woman shook hands with Koweena. "Hi, Dear, I'm Mrs. Harris, my, you sure are a pretty young girl." "Thank you, Mrs. Harris," Koweena said with a polite smile. "So, where are you guys from?" Mrs. Harris asked. Koweena, Joe, and Josi looked at each other when she asked that. Once again it was a question they shied away from. "Natchez, ma'am," Nias spoke up. The three just continued to stare at each other as Nias said that. Koweena rolled her eyes at Joe. "Jerk," she whispered under her breath, speaking about Nias. "We finally keep you quiet, and he speaks up," Koweena told Josi. "Natchez huh, nice place, a lot of rich people live down there," Mrs. Harris said. Koweena's thoughts immediately went right to Julie when the woman said that. She had experienced wealth first hand while living with Julie, and it made her think of her beloved friend. "Wow, I really miss her," Koweena thought to herself. Once again, with the journey, she hadn't had much time to think about missing Julie. But now, as she was standing in the house of a total stranger, her mind wondered to those nights spent with Julie and Thomas in their living room playing and talking. "So I bet you guys are hungry, please come into the kitchen for a bite." As the four made their way to the kitchen, they ran into Mr. Harris who was getting ready to head out for work. Mrs. Harris stretched her arms out toward the four slaves. "Tom, I would like for you to meet our new friends," she said. "Hi," Mr. Harris said as he shook hands with all four of them. "I know a Tom," Koweena spoke up. "Actually his name is Thomas," she continued. "Yeah, that's my name too, I just go by Tom though, much more simple to remember by my friends and strangers." Koweena chuckled. "Yeah," she said. As the four finished eating, Joe, Josi, and Nias made their way into the living room while Koweena stayed behind in the kitchen to help with the dishes. She wanted to talk to Mrs. Harris. "If you don't mind me being so blunt, Mrs. Harris, why do you do this?" "Do what, Dear?" Mrs. Harris asked as she stood over the sink cleaning the plates the four had just previously used. "Why do you harbor slaves?" Koweena asked. "Well, Dear, it's actually a simple answer. We don't agree with slavery at all, my husband and I. We think it's a cruel practice and we want to help out any way we can, you know, to further the slaves cause, and, well, this is the way we do it, by bringing in slaves to stay with us. We can't have children, so this kind of keeps us from being too lonely here." "I'm sorry," Koweena said as she placed her hand on Mrs. Harris' shoulder. "Oh, it's okay, Dear, we've come to accept it by now, children just aren't in our future. Why did you ask that question, Dear?" "Oh, I don't know. I've just read in my books growing up about white people being anti-slavery and all, and well, I just wanted to ask a real person like yourself, whom I've only read about, why you do what you do." "So you're educated?" "Yes, ma'am, very well educated." "Your teacher must be proud." "More than you know, ma'am, more than you know." "I sense a touch of deep emotion in your answer. Were you close to your teacher?" "Close is not the right word, ma'am, she was like a sister to me. She basically raised me and turned me into the brave woman I am now. I miss her *so* much!" Koweena's thoughts once again drifted to Julie. "If I could just talk to her for five minutes and tell her all we've been through already, that would be enough to get me through the rest of this journey" she thought. "How old are you?" Mrs. Harris asked Koweena. "Sixteen." "Well, you're not quite a woman yet, but I suspect with you on this journey you will quickly become one. You know, Koweena is it?" "Yes, ma'am." "Koweena, you sure don't look like the slaves we've been keeping here. Did something happen with your mom and dad?" Koweena had dealt with this her entire life, and no matter where she went, she just couldn't escape people being curious as to why she looked the way she did. "I don't know, ma'am, my mom used to say that God spent extra time in making me. That's why I look the way I do." "Well, I don't want you to think I'm putting you down, Dear, I'm not putting you down, I'm complementing you, you are truly the most beautiful slave I've had here." Koweena smiled. "Thank you, Mrs. Harris." She had been complimented like that many a time in her life, she never got quite used to hearing it though, it seemed new to her each time she heard those words, she always got a kick out of hearing those compliments.

"I think we should stay the night," Nias told Joe as they were sitting in the living room. "Why, Nias, shouldn't we get our rest during the day, and head back out tonight?" "Well, Joe, we've walked a lot of miles, I think we could use the extra rest. I think we're making good time." "Well, Nias, you is more experienced at this than I am, you would know best. Okay, we'll stay the night."

That night, as Koweena and Josi were lying in bed together, there was only one bed in the room, Joe and Nias were sleeping on the floor, Koweena began to talk about the Plantation. "Do you miss the Plantation, Josi?" Koweena whispered. She didn't want to wake Joe and Nias. "Are you crazy, Koweena? I don't miss it one bit. I have no ties to that place like you have. My mother was ripped away from me as early as I can remember. I don't have anybody, Koweena, except you of course, and you're right here with me. So no, I don't miss that place, but I know you miss Julie don't you?" "Something awful, Josi. Any little thing that happens on this journey makes me think about her and how I wish I was still with her; but you know, then I think of being shipped off and it makes me happy that I'm right here with you. Not having to worry about that is a huge weight taken off my shoulders." "I bet," Josi said. "How's your knee?" Koweena asked. "It's fine." "Josi, I know I don't tell you enough, but I'm proud that you're my sister. I love you." "I know you are, Koweena, you've shown it by inviting me to the big house when we were little, by educating me and allowing me to stay with you at Julie's, and by taking me on this journey with you. I love you too." "Good night, Josi." "Good night, Koweena."

After several minutes of dead silence, they both began drifting off to sleep. Suddenly, out of nowhere, a man lunged onto the bed wielding a knife in his hand. It all happened so fast. Koweena was in an in between state of sleep, and being awake, when the man jumped on the bed. As she rolled over, still too asleep to panic or even to defend herself, she noticed that the man was on top of Josi. "Get off her!" Koweena shouted out. That yell by Koweena caused Joe to stir from his sleep. Through the moonlight streaming through the bedroom, Koweena could make out that the man was wielding a knife. She could see the man's arm rise up with the knife tightly clutched in his hand. The man propelled the knife toward Josi. "No!" Koweena screamed out. Josi was sound asleep when the man jumped on top of her. She didn't stand a chance. The knife penetrated Josi's chest, and enter her lung on the opposite side of her heart. "Please stop! Joe, help!" Koweena again screamed out. No sooner had she said that, when suddenly the man turned toward her and raised his arm once again, this time with the knife covered in blood, he lunged at Koweena's chest. Koweena instinctively lifted up her right arm to block the knife from penetrating her. As the knife swiftly came down it grazed her forearm. Suddenly Joe leaped from the floor and landed on top of the man's back. They both were now on top of Koweena, wrestling. The man's knife was just inches from Koweena's face. She tried her best to turn away from the knife, but with the two men on top of her, she couldn't stretch her neck far enough to get away from it. The knife was flashing back and forth right by her right cheek. Joe finally maneuvered to a position where he was able to grab a hold of the man around the neck with both arms. Joe now was able to jerk the man off of Koweena and drag him off the bed completely. They violently landed on the floor. The man, with knife still in hand, was trying to stab Joe as Joe was now on top of him. Joe could clearly see now who the man was, it was Nias. Joe was blocking Nias' arm that held the knife with his one arm, and had his hand clamped down on Nias' neck with the other arm. Joe let go of Nias' neck and used both arms to slam Nias' arm that was holding the knife against the bed's railing.

Meanwhile, Koweena had pulled the covers over her head and was lying there petrified. Joe finally managed to get the knife away from Nias. He now had Nias pinned to the floor. "Why did you do this!?" Joe yelled out. "I'm a secret agent for the U. S. Marshals. You don't stand a chance, they're all around you. They will catch you soon." Without hesitation Joe thrust the knife into Nias' heart and left it there. He sat there for a second on top of the now dead Nias trying to catch his breath. "It's okay, Koweena, he's dead," Joe said panting. Immediately upon hearing that, Koweena snapped the covers off her and leaned over Josi. "Josi!" Koweena yelled in a panic. Josi's side of the bed was drenched in blood. "Joe, it doesn't look good, oh my God! She's not going to make it!" Koweena said with a shaky voice. Suddenly, Mr. Harris entered the room. "What in the hell!?" He hollered out as he noticed the blood on the bed, as well as all over Josi, and the knife sticking out of Nias' heart. "Sir, we need your help! If you could bring a lantern in here along with a bunch of towels, please hurry!" Koweena yelled. As Koweena was leaning over top of Josi she could hear Josi struggling to breathe, gasping for every breath. "Hang in there, Josi, please don't die on me!" As Koweena said that she was thinking of Julie and wondering what she would do in this situation. She was so good at making Koweena feel better under the worst of circumstances, and Koweena wanted to do the same for her sister. But it was gravely too late. Koweena could tell as Josi was struggling all the more to breathe with each passing second, that time was not on her side. She felt helpless. "Koweena," Josi said gasping for air. "Yes, Josi, I'm right here," Koweena said, holding on tightly to Josi's hand. "You're going to make it up north you know. You have that fighting spirit that I admired so much," Josi said as she was choking on her own blood. "Don't talk in the past tense, Josi, you're going to make it," Koweena said as tears streamed down her face. "I see bright lights," Josi said as she stared up at the ceiling. Mr. Harris brought in a lantern; the flame was now flickering throughout the room, and he had the towels with him as well. "Joe, go get the medical supplies, hurry!" Koweena shouted while crying. Koweena noticed that Josi's breathing had slowed dramatically. She was wheezing heavily and loudly with each breath. The breaths she was taking were getting further and further apart with each passing moment. Koweena now new there was nothing she could do. She was about to watch her sister die right in front of her. As Joe hurried back into the room with the supplies, Koweena gave him the grave news. "She's gone, Joe. I never even had the chance to say goodbye to her." Joe dropped the medical bag. "Oh, Koweena no," he said. It was the first time a slave had died on his two journeys. "Why did he do it?" Koweena asked. "He was working undercover, Koweena; he was deceivin us this whole time." Koweena suddenly became infuriated. She got up from the bed with her clothes soaked in blood and ran up to Joe. She slammed her fist against Joe's chest. "You bastard, you bastard! You let him in our group! And now my sister is dead because of you!" Joe said nothing. He just stood there, allowing Koweena to take her frustrations out on him. He knew she was right. Josi was dead because of him. "You bastard!" Koweena yelled. By now exhausted from the yelling, she stopped hitting Joe and leaned forward, putting her head on his chest. Joe wrapped his arms around Koweena. "I'm sorry, Koweena, I didn't know." By now Mrs. Harris had entered the room. "Why don't you stay an extra couple of days," Mrs. Harris said. "We can give your sister a proper burial. We need to get you cleaned up, Koweena, come with me, Dear." As Koweena was walking out of the room she paused, turned back and looked at her sister lying there in a bloody pool. "Goodbye, my beloved sister, your spirit will go with me wherever I go." She then walked out of the room crying.

"Joe, can you help me with Josi here?" Mr. Harris asked. Joe was in a trance, he didn't hear a word Mr. Harris said. He was in shock at the fact that Nias had betrayed them, and what Nias had just done to Josi. "Huh," Joe finally responded. "Can you help me here?" Mr. Harris asked. "Yes, sir."

A week later, back in Natchez, Julie finally received the letter Koweena had written her. She noticed that it came from Doctor Wilson's place. She became immediately worried. "Are they alright? Is she hurt?" She whispered to herself. Julie opened it up and began reading. When Julie got to the part of the letter where Koweena was writing about how Doctor Wilson had been staring at her, and wondering if he had some kind of secret that he was keeping from her, it made Julie break down and begin crying. After what her parents had told her just a week prior, and realizing the dilemma Koweena was in with Doctor Wilson, she just flat out lost it. Thomas was in the kitchen as he heard Julie wailing in the living room, he came rushing into the living room. "Honey, what is it?" "It's Koweena, here, read it and you'll understand why I'm so upset." After Thomas read it he just looked down at the floor. He then sat on the sofa and grabbed a hold of Julie and cuddled her up to him. "I know after what you just learned from your parents that it's very hard on you, and I can't even imagine what you're going through right now, Sweetheart; but hey, look at it, she's alright, and she seems happy, right?" "I'm so proud of her, Thomas." "I know you are, Jules. Don't worry, she's going to make it. If you just wait a little longer, you will get to share with her what you just found out. You just have to wait for her to make it to her destination though." "But I can't wait, Thomas." "You have to, Jules. You have no choice."

Two months later, still on the Natchez Road, Koweena was still grieving from Josi's death. Not only was it a traumatic event to see her sister stabbed to death by an attacker just inches away from where she was lying, but she also watched her die right before her very own eyes. It was something horrific to try and overcome and put behind her. She had been through so many traumatic events in her life though that she was able to whether the storm of losing her only sister with great courage and perseverance. She was riding in Mr. Kitchens' horse drawn carriage along with Joe, both of them were lying underneath some hay inside the carriage, while Mr. Kitchens was in the front, steering the horses. Mr. Kitchens was an abolitionist from the town of Hampshire, Tennessee. He had allowed Koweena and Joe to stay with him for a couple of days. He told them that he would take them to Griner's Stand, a station just a few miles south of Nashville. Joe stuck his head out from under the hay. "We is almost at the end of this road, Koweena," he said. "What does that mean, Joe?" "Well, first off, it means that were really goin to have to depend on the North Star like never before from here on out. It also means that were probably not goin to find a better lookin path the rest of the way north. We will have to go through a lot of woods." Koweena instantly became depressed. "Great," she said. "Don't worry, if we just follow the Star we will be just fine." "Are you familiar with any part of the rest of the way past Nashville?" Koweena asked. "I'm very familiar with the back woods of Kentucky, so familiar, in fact, that we can travel by day during that part of the journey." "Great! Walking this trail at night is just too scary." "Don't get used to it though, Koweena, after Kentucky, we will have to travel the rest of the way mostly at night."

It was a cold, fall morning that day as they approached the station. There was a Marshal standing at the entrance to the station wearing a black cowboy hat with a leather trench coat, with his badge pinned to the left pocket of his coat. "We're almost here," Mr. Kitchens yelled out. Koweena decided to get up and peer through the curtains just over Mr. Kitchens shoulder to get a view of the station. Koweena quickly spotted the Marshal leaning against the wooden building under the awning, smoking a cigarette. "A Marshal!" Koweena shouted. "Shhh, quickly over here!" Mr. Kitchens said, pointing to an area to their right, an open circular space between the road and the woods. As they made their way into the open area, they were positioned at an angle to where the horses and carriage were behind some trees, located in between them and the station. Joe quickly got up and peeked through the curtains and got a good look at the man through the trees. "He's holding a piece of paper!" Joe whispered in a sharp tone. "Yes, it looks like a wanted flier. I've seen plenty of those in my journeys." Mr. Kitchens said. "It could be for me," Koweena said. "It couldn't be, Koweena, they is a bunch of slaves on the run, and besides we is far away from Natchez," Joe reassured her. "Well, there's only one way to find out," Mr. Kitchens said. "What?" Koweena asked. "I'm going to have to go up there and talk to him, and try to get close enough to see just what he is holding. You guys wait right here, and stay under the hay, you hear." Koweena wasn't worried. She felt safe with Mr. Kitchens, and she definitely felt safe inside that carriage. If that Marshal was specifically after her, she believed all they had to do was go back to Mr. Kitchen's house and think of another plan.

Mr. Kitchens approached the Marshal. "Good day, sir," Mr. Kitchens said as he stuck out his hand to shake the Marshal's. The Marshal responded by shaking Mr. Kitchens' hand. "Good day," the Marshal said. "What do you have there?" Mr. Kitchens asked. "It's a wanted poster. We're looking for a runaway fugitive slave girl who escaped from Mississippi about two months ago. Here, take a look at it and tell me if you recognize any of this." Mr. Kitchens grabbed a hold of the flier, it said:

WANTED DEAD OR ALIVE

From the owner of the Defour Plantation in Natchez, Mississippi,

A runaway slave from her master. A $2,500 reward for the capture of the following slave dead or alive. She is about 16 years of age, 5'8" tall, light brown skin, and long, curly brown hair. She has the appearance of being of a mixed race origin. She escaped from the Defour Plantation on or about August 10th, 1845. She is accompanied by two other slaves, one female and one male. All Masters of vessels and others are hereby cautioned against concealing or carrying off said servants, of penalty of the law.

Natchez, Mississippi

August 12th, 1845

As Mr. Kitchens was reading the flier, the Marshal was watching him intensely, looking for any type of unusual reaction from the man that might tip him as to whether or not he was indeed harboring any slaves. As Mr. Kitchens finished reading the flier he made a grave mistake. He quickly glanced over his shoulder, looking at his horses and carriage. The Marshal quickly picked up on it. He too glanced in the direction Mr. Kitchens was looking. The Marshal noticed the carriage off in the distance. He swiftly pulled out his pistol from his holder and put it to Mr. Kitchens' head. "Alright, you bastard, take me to them," the Marshal said. "I, I, I don't know what you're talking about," Mr. Kitchens responded.

Koweena peered through the curtains once again, this time to see how Mr. Kitchens was faring. "He's got a gun to his head, Joe!" Koweena yelled out. "What!?" Joe blurted out. "Look! Look!" Koweena whispered out loudly. Joe looked through the curtains that Koweena was holding open for him. "They're walking this way!" Joe whispered. "What!?" Koweena shouted. "Be quiet, Koweena." Koweena stood to her feet, now with her head completely through the curtains. "Now is not the time to be quiet, we have to do something, and do it quick," she said. "I have to ride these horses like I've never ridden before!" Koweena yelled out as she quickly hopped into the driver's seat of the carriage."Hah, hah!" She yelled at the horses. They immediately took off. "Joe, there's a rifle on the floorboard of this seat, quickly, get up here and grab a hold of it." As Joe was making his way through the curtains and onto the front seat, a shot rang out. One of the horses bellowed out and hit the ground, the movement by the horse almost sent the carriage over on its side. "Koweena, we is goin to have to get on that horse there." "Do you know how to unhook the straps that are holding the horses together?" Koweena asked. "It doesn't matter, we is don't have time to think about it, come on let's get out, keep your body low, stay behind this horse that's still standing." Joe immediately untied the straps holding the two horses together. Another shot rang out, this time hitting the carriage. "Koweena, are you alright!" Joe yelled out. "Yes," Koweena yelled back.

Joe peered up over the horse and noticed that the Marshal was about ten yards away, still holding onto Mr. Kitchens. "Quickly, Koweena, hop on that horse!" Joe hollered out. "Do you have the rifle?" Koweena asked. Joe quickly went back to the carriage and grabbed the rifle. He then swiftly mounted the horse with Koweena. "Do your thing, Koweena, get us out of here." Koweena snapped the reigns, the horse took off. Joe realized that they were headed right for the Marshal. He then realized that he would have to shoot first, or it would be over for the both of them. Joe quickly cocked the rifle and aimed it at the Marshal, no easy task shaking up and down on a horse like he was. He came to the conclusion quickly that he had only one chance at this. The Marshal pointed his pistol at Koweena and Joe as they were getting ready to pass by him. The three were on a collision course. It was a certainty, a fatal situation; the three of them were going to collide with two pistols armed and ready to fire. Someone was going to die as Koweena and Joe headed right for him. "Fire! Fire, Joe!" Koweena frantically yelled out. With just a few feet now between them and the Marshal, with Koweena and Joe flying on the horse, another shot rang out. Who fired the fatal shot and who was hit? The Marshal grabbed a hold of his chest and then looked at his hand; it had blood all over it. He quickly fell to the ground. "Are you hit, Joe!?" Koweena asked. "No, I got him though." The two rode off on the horse through the road.

The two stopped some ten miles away from the confrontation. "Now we is really done it." "What do you mean, Joe?" "Now, not only are we wanted fugitives, but now we is gone and killed a Marshal. Every law enforcement in the country is goin to be after us. I have to ditch this rifle." "No, Joe, don't!" "I have to, Koweena. It will surely give us away if I walk around with a rifle, and besides, no safe house in their right mind would allow a black to stay brandishing a rifle." "Good point, Joe." "The road is going to end soon so we is goin to have to get rid of this horse," Joe said. "I tell you Joe, we've lost more horses since we started on this journey than I can count, not to mention Josi. How much longer can we survive, before it will be us that's next to fall prey to death?"

Chapter 12 Trauma

"Is you ready, we have to make it to that house!?" Joe yelled to Koweena. Another shot rang out in the Western Kentucky woods, this time skimming by Joe's head. "Junior, I think you hit one of them," the man yelled out. "Koweena, if we is don't go now, we is finished, do you understand me!?" Koweena was nervous. "Oh, I'm scared of falling down that embankment, it's just looks too slick," she said. "Come on, Junior, let's go!" The men started running toward the log Koweena and Joe were hiding behind. "Here they come, Koweena, let's go, now!" "Okay, okay, ready, set, go!" Koweena said as they pushed off the log that was jutting out onto the path of the thick woods, the same log that had been there barrier for hours. It had just started raining, once again, as it had earlier on that cold, frigid, wintry night when Koweena and Joe began their descent down the sharp embankment. As Koweena and Joe were running, the lantern Joe was carrying to guide them as their only source of light, was shaking so bad in Joe's hand that it was giving off a strobe light effect. The light was shaking and dancing around wildly, making their already impaired vision in the dark, even worse. "Those Niggers are running, Junior, shoot!" Another shot rang out, this time hitting the tree right next to Koweena. "Damn, Joe, that just missed. Woe!" Suddenly they both slipped on the wet leaves and tripped over a giant rock. "Oh my God!" Koweena shouted out as they both slammed to the damp, cold ground. They tumbled down the mountain about thirty feet when they both crashed against a log. On the other side of that log was a ten foot drop down an even steeper embankment, at the end of that embankment was the house. "Are you alright, Koweena?"

"Yeah, no, I think, I don't know, I might have sprained my ankle."
"See if you can put any pressure on it," Joe said. Koweena stood up. "A
little," she said. "Well, you is goin to have to suck it up, I don't know
what else to tell you. We still have to go down that even steeper hill."
"I can do it, Joe."

Suddenly, another shot rang out, this time it went straight up in
the air. "Woe, Junior!" Both men thumped to the ground and began
skidding down the slope. "My rifle!" Junior yelled out. "Hold on, Junior,
we have to wait until we stop here!" "Quickly, Koweena! They is stuck,
now's our chance!" They both jumped off the ledge onto the much
steeper hill. Koweena went down, wincing in pain. "Owe!" Koweena
hollered out in extreme pain. They both stopped. Joe became emphatic.
"Koweena, you have to suck it up!" He said. "Okay, I can do this, let's
go," Koweena said as they took off running again. Koweena was limping
her way down the slope, running on mainly just one leg. Joe was leaving
her behind because of it. "Joe! Joe! Wait up!" Koweena yelled out. Joe
stopped. He frustratingly took a deep sigh and went back up the hill.
Meanwhile, the other men were still back up on the less steep slope,
gathering their footing. "Come on, grab your gun, Junior!" Junior
went back up and grabbed a hold of his rifle. They proceeded back
down the slope. "Come here, you coons!" The man yelled out. "Hurry,
Koweena, they're on the move again!" "I can't, Joe, I can't run on it."
"Here, put your arm around my shoulder and hold on!" As they made
their way down the hill, Joe was trying to run, not only down a steep
embankment, but he was trying to hold onto Koweena around his
shoulder at the same time. "Is you okay, Koweena?" Joe asked, panting
heavily. "Yeah, I'm fine, are you okay?" Koweena asked, realizing Joe
was struggling to run and carry her at the same time. "Yeah, we is goin
to make it," Joe said.

"Larry, you clean the dishes tonight," Robert told Larry as they were
finishing up their dinner. Larry and Robert were brothers who lived
together in the log cabin at the bottom of the hill. They both worked
in the local mine situated in the mountains of the area. "While you're
doing that, Larry, I'm going to go out and get some more wood for
the fire." Inside the cabin was a kitchen, a small living room and three
bedrooms. Robert came back inside with the wood. As he put the wood
in the fireplace, and while Larry was doing the dishes, a loud bang came

from the front door. "What in the hell!?" Larry said as he turned from the sink toward the front door. "Robert, get the gun!" Larry shouted. Robert grabbed the rifle that was next to the fireplace and proceeded to the front door. Larry grabbed a knife from the kitchen and met Robert at the door. "Who is it!?" Robert shouted. "A friend of a friend!" Joe yelled back. Joe and Koweena just stood there trying to catch their breath. Their stomachs were churning inside. They both realized as they stood there, wondering who was on the other side of the door, that they could be standing right in the middle of a trap. For the first time in their journey, they were at a house, not knowing for sure if it was a safe house, or the house of some slave hater. They had no choice though; the men chasing after them left them with no alternative. "I can't believe you got us into this situation," Koweena told Joe. "I didn't know those men were out there, Koweena. What was I suppose to do?" It was a tense few moments as the four of them waited for some sign on both sides of the door. "If they don't open soon, we is done for," Joe said.

"I can hear two people talking," Robert said as he had his ears pressed against the door, with the rifle cocked and ready to go in his hands. "Why is nobody answering the door? You said you were a friend of friend. Oh, I don't like this, Joe. This is a bad sign. They could be waiting and ready to turn us in once they open the door." "I'm really getting tired of your pessimism, Koweena. Ever since we got stuck up there on that hill you've been saying that there's no way out." It was apparent that the stress and pressure of what they were going through was taking its toll, as Koweena and Joe snapped back and forth at each other. "Look at us, Joe. We've been waiting out here for several minutes now. You said what you were supposed to say, and they haven't opened the door yet, and we have men just a few yards from us trying to kill us. How bad do you want it to get?" "Just be quiet, Koweena, let me try it again. We is friends of a friend." Joe said again to the men on the other side of the door. "Why does that man keep saying that?" Larry asked. "I don't know, Larry, I don't understand it either. It sounds like their harmless though, whoever it is." "What's your name, and what is your business here!?" Robert yelled out to the other side of the door. This was the moment for Koweena and Joe. What Joe was about to say next would determine whether or not they would be saved from their attackers. Koweena noticed that Joe was taking a deep breath to speak.

Koweena grabbed Joe's arm. "Joe, wait!?" She whispered. "Koweena, we's a don't have a choice." Koweena let go of Joe's arm and took a deep breath. Joe spoke up. "We is runaway slaves. There is men chasing us. We need a safe place to stay." "Robert, I don't want to get caught up in the middle of this," Larry said. Robert thought about it for a moment. "Larry, we can't just leave them out there to die." "Yeah, but we could get killed too, Robert, if we let them in." "Nobody is going to kill me," Robert said as he flashed his rifle in the face of Larry. "I'm letting them in." "Robert, don't!" As Larry was saying that Robert opened the front door. "Quickly, come in!" Robert exclaimed as he grabbed a hold of both Koweena and Joe. Koweena quickly saw the rifle in Robert's hand and spoke up. "Don't hurt us, sir, please don't hurt us. We didn't mean to barge in here like this. We will leave, and you will never see us again." "Koweena!" Joe blurted out. "Relax, young girl, its okay, have a seat here in the kitchen," Robert said. Koweena and Joe, both exhausted by their long stand off in the woods, took a seat. "So there are men chasing you you said," Robert said. "Yes, sir, they is probably right out in front as we speak," Joe said.

Meanwhile, Junior and the other man stopped when they got to the bottom of the hill. "They went inside that house," the man said. "What do we do now, Boss?" Junior asked. "Here, let's get behind these trees. We'll wait them out. They have to come outside at some point," the man said. "Do those men have any weapons on them?" Robert asked. "At least a rifle, that's all we could make out," Koweena said. "Yeah, they is least have that," Joe said. "Larry, come with me," Robert said. Larry, with knife still in hand, followed Robert to the front porch. Robert cocked his rifle once more just so the men could hear it. They stood out there for about five minutes, staring out into the dense woods when they finally decided to come back into the house. "Well, we didn't hear or see anyone, so they must have left," Robert said.

"They have weapons, Boss," Junior said. "Like I said, Junior, we'll just wait them out," the man said. "So what can Larry and I do for you guys?" Robert asked. "Well, sir, if we can stay the night, it would be much appreciated?" Joe asked Robert. "Sure, we have the room don't we, Larry." "Sure, I'll go and make sure the bedroom is in suitable condition." "Would the both of you like something to eat? We just finished up with dinner, but we have some leftovers here," Robert said.

"That would be great!" Koweena blurted out, absolutely starving from the long standoff. "Yes, sir, we is lost our food along the way and that would be much appreciated," Joe said. "What's your guys names?" Robert asked. "This here is Koweena, and I'm Joe." "Pleasure to meet you both. Where are you from?" Robert asked. "We is from Mississippi," Joe said. "Mississippi, you're a far piece from there. Say you're escapees are you?" "Yes, sir," Joe said as he took a big bite of the ham in front of him. Koweena looked at the ham, "no more ham," she thought. But she was too hungry to complain much. "I feel for you guys, I would hate to be in your shoes," Robert said. Koweena looked over at Joe as they were eating and smiled. They realized they had lucked up that night in stumbling upon slave sympathizers. They knew they had a fifty-fifty chance of finding themselves sympathizers in the state they found themselves in, as they sat there at the dinner table eating in front of Robert. Luck was on their side that night.

As they finished dinner, Koweena and Joe went into the living room to sit down. "Bedroom is all ready, Robert," Larry said as he walked into the living room where Robert was sitting next to the fireplace. "Great, great, hey listen I have an idea. Koweena, why don't you have the room all to yourself tonight. Joe, you can sleep on the floor in my room," Robert said. "It's only the proper thing to do since we have only one lady in the house," he continued. "Thank you, sir, that's very proper of you," Koweena responded. As they sat there for several minutes in silence, Koweena noticed that the two men were staring at her. She should have been used to it by now, but she got that familiar uncomfortable feeling about her like she had gotten so many times in the past. She had a funny feeling that night, a nervous feeling about the two strange men. She suddenly felt the urge to ask Joe if he would sleep in the room with her. Not only did she feel uncomfortable, which is how she normally felt, but she was feeling something new, as the men just sat there staring at her, she felt scared. She suddenly felt that her beauty was making her very vulnerable. Growing up, her beauty had made her feel weird, and good, at the same time. But now, it was bringing about a panic inside her as she sat there looking down at the floor, afraid to look at the men anymore, afraid that they might still be staring at her, which they were.

"Joe," Koweena whispered to him as he sat there on the sofa right next to her. "What?" Joe whispered back. "Can I talk to you in the kitchen for a moment?" "Excuse us, gentlemen," Joe said as both he and Koweena got up from the sofa and made their way to the kitchen. "What is it, Koweena?" "This doesn't feel right." "What doesn't feel right?" "These men are making me feel scared." "Why?" Joe asked. "They just keep staring at me, it's weirding me out." "I thought you were used to men staring at you all the time." "Not like that, they're looking at me all creepy like; I just don't trust them, that's all." "Koweena, just relax." "Will you stay with me in the room tonight?" Koweena asked. "I thought you would enjoy having a room all to yourself." "Not with these two men in the house I don't." "Listen, I'm goin to be in the other room right across from yours. If anything happens, I will hear it, okay." "That's not good enough," Koweena said. "Koweena, I'm not goin to let anything happen to you, alright. You leave your door open and I'll leave mine open, okay." That made Koweena take a deep sigh of relief. She had been on this journey long enough with Joe that she trusted him completely, even to the point of putting her life in his hands like she felt she would have to do on this night. As Koweena and Joe made their way back into the living room, Koweena thought she would try and get a feel for the two men to see if they were indeed as creepy as they appeared to be when they were staring at her. "So, do you both have wives or girlfriends?" She asked. Robert sat up at attention when Koweena asked him that. "Yes, we both do," he said. "Catherine and Isabelle," Robert continued. "Catherine is my Sweetheart, and Isabelle is Larry's." That answer made Koweena stop rubbing her hands in a nervous fashion. "How long have you been seeing them?" Koweena asked. "About a year now, we plan on getting married, the four of us, on the same day," Robert said. "Oh, that's romantic," Koweena said. "Yeah, we like it," Larry spoke up, finally joining in on the conversation. "So, I guess you guys will need some food to take along with you when you leave?" Larry continued. "Yes, sir, if you don't mind that would be great," Joe said. "Let me go in the kitchen here and see what we have," Larry said as he got up and headed into the kitchen.

"So, what's it like being a slave?" Robert asked. "It's hell!" Joe blurted out. "Yes, I can only imagine." "No you can't sir, with all due respect it's hard for someone who hasn't actually been a slave to understand just how bad it is," Joe said. "True, true, it must be really bad for the both of you to risk your lives out here in the Kentucky woods, so far away from home like you are." "Home sir? A plantation isn't home," Joe said. Koweena just sat there thinking how she didn't necessarily agree with Joe on that statement. Yes, slavery was hell, she agreed with that, but she did have a home on her Plantation, and she did have a family. Her thoughts went right to Julie. She began thinking how Julie was fairing without her in her life. "I wonder if she even misses me at this point," she thought to herself. She grabbed her ring and began twirling it around her finger as she thought of the person that molded her into the person she was on that day. "I wonder if she is pregnant yet," she continued thinking. "Sir, I really didn't have it as rough as most slaves," Koweena told Robert. "Oh yeah, how's that?" Robert asked. Koweena's eyes began to well up with tears. "Well, I had a very dear woman who took me under her wings. She cared for me, treated me like one of her own, and even let me live with her. We were like a family." "I can see it in your eyes that you were very close to this woman," Robert noted. "I depended on her for everything, sir. She was my sunrise, my Christmas morning, she would always lift my spirits when I was down; she was like a sister, a mother figure to me growing up. Excuse me please." Koweena quickly got up and ran into the room that was meant for her. She lied down on the bed and began balling. She yearned for Julie as she laid there crying. "Just to hear her voice, and see her smile, I would give anything," she said to herself as she continued sobbing. "Well, I think it's about time we call it a night," Robert told Joe. "Yes, sir."

Meanwhile, outside, the two men were crouched behind a tree, just yards from the house. "Boss, we're running out of food," Junior said. "Don't worry about that, Junior. We can't worry about that at this point; we have these two fugitives to catch." "We are sure far away from home, Boss." "Junior, there's no backing out now, especially when we're so close to catching them." Junior noticed that his boss began pacing back and forth while rubbing his hands. He seemed like he was getting very excited about something all of sudden, Junior was thinking to himself. "What are you thinking about, sir; you seem very hyped about something all of sudden." "Don't worry about it, Junior, hey, it's time for bed, why don't you get your sleeping bag and lay down." Junior got the impression that his boss was up to something, but he didn't press it any further. Junior got in his sleeping bag and lay down for the night. His boss just continued to pace back and forth, from the tree they were hiding behind, to the other tree that was right next to them, he was pacing and pacing, like he couldn't wait for something to happen. "Oh, I've been waiting for this moment for such a long time," the man said with great anticipation.

As Koweena was lying there in bed, she was enjoying the fact that for the first time on the journey she actually had a bedroom all to herself. She was thinking about all she had been through since leaving the Plantation. From almost getting shot at at the barn when they first started, to getting shot at when they were making their escape off the Plantation, to Joe getting shot, to losing two horses to gunshot wounds, to almost getting shot at by a Marshal, and of course, losing Josi. And now, the stand off she had just experienced in the woods. It was almost too much for her to bear, and they weren't even halfway to their destination yet. She could remember as she lay there, Julie telling her that if she thought about her, or called on her, that she would be there, right next to her. So Koweena began to call out Julie's name. She instantly began to feel much better. She also remembered Julie telling her to keep her head up no matter what the circumstances. She then began to remember Julie's face when they said there final goodbyes, and how she looked. How sorrowful Julie appeared. It made Koweena yearn for Julie even more after visualizing that. "Her face was so heart-breaking to look at," she thought. "It was so frail and weak looking, like she had really gone through some hell in letting me go," she whispered to herself. "If I had just told her how much she meant to me, and how much I truly can't live without her that morning, but I didn't," she continued to whisper.

Meanwhile, there was loud bang in the kitchen area, the sounds of pots being turned over, but Koweena was too deep in thought to hear it. She turned over on her side in the bed, to where her back was facing the door, to focus on going to sleep.

As she was drifting off to sleep, all of a sudden, a dirty, muddy hand covered her mouth. Her eyes opened wide when she instantly heard a voice in her ear. "Scream, or say one word, and I'll kill you, you understand." She immediately thought that it was either Robert or Larry. The man violently slammed her on her back. He ripped her clothes into pieces, tearing them completely off her. She felt scared and humiliated as she lay there on her back, naked. The man quickly whipped out a piece of rope from his back pocket with one hand, while he had a hold of her ankle with his other hand, pressing it against one of the bedposts at the foot of the bed. He quickly tied both her feet to each bed post. As he took off his pants, and began to lay on top of her, the moonlight shined on his face. As he was now lying on top of her, she got a clear view of his face, it was Ray. She was stunned. How? Where? When? She thought to herself as he began thrusting into her. As she suddenly began to wince in pain at Ray's thrusting, she questioned herself. "How in the world did he find me in Kentucky, way up here in these isolated woods, all the way from Southern Mississippi?" Ray began kissing her mouth; she could taste the tobacco from his mouth as he put his tongue down her throat. Tears began flowing down her cheeks as she held on tightly to the sheets next to her head with one hand, and with the other hand she held on tightly to her necklace. She tried not to stare at Ray as he was grunting, she was floored that it was Ray that was doing this to her. As her head slammed against the headboard, she was thinking that this was so much worse than her beatings she had to endure from the same man that was doing this to her now. She was now being internally violated; something that didn't happen during her beatings. Ray was ramming her hard and violently as she just laid there gritting her teeth from the pain. The bed post that were holding her feet were jerking back and forth, they were about to snap in two as her body was being tugged back and forth. She couldn't help but think that this moment was suppose to be a special one between her and the man she would give her whole heart to. Her innocence was robbed from her when she was beaten as a child, but now her chastity was ripped away from her as Ray was ripping into her. Koweena held on tight to her necklace as her body shook with each drive Ray was putting into her. That infamous song that Julie wrote her when she was five began playing over and over in her mind, as the large man pounded all his weight on top of her.

She needed consoling that night like never before in her whole life, even more than she did when she was beaten, and there was only one person who could do it, and yet she was so far away. She needed Julie that night desperately, but this time there would be no Julie there to comfort her. She would have to get through this traumatic event on her own for the first time in her life. When she was beaten the first time she had her mom and Julie. When she was beaten the second time, she had Julie. When she was depressed, she had Julie to hold her and tell her uplifting things. Now, she had no one. She would have to go through this alone. "Please stop, you're hurting me. Why are you doing this to me?" Ray continued violently and forcefully pounding her, while holding onto her hip with one hand, and slapping her face with the other. "Shut up, bitch, and let me enjoy this," he said. As he finished, Joe and Robert came rushing into the bedroom. They leaped onto the bed and tackled the giant Ray, slamming him to the floor, with both Joe and Robert on top of him. They began wrestling on the floor at the base of the bed. Koweena grabbed the covers and pulled them over her with her feet still tied to the bed post. "He's too big for us!" Robert yelled out. Ray threw Joe and Robert off of him, stood up and began kicking the both of them. He quickly pulled up his pants and ran toward the bedroom door. As he made his way out into the hallway, Larry came out of nowhere and leaped on his back. Ray fell backwards and slammed Larry against the wall, knocking him off his back. "Grab the gun!" Larry yelled out to Robert. As Ray was running toward the front door, Robert went into his room and grabbed his rifle. He immediately ran into the hallway and pulled the trigger. Ray was halfway out the door when the bullet grazed his upper arm. "I got him!" Robert yelled out. "How do you know, Robert?" Larry asked. "I could tell by his reaction, he grabbed his arm." "Sounds like it wasn't a fatal shot, Robert," Larry said. "Yeah, but I still got him," Robert replied. "Junior, come on, let's get out of here!" "What did you do, Boss?" "Just grab our gear and let's go!"

Koweena was lying on the bed, with her pillow over her face, sobbing. Robert and Larry went back into the room where Koweena and Joe were. Koweena took the pillow off of her head and spoke, chocking back the tears. "Please guys, I just want Joe in here with me right now." "Sure, let's go, Larry," Robert said as he grabbed a hold of Larry's shoulder and led him out of the room. "Let me untie you, Koweena," Joe said as he began untying Koweena's feet gently. The ropes had left burn marks on her ankles the rape was so violent. "I'm so sorry, Koweena, my God I should have heard something but I didn't." "I need Julie; can you get

Julie for me?" Koweena was in obvious shock. She was so shaken up, that she thought Julie was nearby. "Koweena, Dear, we is in Kentucky, Julie is nowhere near us." Koweena was holding onto her necklace so tight that she was about to rip it off. "I need Julie," she said. "Koweena, Julie is in Mississippi," Joe said.

"It was then that I realized," Koweena recalled. "I was on my own. I would have to get through this without the comforting touch and words from the one I had depended on for so long. But how though? I was in shock. How was I supposed to pick up the pieces after what had just happened to me? I was an emotional wreck. I knew, without Julie, it would be a lonely, uphill battle."

Meanwhile, back on the Defour Plantation, Julie was sitting on her sofa rubbing her hands together in intense worry. "I wonder how Koweena is doing, Thomas. I wonder if she needs me right now." "Jules, you're going to worry yourself to death, just relax." "I can't relax, Thomas, not when Kowie is out there, in God knows where, fighting for her life. Oh, I shouldn't have let her go." "Jules, she could have been shipped off, and at any moment too. You heard your father say that didn't you?" "Yes, but that was before all this. Now, he's on my side. If she would have just stayed a little while longer, everything would have been okay." "But you didn't know what your father knew at that point, Julie, when he threatened to ship her off. You made the right decision at the time, with what information you had in front of you." "God, I hate my father for doing that to me. Why did he have to wait so long to tell me? Why did he decide to tell me after Kowie had left?" "Jules, you're going to have to quit worrying." "I can't quit, Thomas, I need to worry and stress over her, it helps me get through this. It makes me feel close to her. You know as well as I do, that I'm the only one who can calm her, and soothe her, when she's upset. What if she's upset right now and I'm not there for her." "Julie, she's fine, you're going to have to quit getting all worked up over it." "Thomas, you don't know the relationship we have. You've only seen parts of it. She's been through a lot, and each time I've been there to see her through it." "What about Joe? I mean, Julie, he's right there with her. I'm sure he can console her." That made Julie think long and hard about Joe, maybe he could be someone Koweena could lean on. "He did seem like he had his act together when he was here at the house, and he did seem to genially care for Koweena. Maybe she can depend on him when times get tough," she thought to herself. "You know you're probably right, Thomas, Joe does seem like the kind of person that would be there for Koweena if things got rough. You always seem to know just the right words to say, Dear, to ease my fears." Thomas was seated on the sofa, next to Julie as he put his arm around her. "That's what I'm here for, Jules. That's what I'm here for."

The following morning, Joe realized that Koweena wasn't getting out of bed. Robert and Larry were at work, and it was just Koweena and Joe in the house. By noon; and with Koweena not stirring, Joe realized that she had been severely traumatized. Joe went into the room Koweena was in, he noticed that Koweena was not only in bed, but every part of her body was covered by the sheets, even her head. "Koweena, are you awake?" "Go away, Joe!" "Can we at least talk about what happened?" That comment by Joe made Koweena swiftly throw the covers aside, and run into the hallway, toward the bathroom. She didn't make it in time; she threw up all over the hallway floor. "I'll clean it up, Koweena; you just go back to bed, okay." Koweena slowly walked back into the bedroom and got back into bed, and covered herself back up again, with the covers once again over her face.

It was early evening, and Robert and Larry had returned from work, this time with Catherine and Isabelle. "How is Koweena?" Robert asked Joe. "She hasn't gotten out of bed all day, well, except to throw up." "Oh, poor Dear, she's traumatized," Catherine said. "We brought the ladies home with us thinking they could help her," Robert said. "Maybe a woman's touch is what she needs right now," Catherine said. "Come on, let's go see about her Isabelle," Catherine said as they both walked into Koweena's bedroom. Koweena still had the covers over her. She was on her side, with her back facing the door. Catherine and Isabelle walked over to the other side of the bed and knelt down to Koweena's level. "Koweena, Dear, I'm Catherine, and this is Isabelle. Do you want to talk about what happened last night?" Once again, Koweena immediately got up from the bed and ran into the bathroom where she threw up. "Bless her heart," Catherine said. This time Koweena was so depressed, and so emotionally drained, that she just sat there on the bathroom floor. Catherine and Isabelle walked into the bathroom. "Is there anything we can do to make your situation better for you, Dear?" Catherine asked. "No, I just want to be alone." "Oh my God, she's got blood all over her Catherine," Isabelle noticed. "Koweena, Sweetheart, you have dried blood all over your legs," Isabelle said. "Catherine, she's got blood all over her here," Isabelle said. She went over and knelt down to get eye level with Koweena. "Koweena, Catherine here is going to get a sponge, and a tub basin full of water, and we're going to clean you up, alright." "Don't touch me!" Koweena screamed out. "Koweena, Dear, I understand you are in shock right now, but we're going to have to clean you up," Isabelle said. Catherine brought the sponge, and the tub basin full of water, back into the bathroom. "Catherine, I need for you to go into her bedroom and replace those sheets, I'm sure there's blood all over them." As Isabelle began applying the sponge to Koweena's legs, Koweena began fighting her off with her fists. "Catherine, I need you, she's fighting me here!" Isabelle hollered out into the bedroom where Catherine was changing the bed sheets. Catherine rushed into the bedroom to hold Koweena's arms down as Isabelle cleaned her legs. Koweena, wailing her arms and kicking her legs, gave them a struggle, but they finally managed to clean her up. "Okay, we'll leave you alone now, but if you need us we'll be just around the corner, okay," Catherine said. "Okay," Koweena replied. "You know, Koweena, being around people will help," Isabelle said. "Can you go get Joe?" Koweena asked. "Sure, I'll go get him," Isabelle said. "Joe, she wants to talk to you," Isabelle said as she walked into the kitchen with Catherine. Joe entered the bathroom.

"Goodness, she was a mess, Robert, you should have seen the blood," Isabelle told Robert in the kitchen.

"Yes, Koweena, what is it, Sweetheart." "Joe, I don't know if I can get through this." "Koweena, I can't imagine what you is goin through right now, I wish there was somthin I could do to make it better for you." "Just you being here, Joe, helps." "Listen, I hate to bring this up right now, but we have to get movin, Koweena. I know you is traumatized, but if we don't get to movin, we could die." "That wouldn't be such a bad thing, Joe." "Koweena, you don't mean that. I know it's hard, and I know it's goin to be hard, but you have to get back on your feet and be my tough partner, like I know you are." "I can't Joe, I just want to crawl up into a hole and die." "Koweena, I'm not givin up on you, without you, I wouldn't have made it this far." "Was your other journey this hard?" Koweena asked. "No, not even close, but I didn't have you. You is resilient, Koweena, you can do this."

As Koweena lay there that night in bed, she was still in shock. She was shaking with fear, even though Joe was lying on the floor right next to her bed. Oh, how she needed Julie desperately to calm her fears. She remembered that night, right before she began this journey, Julie laying with her beside her bed, cuddling up close to her, protecting her, consoling her as she always did. She had no one to cuddle up to on this night. She just stared out into the nighttime sky with her blankets pulled all the way up to her neck, thinking about how one act the previous night had destroyed her life, as she shook with fright, fearing that Ray could return at any moment. As the pain that had transpired the night before was still fresh on her body, and in her mind, she felt so alone. The lonliness and pain was unbearable.

"Joe, Joe, are you awake?" Koweena asked in the silence of the room. Koweena called out in the darkness of the night, hoping for a response from Joe. "Joe, wake up please?" She continued asking. Finally, a response, "What is it, Koweena?" Joe asked as he stammered to sit up. "Will you come up here and lay with me in bed please; I really need someone up here with me?" Koweena asked. She needed someone to replace Julie, and she was determined that on that night, it would be Joe. Joe got up, went over to the bed and laid on top of the covers Koweena was under. "Will you put your arm around me, Joe?" Koweena asked in a soft, vulnerable voice. "Are you sure about this, Koweena?" Joe asked. "Just do it, Joe." Joe put his arm around Koweena as she placed her head on the pillow that he was lying on. She felt somewhat at ease by Joe's presence. She did feel better with Joe being in bed with her, it was a warm body, and her and Joe had become close since the journey began. Though she did trust him, it still wasn't Julie holding her. However, for the first time in her life, she found herself growing emotionally attached to someone other than Julie, as she lay there feeling protected by Joe.

After a sleepless and agonizing night, Koweena did get out of bed that next morning, but she was back to staring at the floor, just like she had done during her beatings. This time, however, there was no Julie, and there was no time to properly heal from her trauma either. Koweena and Joe had to leave right away. They packed up their supplies and got ready for their next destination. "Thank you, Robert. I mean, really, you helped us on so many levels these last few days," Joe said. "I just feel bad for Koweena," Robert said as he glanced over at Koweena who was choking back the tears as she just stared at the floor, with a lifeless look about her. "She'll make it, Robert. She's tough," Joe said. Robert shook hands with Joe. "Okay, Joe, be careful, you hear," Robert said. "Good bye, Robert," Joe said. Joe wrapped his arm around Koweena's shoulder and led her out of the house. With what just happened to Koweena, the crushing shock of being raped, and no Julie to comfort her, the question would be, would she have enough strength and fortitude to make it the rest of the way? One thing was for sure, Joe wasn't going to give up on her.

"With what happened to me that night in Kentucky, and without Julie in my life now, Joe was thrusted into becoming my rock, someone I needed to depend on," Koweena recalled. "I would need Joe like never before. As a result, that caused me to start having stronger feelings for him. Strange feelings, feelings I had never felt before. Even though my rape had just happened a few nights earlier, the feelings I had for Joe were developing. Those feelings I started having for him most definitely scared me."

Chapter 13 More Than Friends

$\mathcal{I}$t had been a month and a half since the horrific rape of Koweena, and she and Joe were cutting across a field on a sunny April day, just south of the town of Anderson, Indiana, which was about fifteen miles away. They were in between Anderson, which was to the North, and Indianapolis which was to the South. Koweena had been in a saddened, depressed state for most of the journey from the Western woods of Kentucky to this small enclave in Indiana. But with the dawning of each new day, and not running into any Marshals or bounty hunters, or Ray for that matter, Koweena realized she was getting closer to the finish line; and her chance at freedom. This fact was helping her to shake off the overbearing weight of her burdensome depression. As they were cutting across the field, Koweena spoke up. "Joe, hold on a second." She immediately stopped, turned around and threw up. She just stood there, bent over, throwing up, on and on, she couldn't stop. "Koweena, you sure have thrown up a lot over the last month. I'm worried about you. Is you alright?" "I don't know what's wrong with me, Joe, I just can't stop getting nauseous, I seem to be throwing up all the time." "That safe house is right over this ridge, when we get there, we'll see if those folks have an idea as to why you is so sick. Or maybe they can get us a doctor to look at you."

Joe was very worried about Koweena. He had grown so fond of her since their journey began, and he needed her in order to make it the rest of the way. They had, since the journey began, become more dependant on each other emotionally. "You know, Koweena," he said to Koweena as she continued throwing up; "this is as far as I's ever made it up here in the north. I's never went this far." Koweena wiped the vomit from her mouth. "Is that a good thing or a bad thing, Joe." "Well, it depends on how you look at it, Koweena. We is made it this far, right? But, on the other hand, I don't have a clue about how to get the rest of the way up north." "Take the good with the bad huh, Joe." "Something like that, Koweena." "Julie taught me long ago that that means to compromise. So, Joe, this is me saying that I'll compromise with you. You got us this far, right?" "Yeah." "So I'll compromise with you, since the bad thing is that you basically don't know where you're going, I'll compromise and help you get the rest of the way." "But you don't know where we is goin either," Joe said. "Take the good with the bad, Joe; take the good with the bad." "Is you tryin to be funny, Koweena?" "Joe, let me help you out a second. It's *are* you trying to be funny not *is* you trying to be funny." Joe began laughing out loud. "Teach me, Koweena! Teach me!" He said sarcastically. Joe pointed to the ground. "Let's sit right here and eat and rest until it gets dark," he said.

They sat down on a grassy embankment on top of a hill overlooking the little village where their next safe house was located. As they were eating, a little boy approached them on a horse. Koweena chuckled. "Not another horse, I'm sick of horses on this journey," she said. She was just kidding; she loved horses too much to truly be sick of them. The little boy was enthusiastic as he approached them. "Hi there!" The little boy said. He didn't look any older than eleven as he rode up right to the spot where the two were eating. "Just act cool, Koweena; we don't know whose parents this little guy belongs to." Koweena and Joe were suspicious and paranoid of anyone they didn't know who wasn't expecting them along the journey, even someone like this little boy. "So, are you guys runaway slaves?" The boy asked. Koweena had a sideways grin. "What do you think?" She asked right back. "Well, okay," said the little boy, "you have a sack of food there, and you have a bag of clothes. I would say that you are runaway slaves." "You're right little fella," Koweena said. Joe gave Koweena a disappointing look after she said that. "Joe, I can't eat this stuff, it sickens my stomach to even look at it." "Koweena, you's need to eat. You haven't eaten anything in weeks. You need to keep your strength up for the rest of the journey." "I've seen lots of runaway slaves before, you meet the typical profile," the boy said. "I just can't stand to look at it, Joe, get it out of my face before

I throw up again," Koweena said. "What do you mean you've seen a lot of runaway slaves before?" Koweena asked the boy. "Oh, my parents have kept a lot of them while I was growing up. They would just come and go." "What is your parents last name boy?" Joe asked. "We're the Wilkins family," the boy said. "Wilkins, isn't that the place we're going next?" Koweena asked Joe. "It sure is," Joe replied. "Why don't you go home kid, and let your parents know that we'll be there tonight?" Joe asked the boy. "No, I want to stay here; I'm interested in knowing what all you guys have been through along your journey." Koweena began to chuckle again. "What's your name, boy, or should we just keep calling you boy?" She asked. "My name is Mitchell." "Okay, Mitchell, what would you like to know?" Koweena asked. "Well, how did you," "hold on, Mitchell," Koweena interrupted as she leaned over to throw up once again. "Are you alright, ma'am?" Mitchell asked. "She's been throwing up a lot," Joe told Mitchell. "Do you guys have a doctor in this little village?" Joe continued as he asked Mitchell. "Yeah, we have a doctor, Doctor Rosinborough." "Good, you hear that, Koweena, we can get you a doctor here," Joe said to Koweena. Koweena was turned over on her side, with her back to Joe and Mitchell, exhausted from all the vomiting. Joe was getting very concerned about Koweena, he knew she was sick, but he didn't know why, and he knew it could jeopardize the whole journey. "So tell me about your journey?" Mitchell asked Joe.

For the rest of the afternoon, as Koweena lay there, sleeping on her side, Joe told Mitchell all about their journey, leaving out no details. Mitchell was gripped and moved by what Joe was telling him, intensely listening to every word that proceeded out of Joe's mouth. "Wow, you guys have been through a lot. You know I don't know a lot about being pregnant, but it sounds like the misses over there is pregnant," Mitchell said, observing Koweena as she slept. Joe began to panic. "What!?" He said. "Yeah, my mom just had my sister not along ago, and she went through some of the same things you were telling me that your partner has been through," Mitchell noted. Suddenly, Joe became sickened by what he all of a sudden was thinking. "Could that mad man have really gotten Koweena pregnant?" He thought. "Congratulations!" Mitchell said with a big grin on his face. Joe gave him a perplexed look. "She is your partner right?" Mitchell asked. Joe became a little depressed. "No, no, it's not like that, Mitchell, not like that at all," Joe said. He could only wish that that was the case. Joe, in mentioning the details of the journey, left out the rape incident. He felt Mitchell was too young to hear about such a gory detail as that. "She's having what they call morning sickness," Mitchell added. "Morning sickness, but she's sick all the time, not just in the morning." "No," Mitchell continued. "They just call it morning sickness. It's where they throw up all the time the first few months after getting pregnant." That statement by Mitchell hit Joe like a ton of bricks. He realized at that point that that was exactly what Koweena was going through, and he also realized that it started happening right after the rape, it fit perfectly to what the boy was describing. "What do you do for it?" Joe asked. "You just have to let it run its course, there's really not a whole lot you can do about it," Mitchell replied.

As nightfall fell, Koweena, Joe, and Mitchell made their way down the hill into the village, with Mitchell riding his horse, while Koweena and Joe were on foot. "Wait a minute!" Joe whispered in a sharp tone as the three approached Mitchell's house. "What is it, Joe, what's the matter?" Koweena asked. "The statue in the lawn, it has no lantern or flag in it!" Joe whispered strongly. Mitchell, now galloping onto the driveway, new exactly what that meant. "Mitchell, we's a gots to go, nice meeting you. Come on, Koweena, lets get out of here!" Joe said as he grabbed a hold of Koweena's arm and began pulling her on past the house. Koweena stopped, bent over, and placed her hands on her knees. "Joe, I can't, hold on." "Koweena, come on, we can't be out in the open like this." "I can't, Joe; I'm too exhausted to move." After what Joe had learned from the boy earlier that day, he decided that he wasn't going to tell Koweena what actually might be making her so sick and tired. "Koweena, I know you is sick, but we have to keep moving. This is a dangerous place right now. Marshals could be stakin this place out as we speak." "What about those woods over there," Koweena said, breathing heavily, trying to catch her breath as she pointed over to the woods located on the opposite side of the street. "What if there's Marshals in there, Koweena?" "Joe, I just can't go on any further, I just can't." "Okay, come on," Joe said as he took Koweena by the arm once again and led her into the woods about ten yards, where they sat down behind an oak tree, with the tree separating them from the houses on the other side of the street. "Joe, I'm going to throw up again." As Koweena sat there throwing up, Joe realized he had to get her to a doctor, and fast. "Here, Koweena, can you eat some of these crackers? You have to eat something." "I think so," Koweena said, holding her hand to her mouth as she convulsed trying not to throw up again. "You wait right here and eat those crackers. I'm goin to go up the street and see if I can't spot another statue, maybe we is get lucky." Koweena clutched onto Joe's arm. "No! Wait! What if you don't make it back? I can't go on like this alone," she said. "Koweena, we's don't have a choice. You is too sick, I have to do something. Anyways, if I don't, we could be stuck here, and we don't have enough food to last another day." Koweena became depressed as she looked down at Joe's feet. "Okay," she said. "Hey, look at me," Joe said as Koweena looks up at him with teary eyes. "We's a goin to make it, you hear. I'm not goin to leave you stranded here, okay, I promise." "Promise?" Koweena asked. Joe grabbed a hold of Koweena's hand as she held onto the cracker with the other hand. "I promise," he said. Once again, like the time when Koweena was wrapping Joe's arm, after he had been hit with a bullet, they just stared at each other in silence for several seconds; Koweena was just sitting there biting her bottom lip as she stared at him. "Um, um, I have to go," Joe said, almost speechless as he stared into Koweena's eyes. Koweena stroked her hair from her ears while looking back and forth at Joe and the ground with a nervous grin on her face. "Yes, Joe, you must go," she replied. As Joe left, Koweena began thinking about him. Thinking of him only in ways a young girl would do when dreaming about love. Her thoughts then quickly shifted to Julie. "I haven't had a chance to write her in so long. God, I've only written her once, and that was at the beginning of our journey, she must be worried sick." She just sat there rocking back and forth against the tree, holding her necklace tightly and staring at her ring. "I wish Julie were here with me, with me being sick, she would know just what to do."

Meanwhile, all the way back down South at the Defour Plantation. "God, I wonder how she's doing." Julie said as she paced back and forth in her living room. "She could be dead, Thomas, that's why she's not writing. She could be dead!" "Jules, Baby, you're going to have to calm down, you're pregnant now, you don't want to upset yourself, or the baby." Julie wiped away the tears from her face. "Thomas, we're talking about Kowie here, you know she's my life." "Honey, I know she's your life, but she's probably too busy right now to write. She's probably almost up to Michigan by now." "You don't know that for sure, Thomas. What if something bad happened to her? I would never know. There's got to be something my dad could do." "Sweetheart, he's already sent an overseer, Mr. Williams, up north to try and find her and bring her back down here." "But what if he never finds her?" "He already wrote your father last week, and told him that he learned that they were heading through Indiana. He will find her, you have to have faith." "You're right, Thomas, we do have someone that is trained and equipped to locate Kowie. If she was dead or hurt, I'm sure Mr. Williams would have found out and let us know." Thomas always had a way with Julie, calming her down and making her see the big picture, similar to the way Julie used to do with Koweena. "Mr. Williams will find her, Darling, now just try and relax, for the baby's sake, okay." "Your right, Thomas, Mr. Williams is hot on her trial." "Right, and the letters he's sent your father," Thomas added. "Yes the letters," Julie said, "even if I haven't gotten any from Kowie, at least we have his letters telling us that he knows where she's headed." "Exactly, now come here and let me hold you on the sofa here and calm you down, and put my hand on your stomach." As Julie cuddled up next to Thomas, with Thomas rubbing her belly, she asked. "Do you think Mr. Williams will find her?" "Yes, Jules, he will find her. From the letters he's sent, he's right on her path. It will be just a matter of time." "What if she doesn't want to come back down here?" "Once she finds out what we know, she will want to, Dear, don't worry."

After three miles of walking, Joe finally spotted a statue with a lantern in it. "Yes! A safe house!" He whispered out loud. "Dempsey, huh," Joe noted to himself as he read the wooden sign with the burnt inscription of their last name hanging under their mailbox. "I've got to hurry back to Koweena and tell her the good news. Wait a minute; I had better introduce myself first before I do that," Joe whispered to himself.

"Sweetheart, would you like some tea?" Mr. Dempsey hollered into the living room from the kitchen at his wife who was sitting at her favorite chair doing her favorite thing, knitting a sweater. The Dempsey's were an older couple, in their mid-fifties, and they lived alone. As Mrs. Dempsey was knitting, waiting for her husband to come into the living room, she caught a glimpse of something moving outside her window.

She took a deep breath and held it; it startled her so much that she was too scared to breathe, too scared to yell out to her husband. As she stared into the blackness of the night through the window, suddenly a coal-black face appeared, pressed up against the window pane. She became gripped with fear as she stared at the face. "Ah!" She blurted out in fear. "What is it, Honey!?" Her husband yelled from the kitchen as he heard his wife yell out. "There's someone at the window, Honey, quick, come in here!" Mr. Dempsey quickly ran into the living room and peered out the window. Suddenly, a knock came from the front door. "You wait right here, Dear, don't move." Mr. Dempsey went upstairs and grabbed his rifle and headed back downstairs to the front door. "Who is it!?" He yelled out to the other side of the door. "A friend of a friend, sir," Joe said as his voice permeated through the door to Mr. Dempsey. Mr. Dempsey put his rifle down next to the door and opened it. As he was opening the door he yelled out to his wife. "It's okay, Dear!"

"Hey, sir, my friend and I were wondering if we could stay the night," Joe said. "Sure, but I don't see your friend, where is he?" "It's a she, sir. She's a few miles down the road, she's very sick, sir, she needs a doctor to look at her." "Doctor Rosinborough, yes, he can look at her. You guys come on in once you get her here, and we'll see about getting the doctor to look at her," Mr. Dempsey said. "Yes, sir, I is be right back."

Joe returned to the woods where Koweena was slumped over lying on the ground. "Koweena! Koweena! Are you alright?" No response came. "Oh my God, Koweena! Wake up!" Finally, a response, "I'm feeling very weak, Joe, I feel like I'm going to faint." "Don't worry, Dear; I have a place for you now." "I can't walk any further." Koweena said with a very faint voice. It hit Joe, he was losing her. She was sicker than he realized. "Koweena, I'm goin to carry you, okay." "But what about our food and clothes?" "We will have to leave them here, we have no choice. I have to get you to a doctor; the man at the safe house I found said he would get us a doctor." "I'm scared, Joe." "I know you are, Dear, but it's goin to be alright." Joe scooped her up under his arms and began carrying her. Joe was of average size, a little over six feet tall and around one hundred and seventy pounds; this wasn't going to be an easy task for him to carry her all the way to the Dempsey's. Every fifty yards he would have to sit her down so he could catch his breath. Each time he would sit her down, he noticed that her breathing got slower and slower. "Hang on, Koweena, don't you die on me now, we is made it too far, and you is been through too much to die."

After struggling for several miles, Joe finally got Koweena to the Dempsey's. As Mr. Dempsey opened the door, he noticed Joe bent over gasping for air, and Koweena lying on his porch. "There's a room upstairs we can put her in, quickly let's get her up," Mr. Dempsey said. "I can't pick her up, sir, don't have enough strength." "Okay, let me have her." Mr. Dempsey lifted Koweena up and carried her to the upstairs bedroom that was used by the Dempseys as a guest bedroom. Mrs. Dempsey made her way to the bedroom. She quickly noticed Koweena's condition. "We have to get Doctor Rosinborough here quickly," she said. She quickly ran downstairs and grabbed some cold, wet towels from the kitchen. She swiftly ran back upstairs. "What's your name?" Mrs. Dempsey asked Joe. "Joe, ma'am." "Joe, I need for you to place these towels on her head and arms, hurry, let's go." "Joe," Koweena faintly yelled out from the bed. "I'm right here, Koweena," Joe said as he was placing the towels on Koweena. "I'm really scared," she said. "It's going to be okay, the doctor is coming," Joe said. As Joe said that, he had this feeling in the pit of his stomach that things were not going to be alright. Looking at Koweena lying there, struggling to breathe, he felt she didn't have long. He just stood there over top of her in anguish; he had grown too attached to her to lose her now.

After an hour had passed, Doctor Rosinborough finally made his way to the house, and into the room. With the lights on, and with the apparent stuffy heaviness filling the room, making Koweena hot, he began to work on her. After several hours of checking her over, Joe finally spoke up. "Tell me, doctor, what is it? What's wrong with her?" The doctor got up from the bed and turned to Joe, now eye level with him. "Well, son, I'm going to be frank with you, it doesn't look good." Joe's head dropped. "I believe she has what is known as Gestational Diabetes." Joe was deeply concerned. "Doctor, that's a big word. What does it mean?" Joe asked. "Well, Joe, we don't know what causes it. What we do know is that the hormones from the placenta block the action of the mother's insulin in her body." "So she's pregnant?" Joe asked. "Yes," the doctor replied. Joe's worst fears had come true. Over the journey that had lasted almost a year now, somewhere along the way

Joe had fallen in love with Koweena. He was crushed at the news. "So, what does all of that mean, Doctor?" Joe asked. "Well, it means that Koweena is suffering from very high blood pressure, and extremely high blood sugar levels." Joe had his hands squeezed together. "What is the worst case scenario, Doc, just tell me?" He asked. "Well, Joe, I hate to tell you this, she could very easily have a heart attack at any moment. That's why her breathing is so slow." "Is there nothing you can do, I mean you are a doctor, there has to be something you can do." "Son, if I could I would, but I can't. There's nothing more I can do." "Is there anything that will help her out of this?" Joe asked. "Well, she's not moving, and she's resting, that could possibly bring her blood pressure down. Son, the only way she's going to make it is if she's bed ridden for the rest of her pregnancy, that's the only way."

Joe walked over to the bed where Koweena was sleeping. He could hear the wheezing in her breathing as he placed his hand on top of hers. "Don't die on me, Koweena, please don't die." As he stood there holding Koweena's hand, his thoughts jumped from her, to the fact that they would have to stay in one place for however many months it would take for her to have this baby. Joe thought back to when the rape happened, and calculated that they would have to stay there for seven months. "That's way too long," Joe whispered to himself. "What choice do I have, I'm not leaving without her." After hearing the news from the doctor, Mrs. Dempsey went into the room and approached Joe. "Joe, you don't have to worry. You can stay here as long as it takes, okay?" "Thank you, ma'am."

That night Joe didn't sleep at all, he just sat in a chair pulled up next to the bed alongside Koweena, holding her hand. Periodically he would put his head down on Koweena's hand, and sob quietly. It was the first time Joe had cried since being a little boy living on his Plantation.

After several days, and several visits from the doctor; and from the medicine the doctor figured may help her, Koweena showed signs of improving. Her breathing was still heavy though, and she was still too weak to get out of bed. That night, Joe was sitting in his chair by her bed, as he had since their first night there, he never got up from that chair, when Koweena, who was mostly unconscious during the entire time there, turned her head over in the direction of Joe. "What's wrong?" Koweena asked Joe in soft loving tone, with a consoling look on her face. She noticed the obvious stress on Joe's face. Joe placed his hand on Koweena's cheek. "Hey you, how are you?" He asked. He was trying to be strong for Koweena's sake. "Very weak," Koweena responded, "but this medicine has made me relaxed, and it's helped my breathing somewhat. How are you?" Joe didn't want to tell her why she was so sick, and how sick she truly was, nor did he want to tell her how worried he was about how much danger they were in, with them having to stay so long in one place. He wanted so desperately to tell her how much he loved her, especially looking at her so weak and vulnerable as she was that night in her bed. But he just couldn't muster up enough nerve to do it. He was, however, able to muster up enough nerve to tell her why she was sick. He knew by telling her that she was pregnant, that it would crush her though. But he felt she had to know. Joe had a strained look on his face. "Koweena, you is pregnant," he said. "What, Joe?" Koweena was too weak to show any emotion. "Yes, Koweena, the rape, you is pregnant." With one hand on her cheek, Joe grabbed a hold of Koweena's hand with the other. Koweena, trying to process what she had just heard, laid there and just stared at Joe. Finally the emotions came. Tears began streaming down her face as her eyes went from Joe to the ceiling above. The wind was knocked out of Joe as he sat there watching Koweena cry silently, knowing she was too weak to actually cry out loud. Koweena's mind began to race, thinking back through all the hardships she had been through. She thought by escaping the Plantation, her troubled days would be behind her. Then she began to think of that one man that was behind her troubled past, Ray. It didn't matter where she was in the country, he would be there to destroy her innocence over and over again she thought. After thinking that, she quickly clutched Joe's hand with a firm grip. It was the first real movement from Koweena since she arrived at the house. Joe quickly became alarmed. He knew something was wrong. Suddenly, Koweena blurted out. "Ray! We have to go! Ray will find me here! He will hurt me again!" Joe could see that Koweena's airways were tightening up, her breathing was getting louder. "Shhh, Koweena, Ray's not goin to hurt you, I'm here," Joe said, now standing up trying to keep Koweena still. "Ray!" Koweena continued to shout out with what breath she could gather. Joe continued to hold her down. "Ray's not going hurt you, Dear, I promise, you is safe," he said. She suddenly became silent, but her eyes were as big as saucers. Ray was on her mind, and it terrified her. "Mrs. Dempsey!" Joe yelled out. Mrs. Dempsey came running into the bedroom. "What is it, Joe?" "Get the medicine, hurry!" Joe screamed. After swallowing a dose of the medicine, Koweena calmed down, so much so that she fell asleep.

Koweena remained stable for the rest of her pregnancy. After seven months of staying at the Dempsey house, it was now time for Koweena to deliver. She was lying on the bed on her back, with her legs bent and spread far apart. Doctor Rosinborough was there crouched over at the foot of the bed as Koweena was breathing heavily and panting as she pushed. The doctor knew that this could be a hazardous moment for Koweena with her high blood pressure; with all the straining she was doing she could easily have a heart attack. Joe was in the room holding her hand, with Mrs. Dempsey standing alongside of Doctor Rosinborough.

Suddenly, there was a loud knock on the front door. Mr. Dempsey went to open it. As he did, he quickly noticed two men standing there with badges attached to their coats. It was a cool, rainy, November evening. "Excuse us, sir, this is Marshal Johnson, and I'm Marshal Turner. We are of the understanding that there are some runaway slaves that are staying here at your residence." "I don't know what you're talking about, officers; there are no runaway slaves here." "Sir, we've heard from several folks in the area that there are indeed slaves here, we need to come in and check for ourselves." Joe quickly heard what the two men were saying. Instinctively, he felt the need to protect Koweena. He quickly pulled his hand from Koweena's. "Joe! Where are you going! I need you!" "Koweena, I have to do something, but first I have to tell you something." "What is it, Joe?" "I, I, I love you, Koweena." "I," Koweena didn't get a chance to finish what she was going to say as Joe let go of her other hand and immediately went downstairs. "Here I am, I'm the one you is looking for." "Joe! No!" Koweena yelled out. "Who is that?" One of the Marshals said looking in the direction of the upstairs bedroom where Koweena had shouted out. "That's my daughter," Mr. Dempsey quickly responded. "She's giving birth." "What's your name, Nigger?" "Joe," Joe replied as he made his way from the stairs to where the Marshals were standing. "Alright, come with us." They quickly led Joe out of the house. The Marshals had bound both his hands behind his back with a rope. Mrs. Dempsey hurried down the stairs and approached her husband. "What happened?" She asked. "They took Joe," Mr. Dempsey replied. "Are you going to do something?" Mrs. Dempsey asked. "Yes, I'm going to gather some of the guys from the church, and we're going to get him back," Mr. Dempsey said as he quickly grabbed his shotgun and went out the front door.

"Push, Koweena, I need for you to push," Doctor Rosinborough said as he saw the crowning of the baby's head. With each strenuous push Koweena gave Doctor Rosinborough, he would hold his breath in fear that she would go into cardiac arrest. "One more good hard push, Koweena, you're almost there," the doctor said. She needed Joe there with her, to hold her hand as she gave her one final giant push. Finally, she heard crying. "You have yourself a healthy baby boy, Koweena," the doctor said with a smile. Koweena just turned her head away from all the action. She didn't want to see the baby. All of a sudden, Koweena began choking. "Doctor, she's foaming at the mouth!" Mrs. Dempsey yelled out, pointing at Koweena. The doctor quickly handed the baby over to Mrs. Dempsey and ran over to Koweena. "Koweena, Koweena, can you hear me?" The doctor put his ear up to Koweena's throat. "Her esophagus is constricted; I'm going to have to cut her open right here. Mrs. Dempsey I need for you to go get a lot of wet towels, now, hurry!" Mrs. Dempsey hurriedly put the baby down on the blanket on the floor, with the baby crying aloud, and ran downstairs to get the towels. "Koweena, Koweena, I need for you to stay with me here," the doctor said as he quickly checked her pupils, and then grabbed a scalpel from his bag. He bent over on the bed, with scalpel in hand, and proceeded to cut into Koweena's neck. Koweena's body was convulsing so badly from the choking, that it was hard for the doctor to make an accurate incision into the exact location of the esophagus where he needed to cut. Mrs. Dempsey, now out of breath, arrived back into the room with the towels. "Hurry, Mrs. Dempsey, I need for you to come over here and hold her down so her neck will remain steady, I'm going to have to perform a tracheotomy." Mrs. Dempsey came over to the bed, laid the towels down next to Koweena. "Hold her head," the doctor said. Mrs. Dempsey grabbed a hold of Koweena's head as Koweena was gasping for any kind of air she could get a hold of. "I have to hurry before she chokes to death," the doctor said. He quickly made an incision into her throat, cutting her vertically, and then making a cut horizontally. He then was able to reach her esophagus, cutting it open. It was an intense several minutes as Koweena began to turn blue. Blood and mucus began pouring out of Koweena's esophagus. Koweena's body immediately ceased convulsing. "I'm going to have to stitch her up. Mrs. Dempsey, go check on the baby if you would please." Mrs. Dempsey went over to where the baby was lying, she noticed that he was giving off a healthy cry and went over to him and picked him up. "Such a beautiful baby, yes you are," Mrs. Dempsey said with a smile on her face. After the doctor stitched her throat up, he put a bandage on her neck. "Koweena, can you hear me?" The doctor asked. Koweena nodded yes. "It's important that you not talk for several days, alright." Once again, Koweena nodded yes. "Would you like to hold your baby?" The doctor asked. Koweena nodded no, and then turned away. The doctor went over to Mrs. Dempsey. "I'm concerned about the mother and the baby. It seems as though she wants nothing to do with the baby. This could be just a temporary thing because of the fact she's so young, I don't know. The problem is, if she doesn't respond to it soon, the baby will have no way of eating. It's vital Mrs. Dempsey, that she breast feeds by day two, you must get her to respond to the baby." "What if she doesn't?" Mrs. Dempsey asked. "Then he will starve. Give him some sugar water for the first couple of days, and we'll see what happens from there. I'll be back in two days to check on her throat, and to see where we stand with the feeding process." "Yes, Doctor." "She's stable now, but her esophagus could constrict again, if that happens, get a hold of me immediately." "What do I do in the meantime if that happens?" "The only thing you can do, if it happens again, is to try and massage her throat in a firm manner. It may unclog her esophagus, but hopefully there won't be a next time." "Thank you, Doctor." "I'll be back in a couple of days." "Again, thank you for everything," Mrs. Dempsey said.

As the drama was unfolding with Koweena, Mr. Dempsey, along with six of his men, who were members of his local American Baptist church, headed out toward the jail in Anderson on horseback. "Sit in that cell and remain silent, Nigger," Marshal Turner told Joe. Joe sat there inside the cell worrying about Koweena, wondering how she was faring with her pregnancy. He also wondered how she responded when he told her that he loved her. He didn't have time to even notice the response on her face when he told her. "I had to tell her, it had been bottled up inside me for most of the journey," he whispered to himself. "I know she's only almost seventeen, but I'm only in my mid-twenties, I would make a suitable husband for her," he thought. "I have to get out of here; I have to see her again. For the first time I have something else to live for other than helping more slaves," he continued thinking to himself. He got up and approached the bars of the cell. "What is you goin to do with me?" He asked the Marshal. "That's for your master to decide, now sit down, Nigger, and shut up."

Suddenly, a loud crash came from the front door of the jail. "Don't even think about it, Marshal, put the weapon down," Mr. Dempsey said in a sharp tone. Marshal Turner, who was the only officer in the jail, with Joe being the only prisoner, realized that he was outnumbered. He quickly put the pistol down. "Do you realize that you are interfering with government business here? That's a serious crime, boys," Marshal Turner said. "That's why we're taking you with us," Mr. Dempsey told the Marshal. "Quick, Bob, get the keys from the Marshal and let Joe out," Mr. Dempsey ordered. The Marshal hesitantly gave the keys over to Bob, who let Joe out of his cell. "Do you realize that this man you are freeing killed a fellow Marshal?" The Marshal said. "I'm sure he had good reason," Mr. Dempsey said. "Where are you taking me?" Marshal Turner asked. "To our church," Mr. Dempsey responded. "We're going to handcuff you to one of the pews." "Are you crazy!? There will be Marshals combing this whole area looking for me!" "Not in a church they won't," one of the church members spoke up. "Come on, Joe, let's go, you can ride with me," Mr. Dempsey told Joe as he put his arm around him and lead him out of the jail. "I get to see my Koweena," Joe thought to himself with a big smile on his face. "Come on, Marshal, you're riding with me, let's go!" Another church member hollered out. It had just finished raining when the men mounted their horses. Just as they began galloping off from the jail, Marshal Johnson, the other Marshal that had been at the Dempsey's house that night; arrived and quickly noticed that his partner was riding off with the men on horseback. He quickly ran into the jail and noticed that Joe was gone. The Marshal ran back outside and fired his pistol up into the air in hopes of scaring the men. It worked. "Come on, boys, hurry, let's get out of here! Ha! Ha!" Mr. Dempsey yelled as he kicked his horse.

Their horses began galloping at top speed, through the dirt road that was guarded by woods on both sides. Marshal Johnson was galloping right behind them, snapping the reigns on his horse, picking up speed. "Bob, you're going to have to shoot him!" Mr. Dempsey yelled out, just ahead of Bob, who was in the very back of the group. "I'm not killing anybody!" Bob yelled out. "Bob, you have to, it's either us or him, now shoot!" Mr. Dempsey yelled out once more. Bob was very hesitant to pull the trigger, that was, until the Marshal fired a shot that just barely grazed Bob's calf. Bob turned around and cocked his rifle and pointed it at Marshal Johnson, no easy task while galloping on a horse at top speed. He fired; he quickly noticed that the Marshal instantly fell off his horse and onto the ground. "I hit him, guys!" Bob hollered out. "Whoa, whoa!" The men yelled out to their horses in unison to stop. "We have to dispose of the body. We'll take the horse with us," Mr. Dempsey said. Bob placed his hands on his head. "Oh my God, what have I done!?" He yelled out. Mr. Dempsey walked up to Bob. "Bob, I know this was difficult for you, but listen, the Lord understands. You had to defend yourself. He will not hold that against you. Give your conscience a rest, alright, you did the right thing." They disposed of the Marshal's body in the woods, and proceeded to their church. When they arrived at the church, they handcuffed Marshal Turner to one of the pews. "You're not going to get away with this," Marshal Turner told the men. "We'll come back several times a day and feed you. Here are some blankets, and a pillow to lye down on, and you have this lamp to keep you company at night. We'll be back in the morning to check on you. We'll let you go once the slaves are clear out of sight," Mr. Dempsey said. "You won't get away with this!" Marshal Turner hollered out as the men closed the door behind them.

Joe, now back at the Dempsey house, entered Koweena's room. As he walked in, he quickly noticed Koweena's throat, and the giant bandage covering it. His eyes began to tear up. "What happened?" He wondered. Mrs. Dempsey walked into the room. "What happened?" Joe asked her. "She had a tracheotomy performed on her after the baby was born." "What's that?" Joe asked. "She was choking to death, Joe, she was in grave danger. But the doctor basically cut a hole in her throat and saved her. She can't talk though for several days. She wants nothing to do with her baby, Joe." "My Sweetheart," Joe whispered softly. "You really care about her don't you?" Mrs. Dempsey asked. "It's that obvious huh." "Yes, Joe, it is. I'm really rooting for you on this one. I hope the two of you make it, and become very happy together." "Thank you, Mrs. Dempsey." "I'll leave you alone with her," Mrs. Dempsey said. Joe quietly and softly walked up to Koweena, grabbed that familiar chair that he had been sitting on for months, and sat down next to her bed, he quickly grabbed a hold of her hand and began crying. Koweena awoke and instantly noticed Joe crying on her hand. She nudged his head with her hand. Joe looked up at her, she had a look like she was about to cry. She then lifted her hand up, and with the other hand, began writing on her hand with her finger, signifying to Joe that she wanted to write something. "I'll be right back, Dear," Joe said. He returned with a pencil and a note pad. He handed them to Koweena. She began writing. After writing for a moment, she handed the pad to Joe. "Why are you crying? Don't cry, I'm going to be okay," the note said. Joe wiped away the tears from his face. "I know you is goin to be okay, I just care about you so much, that's why I'm cryin," he said. Koweena signaled for the note pad again. She began writing something else. She again handed the pad to Joe. "I care about you too!" The note said. "I should have told you how I felt a long time ago, but with the rape and all, it just didn't seem like the right time. Koweena, somewhere along this journey, I fell for you hard. I'm crazy about you. I will take care of you when we get to Canada, you, and the baby." Koweena smiled as a tear fell down her cheek. She again made the signal to get the pad back from Joe. Joe handed her the pad and she began to write. She handed it back to Joe with a smile on her face. "I want to see my baby," the note said. Joe laughed with happiness and smiled. "I'll go get him." Joe returned to Koweena's bed and placed the baby in her arms. The moment Koweena held her baby; she fell in love with him instantly. She requested the pencil and note pad once again from Joe. She began writing. "I never thought I could love something so much!" The note said. That night she just laid there and cradled her baby in her arms, with Joe sitting alongside her.

The doctor returned several days later to find Koweena breast feeding her baby. "Thank God," the doctor said with a deep sigh of relief. "I see she's finally taking to her baby," he told Mrs. Dempsey. "Yes, she took to it that very night, we were all relieved." I need to check her throat, but I'll wait until she's finished here. I'll wait downstairs." "Okay, Doctor," Mrs.

Dempsey said. After Koweena had finished breastfeeding, the doctor returned to the room to check on her throat. When he peeled back the bandage, he had a serious look on his face. Koweena, who was now able to speak, spoke up. "What is it, Doctor?" She said with concern. "Well, Koweena, you've developed a serious infection. It looks like it's almost to the point of gangrene. I can tell you this much, you're not going anywhere any time soon." "How long will I have to be here, Doc?" "Well, looking at this infection, it's going to take a lot of attention. We're going to have to clean it around the clock, and bandage it over and over again." "But, Doc, I have to get on the road. Joe and I, and my baby, we have to keep moving, I can't stay here much longer." The doctor looked at her with raised eyebrows. "Koweena, if this goes untreated, you could die. Then your baby won't have a mother. Is that what you want?" "We'll stay," Joe said, as he was seated next to Koweena. "Now, I'll be back in a couple of days. In the meantime, Joe, you and Mrs. Dempsey will have to remove this bandage and clean the wound four times a day. Is that clear?" "Yes, Doctor," Joe said. "Okay, Koweena, remain in the bed, you got it." "Yes, Doc," Koweena depressingly said. "Okay, I'll see you in a couple of days," the doctor said as he left the room. Joe began stroking Koweena's long, flowing, curly hair. "It's okay, Koweena, you and the baby are goin to be just fine," he said. Koweena cared deeply for Joe, and she loved him dearly, but she was scared. She was scared because of how strongly Joe loved her. She thought his love for her was just too good to be true, and just like Julie, he would be ripped away from her, it would only be a matter of time. So she held back from showing her love toward him. Joe made her feel similar to the way Julie used to make her feel. She felt the affection and love from him that Julie used to give her growing up. He also made her feel safe and reassured; something she also felt growing up with Julie. With Joe stoking her hair, and the fact that she was having all those feelings that she used to feel with Julie, as she laid there holding her baby, she couldn't help but think of Julie. She missed her voice so much, her consoling, soft voice. She wanted to share the good news about her baby so desperately with her. She had no doubts as she lay there holding her baby, she knew how to be a good mother, she had a great teacher growing up, she would just simply follow the example she had observed from Julie.

Meanwhile, the overseer, Mr. Williams, had learned during one of his stops at a station in Evansville, Indiana, a town on the southern border of the State, that Koweena had indeed stopped by there some time ago. "Yes, she came by here a couple of months ago, cute little girl," the Station Master told Mr. Williams. The Station Master, after learning that Mr. Williams was sincere in not capturing Koweena, Mr. Williams explained the story to him, that he was simply trying to get to her for the sake of the Plantation owner's daughter, the Station Master felt comfortable in sharing the information he had on Koweena. "Well thank you, sir, I'll surely pass this onto the owner's daughter. Did they say where they were headed by chance?" "No, they just said they were headed up to Canada, that's all." "Was she with anybody?" "Yes, I believe his name was Joe." "Great, thank you, sir," Mr. Williams said as he stayed at the Station that day writing a letter to Julie, and making sure that the Postman received it. "Well, sir, I'm headed north, I guess," Mr. Williams told the Station Master. "Okay, good luck!"

Weeks later Julie got the letter. She began reading it, it said:

Dear Mrs. Callahan,

I spoke with a man today who actually talked with Koweena just months prior to me being there. He told me that she was doing fine, and that she was headed for Canada. I have some good news to report. Joe is still with her. It just seems to be the two of them however, so I don't know what happened to her sister. I am headed north, and I feel assured that I am hot on their trail. Mrs. Callahan, with all indications pointing to the fact that I'm on the right direction, I feel that I will soon catch up to them. The people that are helping them along the way seem friendly. They also seem very obliged to help me with whatever questions I have regarding them. I will write you again as soon as I find out any more pertinent information about them. Mrs. Callahan, don't worry, I will find them.

Mr. Williams

After reading the letter, Julie put the letter to her chest, closed her eyes, and gave a deep sigh of relief. "What does it say, Sweetheart?" Thomas asked. "Mr. Williams has learned that they're doing fine. Koweena and Joe are still together. Josi is not with them though, that concerns me greatly." "Maybe she found her someone, and settled down somewhere up north, leaving Koweena and Joe behind." "Yes, that's possible. Speaking of finding someone, I wonder how Koweena and Joe are fairing. You know, I mean, I'm just thinking out loud." "What are you getting at, Dear?" Thomas asked. "You know, Thomas, if there are any sparks between them." "You mean romantically?" Thomas asked. "Yes, why not, I mean they've travelled almost the entire country together, they're bound to be close to one another by now, and I always thought they would make a cute couple the moment I met Joe." "I agree, Jules, I didn't want to say anything to you because I wasn't sure if it would upset you, but I'm rooting for the both of them to get together. They have a lot in common, they're both slaves, or about to be former slaves, they're on this journey together toward freedom, I think they would make the perfect couple." "Oh, it would be perfect, Thomas. Koweena has talked so much about having a family of her own, especially the last few years before she left, and now with Joe by her side, it just seems right, you know. They can come down here and start a family. Now with my dad's approval, it will all work out just fine." "That makes you happy, doesn't it, Julie?" "Yes, Thomas, knowing that Koweena is still surviving out there, and the fact that she still has Joe by her side, I'm very happy. It will just be a matter of time before she's back here."

As spring approached, Koweena was now well enough to leave the Dempseys, with Joe and her baby, and begin again on her journey. "Thank you so much, Mr. and Mrs. Dempsey, I stayed longer than one day, much longer," Koweena said. Mrs. Dempsey laughed. "Eleven months," she said. "Yes, but seriously, thank you; I wouldn't have survived without the both of you. And, Mr. Dempsey, thank you for bringing Joe back to me. You truly are my hero." "Your welcome, Koweena, I guess that old Marshal is about ready to get out of that church after being cooped up in there for so long." Koweena chuckled and smiled. "Yes, sir, I guess he is," she said. "Good bye, Koweena," Mrs. Dempsey said as she gave Koweena a kiss on the cheek. "Good bye," Koweena said as she walked out the front door with her baby in her arms. As Joe proceeded to the door behind Koweena, Mrs. Dempsey grabbed Joe by the shoulders. "Treat her right; she's a beautiful, sweet girl, a rare breed these days, Joe." Joe smiled down at Mrs. Dempsey. "Yes, ma'am."

With the baby now a part of their team, it slowed Koweena and Joe's travel time down tremendously. They would only be able to travel about five to seven miles a day; and their stay at safe houses would have to be much longer than the normal couple of days. As they travelled north, toward Michigan, the three of them were inseparable. They would play together when they stayed at safe houses, just the three of them. Joe would always sleep on the floor next to the bed Koweena and the baby was sleeping in, in every single safe house they went to. He never let them out of his sight. Joe had become a father to William, the name Koweena finally gave him about halfway through their journey to Michigan. He would bathe him, clothe him, and he would even carry him during their walks from one safe house to the next. As a result of Joe's great treatment of Koweena and the baby, Koweena fell hopelessly in love with Joe more and more as each day passed. She didn't want anyone else in her life, she just wanted Joe, and the love that she was once scared to show Joe, and hesitant to allow to strengthen, was now equal or even stronger than Joe's love for her. They were crazy for each other.

One night, in a safe house in Southern Michigan, Joe approached Koweena on the subject. "Koweena, we've been travelling now for quite some time, and it's been troublesome free, right?" "Yes, Joe." "I know I don't have much education like you do, and well, I was just wondering, does that make you love me any less?" "Does it make me love you any less, Joe, are you kidding me, I couldn't be more in love with you, you know that. You treat me and the baby so well, I couldn't ask for more. God, I thought Julie spoiled me, that was, until I met you. On this journey, especially since we left the Dempseys, you've done nothing but spoil me. You always do everything in your power to make sure me and the baby are just as perfect as we can be. And now that were getting so close to freedom that I actually can start tasting it, I want to start a family together. I watch how you handle William. I watch you when we have play time together at these different safe houses. You're so gentle and sweet, you're all a woman could ask for Joe. Sure, these safe houses aren't home, but we have a set routine, despite that. No matter what safe house we're at, you always seem to find time to set William and me down to spend family time together. Joe, I know I tell you that I want to start a family with you someday, but we've already started our family, right here, right now. And, Baby, we have so much in common, we both grew up in Natchez, we're both former slaves, and we're both on this journey together toward freedom. You're the best thing that has ever happened to me, besides William of course, and I really do love you, with everything I have. God, I can't wait to marry you and be called your wife." "Koweena, I would die for you, that's how much I love you. I am nothing without you and the baby. Now I know why I left the north and went back down south." "Why, Joe?" "It's simple, Koweena, it was to find you. We were destined for each other." Koweena put her hand to Joe's cheek. "I feel the same way about you, Sweetheart, oh, I'm so glad to hear you say that," she said. "You know, Joe," Koweena went on, "I know that God loves me, and how do I know that? Because he took time out to create you for me." Joe got down on one knee in front of Koweena. "Koweena, I want to do this right," Joe said. Koweena took in a loud gasp of air when she saw Joe approach her on one knee. "Are you alright?" Joe asked her. "Yes, I just can't believe this is about to happen." "Koweena, my soul mate, my everything, will you be my wife?" "Yes! Yes! Yes, Joe! A thousand times yes!" "I don't have a ring so." "It's perfect Joe, it's perfect. You don't need a ring." They then embraced each other tightly. Over the last fourteen months of traveling, they had grown co-dependant on each other. One couldn't do without the other. Koweena thought of Julie right then. Joe called her his everything, something she had only heard Julie call her. She thought she would never meet anyone that treated her as well as Julie had treated her. But now she had, and she realized that night hugging Joe, that she was lucky enough for that person to be her future husband.

Over those last fourteen months, Julie had received two letters form Mr. Williams, both letters were telling her the same thing. That Koweena was doing fine, and that he was still hot on her trial.

"God, I miss her, Thomas!" "I know you do, Julie, but, Sweetheart, her journey is almost over. Mr. Williams is going to find her." "I'm glad she's still with Joe, that makes me sleep a little easier. I just wonder if they've grown fond of each other yet. I think Joe would treat her right if they did get together." "Yes, I agree, Julie." "I just wonder if he's able to console her when she's upset, like I did when she was here, God, I hope so." "Don't worry, Jules; I'm sure he has everything under control. You know, when he was here, he seemed like a very level headed young man. I know he's taking very good care of Koweena." "Do you think she misses me, Thomas?" "I think she thinks about you all the time, Julie." "I just don't want her to forget about me, you know." "There's no chance of that, Julie, you've made too big an impact on her life, I know she misses you like crazy." "I just wish she knew what I know, Thomas, it would change everything."

It took Koweena, Joe, and William two years to get to Manistee, Michigan from the Dempsey house in Indiana. Manistee was a wealthy town, situated on the banks of Lake Michigan, in the Northwest part of the State. "We're almost home free, Baby!" Joe said with excitement, as he hugged Koweena around the neck with one arm while holding William with the other arm, as they walked to the next safe house. Joe became greatly enthused. "All we have to do is get on a steamer and go across Lake Michigan and Lake Superior, and we are there! Can you believe it!?" Joe asked. Koweena kissed Joe on the cheek. "I love you so much, Sweetheart," she said. They arrived at their next safe house. Joe stared on with amazement. "Wow, look at this house!" he said. "There's a lantern in the statue, Joe," Koweena noted as she observed the statue standing in the front lawn.

The house was the largest house by far in the entire neighborhood, and the largest safe house that they had ever been to. It was two stories, with three sectional structures connected together to make one giant house. It had a total of thirty two windows that stretched all around the house. Joe approached the front door and knocked. After several minutes of no response, Joe became worried. "Who is it!?" A man's voice finally yelled from the other side of the door. "A friend of a friend," Joe replied. The door opened. "Hi, sir, I'm Joe." Joe stretched his arm out in the direction of Koweena and William, who were standing at the bottom of the front porch steps. "This is my baby William, and my fiancée Koweena," Joe said. When Koweena heard Joe call William his baby she melted inside. She was so in love with Joe that it made her leap for joy inside when she heard Joe say that. She just stood there with a sideways grin, looking at Joe right in the eyes as her eyes began welling up with tears. Joe looked at her and smiled. He then motioned with his mouth without any sounds coming out, "I love you," to her. Koweena did the same right back. "Joe, come in, pleasure to have you. I'm Mr. Tulley, and this beautiful lady sitting in the living room is my wife." "Come on, Honey," Joe said as he motioned with his head for Koweena to come into the house. Mrs. Tulley got up from her chair in the living room and went into the foyer. "Hi, Koweena, I'm Mrs. Tulley," Mrs. Tulley said as she extended her arm toward Koweena. Koweena extended her arm right back to shake hands with the middle aged woman. "Hi, Mrs. Tulley," Koweena said. Mrs. Tulley noticed the baby. "Koweena, you can stay here as long as you would like, for the baby's sake." "Thank you, ma'am." The Tulley's showed Koweena and Joe to their bedrooms. "Sir, I stay in the same room as Koweena," Joe noted as he realized that Mr. Tulley was showing him a room of his own. "Fine, Joe, that will be just fine," Mr. Tulley said.

That night Koweena, Joe, and William were lying down, getting ready to go to sleep, Joe was on the floor, while Koweena and William were in the bed, as was normal for them to do during their nights for the past two years. The room was silent for several minutes, as Joe was trying to go to sleep. The room was bright due to the moonlight shining through the window, when Koweena spoke up. "Joe, Joe, are you awake?" Koweena whispered. "I was almost falling asleep, what is it, Baby, is something wrong with William?" "No, nothing's wrong. I want you to come up here and sleep with me, Joe." "It will be too crowded, the three of us on that twin size bed." "No, Joe, I meant just the two of us. We can put William down on the floor where you are. I *really* want you to sleep with me, Joe." Joe didn't need an interpreter, he knew exactly what Koweena meant, and he could sense it in her voice how desperately she wanted him in that bed with her. Joe desperately wanted to as well, but being the gentlemen that he was, said. "Koweena, please don't take this the wrong way, I want you so bad right now I can't stand it, but I want to wait until we is married. "Come on, Joe, one night." "Baby, I want to wait and do it properly, you mean too much to me. I want to wait until you is my wife." "Alright," Koweena said, taking a frustratingly deep breath. She never thought she would feel those feelings she had that night, all due to the rape. But her feelings for Joe were so strong, and Joe's love for her was so perfect, it helped heal her once damaged soul that had been crushed on that wintry night in Kentucky.

The third night of staying there, Joe was upstairs giving William a bath. Mrs. Tulley and Koweena were sitting downstairs in the living room. Mr. Tulley was off on some business, he was a very successful entrepreneur. Suddenly, there was a knock on the door. Mrs. Tulley went to answer it. Koweena made the grave mistake of not running upstairs to get Joe and William, and hiding with them somewhere in the house. Two years of not running into any opposition from authorities or bounty hunters caused her to let her guard down and not even entertain the idea. "Hi, ma'am, my name is Marshal Turner, I would like to come in and talk to you about some runaway slaves that have been spotted in the area." "I'm not harboring any slaves." "That's not what I said, ma'am." Marshal Turner gave her a suspicious look when she said that. Marshal Turner was the man who was cooped up in the church for months by Mr. Dempsey in Indiana. Marshal Turner immediately went through the front door entranceway by Mrs. Tulley. "Hey, wait a minute, you can't just go marching in here," Mrs. Tulley said as she stumbled back from the Marshal pushing her out of the way. Suddenly, Marshal Turner was standing there face to face with Koweena. The Marshal was standing at the threshold between the foyer and the living room. Koweena heard the Marshal talking at the front door, but everything happened so fast that all she could do was stand up before the Marshal was there, standing right in front of her. "Is there anyone else in here with you?" The Marshal asked with his pistol drawn at her. "No one else, just me," Koweena responded. Koweena realized she was at the end of her road. It suddenly hit her, "I'll never get to see William, or Joe, ever again." She suddenly began chocking back the tears as she held on tightly to her necklace. "Come with me," the Marshal said whipping his pistol back and forth from Koweena to the front door. She quickly grabbed her ring from her finger and placed it on the sofa. As she walked by Mrs. Tulley, she whispered in her ear. "Give Joe the ring," she said as she walked out the front door with Marshal Turner.

After Joe had finished giving William his bath, he carried him back downstairs expecting to see Koweena sitting on the sofa. When he arrived at the bottom of the stairs he noticed that Koweena was not in the living room. He saw Mrs. Tulley with a sad look on her face. He also noticed her holding Koweena's pink sapphire stone ring. Joe was absolutely devastated. He knew Koweena didn't go anywhere without that ring on, and with it now in Mrs. Tulley's hands, he knew she was gone. "Where did they take her?" Joe asked Mrs. Tulley. "I don't know." "Who was it?" "His said his name was Marshal Turner." Joe remembered that that was one of the men from Indiana. "Where's your jail?" Joe asked. "It's on Poplar Street, about five miles from here." "Can I borrow one of your horses?" "Sure, Joe, they're around back." "Here, watch William, ma'am, I'll be right back." Joe handed William off to Mrs. Tulley and ran out the front door.

"So Marshal Turner, where are you from?" The Sheriff of Manistee asked the Marshal. "I'm from Indiana. Been asked to track down several slaves, caught them all too. Chased this little pretty one you see here in your cell, for years, finally caught up with her though." "Pretty girl, yes, you sure she's a slave?" The Sherriff asked. "Oh yeah, she's wanted for killing a Marshal down in Tennessee, pretty serious stuff." "Is she wanted dead or alive?" "Either way, but I tell you what, with her killing a Marshal, she'll probably be dead."

"I just sat there in that cell listening to the Marshal go on about my fate," Koweena recalled. "I remember opening up my heart shaped locket and looking inside. What I saw in that locket had helped me get through so many tough times, and this time was no exception. I was at peace with dying. I realized that William was a little piece of me, and that my life would go on in him. I also knew that Joe would take good care of William, and get him safely to Canada, and that they would be together from there on out. I was so close to my dream marriage that I had dreamt of since I was a kid. It just seemed like me and Joe were meant to be. How could it all end like this? I thought to myself as I waited in that jail cell to be executed. I knew, with what had happened to that Marshal in Tennessee, that execution is what I would be facing. As I waited to die, my life flashed before my eyes. As I stared at the locket, I thought of the first day I met Julie, and how I was such a fragile little girl back then. I thought about all the times Julie had come through for me growing up, and how she gave me stability by letting me live in her home. I thought about the beatings, and how Julie had fought so hard to bring me back from the total brink of collapse. Maybe I'll get to see the three most important people in my life, William, Joe, and Julie, in heaven someday, I thought to myself. I thought about William and Joe. I was confident that they would get along just fine without me. Joe will take such good care of him. I had no doubts about that. I thought about how strong Joe loved me, I knew he would do everything in his power to make sure William was safe, and treat him as if he was his own."

Suddenly, the door to the jail flew open. Koweena ran to the bars of the cell, she could see that it was Joe. "What are you doing, Joe!?" Koweena yelled out. "Let me handle this, Koweena." Joe walked right up to Marshal Turner. "Marshal, take me instead." "No, Joe!" Koweena hollered out as she grabbed tightly to the bars. "I'm the one who shot the Marshal in Tennessee, not Koweena. You've been tracking us down to get this notch under your belt, to be able to say you were the one who did away with the person responsible for killing one of your men, well, here I am." "You have a good point, Nigger, but why shouldn't I just kill the both of you?" "She has a child, Marshal, please, have some compassion and humanity about you. Let her go." "Joe, stop it!" Koweena yelled out, still clutching onto the bars. The Marshal pulled out his pistol from his holder and put it to Joe's head. "Killing you is going to be fun. Sherriff I'm going to take him out back and kill him, you let the girl go." Koweena looked at Joe with tears running down her face. Joe looked back at her and smiled as the Marshal grabbed a hold of him. He held up the ring that Koweena had worn for so long into the air to show Koweena, and then he clutched it into his hand, making a fist. "Joe, don't do this!" Koweena yelled in desperation. "Marshal, before you take me out back and kill me, can I have a moment?" "Go ahead," Marshal Turner said. Joe walked over to Koweena. He began kissing her hands that were still clutched tightly to the bars. "You is goin to find somebody who loves you as much as I do." "Don't talk like that, Joe," Koweena said as they both were kissing each other through the bars. "And you is goin to have a bunch of kids, and you is finally goin to get that dream marriage you's always wanted. Promise me that, Koweena. Promise you'll never give up, no matter what. Carry my love with you wherever you go." Koweena was to the point of almost becoming hysterical. "Please, don't do this, Joe!" "Remember, your ring is always with me, forever, my beautiful everything." "No one will ever treat me the way you have, I'll never find anyone better. I will never be loved

like you love me," Koweena said. "Come on let's go," the Marshal said
as he grabbed Joe by the arm and pulled him away as he was kissing
Koweena.

As Joe was lead out the entranceway of the jail, Koweena collapsed
onto the floor. Once again, she held on tightly to her necklace. She
needed Julie desperately right then to hold her and tell her everything
was going to be alright. "Come on, Miss, you can go," the Sheriff said
as he opened the cell door. Koweena didn't want to move. She had just
lost the love of her life, she wanted to crawl up in a ball and die. "There's
a horse out front waiting for you, you can ride back to your house on
it," the Sheriff said. He felt sorry for Koweena, and the emotion on
his face was evident of that. "Are you going to be alright?" The Sheriff
asked her in a concerned, soft voice. Koweena didn't respond. She just
slowly got up and walked to the door of the jail with her head drooped
down, sobbing, looking at the floor. This was worse than anything she
had gone through before, and that was saying a lot considering all she
had been through up to this point. As she touched the door to open it,
she heard a gun shot. She put her hands to her face and began crying
so hard she could hardly breathe.

Back at the Tulley house, Koweena was lying on her side on the bed,
sobbing. She was too upset to even think about William. Mrs. Tulley
had him in the living room rocking him in her wooden oak rocking
chair. Koweena just lay there, thinking about Joe, the man who had
treated her better than Julie had. She had lost her partner, the one who
had given her hope, and strength, and a future along this journey. "How
can I go on?" She thought, as she just stared out into the blackness of
the night through the window, with tears running down her face. Joe
was her rock, her inspiration, and now he was gone. She would have to
raise William on her own, and they still weren't in Canada yet. "How
am I going to make it without Joe?" She whispered to herself. The man
of her dreams was now dead, she was hopeless, and she had no one to
console her. She felt like she was going to completely collapse.

She had her right hand lying on her hip, as her back was to the door.
Suddenly, out of nowhere, a hand gently touched her right hand. The
hand lifted her ring finger. Suddenly, she felt a ring slide on her finger.
Her eyes got real wide. She quickly turned over and noticed Joe standing
there over top of her with a gentle smile. "Oh!" Koweena yelled out as

she clutched on to Joe with both arms around his neck. She was crying so hard and laughing at the same time. While she was hugging him she was beating on his back with both hands and tugging on his shirt, almost ripping it off. After several minutes of this, she looked Joe right in the eyes. "I thought I lost you! Oh my God! What happened? How? I heard a gunshot." "I know, just as the Marshal cocked the pistol to shoot me in the head, a shot did ring out, but it wasn't the Marshal's gun. It came from behind us." As Joe was talking, Koweena was kissing on both his hands. "The shot hit the Marshal, and down he went, he was dead in a second." Koweena had a puzzled look on her face. "But how?" She asked. "His name is Mr. Williams. He's an overseer from the Defour Plantation." "Oh no!" Koweena yelled out. "No, it's not what you think. He tracked us down because of Julie. Mr. Defour sent him up here for Julie, to make sure you were safe." Koweena sat back down on the bed with her legs crossed, overlapping one another. "But why? I don't understand," she said. "I don't know, he just said Julie had something important to tell you, that's why he's up here." "What could be so important, that Julie sent a man all the way from Natchez, up here to find me? What could she possibly want so desperately to tell me?" "I don't know, all I know is that he saved my life." "Did you tell him about William?" "No, I didn't tell him anything personal about you or me."

Koweena's dream had come true, she had Joe back in her grasp; but now she had so many questions floating around in her head. "Julie cares that much about me to send someone all the way up here. But why did Mr. Defour send him to make sure I was alright?" She thought to herself. Once again, she was surprised at just how much Julie loved and cared for her, that thought dominated any questions she might otherwise be entertaining. She quickly ran downstairs and grabbed William. Koweena was so overly excited. "My fiancée is back, the love of my life is alright!" Koweena said to Mrs. Tulley as she patted her on the shoulder while grabbing a hold of William with one arm. She ran back upstairs and into the bedroom they all three were sharing. Koweena got so excited. "Look William, daddy is home!" "Daddy!" William yelled out. She walked over to Joe and hugged him. "I'm so glad you're back, Baby, you are absolutely my hero, confidant, and inspiration, you are my everything." Koweena had heard that word, everything, used to describe her by two of the most important people in her life, Joe, and Julie, and now, for the first time in her life, she was using that word right back to describe someone, in this case, Joe. After she said that, the three just stood there for several minutes in one big hugging circle.

Chapter 14 From Rags To Riches

M rs. Tulley approached Koweena one Thursday night, as Koweena was dressing William in her bedroom. "Koweena, I have an idea," Mrs. Tulley said. "What is it, Mrs. Tulley?" Like all the safe house owners that Koweena and Joe stayed with, the Tulleys fell in love with both Koweena and Joe from the outset. "I would like to ask you a question?" "Sure, Mrs. Tulley, go ahead." "Once a year we have this black tie event at the local town dance club. It's a very prestigious event, and the club is beautiful. It's for all the well to do people in the town. It's called the Manistee Ball. I would like for you and Joe to come with Mr. Tulley and I tomorrow night. How does that sound?" "That sounds great; Mrs. Tulley, but I don't have anything to wear, and what about William?" "I have all that covered, Koweena. My daughter is about your size, an exact size actually. She has a beautiful dress that she left here when she moved out when she got married, it would fit you perfectly, and it's very elegant. And my husband has an extra tuxedo that Joe could wear. Oh, it would be perfect, Koweena." "But, Mrs. Tulley, we're runaway slaves; we can't be running around in public like that." "Dear, you're up north now; there will be plenty of free blacks at the ball. No one will suspect a thing, especially with the two of you looking the way you'll be looking." "I don't know," Koweena said. "Koweena, you'll blend in just fine." Koweena thought about the Sherriff at that point. "What about the Sherriff, will he be there?" "Yes, dear, he'll be there, why?" "What if he seizes us?" "Koweena, he's not in the business of slave catching. There's no slavery that goes on here. Like I said, there will be plenty of free blacks there." "But the Sherriff has seen me; he'll know I'm a slave." "Koweena, I have that all covered as well. My husband has talked to him. He does know about you, yes, but he has assured, both me and my husband, that everything will be fine. He said you could stay here as long as you wanted, and there would be no trouble. He also said that he would be honored for the both of you to be there." "He said that. He said he would be honored?" "Yes, honored, Koweena." "The Marshals are out of the picture now," Koweena thought to herself. "But what about William?" Koweena asked Mrs. Tulley. "Mrs. Lane will take care of him; she's been babysitting for years. She babysat my daughter for sixteen years while she was growing up; she's a great babysitter, very trustworthy." "I don't know, Mrs. Tulley; I've never been away from William." "You can trust Mrs. Lane; she will take good care of William. He's two, right?" "Yes, two." "He's a perfect age to babysit, Koweena, everything will be just fine. Come on, you will have fun. You deserve some fun after the long journey you've been through." "Let me talk it over with Joe first, okay." "Talk what over with me, Koweena?" Joe asked as he entered the room. "Mrs. Tulley has invited us to a black tie ball tomorrow night, Joe. What do you think?" "Mrs. Tulley, can you give us a moment?" Joe asked. "Sure, take all the time you need. Koweena, try and give me an answer by tonight, okay?" "Sure, Mrs. Tulley." As Mrs. Tulley left the room Joe began to talk to Koweena.

"Koweena, we is fugitive slaves, we can't be going around in public, especially to some public party." "But, Joe, Mrs. Tulley has worked everything out for us." "What about the Sherriff, Koweena? He knows what both of us look like." "Mr. Tulley talked to the Sherriff. The Sherriff told her that he would be honored to have us there." "That's what Mrs. Tulley said, honored, you sure she said that he said honored?" "Yes, Joe, she said he said honored." "It would be fun, I guess, and you deserve some fun after all you is been through." "So that means we can do it?" "What about William?" Joe asked. "Mrs. Tulley has all that covered too. She has a great babysitter lined up; this babysitter is very experienced as well. She seems to have really gone to a lot of trouble to make sure we are able to go." "I don't know, Koweena, what if something goes wrong? I can't afford to almost lose you for the second time." "Damn, Joe, we deserve this. My God, we've been through hell almost the entire trip, and I've been through hell my entire life. I want to share this special night with you, Baby. I want a night out, just the two of us, without William, and without having to worry about those damned Marshals, or bounty hunters. Just us, on the dance floor, let's put everything aside for one night. We may never get another opportunity like this again." Koweena began bouncing up and down, pleading as though her life depended on it. "Oh, please, Joe!?" She begged. "Okay, okay, if it means that much to you. You know I could never turn you down anyway." Koweena gave him a gentle kiss on the lips. "That's my man," she said.

Friday evening had arrived, and Koweena was getting dressed for the ball. She couldn't help but think of Julie as she was putting on her gown. She felt like Julie, as she thought back to all those times she watched her put on all those ritzy dresses. She also felt like those princesses she had read about growing up. It was a dream come true, as Koweena slipped her five foot, ten inch frame, into her burgundy, diamond studded dress, that stretched from her neckline down to her ankles, with an opening in the back, exposing her entire backside. She felt somewhat embarrassed by her scars on her back, but her skin had such a beautiful tone to it that it washed the scars out, making them almost invisible. The shoes she chose for the dress were black patent heels. She had never felt, or looked better, as she stared at herself in the mirror looking ten times better than all the times Julie had spent making her over in the past. Julie had spent a lot of time showing her how to fix herself up as she was growing up, and she used that knowledge well, making herself beautiful, her beauty radiated the room. Her hair was pinned up in a twisted ball, with ringlets all around her neck and sides. "You look stunning!" Joe exclaimed as he walked into the room with his tuxedo on. "So do you, Baby!" Koweena said, checking him up one side and down the other. "I mean really, Koweena, you look stunning, I'm the luckiest guy in the world. I'm goin to have to keep an eye on you; they'll be men waiting in line just to talk to you if I don't." "Oh, Sweetheart, you know my eyes will only be on you," Koweena said as she winked at him with a smile. Joe put his hand to his chest. "Just looking at you makes my heart race, Darling," he said. "You know, Joe, Julie did a great job of making me feel beautiful growing up, but right now, I feel the most beautiful I've ever felt in my whole life." "You certainly have that glowing look about you, Koweena, that's for sure," Joe said. Mrs. Tulley walked into the room, immediately upon seeing Koweena, she put both her hands up to her face in amazement. "Wow, you look amazing, Dear!" She said. "My daughter's dress fits you perfectly, I knew it would. You look absolutely amazing, you truly do," Mrs. Tulley said. "Thank you, Mrs. Tulley," Koweena said with a smile, with her head held high. "Are you guys ready to go?" Mrs. Tulley asked. Koweena and Joe both looked at each other and took a deep breath together, and then smiled. They both gave out a nervous laugh. "Yes, we're ready," they both said in unison. "Okay, when you're ready, just meet me and my husband downstairs, we'll be waiting. You two are going to have the best time of your lives." Koweena shrugged her shoulders and patted her hips with her hands. "Well, Joe, I guess this is it." "You is goin to be the best lookin woman there, hands down," Joe said. "Oh, I love you," Koweena said as they embraced one another one last time before they headed downstairs. As they headed down the stairs Mr. Tulley glanced up at Koweena. "Wow, Koweena, you look beautiful!" "Thank you, Mr. Tulley." "Are we ready, everyone?" Mr. Tulley asked. Koweena was nervous. "Yes, I think so," she said. Mrs. Tulley walked right up to Koweena and whispered in her ear. "Don't worry, Dear, you're a knock out. You'll be the best looking woman there, no need to be nervous." "Let me go say goodbye to William, one last time, Mrs. Tulley, I'll be right back." Koweena made her way into the living room where William was playing with Mrs. Lane. Koweena bent down to get eye level with her son. "William, Sweetheart, I want you to know that mommy will be right back as soon as she can, alright. I'll miss you. Will you miss mommy?" Koweena asked. William nodded his head yes and went back to playing. Koweena placed her hand on William's head and gently kissed him on his head. "I'll be right back," she said. She walked back into the foyer, grabbed a hold of Joe's arm, and said, as she gave a deep sigh. "Okay, I'm ready, let's do this."

As they were walking in the parking lot, on a clear, moonlit, starry, warm spring evening, heading for the Manistee Ball building, Koweena began to get really nervous. She had never been to such a fancy outing as this before. The closest she came to being part of something so fancy was when she was the ring bearer at Julie's wedding. But she was just a child then. Now, she was nineteen, and she felt the pressure of being an adult, and having the pressure of behaving classy amongst such important upper-class people. As she made her way into the entranceway, she removed her arm from Joe's grasp and grabbed on tightly to his hand. She whispered into his ear. "Don't let go of my hand, Joe." "I won't, Sweetheart, everything is goin to be alright, okay, I promise."

As Koweena walked into the ball room, she felt like she did that day when she was five, when she entered the Defour house when it was being decorated for the Christmas holiday. Her eyes opened wide, she was trying to take it all in. She noticed the band that was on stage, directly in front of her, on the opposite side of the building from where she was standing. The band members were all dressed in tuxedos. They were bellowing out the familiar sounds of that era, big band music. The music echoed throughout the building. Her eyes then moved to the dance floor. It was a smooth, slick, pine wood finished floor, varnished to a brilliant shine. She visualized herself dancing up there with Joe, just the two of them. Her eyes then moved to the tables. They were covered with white laced cloths over white linen. They had rose pedals sprinkled all over them, with a bouquet of roses anchored in the middle. The look made her gasp as she put her hand to her mouth. She then glanced over to her right and noticed a corner bar, tucked tightly in the corner, right next to the entranceway. With the dance floor, the music, and the rose pedals, it was the most stimulating place she had ever been in. She went from being nervous, to feeling romantic.

Suddenly, all eyes turned on her. She instantly became the center of attention. Everyone in the building stopped their dancing and talking, and fixated their eyes on her.

"I had arrived," Koweena recalled. "I mean, I knew I wasn't in Canada yet, and technically I was still a slave, but as I stood there with all eyes on me, I knew I was no longer that slave girl back in Mississippi. I was beautiful, and that night, I knew it. What a long way I had come from the days of fearing a beating from an overseer. All those books I had read about princesses, I was now experiencing it, I was one of them."

Joe whispered in Koweena's ear. "They're all staring at you, Sweetheart, I told you that you would steal the show." Koweena was in shock as she gazed around the room. Yes, she was used to people staring at her, but nothing of this magnitude. For that brief moment in time, she felt like a queen, definitely not like a former slave from Mississippi.

She thought at that moment of Julie, and how proud she would be of her standing there looking like an elite woman. After all she had been through in her life, no one deserved that moment more than her. It was at that moment that she truly realized just how beautiful she really was. Her rough childhood, her beatings, her many threats as a result of being a slave, the rape, they all faded into the abyss that night as the spotlight shined on her. "Dear, they love you," Mrs. Tulley said to Koweena. "Wow, look how far I've come, from not being considered a human being on that Plantation, to now feeling like a goddess," she thought to herself as everyone continued staring at her. As she proceeded further into the room, everyone finally went back to what they were doing. "How did that feel, Darling?" Joe asked. "That was awesome, every girls dream, and I got to experience it. Julie would have been proud."

A couple of weeks prior to the ball, Mr. Williams wrote Julie once again, this time telling her about his run in with Joe.

Dear Mrs. Callahan,

I'm writing to let you know that I ran into Joe a few days ago. I finally caught up with them in Manistee, Michigan. Although I didn't see, or talk to Koweena, Joe told me that she was doing fine. Unfortunately, I don't have any details to tell you about Koweena, other than the fact that she seems to be healthy, and in good condition. Joe was as well, although he did run into a problem with a Marshal here in Manistee. I don't want to alarm you, but I feel I must tell you the following. The Marshal was about to execute him, that was until I arrived on the scene. I shot the Marshal just before he pulled the trigger on Joe. It seems as though Joe murdered a Marshal in Tennessee some time ago. Like I told you before, I don't have very many details to give you, Joe didn't talk to me long. I got the impression though, in what time I did spend with him, that he and Koweena seem to be very close. I will try and catch up with them again before they make their way across the border. Just to let you know, I did tell Joe that you desperately needed to speak with Koweena.

He asked why, but because of the fact that I don't know why you want to speak with her, I couldn't give him a straightforward answer. My only hope is that this letter eases your mind a bit about the condition of Koweena. If you want to write me, you can do so by using the address on the envelope. I'm not sure how long I'll be at this location, but you can give it a try. If you do decide to write, and I receive it, I'll make sure Koweena gets it immediately.

Mr. Williams

"I knew I should have told Mr. Williams about why I need to speak to Koweena, that way he could have told Joe," Julie said as she lay there in bed. "Don't beat yourself up over it, Dear, remember what the doctor said, you need your rest, and you need not get too upset," Thomas told her. "And what about this murder in Tennessee, what happened? Was Koweena hurt?" "Jules, Mr. Williams told us that she is doing fine." "Yes, that does ease my mind a bit." Julie coughed as she continued. "What about the fact that she and Joe seem to be close. I knew something like that would happen," "Aren't you happy about that, Jules?" "Yes, very happy, I hope they're romantically involved. I just want her to live her dream, that's all I care about; I want her to find her husband out there so she can get all she's ever wanted. But with the condition I'm in, Thomas, I must tell her soon." "No, Jules, don't talk like that. The doctor said it was nothing, nothing to be alarmed about." "I know, but I want so desperately to tell her." "Try and write her, Jules." "But what if Mr. Williams doesn't get it; it's a long shot to expect him to still be there by the time the letter arrives." "You never know. It's worth a shot. She needs to know," Thomas told her as he held a glass of water up to her mouth for her to drink. "You're right, I can't waste anymore time. I wanted to tell her in person, but if this is the way I have to tell her, then this is the way it has to be," Julie said as she gulped down the water. Thomas placed a wet cloth on Julie's forehead. "I think you should write, Sweetheart, she needs to know. I don't think it matters how she finds out, just as long as she finds out," Thomas said. "Okay, I'll write, it's worth a shot. My Koweena deserves to know, regardless of how impersonal a letter is."

Back at the ball, Koweena got her chance to dance with Joe on that beautiful dance floor as the band was playing a slow song. As she was pressed up against Joe, holding onto him tightly, she thought she was in a dream. She felt the most beautiful she had ever felt, and she was dancing with the man of her dreams in this gorgeous setting. "Hold on, Koweena, I'll be right back." Joe let go of the tight grip he had on Koweena and proceeded to one of the tables where he picked up one of the roses from the vase. With the slow song still playing, he approached Koweena with the rose in hand. He walked right up to her, grabbed her by the hips, pulled her tightly to him, and placed the rose in her hand. Koweena's eyes began tearing up as she wrapped her arm that was holding the rose around Joe's neck, as they picked up right where they left off, dancing to that slow song.

As the song finished, Joe glanced over his shoulder and spotted Mr. Williams sitting at one of the tables sipping on some bourbon. "Koweena, I see an old friend, are you goin to be alright on your own for a minute?" "Sure, Joe, go ahead." Koweena was a little curious at the fact that Joe mentioned that he had seen an old friend. "Who does he know up here?" Koweena questioned to herself. She was too busy taking in all the pageantry around her to be too concerned about what Joe said.

"Hey, Mr. Williams, its Joe, remember me?" "Have a seat, Joe. Would you like a drink?" "No, I don't drink." With the music playing in the background, Mr. Williams knew that this was his chance to finally talk to Joe about bringing Koweena back down south. "Mr. Williams, I really didn't get a chance to thank you the other day for saving my life. Koweena and I both owe you a lot of gratitude." "So you and Koweena are tight huh?" "Yes, sir, we is very close." "Romantically close?" Mr. Williams asked. "Yes, sir, that close." "Joe, I need to talk to you about something. As you know, I've been tracking you all the way from Natchez to try and get a hold of Koweena." "Why, sir?" "Well, Joe, as you also know, it's because of Julie." "Yes, you told me that before, but what does Julie have to say that's so important as to make you follow us all the way from Mississippi, up here?" "Well, I don't know, Joe, she didn't tell me. I think she wants it to be personal, you know, between her and Koweena." "So what is it exactly that you is tryin to do here, Mr. Williams?" "Well, Joe, I need to bring Koweena back down south with me." "No way, Mr. Williams, with all due respect, we is made it too far just to turn around and go back, no way. We is just too close now to our freedom. We have plans now, we have a child." "You have a child?" "Yes, sir, a two year old." "Congratulations, Joe." "Thank you, sir." "What's his name, if you don't mind me asking?" "William, sir." "William, that's a very strong name, you must be proud?" "Yes, sir, we are." "Joe, will you at least mention it to her. Tell her that I really need to talk to her. I need to try and convince her to come back with me, you understand don't you?" "Well, sir, like I said, there's no way we is goin back down south. I don't see how tellin Koweena any of this is goin to change her mind." "Maybe true, Joe, maybe true, but I would at least like the chance to talk to her myself, I think you owe me that much after I saved your life." "Your right, I'll see what I can do, Mr. Williams." "Thank you, Joe."

Meanwhile, as Joe was talking to Mr. Williams, Koweena was standing off to the side of the dance floor by herself sipping on some water, when a man approached her. His name was Will McDonald; he was one of the most handsome and wealthiest men in Manistee. He had very well groomed short cut black hair, that was combed back, with a part down the left side. He had olive skin, which gave him a light tan tone complexion. He had very well defined cheek bones, and dark eyebrows. He had long eyelashes, which gave his eyes a seductive look. As he stood there in front of Koweena, smiling, Koweena hardly noticed him; she was too busy staring at the band as they were playing. "Now, I must admit," he said as he began talking to her, "on the one hand, it is almost impossible to speak to someone who looks like you, but on the other hand, should that be your problem?" Koweena turned to him and was taken back at just how handsome Will was. The music began to fade into the background as Koweena stared at Will while biting her bottom lip. Koweena grinned. "So, I guess life's hard all around huh?" She said. "No, not if you pay attention. You're standing here alone, which means you're obviously not here with anyone; and you have that 'Don't bother me' sign stamped on your forehead." Koweena laughed out loud at that remark. "Well, you could be funny, and interestingly charming," Koweena said as she checked Will out from head to toe. "This man is too damn fine," she thought to herself as she stared into Will's eyes. Sure, she thought Will was good looking, but she in no way was tempted by this man, she was too in love to be tempted. "Don't take this personal, or the wrong way. I know it takes a lot of guts to come over here and try and generate a conversation out of thin air, especially when you're trying to woo a girl, but I'm just not interested. But thank you for coming over, I take it as a compliment," Koweena told him. "Well, that's the way you should take it miss…" Will was trying to get her name, but Koweena was having none of that. She just stood there with raised eyebrows and a smile, as Will was waiting for a reply. Will gave a flirtatious smile. "Well, miss, you should take it as a compliment," he said. "You know what you need," Will continued. Koweena just smiled. "No, tell me, what do I need?" She said sarcastically. "You need a man that will treat you like a natural born," "woman?" Joe said in the form of a question as he interrupted Will and completed his sentence for him. He stood there and smiled at Will. "Sorry I'm late, Honey; how is everything?" He asked Koweena. "Just fine, Sweetheart," Koweena said with a smile as she looked at Joe for a second and then looked back at Will with that same grin. Will stared at Joe for a few seconds and then grabbed Koweena's hand. He kissed it. "Your man is a lucky man, good evening, miss," he said, and then he walked away. Joe put his arm around Koweena and gave her a gentle kiss on the cheek. "You're just miss popular tonight aren't you, my little Miss Beautiful," he said. Koweena laughed. "What can I say, I'm just blessed I guess." It was the best night she had ever had. She was with the man in whom she loved more than anything, she was the most beautiful woman there, and she was being wooed by the most handsome of men. She felt like the most important person in the world, a sharp contrast from the fields of Natchez from whence she came.

After three more weeks of staying with the Tulleys, it was time for Koweena, Joe, and William to move on. Joe was waiting for the next steamboat to arrive at the Manistee port to take them on into Canada, and finally after three weeks, one had arrived. Since the party, and as a result of it, Koweena was feeling more confident than ever. It looked like her nightmare past was behind her. She felt more beautiful than ever. She was about to marry her dream man, and William was healthy, and seemed to be getting smarter with each passing day. Things couldn't be going any more perfect for her, and things were about to get even better. "Koweena, I want to marry you the minute we get to Canada,"

Joe said. Koweena almost began crying as she kissed Joe. "Oh Joe!" She said. "Koweena, there's one problem that stands in the way. It's not a big problem, it can easily be solved, but I want you to make the decision. I want it to be from you." "What is it, Joe?" "We need to pick a last name for me, for us." That was an easy one for Koweena; she could only think of one last name that she wanted. Koweena held her head high as she spoke. "Mr. and Mrs. Joe Defour." "But, Koweena, that's the last name of the Plantation that you slaved and suffered on." "I know, Joe, I know it sounds a little strange to want to have the same last name as my plantation owner, but it was Julie's last name, and that's all that matters to me. I've wanted to be related to Julie all my life, and doing it this way, I will sort of be. That's what I want, Joe." "Okay, Dear, Defour it is." "Oh, I can't believe it's all about to happen, reaching freedom, marrying you, starting a family with William. It's really happening isn't it?" Koweena asked. Joe smiled as he hugged Koweena. "Yes, Dear, it is," he said. "Okay, guys, are you ready?" Mrs. Tulley asked as she entered the room with William. She handed William to Koweena and continued to talk. "Now, remember, Mr. Larson will be expecting you in Sudbury when you reach the other side." Koweena was overly excited. "Yes, ma'am!" She said. "Once you reach the other side of Lake Superior, it will be about a day's journey to the town, okay," Mrs. Tulley said. Joe was brimming with enthusiasm as he punched his fist in the air. "Sudbury, Ontario, here we come!" He yelled.

As Koweena, Joe, and William waited on the banks of Lake Michigan for the steamboat, Koweena knelt down and grabbed a handful of sand, and began slowly pouring it from her hand. "You know, Joe, looking at this water, and holding this sand in my hand, it just makes me think of just how beautiful life is. I mean, here we are about to become free. All those years of slaving as a child, I never thought in a million years that I would be here, with a child of my own, and about to get married to the most beautiful man in the world. I used to dream about this day so many times growing up, I just never actually thought it would come true, you know. Life is just so unpredictable. When you think it has you beaten down, someone, or some thing, comes along that changes everything. Like Julie, without her coming into my life, I would still be there on that Plantation, living a miserable life, with no hopes or dreams. She really spent a lot of years instilling hopes and dreams into me. And you and William, Joe, pouring love into my parched, empty soul, that had only Julie in it, not that I'm complaining of only having Julie in my life, but growing up, I wanted so desperately to have what she and Thomas had, and now I do." As Koweena was saying that, she was just shaking her head, it just hit her as she was talking, all she had actually been through, she was in utter amazement at all that had transpired over her life.

Suddenly, a man approached them who was also waiting for the steamboat. "So, where are you guys headed?" The man asked. The three had come too far to blow this one. They weren't about to answer that question, they didn't even acknowledge the man who was standing right next to them. "Why are you guys headed to Canada, vacation, work, or something entirely different?" The man asked. Joe leaned into the man, now just inches from his face. "Listen, I'm only goin to tell you this one time, if you don't get away from us, I'm goin to kick your ass, and then throw you in the lake, do you understand me?" Joe said to the man. It was obvious; they were too close to freedom. Joe was going to do whatever it took to make sure he and his family reached their destination. Koweena just stood over there, listening to Joe, with a big smile on her face. She was so proud of her man taking such a brave stand like that. "Sorry, sir, I was just trying to be polite," the man said. "Well, be polite somewhere else, now get the hell out of here," Joe said as he motioned with his head for the man to head back up the bank. Koweena smiled, and nudged Joe with her shoulder. "Way to go, my knight in shining armor," she said. "We is too close, Koweena. I'm not about to let some punk ruin it for us."

As they got on the steamboat, Joe took William from Koweena's arms, and put him up on his shoulder. "Look, William, the only thing that separates us from freedom, is this water you see right here," Joe said. Koweena stood there against the railing of the boat, and took in a deep breath of northern lake air. She realized her goal was within striking distance now, as she exhaled the deep breath in a relaxing, satisfying manner. She was trying to remain calm as she realized that Canada was just over the horizon, as the boat began to sail off toward the land, where she would no longer have the stigma attached to her of being a slave that had been clinging to her for her entire life.

There were about seventy five people on board the steamboat that was churning through Lake Michigan on its way through Lake Superior, toward Canada, when Koweena noticed a strange man standing some ten yards behind them, wearing a cowboy hat. She noticed that he seemed to be looking over in their direction. She couldn't make out the face of the man as he had his head in a downward position so as to make his cowboy hat hide his face. "Joe, there's a man that's standing behind us, don't look!" She whispered strongly at Joe as he was about to turn around and glance at the man. "I don't want him to think we notice him, so don't look behind you. He just gives me a funny feeling, Joe, I don't know, there's just something off about him." Like in the past, Koweena's instincts were usually right on target about people. "Koweena, I need to look at him so I know who you is talking about." "Okay, go ahead, but be discreet about it," Koweena said. Joe glanced over his shoulder and noticed that the man was indeed glancing over in their direction. "Wait right here, Koweena," Joe said as he took William off his shoulders and placed him in Koweena's arms. "No, Joe! Just don't go, okay; I have a funny feeling about this." "Don't worry, Koweena, I'm not goin to do anything, I just need a closer look at him to see if I recognize him, that's all."

Joe took the long way around the boat, so that he could walk up to the man from behind him; he wanted to sneak up right beside the man without being noticed by him. As Joe approached the man from the man's left side, the man realized, upon looking at Koweena, that Joe was not with her. As Joe was standing just a few feet from him, he tried to sneak a peek under the man's hat to see if he indeed recognized the man. Joe took his eyes off the man for a second to look over at Koweena and William, that gave the man just enough time to pull his pistol, keeping it under his coat; he then put it to Joe's side. The man whispered in Joe's ear. "Don't make a sound, or you die, if you do make a sound you'll never get to see that pretty little girlfriend of yours again, understood?" The man led Joe to the downstairs boiler room. When they finally got down there, Joe turned around to look at the man, when he did, he was instantly greeted by the butt of the man's pistol. Joe crashed to the ground. The man stood over top of him and beat him over and over again with the pistol. Joe was completely knocked out, but the man continued his assault with one blow after another on

Joe's head, with the pistol gripped firmly in his hand. He reared back with all his might, and blow after blow, continued to smash the pistol against Joe's head. Blood was splattering everywhere with each blow. It was apparent; the man was trying to kill Joe. "Hey, what's going on over there!?" One of the steamboat workers hollered out from behind the boiler. The man stopped his assault and ran back upstairs. "Oh my God, Jerry, get over here; we have a man severely hurt here!" The steamboat worker yelled out.

Meanwhile, back up on the deck, Koweena was looking all around for Joe. She glanced over to where the man had been standing and noticed that he was no longer there. She then became extremely worried. Not thinking about what she was doing, she put William down on the wooden deck floor and began walking around, trying desperately to find Joe. She assumed that William was walking along with her, after several minutes of pacing the deck; she looked down and noticed that William was not there. Her thoughts quickly went from Joe to William. "William! William!" Koweena frantically screamed out. She pushed and pulled people out of the way, deliriously whipping her head all around, desperately searching for William. "Ma'am, ma'am, what have you lost?" A man asked Koweena, noticing that she was eagerly searching for something. "My child, my mind," Koweena, now hysterically crying, said. "I tell you what," the man said, it was Mr. Williams. "Why don't you grab that curious little fella over there playing with that mother's boy, while I try to help you look for him?" Koweena swiftly glanced over in the direction Mr. Williams was pointing, and noticed that it was William. "William!" Koweena yelled out. Koweena picked William up and walked back over to Mr. Williams. "Oh, thank you so much, sir, what can I do to repay you?" Koweena asked Mr. Williams. "I'm sure you'll think of something, ma'am." Koweena was puzzled by that response. "What on earth could he be talking about?" She wondered. She didn't wonder long though before she picked up right where she had left off, and began wildly looking for Joe. She was so consumed with finding Joe that she didn't even notice that the boat had docked on the shores of the small town in Canada called Blind River. It should have been an ecstatic moment for Koweena. Finally freedom, her long journey from the southern most reaches of Mississippi to Canada, had finally come to its conclusion; she had made it to her destination. But instead of being happy, she was losing her mind, wondering where Joe was. She had searched all over the boat, but to no avail. She hurriedly approached the dock worker who was letting the passengers off the boat. "Sir, my husband," she instinctively called Joe her husband without thinking. "He has been hurt. I know it; you have to help me find him."

No more had she just got those words out of her mouth, when out of nowhere, she was tackled from behind. Her face slammed to the ground, William went flying out of her arms as he pounded hard to the ground. Koweena was in a semi-conscious state as her face was scratched up from the fall. She could hardly breathe as the man's weight was crushing her lungs, as she laid there on her side. He instantly jerked her over. Koweena, even though she was groggy, could quickly make out the man who was standing over top of her, it was Ray. Ray instantly put his hands around Koweena's neck, and began violently choking her. "Finally, bitch, die," Ray said with a deep strain in his voice as he was giving everything he had to choke the very life out of Koweena. Koweena grabbed a hold of Ray's wrists, trying her hardest to pry them off her. "How long have you been stalking me?" Koweena asked as she was struggling with Ray's arms. Ray eased up for a second to answer. "Damn, bitch, why I've been stalking you ever since you were a child. Everyday on the Plantation I was stalking you, watching your every move for years." Ray then continued his tight grip on Koweena's neck. As the crowd was getting off the boat, no one offered to help. "Dear, do something!" One of the female passengers told her husband as they walked by Koweena, jerking violently and pounding the ground with both hands as she was trying to gasp for any kind of air she could get. "I'm not getting involved," the husband told his wife. That was the sentiment of everyone around that was witnessing the event. Ray was just too big, and no one wanted to mess with him. With the combination of Ray's heavy weight resting on her chest, and his large hands squeezing her throat firmly, Koweena could feel herself slipping away. William was lying on the ground face first, crying hysterically. With the looks of things, he was about to lose both his parents on what was suppose to be a happy boat ride for the three of them. Suddenly, a loud boom rang out. Ray slowly let go of the strong grasp he had on Koweena's throat, and tilted over, and landed on his side on the ground. Koweena quickly grabbed her throat as she tried to catch her breath.

Mr. Williams ran over to Koweena, with his pistol still in his hand. "Are you alright, miss?" He asked Koweena. "Check on my son," she said with a raspy voice. Mr. Williams went over to William and picked him up; he was shaken up, but was alright. He was more scared than anything. Joe, with a bandage around his head, ran up to Koweena and began kissing her on her forehead. "What happened?" He asked her. "What happened to you?" She asked, as the dock worker walked over, rolled Ray's body out of the way, and began wiping her scratched up face with a towel. "Ray attacked me," Joe replied. Koweena put her hand to Joe's cheek. "He attacked me too," she said. "Well, he won't be attacking anybody else," Mr. Williams said, walking up to them both with William in his arms. Joe was surprised. "Mr. Williams!" He yelled. "Is this the Mr. Williams that saved your life that time?" Koweena asked Joe. Joe became emphatic. "Yes!" He said. "Did you kill Ray?" Joe asked Mr. Williams. "Yes, and it was none too soon," Mr. Williams replied. "This little miss here was seconds away from going under for good," he continued. Joe was amazed. "So you have saved both our lives," he said. "Yes, I guess I have, Joe." "He also helped me find William, Joe," Koweena said. Koweena sat up slowly, holding her neck. "How can we repay you, Mr. Williams?" She asked. "Well, Koweena, you can listen to what I have to say. I've travelled a long way to talk to you, and I now have something in my possession that I think you're going to want to read." Mr. Williams pulled out an envelope from his shirt pocket and stretched it out toward Koweena. "What is this?" Koweena asked him as she grabbed the envelope. "It's a letter from Julie," Mr. Williams replied. Koweena was surprised. "From my Julie?" She asked. "Yes, from your Julie," Mr. Williams replied. "Mr. Williams, you have to stay with us," Joe said as he received William from Mr. Williams' arm. "Where are you staying?" Mr. Williams asked Joe. "We is staying in a town called Sudbury, it's about a day's journey from here." "That sounds excellent, Joe, I would like to do that, it will give me a chance to talk to Koweena." "Great!" Joe said with enthusiasm as he stretched out his hand to shake Mr. Williams' hand. Mr. Williams returned the gesture as they shook hands. Joe then moved in closer to him and clutched his arms around Mr. Williams' neck, giving him a hug.

Chapter 15 Coming A Long Way

As Koweena, Joe, William, and Mr. Williams finally made their arrival at Sudbury, the four of them approached Mr. Larson's house. "What is, Dear?" Koweena asked Joe as he stopped at the edge of Mr. Larson's yard. "This is weird. I'm so used to seeing a statue, and here, there's no statue." "Baby, we're free, we're free, that's why you don't see a statue. Be happy about that, not worried." "You is right, Darling, let's go on," Joe said as he approached Mr. Larson's front door and proceeded to knock. "Who is it?" A voice responded on the other side. Once again, Joe thought for a moment as if he was still a runaway slave. He almost responded to the voice on the other side with what he had been saying for years now, "a friend of a friend," but he caught himself before he said it. "It's Joe and Koweena, sir," Joe said. The door opened, "Joe and Koweena, come in, I've been expecting you." Mr. Larson noticed the bandage around Joe's head and the scratches on Koweena's face. "My goodness, what has happened to the both of you? You look like you've come from a war zone," Mr. Larson said. Joe grinned. "Sir, believe me, we is used to it by now, we'll be alright," he said. "Well, I'll have our local doctor look at the both of you just to be on the safe side," Mr. Larson said. "Mr. Larson," Koweena said, "do you mind if Joe and William go in your living room for a moment so Mr. Williams and I can talk?" "Not at all, Koweena, Joe you come in here and sit down on the sofa and relax a bit," Mr. Larson said as he led Joe, with William in his arms, to the living room. "Koweena, you and, what did you say your name was, sir?" Mr. Larson asked. "Sorry, I didn't introduce myself, sir, I'm Mr. Williams." "You and Mr. Williams are more than welcome to use my kitchen to talk. Meanwhile, I'll go and call the doctor." "Really, there's no need to Mr. Larson," Joe said as he sat on the sofa rocking William on his lap. "You have some serious blood coming from that head bandage of yours, Joe, I think it's best if I do," Mr. Larson said. Joe just nodded his head yes, and continued rocking William.

Koweena and Mr. Williams sat at the kitchen table. "You need to come back down South with me, Koweena, it's of an urgent matter," Mr. William said. It was a dark, cloudy day, so all the lights in the house were on. "I can't, Mr. Williams; I have a life up here now. I've met a great man, we're going to get married and start a family here." "Koweena, Julie has some very important news to tell you, that's why I came all the way up here to track you down." Koweena listened as she held on with a firm grip to the letter Mr. Williams had given her the day before. "Wow, it must be some very important news, what is it, Mr. Williams?" Koweena wondered what was so pressing as to make this man travel all the way up here just to bring her back down south to have Julie tell her something. "Don't know, ma'am, Mr. Defour just asked me to track you down and bring you back with me." Koweena looked puzzled. "Mr. Defour?" She asked. "Yes, Mr. Defour, is there something strange about that?" Mr. Williams asked. "It's just that right before I left, Mr. Defour was going to ship me off to another plantation, and now he has sent you all the way up here just to make sure you brought me back there safely. Sir, forgive me, but it just doesn't make any sense." The thought quickly entered Koweena's mind that maybe Mr. Defour had gone to such trouble in order to really ship her off. "Koweena, Mr. Defour sent me on this journey with specific instructions to make sure, one, you were alright, and two, to assure you that everything would be safe on the Plantation, and that no harm would be done to you when you returned. He really stressed that you would be safe if you indeed decided to return." "Well, forgive me, Mr. Williams, if I don't completely trust Mr. Defour. Besides, I can't, Mr. Williams; I have a life up here now. I have this letter in my hand from Julie anyway." Koweena lifted the letter in the air, shaking it. "I'm sure she has told me all she wants to tell me in here," Koweena said. "I will read the letter and learn for myself what she has to say, without having to come along with you back to Natchez. I tell you what you can do for me though. I'm going to write Julie and tell her all that has happened to me, you can deliver it to her first hand when you arrive back down there, okay." "Koweena, I really need to take you back down there with me." "What's wrong, Sweetheart?" Joe asked as he overheard Mr. Williams trying to press the issue of trying to return Koweena back down South. "Oh, nothing, Dear, Mr. Williams was just trying to get me to go back down south with him, that's all. I told him that I have a life here, with you now." Joe put his arm around Koweena. "Yes, she does, Mr. Williams," Joe said. "I tell you what, Koweena, if Mr. Larson will allow me to stay here overnight, I'll wait for you to write that letter and then I will indeed take it back down south with me and deliver it to Julie first hand." "Thank you, Mr. Williams, that sure would mean a lot. You have done so much for our family during this journey. Without you, neither one of us would be standing here right now. William wouldn't have any parents." Koweena grabbed a hold of Mr. Williams' hand. "You will not be forgotten, Mr. Williams, I can assure you of that," she said. "Thank you, Koweena, I'm just glad I was here to help." "Yes, thank you, Mr. Williams," Joe chimed in, as he placed his hand on Mr. Williams' shoulder. "Joe, the doctor is here!" Mr. Larson yelled from the foyer area into the kitchen. "Here, Honey, you hold William for a minute while I go get checked out," Joe said as he handed William over to Koweena and proceeded out into the foyer area.

"You're fine, Joe, we'll keep the stitches in for a while and I'll be back to take them out later," the doctor said after he stitched up Joe and rewrapped the bandage around his head. "Thank you, Doctor," Joe replied. After Joe said that, Koweena came into the living room holding William, and approached Mr. Larson. "Mr. Larson, can I ask you for a favor?" "Sure, Koweena, anything." "Can we have a special dinner in honor of Mr. Williams tonight?" "Sure, I'll fix my special lamb covered in mint jelly, with my special mashed potatoes and peach cobbler. How does that sound?" "Great, Mr. Larson, thank you. It' just that he's done so many things for us along our journey, well, simply put, without him, Joe and I wouldn't be here, breathing, you know what I mean?" "I gotcha, Koweena, don't worry, it will be special."

As Mr. Larson was in the kitchen preparing the special meal, Koweena was in her guest bedroom holding the letter from Julie, tightly, with both hands. It was the perfect time to open it and read what it contained, but she was too scared. Joe was in the living room with

William, while Mr. Williams was in the other guest bedroom, resting. It was the perfect opportunity for Koweena to relax and read what Julie had written, but she just didn't have the nerve to peel back the envelope. For Julie to go through all this trouble just to tell her something, meant that the contents inside must be explosive, Koweena thought to herself. Her fear was greater than her curiosity that night; she just felt she wasn't ready emotionally to open it, so she didn't. "I will do it tomorrow, that will still give me enough time to write her back before Mr. Williams leaves," she whispered to herself. "I better ask Mr. Williams tonight at dinner when he plans on leaving tomorrow," she continued to whisper. She placed the unopened letter on the nightstand by the bed and went downstairs.

As she approached the living room, Joe could sense that something was wrong. "Everything alright, Honey?" Joe asked as he could see on Koweena's face that something heavy was weighing on her mind. "It's Julie's letter, I'm too terrified to open it." "Why?" Joe asked. "If she's gone through this much trouble just to tell me something, it must be earth shattering. I'm just not prepared to open it right now." "Do you want me to be alongside you when you read it, will that help?" "No, Joe, I need to read it when I'm by myself."

"What time will you be leaving tomorrow, Mr. Williams," Koweena asked as they were sitting at the kitchen table eating their special dinner. "I can leave whenever you finish with your letter. Do you know when that will be, Koweena?" Mr. Williams asked. "I will have it written by the afternoon, Mr. Williams." "Great, that will work out perfectly," Mr. Williams said as he took a big bite of the lamb with bits of mint jelly and mashed potatoes covering it. Mr. Williams spoke up with his mouth full. "This is a mighty fine meal, Mr. Larson." "Thank you, Mr. Williams, Koweena asked me to make it in your honor." Koweena looked over at Joe waiting for him to look at her. When he finally did, she motioned with her head for him to stand up. "Oh, yes," Joe said under his breath. Everyone at the dinner table heard him though. Mr. Williams gave him a funny look as Joe stared over at him as he proceeded to stand up with his drinking glass in hand, tapping it with his fork. Joe raised his glass toward Mr. Williams. "I would like to make a toast. Mr. Williams, I just want to pause for a moment from eating to thank you, on behalf of Koweena, myself, and William, thank you from the bottom of our hearts for all you is done for us. Truly, without you, the three of us would not be here today, and we will make sure that William knows all about you, and what you did for us too, Mr. Williams!" "Here here," Koweena said as she raised her glass toward Mr. Williams and clanged it against Joe's glass. Mr. Larson joined in, as well as Mr. Williams, and the four of them tapped their glasses against one another in unison. Mr. Larson smiled in the direction of Mr. Williams. "Mr. Williams, you sure mean a lot to this young couple, it's very evident," Mr. Larson said. "Yes, it's a good feeling," Mr. Williams said. Koweena clutched her hand onto Mr. Williams' arm, patting it over and over again. "Mr. Williams, I never realized that there was such an honorable overseer on the Defour Plantation. It's been a pleasure to know you," Koweena said as she got up from her chair and gave him a kiss on the cheek. Mr. Williams' eyes began to tear up. "Thank you, Koweena," Mr. Williams said with his head down in humility, still with tears in his eyes. After several minutes of eating, Koweena spoke up, "So, Mr. Williams, are you married?" "Yes, Koweena, it will be twelve years next month." "Do you have any children?" Koweena continued asking. "Yes, I have one, Douglas, he's nine." Koweena smiled. "Well, I pray nothing but the best for the three of you," she said. "Thank you, Koweena," Mr. Williams responded.

That night, as Koweena was lying in bed, with William asleep alongside her, and Joe asleep on the floor, she was laying on her side staring at the letter on the nightstand. The letter stared back at her like some ominous rain cloud, full of lightning and thunder. If she could just touch it and quickly open it, half the battle would be won, she thought. She was now even too afraid to put her fingers on it. "I have to overcome this, I've got to read it in less than twelve hours," she thought. With her hands shaking the entire time, she took a deep breath, grabbed a hold of the envelope, and ripped it open. Once she got the envelope open, she quickly put it back down and put her hands and head under the covers. But suddenly, the curiosity that was overshadowed by fear earlier that day, was now coming to the forefront as she realized that she had come this far by opening the letter. She pulled the covers from her head and looked at the envelope once again. With the envelope open now, and with the appearance of the crease and rip on the top of the envelope turned in her direction, it gave it a look as if it was smiling at her. She inadvertently let out a little laugh. With the letter appearing less ominous now, she grabbed a hold of it once again, this time her hands were not shaking. She slowly and gently pulled the letter from the envelope and opened it up. It was still just as cloudy as it was earlier in the day, and the clouds were blocking any chance that the moonlight might have of shining its light onto the letter. All she could do was vaguely make out the outline of the letter, and how long the letter was. "It seems pretty lengthy," she thought to herself. She was somewhat relieved that there was no moonlight, she definitely wasn't ready to read it that night, and with moonlight, she would have been tempted to read it. She placed the letter back on the nightstand, this time with the letter on top of the envelope. She couldn't sleep that night, all she kept thinking about was that letter. Her entire night was spent glancing over at the letter every few seconds. As the night grew on, with each passing second, she increasingly grew more and more curious about its contents, by morning, she was ready to read it, although still nervous about what it contained.

As the early morning turned into to mid-morning, Koweena found herself once again paralyzed by the letter. With William playing at her feet, she just stood there over top of the folded letter. It was as if someone was physically holding her arm down, keeping her from reaching for the letter. Finally, after moving her arm back and forth toward the letter, she mustard up enough courage to grab a hold of the letter. Her heart was pounding inside her chest, and she was struggling to breathe as she grabbed a hold of William with letter in hand, and proceeded to the living room. She had to do this quick or she would put the letter down, freeze up again, and it would take her God knows how long to get up the nerve to hold the letter once again. She quickly put William down on the floor, sat down on the sofa, took a deep breath, and with her heart about to explode inside her, she began to read:

My Dearest Koweena,

I feel like it has been a lifetime since I've seen your pretty face, or heard your beautiful voice. It seems like just yesterday that you were singing to me that song I taught you when you were five, you could sing so well, and it's that voice that I crave to hear once again. I can remember so vividly the days when I would dress you up and fix your face up; it's that beauty that I crave to see once again.

"So far so good," she whispered to herself, closing and opening her eyes, trying to focus them as a result of her extreme panic:

My hope is that this letter finds you, and finds you well and free. If you're reading this letter, it means you've either crossed the border, or are getting ready to. I just want to tell you that I'm so proud of you Koweena. I knew you had the strength and fortitude to do it. It also means that you've run into Mr. Williams. I know you're wondering why I sent someone all the way up there to find you when we agreed that we would wait until you got settled in Canada before you would really try and reach out to me. Well, what I found out just after you left just couldn't wait. I had to let you know as soon as possible. I lied awake many a night since finding out what I know, dreaming of this moment when I would be able to tell you what I now know. My plan was to tell you in person, that's the way it should have been done, but if this is the only way it can happen, than this is the way it will have to be. Koweena, you might need to sit down before you continue to read on.

Koweena looked up from the paper, glanced over at William who was playing, took a deep breath, and proceeded to read on:

Are you sitting down? Okay, here it goes. God I want you to be happy when I tell you this. Koweena, I'm your mother.

Koweena immediately glanced up from her paper and looked out the window of Mr. Larson's living room, with a blank stare on her face. Her mind was blank at that moment, she couldn't think of anything, good or bad. She was in total shock as the sunlight streamed into the living room through the window she was staring out of. "I wish I would have read this with Joe with me after all," she thought. After staring out into the clear, sunny sky for a moment, Koweena finally proceeded to look back down at her paper, still stunned, and continued reading on:

My parents told me just after you left. I was so irate with them because of the timing of the whole thing. Why did they have to wait until you had just left to tell me? I guess it doesn't matter now, what matters is that you now know. I'm sure you have so many questions you're wrestling with right now. I know you want to know how this all happened. When I was thirteen I was raped by a slave inside his shack. How did I end up inside his shack? I decided to take a different route one night from the horse stable and walk by the slaves living quarters, as I did, a large black man grabbed me and threw me through the door of his shack where he then proceeded to rape me. My father hung him not long after that. I want to stop right here for a moment because I can only imagine what must be going through your mind right now. Koweena, I'm so sorry you had to find out this late in your life, and in this fashion. Like I said, I really wanted to tell you in person. Doing it this way, I have no idea if you're happy right now, or sad, or both. It's just so frustrating, all that time we spent together and we just didn't know. But then I look at it a different way, even though neither one of us knew, God still brought us together on that fall afternoon when you were five so that we could spend all those years together. What's ironic about this whole thing is that I treated you like my own daughter. That's how I see the beauty in all of this. Getting back to the rape incident, my mother decided to keep it hidden from everyone. She kept me hidden from the outside world for nine months. I don't want you to think that I didn't want you in my life with what I'm about to tell you, but those nine months were hell. My mom made me feel so ashamed to be pregnant. Oh, but during that time, as the months grew on, I wanted you so bad. My mother had made the decision that she was going to give you up after you were born. So she proceeded to find a slave mother who would be giving birth around the same time as me, and give you up to her. That is where Amitha comes into the picture, she had just had a baby, I'm assuming it was Josi, and therefore, she was able to breast feed during that time. So my mom thought it would be the perfect fit. I had no say so in the matter Koweena. You're probably thinking that I could have fought for you better, but I was only a child myself, I didn't want to give you up, but ashamedly I was influenced by my mom. I had no choice Koweena, please try and understand that. Your birth was a difficult one; I had a lot of trouble having you. But my mom had it all set up when the moment arrived. She had slaves all around my bed ready to take you to Amitha once you were born. I was depressed for years after the ordeal. I felt like a part of me had been ripped away from me. There wasn't a day that went by that I didn't think of you and how you were doing. It was the toughest years of my life. I can't say that the rape was a terrible thing that happened to me, because it brought me you. My only hope is that you're not mad at me for all of this. Please know that as soon as I found out that you were my daughter, your beautiful, perfect self, who had been stripped from me years ago, I did everything in my power to track you down in order to tell you. I just hate that I had to do it in this fashion. I wish I could be there to respond to your reaction to all that I'm telling you, to be able to talk to you and hold you. I want you to also know that you have a sister. She's two now, it too, was a difficult birth, I named her after you, her name is Kowie. She's a curly, blonde headed bundle of joy. She has your beautiful eyes. I have visions one day of the both of you running through the fields somewhere, holding hands. I want you to be a part of her life Koweena. I love you more now than I ever have, if that's possible, you are still my everything Koweena. I want you to come back down here and live with me. If you don't want to however, then I will come up there and spend time with you. I have to see you now that I know you're my daughter, my only wish is that you feel the same. I love you Koweena. By the way, remember when we talked about you not knowing when your birthday was that day in the living room when you were five. You will be happy to know that you were born on May 8th, 1829.

Your loving mother,

Julie

Koweena dropped the paper to the floor and just sat there, hunched over on the sofa, speechless. She was trying so hard to process all that she had read. Suddenly, a thousand thoughts came flooding into her mind. "Why didn't she fight for me? Why did Mrs. Defour do that? All these years of thinking that Amitha was my mom. All those years spent with Julie, not knowing that she was my mom." The thoughts just bombarded her brain. "What is it, Sweetheart?" Joe asked as he came back from one of his many job hunting expeditions. He was looking so forward to telling Koweena that he had indeed found a job as one of two local teachers at one of the local one room schoolhouses in Sudbury. The excited reaction he had on his face because he couldn't wait to tell his fiancée, suddenly became one of concerned seriousness. He could clearly see that Koweena was lost in thought. He could tell by her body expression, and the note on the floor, that she had received some devastating news.

After all the questions that had overloaded Koweena's mind began to quiet down, she then began to think of how great Julie had treated her over all those years. She suddenly went from being mad and confused, to becoming happy that Julie was her mother. Thinking back to all those years spent with Julie, she realized that Julie *was* the perfect mother. "God, I'm so lucky," she thought to herself. "I can't wait to see her and call her mom," Koweena whispered out loud. "See who? Call who mom?" Joe asked. Koweena realized that Joe had heard what she said unintentionally. "Joe, I'm a little stunned right now, I think you better come over here and sit down so we can have a talk." Joe could clearly see that Koweena was upset as a result of the tears she had forming in her eyes. Joe went over and sat next to her on the sofa. "What is it,

Sweetheart?" "Joe, Julie is my mother." "What!? Is that what's on that piece of paper on the floor?" Koweena, so stunned by what she had just read, didn't realize that the letter was on the floor. She reached down and picked it up. "Yes, it's all in this letter, here." Koweena handed the letter to Joe. After Joe read it, he immediately took a hold of Koweena and cuddled her up close to him. They leaned back on the sofa as Joe had a firm grip on Koweena, kissing her head. "Well, Koweena, you can look at this as a very positive thing. You know the exact date of your birthday, and you have a mother who is very good to you, and loves you more than anything. She was good to you growing up, right?" "God yes, the best, that's why I'm so happy. I mean, even though I didn't know she was my mom all that time we spent together, and that makes me sad, at the same time she was so good to me. I mean she *did* treat me like a daughter. If we would have known back then it wouldn't have changed our relationship in the least, because we were that close to one another. I just can't wait to see her, wait a minute; I have to write her right now." "Hold on, Koweena, you might want to wait just a little bit." "Why, Joe?" "I have some good news, two pieces of good news actually." Koweena sat straight up on the sofa, wearing a grin, as her hands were clutched together. "What is it?" She asked. "I can see you is excited," Joe said. "Tell me, Joe, what is it?" "Well, first off, I found a job; I'm a teacher at the local school." "Oh, that's great, Joe, I'm so happy for you." "For us, Koweena, for us." "For us, Joe," Koweena said, laughing out loud. She began bouncing up and down on the sofa. "What's the other good news?" She asked. "I got us a house." "Oh!" Koweena yelled out as she gave Joe a huge bear hug. "What kind of house?" Koweena asked, still clutching on to Joe. "Well, it's not big, but it has a giant field in the backyard with rolling hills and a giant oak tree on top of one of the hills. It's about an eight hundred square foot house with three bedrooms, a kitchen, and a living room." "Oh, Joe, it sounds perfect. Our children can run and play in the field, it will be perfect." Koweena slapped a big kiss on Joe's lips. "Oh, I'm so happy. You are the perfect soon to be husband, you know that," she continued. "When can we move in?" Joe became excited. "Immediately!" He yelled out. Koweena looked at Joe with raised eyebrows. "Let's do it today!" She yelled back. "Don't you think it would be best if we wait until tomorrow? That way we will have the entire day to get settled in. And plus, you need to allow what you just read to process, you need some time to let it soak in a bit," Joe said. "You're right, tomorrow, I'll start getting packed right now though. Oh, I can't wait." Koweena said. She stood up from the sofa and jumped up in the air with her arms held high. Mr. Larson walked in as Koweena was jumping up and down. He gave a big smile. "What in the world is going on here?" He asked. "Mr. Larson, we have a home, we have a home!" Koweena yelled as she ran over to Mr. Larson and gave him a big hug. "Whoa, whoa there young'un!" Mr. Larson said with a smile as he let Koweena hang on to him with a firm grip. Joe started laughing out loud as he watched Koweena show off her excitement.

The two had come along way since that first day of riding that horse through the field of the Defour Plantation, dodging bullets. Koweena had definitely come along way, from the days of carrying buckets of water to the fields on the Plantation as a child, to the beatings; and being threatened to be shipped off to some foreign land as a teenager, not to mention the rape, she definitely deserved this moment. Although Koweena felt like giving up at times as a child, and along the journey, she did exactly what Julie told her to do; she kept her head up and forged on. She was so excited at what she had just learned in just a matter of minutes. Julie was her mom, and she and Joe now had a house to call their very own. It was so much information in just a short amount of time, that it was almost overload for her brain. "You're right, Joe, I need to sit down for a moment and let all this sink in," Koweena said as she took a deep breath, flipped back her curly, thick hair, and proceeded to sit back down on the sofa. After several minutes of just sitting there taking deep breaths, she finally spoke up. "Let's get married, Joe, right now." Joe opened his mouth getting ready to say something, but Koweena quickly cut him off. "I mean it's perfect. It's the right time, we have a house now, don't you agree?" "Do you really want to?" Joe asked. "Yes, more than ever!" Koweena emphatically said as she gave Joe a big hug. "William can be the ring bearer," Koweena said. She immediately thought back to the day when she was a ring bearer in Julie, now her mom's, wedding. Although she had dreamed of a big wedding growing up, especially after Julie's wedding, she didn't care about that now. She was so in love, she just wanted to get married; she didn't care anything about the details. Ever since she fell in love with Joe, she could think of only one thing, becoming his wife. And now, with her being on the cusp of just that, she could care less how they got married, just as long as they did. "About William being the ring bearer. I don't have a ring for you, Koweena." "I don't care about that," Koweena interrupted. "But, I did ask Mr. Larson if I could borrow one his rings from his late wife, and he said yes," Joe continued. Koweena was overflowing with enthusiasm as she held Joe's hands while bouncing up and down on the sofa. "Oh, so you have thought about getting married right now!" William just laughed as he sat there watching his mother carrying on so. "Oh God, I almost forgot. I need to write Julie, I mean my mom, before Mr. Williams leaves," Koweena said. "Me and William will go in the other room and give you some space while you do that. Let's go William," Joe said as he got up from the sofa and grabbed William and left the living room. Koweena got up from the sofa as well and proceeded to the kitchen where she sat down at the kitchen table and proceeded to write Julie. "Mr. Larson! Mr. Larson!" Koweena yelled from the kitchen toward Mr. Larson's room. Mr. Larson made his way into the kitchen. "Yes, Koweena, what is it, Dear." "Do you mind terribly to get me some paper and a quill? I need to write someone a letter." "Sure, I'll be right back with that." Thoughts began to flood Koweena's mind as she thought of all the things she wanted to write. She wanted to give the impression to Julie of just how happy she truly was at that moment.

Dearest Mom,

It hit Koweena after writing those short two words. Koweena never before had had such a complete feeling ever until she wrote those words. It dawned on her after writing them, just how happy at that moment she truly was. Her dreams had come true. She had wanted so badly to be related to Julie, and now, not only was she related to her, but Julie was her mother, it was perfect, and she realized that in just writing those two words:

> Thank you for telling me about when I was born. When I first learned that you were my mom I was confused and upset, but then I realized just how great you treated me growing up, and I suddenly became very happy. I'm proud to call you my mom; I wouldn't want it any other way. There is more to the story about my birth

that you don't know. Amitha, right before I moved in with you, when I was nine, told me about the ordeal and what had transpired that night. I was in very bad shape that night of my birth; the slaves couldn't get me to stop bleeding. But two slaves gave their everything to make sure I would survive. Sam, a fellow slave who lived in the shack with us, gave up his life by getting me some medical supplies from the medical building. He was later shot and killed after arriving back at the shack with the supplies to stop my bleeding. Although I don't know who he is, I can't wait for that day when I get a chance to thank him in person in Heaven. Another slave, Sarena, who was Sam's girlfriend, used her skills that she had learned by watching a white girl get stitched up, and she was able to use the supplies Sam got, to stitch me up. Two slaves, who were in love with each other, worked as a team to save my life. I wouldn't be here today if it weren't for Sam and Sarena. Amitha called it a true love story in action that night. I guess you could say I was meant to be here. One of the reasons as to why I think that is because of my son. You have a healthy grandson, his name is William, he will be three in November. Mom, I can't come back down there with Mr. Williams, I just can't. I have a good life up here in Canada now. Joe and I are about to get married. Yes, the same Joe that I was too shy to talk to when Thomas brought him home with him that night at your home. By the time you read this letter, it will have already taken place. We just bought ourselves a house; it has a huge field as a backyard. Will you, Kowie, and Thomas come up here in the next several months? I've dreamed my whole life growing up, of you coming and visiting me at my home with my new family. I've come a long way mom, and I owe it all to you. You never gave up on me, from the time I was just a little girl, to the final days of me staying on that Plantation, you always supported me. You taught me how to be a lady, a good mom, and a good mate to my man. Whatever I now know, I got from you. I miss your smile and the way you used to console me and cuddle with me when I needed you the most. You gave me hope and inspiration mom, not just while I was growing up, but also on this journey. There were times on this journey that were terribly rough, and during those times I thought only of you. Please come up and see me as soon as you can. I will attach my new address to the bottom of this letter. I love you so much!

Your loving daughter,

Koweena

13 Asbury Street
Sudbury, Ontario

Koweena realized that she was taking a chance by giving out her address like that. She didn't trust Mr. Defour in the least. After all, how did Ray eventually track her down if Mr. Defour wasn't behind it she thought? But then she realized she was in free territory now; there was nothing Mr. Defour could do about it now, even if he wanted to. As she walked up to Mr. Williams to hand him the letter, she noticed that he was getting ready to leave as he was standing in the foyer area. "Mr. Williams, I need for you to do me one last favor." "Anything, Koweena, what is it?" "I need for you to make sure that this letter winds up in the hands of Julie only, nobody else. And I also need for you to make sure that you don't tell Mr. Defour where I'm living." Mr. Williams gently grabbed a hold of Koweena's arm. "But, Koweena, he's my boss." "I know, but you can say you don't know, can't you?" "Sure, Koweena, I'll do that." Koweena leaned over and gave Mr. Williams a kiss on the cheek. "Thank you, Mr. Williams," she said. "I'm going to miss you," she continued. Mr. Williams smiled. "Likewise, Koweena," he said. "I can't thank you enough for what you have done for us, saving both mine and Joe's life, we owe you a lifetime of gratitude," Koweena said while getting choked up as she was about to cry. "Koweena, I only did what was right, you take care now." "You too, Mr. Williams, be careful," Koweena said as she held her hand high, waving good bye. "Mr. Williams, wait!" Koweena yelled out as Mr. Williams was just about to cross the edge of Mr. Larson's lawn. Koweena ran out to where he was standing. "I almost forgot, I made you this yesterday," Koweena said as she handed Mr. Williams a knitted, red, heart shaped cotton cloth with the names of William, Koweena, and Joe embroidered in the middle of the heart, with the words 'We love you' stitched at the bottom. Mr. Williams had a stunned, surprised look on his face. "For me?" He asked. "It's the least I could do for you," Koweena said as she had her hands folded together, looking up at the tall Mr. Williams. Mr. Williams leaned over and gave Koweena a kiss on the cheek. "Good bye, Koweena, I will treasure this, thank you." "No, Mr. Williams, thank you," Koweena said with a smile. As Mr. Williams walked off into the cloudy sky, Koweena just stood there and watched him. "What a great man," she said to herself.

Koweena and Joe wanted to make sure that their wedding day, and their move in day into their new home, would coincide on the same day. Three days after Mr. Williams left, the two, along with William, made their way to the local courthouse to not only get married, but also to finalize their last names. The two were walking toward the courthouse, with William riding on top of Joe's shoulders. "Do you still want our last name to be Defour, Koweena?" Joe asked. "You know, Joe, part of me has had my reservations about the name Defour, after all, it is the last name of that awful man, that grandfather of mine who not only tried to ship me off, but who also sent Ray after me to try and kill me. But now, knowing that Julie is my mom, I really want her last name." "What, Callahan?" Joe asked. "Yes, I mean I just don't think I could live the rest of my life with the same last name as Mr. Defour, or Mrs. Defour for that matter. It would be perfect, all of us, you, William, my mom, Kowie, me, and Thomas, we would all have the same last name, one big happy family. "Koweena, Joe, and William Callahan, I could live with that. Frankly, Koweena, I could care less what our last name is, just as long as you're my wife." Koweena leaned into Joe's side as they continued walking toward the courthouse. "I love you, Joe," she said.

After finalizing their last name, it was now time for the wedding ceremony. Mr. Larson allowed Koweena to borrow one of his late wife's dresses. It was an off white dress, strapless, with ruffles going around her upper arms, over and across her upper chest. The dress reached all the way down to her ankles. She had on some black paten heels, once again borrowed from Mr. Larson's late wife. Her long, flowing, curly hair was down in the back, with it pulled back in the front, positioned by a clip on top of her head with little ringlets coming down both sides, around her ears. Joe had borrowed a black suit from Mr. Larson.

It was the day Koweena had been dreaming about since she was nine, standing up on that stage in Natchez as a ring bearer, holding Julie and Thomas' rings during their wedding. Now, her very own son stood there in between her and Joe, holding an off white pillow with the borrowed ring on top as their ring bearer. It couldn't get any more poetic, Koweena thought, as she looked deeply into Joe's eyes as the judge pronounced their vows. She knew she was looking into the eyes of the man who had healed her after her rape, the one who had literally at times carried her on his back during part of their journey, and it was the man who stayed at her bed side with tears flowing down his face onto her hands as she struggled to breathe. It was the man who risked his own life in order to save hers, on numerous occasions, and finally it was the man who was alongside her when she felt the most beautiful she had ever felt that night at the ball in Manistee. "He stood back and allowed me to shine that night," she thought to herself as she stood there clutching onto Joe's hands. After Julie's wedding, she spent years planning on what she wanted her husband to be like, what qualities she wanted him to posses, Joe surpassed them all, and then some. It was then that she realized that there was indeed a God. She had been through so much; at times, while on the Plantation, she thought this moment would only be a dream.

As she stood there staring at Joe and glancing down at William periodically, she thought back to the days growing up as a slave, years spent beaten and trapped. She never thought she would make it this far, and yet here she was, at nineteen years old, living out her fantasy, a dream she would role play almost daily in Julie's house, wondering if it would ever come true. She had endured those times, and now it was paying off. "I now pronounce you husband and wife, you may kiss your bride, Joe," the judge said. Koweena's heart was doing summersaults inside her at that moment as she kissed Joe. Now, for the first time she was a wife. What had once been a distant dream on the fields of Natchez was now a reality. She was a mother and a wife. She felt like she needed to pinch herself, but she was afraid to, she felt that if she did, she would be right back in those same fields picking cotton. "Is this real, Joe?"

Koweena asked in a soft vulnerable tone after kissing Joe. "Yes, my persevering wife, it's real."

"Oh, I knew she and Joe would make the perfect couple," Julie said as she was reading Koweena's letter in bed. Julie put the letter up to her breast and took a deep sigh. "And, Thomas, she called me mom." "Here you go, Dear, here's your medicine," Thomas said as he leaned over her to give her the cup of medicine. "Thomas, I don't want to take that, I don't need it." "Jules, you need it, you heard what the doctor said, now drink up, Sweetheart." "I have a grandson!" Julie said. She got so excited as she gulped the medicine down. "A grandson, Thomas, I'm a grandmother, can things get any better!" "Be careful, Dear, you need your strength, don't get too excited." "But, Thomas, I have a grandchild. I'm only thirty two, and I'm a grandmother. How exciting is that! Oh, I can't wait to meet him." "Do you think that would be such a good idea, you know, to travel and all, with your condition such as it is." "Thomas, nothing can stop me from seeing my Koweena. I want her to meet her sister, and I want to see my grandson, it will be so perfect. I'm feeling better already just thinking about it. Koweena has her family, she's calling me mom, I have two beautiful daughters, and now I have a grandson, things couldn't be going any better. Thomas, make plans now to leave for Canada." "Sweetheart, don't you think you should wait awhile?" "Thomas, we're going as soon as possible. I have a daughter, grandson, and son-in-law to see."

Koweena and Joe had settled comfortably into their new home in Sudbury. From the time they were married in June until now in November they lived a peaceful, hassle free, successful life. Joe's job as a school teacher was going great, and Koweena was the perfect mother and housewife. She was now three months pregnant, and she was glowing. Her already luminous skin tone was even more radiant as she began to slightly show a bit. Their house was isolated from the town, nestled up in the rolling hills of the Canadian mountains. Their nearest neighbor was a half mile away.

"William, wipe your mouth before you leave the table, alright," Koweena told her now three year old son as he got up from the table one evening to go play. Koweena put her fork and knife down, and proceeded to give Joe a long glare, as she began to smile in his direction while he was busy eating at the opposite end of the table. He glanced up at her for a second and noticed the huge smile she had on her face as she was staring at him. Joe smiled back at her. "What?" He said. "What?" She replied. "You have that look about you," Joe noted. "What look?" "That look like your about to say something very interesting." "We made it didn't we," Koweena said in a soft tone as the oil lamp burned brightly next to the kitchen sink, giving off its light throughout the kitchen. "What do you mean?" Joe asked. "I mean, look at us, we really made it, you and I, we've finally settled down. I mean, no one would suspect that we were former slaves, no one, not our neighbors, not anyone you work with, no one." "Yes, my Darling, we made it." Suddenly Koweena's face went from one of joy to one of sadness. "What's with the changed expression all of a sudden, Sweetheart?" "What do you mean?" Joe put his utensils down and placed his napkin on the table as he stared intensely into Koweena's eyes. "I mean you went from being happy, to all of a sudden having that sad look, what's wrong?" He asked. "I'm just thinking about Julie, I mean my mom." "And that makes you sad?" Joe asked. "It's just that I haven't heard from her in months. I don't know if she's coming up or not. What if something's wrong?" "Nothing's wrong, Dear, I'm sure she's goin to write soon, or maybe she's on her way up here as we speak." "Yes, maybe, I just wish I would have heard something from her by now." "You miss your mom don't you?" Joe asked. Koweena smiled. "It's that obvious huh," she said. "Why don't you write her again, it couldn't hurt?" Joe asked. Koweena clutched on tightly to her necklace. "It's just that I want to show off my family to her, you know, show her how far I've come," she said. "Sweetheart?" "Yes, Joe." "What is in that locket you've been clinging so tightly to all these years?" It was a question she knew Joe would ask at some point during their relationship. "I mean, Dear, you have never taken it off the entire time I've known you. What's so important about it?" Koweena looked down at her plate, still clinging to the necklace. It was the only thing she didn't want to share with Joe. It was something special between her and Julie, and she wanted to keep it that way. She didn't want to keep anything from Joe, that is, except her necklace. It was her intimate secret that she had held onto for years, and she wasn't about to give that up. "It's nothing, Dear. Are you done with your meal?" Koweena asked, trying to quickly change the subject. Joe looked down at the table, dejected. "Sure," he said. He was hurt that Koweena didn't want to share her story behind the necklace with him. Koweena noticed it as well, as she got up from the table and walked over to grab Joe's plate. "Joe, it's just that some things a woman experiences in her life are a part of just her, and sometimes she doesn't want to share them, not even with her husband." "So now you're keeping secrets from me?" "No, Baby, there are just some things that are between me and Julie, and I want to keep it that way, that's all. There's no reason for you to be mad," Koweena said as she leaned over with his plate in hand and kissed him on the lips. "You'll get your chance, Darling," Joe said as he smacked his lips together, soaking up every last drop of that quick kiss from Koweena. "To what, Dear?" Koweena asked. "To see Julie again, you just have to give it some time, that's all."

After she and Joe spent the next hour cleaning up the kitchen table and washing the dishes, she walked back into her bedroom alone. She opened up the locket and began to sob. She thought about that conversation she had just had with Joe, about the locket, as she continued staring at the contents inside the locket, missing her mother terribly. She couldn't help but think back to that time when Julie told her that a woman's heart is full of secrets, and how sometimes a woman just wants to keep it that way, a secret, kept only to herself. "Oh mom, where are you?" Koweena asked herself as she closed the locket and kissed it.

It was a bright, sunny, late November day, the month had almost come and gone, and still no word from Julie. Koweena couldn't take it anymore. That afternoon, after sweeping the front porch, and with William sitting in the living room playing, she began to write Julie. Suddenly, off in the distance, as she began to write while sitting at her kitchen table, she could hear what sounded like a horse drawn carriage coming up her long driveway. She went to the door to see if it might be one of her neighbors, but she didn't recognize the carriage. She stepped out onto the porch to get a closer look. "Oh, there she is," a soft voice said from inside the carriage. "Look at her, she's glowing," the voice said while simultaneously giving off a loud cough. Koweena, not recognizing who was coming up her drive, and a little worried now, hollered into the living room from the porch. "William, get in your room, now!" She ran inside to get her rifle and quickly came back outside. As she was standing on the porch, with rifle in hand, the carriage came to a complete stop right in front of the house. "Don't come any further or I'll shoot!" Koweena yelled out. "Don't shoot, don't shoot!" A recognizable voice said in a laughing manner coming from the carriage. "Wait a minute; I recognize that voice, its sounds like Thomas." No sooner had Koweena said that than Thomas got out of the carriage with his hands up. "Don't shoot us, little Koweena!" Thomas said in a joking tone with his hands still in the air. "Thomas!" Koweena shouted out as she let go of the rifle immediately and ran toward the carriage. As she got to the carriage she quickly gave Thomas a big hug. She was swept away with enthusiasm as she wrapped herself around Thomas with all her might. "Oh, Thomas, it's so good to see you, I thought you would never come!" She let go of Thomas and stepped back as this blonde woman got out of the carriage. Koweena didn't recognize who it was at first because her hair wasn't long like Julie's, it was short and shoulder length. As the woman slowly got out of the carriage, it was apparent that she was in a weakened state. After she slowly got down from the carriage she immediately looked up, it was then that Koweena knew it was Julie. For the first few seconds, they just stared at each other, Julie wearing a smile, while Koweena stood there biting her bottom lip. It was the first time they had seen each other as mother and daughter. They both were nervous because of that, as they just continued standing there staring at each other. Finally, out of nowhere, Koweena began to run toward Julie, leaping in the air and embracing her tightly. The minute she did, Julie fell back against the carriage. "Whoa, Koweena, whoa," Thomas said as he pulled Koweena off Julie. Koweena instantly noticed that something was wrong by looking at Thomas' expression when he pulled her off of Julie. Julie just sat there on the carriage steps, trying to catch her breath. "Koweena, why don't we go inside, huh," Thomas said as he grabbed a hold of her and led her inside the house. Koweena could only look back at Julie, watching her sitting there gasping for air, as she walked with Thomas into the house.

As they got into the house, Koweena quickly jerked her arm from Thomas' grasp. "What's wrong, Thomas? What's wrong with Julie?" "Maybe you should let her tell you, Koweena," Thomas said as he choked back the tears. Koweena suddenly began to panic. She walked back outside and noticed Julie being helped up the yard by her arm by one of the drivers. She approached Julie again, this time careful not to hug her. She noticed the blood shot eyes of Julie's. As they stood there quiet for a few seconds, finally, Julie spoke up. "My beautiful daughter," she said as she held her arms out toward Koweena. Koweena instantly began sobbing. "Mom," she said as she embraced Julie once more. As she was hugging Julie, she noticed that Julie's hug was weak; she didn't have a firm, strong grip on her. Koweena's heart dropped into the pit of her stomach as she began sobbing harder as she stood there hugging Julie with everything she had. She knew something was terribly wrong with her mother. Koweena rested her chin on Julie's shoulder. "Mom, what's wrong?" She asked, choking back the tears. "Oh, my beautiful daughter," Julie said as they continued hugging one another. "Mom, just tell me what it is." "Koweena, we need to talk," Julie said. Koweena let go of Julie and looked at her closely. She noticed her lips were cracked as if she hadn't had anything to drink in days. In addition to her blood shot eyes, she noticed dark, black circles around her once vibrant, beautiful eyes. In Koweena's eyes, as she looked her mom over, the Julie that had been so strong for her over all those years, now had the appearance of one who's once tough, charismatic strength Koweena was so used to, was now suddenly ripped away, right out from under her legs. "Koweena, I need for you to grab a hold of my arm to lead me into the house," Julie said. That comment made Koweena suddenly put her hands to her face and begin sobbing out of control. "Koweena, Sweetheart, its okay, come on, help me into the house, don't cry, everything's going to be alright, I promise." Now that's the Julie that she remembered. That's the Julie she had craved during her journey, comforting, consoling. That was the Julie she had missed all those years. But as she looked at her mother, unable to walk without her assistance, her heart was breaking into pieces.

As Koweena led Julie into the house, Julie's eyes quickly fell on William. She smiled from ear to ear. "So, this must be my grandson," she said. "Oh, he's precious," she said as she slowly sat down on the sofa right in front of William. "Wow, my very own grandson, now I can go," Julie said. Koweena quickly looked over at Thomas, trying to figure out what Julie meant by that statement. As she did, she noticed tears streaming down his face. In a panic, Koweena spoke out. "Alright, if someone doesn't tell me what's going on, and I mean right now, I'm going to lose it." "Koweena," Julie spoke up, "will you let me spend some time with my grandson, then I'll tell you everything, Dear, alright."

Koweena had been so upset by Julie's appearance and actions that she failed to notice the little girl Thomas was holding. "Is this," Koweena said, placing her hands on little Kowie's back. Thomas smiled. "Yes, this is your sister," he said. "Can I hold her?" "Sure," Thomas said as he handed Kowie over to Koweena. Julie glanced up from having her hand on William's head and noticed Koweena holding Kowie. Tears began to slowly fall from her cheek. "All my dreams have come true," Julie said, choking back the tears. "She looks like me," Koweena noticed as she held Kowie up high, now staring at her right in the eyes. "Yes, we thought that the minute she was born," Thomas noted. "Koweena, is it alright if Thomas takes the kids to the back bedroom so we can talk?" "Sure, Thomas," Koweena said as she hands Kowie off to Thomas. "William, will you go with Thomas here into your bedroom, show Kowie some of your toys," Koweena said.

As the living room cleared out, it was just Koweena and Julie now sitting on Koweena's sofa. Julie spoke up. "Koweena, I'm so proud of you, you now have the family you always dreamed about growing up. I knew you had the strength to do it, all I needed to do was let you spread your wings." "Mom, what's wrong, tell me, I can handle it." "I will, Koweena, but first, tell me about you, I want to know everything." "Well, I'm three months pregnant." "I was going to say something. I noticed you've started to show a little bit. Wow, another grandchild, I just wish," Julie suddenly looked down at the floor as tears began to flow down her cheeks. "Mom, you've been there for me so many times in the past as I grew from a child into a woman, please let me be there for you. Tell me what's wrong." "Tell me about your journey," Julie said, trying to quickly change the subject. She was so used to being the strong one in her relationship to Koweena; she just couldn't handle the thought of her being the one who needed a shoulder to cry on. "How old is Kowie?" Koweena asked. "She was born in January of '46." "So William is only two months older than Kowie." Koweena said. "Yes, he is," Julie replied. "So, tell me about your journey." "Well, I don't know where to begin. I was raped, mom, it was Ray. Ray is William's father." "What!?" Julie asked vehemently with every ounce of strength she could muster. "Yes, it happened in Kentucky." Julie placed her hand on Koweena's cheek. "Oh, Koweena, no, I wasn't there for you," she said. The gentle touch from Julie made Koweena start crying. All the memories of Julie being her one constant in her life came flooding back to her as she sat there staring at the weak looking Julie. After composing herself, Koweena continued. "I needed you so bad then I didn't know what to do. If it hadn't been for Joe, I wouldn't have made it." It was then that Julie realized that Joe had replaced her as the strength in Koweena's life. "Baby, I don't know what to say." "It's alright, mom, I really don't have any scars from it, Joe's love just maraculously wiped away all the nightmares." "He's a man of valor, Koweena, hold onto him." "I will, mom, with everything I have." "Tell me about my grandson." "I didn't want William at first, but when I saw him, I don't know, something magical happened. I instantly fell in love with him." Julie quickly thought back to her giving birth to Koweena. "Koweena, I'm so sorry that that didn't happen with you when you were born." "It's alright, mom, I know your situation was different back then, I don't blame you. I'm just glad I know now that you're my mom. We can now have the kind of relationship we deserve." Julie just looked down at the ground. "What is it, mom?" Koweena asked. "Tell me more about your journey," Julie said, trying to dodge the question. Koweena went on and on, telling Julie about her journey, especially that night in Manistee when she felt like a queen at the ball. For a brief moment in time, they were mother and daughter, chatting and laughing. It was like old times, except this time they both new they were family, something they both so desperately wanted all those years in Natchez. They held each other's hands as they talked. Julie would kiss Koweena on the cheek every once in a while during one of Koweena's many tales about her journey. From the time Koweena was five, all Julie ever wanted and dreamed for was for Koweena to be happy, and now Julie was seeing with her own eyes the dream coming to fruition. In watching Koweena's dreams come true, Julie's dreams had come true.

"Julie died two weeks after that conversation, on a cold, cloudy, December afternoon in my bed," Koweena recalled. "She went peacefully in her sleep, as if all she had ever hoped for had come true, and she could now rest from her suffering."

It was a rather warm, sunny, January afternoon, just a month after Julie's death, when Koweena, Kowie, and William made their way up the hill toward the big oak tree where Julie was buried. It was Julie's dying wish as she told Thomas before they made their trek up north to see Koweena, that she be buried on Koweena's property. It was as if she knew she was going to die there once she arrived. As the three arrived at the grave site, they just stood there holding hands, staring at the tombstone. Julie's family, her legacy, now standing there holding hands with one another, with Koweena in the middle, at the foot of Julie's burial site. Koweena was grieving hard that day as she stared at the inscription on the tombstone. She began to quietly sob as she gripped tightly onto both William and Kowie's hands. The tombstone read:

Julie D. Callahan

Feb.7, 1816 Dec.12, 1848

Beloved Mother and Wife

You daughters will always know they are loved by you

"Mom, I wanted to do this right here in front of you, so I hope you're happy by this," Koweena said as she let go of William and Kowie's hands and reached into her pocket and pulled out a gold roped necklace with her pink sapphire stone ring hanging from it. "This cost me quite a bit to do this," she said chuckling as she wiped away the tears from her face. She walked around behind Kowie. She leaned over her and gently wrapped the necklace around her, connecting it behind her neck. "There you go, Kowie, you always wear that okay, our mom gave me that when I was little like you." Kowie just stood there holding the ring close to her face with her hand, with wide open eyes. "Mom," Koweena continued, "thank you for broadening my horizons, thank you for being there for me and cheering me on when life seemed hopeless for me, I love you always." Koweena walked over to Julie's tombstone, bent down, took off her necklace that carried the locket, opened the locket, kissed it, and laid it down at the foot of the stone with the open locket facing away from the tombstone. She remained there, bent down, as her tears dropped onto the foot of the stone. "I will always keep my head up, mom," she said as she touched the top of the headstone. She got up and walked over to William and Kowie, grabbed a hold of their hands once again. "Come on, guys, you want to run across the field together holding hands?" "Yeah!" They both said in unison with enthusiasm. The three took off, running through the field, just the three of them, with Koweena in the middle holding both William and Kowie's hands.

"Julie is gone, but her spirit will live on in me, in William, in Kowie, and in my future baby," Koweena recalled as the three were running through the field with the wind whipping through their hair. "People say it can't work, black and white, but I'm a walking example that it can. Julie taught me that love is color blind. I have certainly lived a rough life, but if I didn't have my mom in my life during those most important years, when I was going through some of the toughest things a young girl could ever possibly face, I wouldn't have made it. My mom taught me everything, she taught me about life, and the long journey ahead. A young beautiful mother told me once that a woman's heart is full of secrets, and my relationship with my mom, the wonderful moments we shared, will remain just that, a secret deep inside my heart. These intimate moments with my mom will remain tucked deep within my soul that will always be between just her and me, wherever I go."

Later on that week, Joe went up to the grave site to pay his final respects. As he stood there staring at the tombstone, he noticed the open locket lying at the foot of the stone. He looked around to make sure no one was watching and then proceeded to walk up to the stone to get a better look at the locket. As he gazed upon the locket he could only smile at what he saw. It was a picture of Koweena and Julie sitting on the sofa in Julie's parent's living room the day her and Koweena first met. There was an inscription on the bottom of the picture, it said: "I knew, this day, that you would be a part of my soul." "Perfect," Joe said with a little chuckle and a smile. "Thank you, Julie, for bringing Koweena into my life," Joe said as he kissed his hand and gently placed it on the headstone.

"I will miss my mom," Koweena again recalled that same January afternoon that she gave Kowie her sapphire stone ring, picking both William and Kowie up and holding them tightly after their run in the field. "But her lasting influence will be with me forever, and I will make sure that William and Kowie, and my future baby, never forget the woman that carried me throughout my life."

Thomas and Kowie, after staying at Koweena and Joe's for several months after Julie's death, decided that they were going to live there with them in Sudbury permanently. Thomas wanted Kowie to be alongside her mother, and Thomas didn't want to leave Julie's side either. So they built a house on the field behind Koweena's house. Koweena later gave birth to a beautiful baby girl. The name Koweena gave her was an easy choice, Julie Koweena Callahan. Thomas and Joe later opened up their own land surveying business together, they're co-founders and co-owners of the company. It's quaintly enough called Callahan Enterprises. While Joe and Thomas would be away on business, Koweena would spend her days, as she did everyday, with William, Kowie, and baby Julie. Although she missed her mom terribly, she was happy taking care of the three children and fixing meals for them, and Joe and Thomas when they weren't away on business. One day, as it was just her and the kids, she was going through some of her mom's boxes and came across the very first book Julie ever read to her. The very same book Koweena clung to as a child. The first book she had ever read. She could remember Julie reading that to her for the first time when she was five. "Guys, come in here!" Koweena yelled out from her bedroom where she and baby Julie were. She was yelling to William and Kowie who were playing in the living room. As the four of them huddled together, all sitting on the floor, Koweena opened up the book and began reading it aloud to them. She paused from reading for a moment, laughed a little and said. "Guys, this is the first book I ever read, and it was the first book your mother, Kowie, and your grandmother, William, ever read to me. I held onto this book with everything I had while growing up." Koweena made it her mission to educate those kids like Julie had done her. She was going to pass on the knowledge and education that Julie had poured into her growing up, to bring those children up right.

As the years passed by, Koweena enjoyed her life as a mother, wife, sister, and step-daughter. With the memory of Julie fresh in their minds, Koweena, Joe, William, baby Julie, Kowie, and Thomas lived on that plot of land in Sudbury as one big happy family. Koweena used her life experiences, all that she had been taught, and all she went through, to take care of her family and her extended family. She was happy, and she did a great job of making sure that they were happy, and that all of them were taken care of.

"Looking back," Koweena recalled one day as she was sitting in her front porch rocking chair, staring out into the edge of the sky where it was red due to the sunset, holding baby Julie. "I've walked a lot of miles, and I've been through a lot. I wouldn't want to go through what I went through again, but you know what, I wouldn't change a thing. I went from being someone else's property, a debased slave as a child, to a great mother, wife, and homemaker, a successful woman. I've accomplished all my dreams, all that I set out to accomplish. I lost a mother and a sister in the process. You know, it takes a lot to be a survivor, and I have survived a lot. I have experienced the good and the bad, even from the time I was born. But now that I look around me at all that I have, if surviving results in this, if this is what it has brought me, I'm proud to call myself a survivor."

NOTES

Chapter 1

- "Signals on the Underground Railroad": philly Burbs.com

- Bob Bankard, "The Passage To Freedom: The Underground Railroad in Bucks, Burlington and Montgomery Counties"

- "History of slavery in Kentucky", www.wikipedia.org

- The Volume Library: 1984, The Southwestern Company, 788.

- "Slavery in the United States", www.wikipedia.org

- "Underground Railroad", www.wikipedia.org

Chapter 2

- "Natchez, Mississippi", www.wikipedia.org